# WHAT BIG RED EYES YOU HAVE



The beast had been thawing for nearly eighteen hours now, since the ice surrounding it had been removed.. Connant poked at it with an unconscious caution; the flesh was no longer hard as armor plate, but had assumed a rubbery texture. It looked like wet, blue rubber glistening under droplets of water like little round jewels in the glare of the gasoline pressure lantern. Connant felt an unreasoning desire to pour the contents of the lamp's reservoir over the thing in its box and drop the cigarette into it.

The three red eyes glared up at him sightlessly, the ruby eyeballs reflecting murky, smoky rays of light. He realized vaguely that he had been looking at them for a very long time, even vaguely understood that they were no longer sightless. But it did not seem of importance, of no more importance than the labored, slow motion of the tentacular things that sprouted from the base of the scrawny, slowly pulsing neck.

Connant picked up the pressure lamp and returned to his chair. He sat down, staring at the pages of mathematics before him. The clucking of the cosmic ray counter was strangely less disturbing, the rustle of the coals in the stove no longer distracting.

The creak of the floorboards behind him didn't interrupt his thoughts as he went about his weekly report in an automatic manner, filling in columns of data and making brief, summarizing notes.

The creak of the floorboards sounded nearer.

—from "Who Goes There?"
by John W. Campbell, Jr.

## BAEN BOOKS EDITED BY HANK DAVIS

*The Human Edge* by Gordon R. Dickson

*We the Underpeople* by Cordwainer Smith
*When the People Fell* by Cordwainer Smith

The Technic Civilization Saga
*The Van Rijn Method* by Poul Anderson
*David Falkayn: Star Trader* by Poul Anderson
*Rise of the Terran Empire* by Poul Anderson
*Young Flandry* by Poul Anderson
*Captain Flandry: Defender of the Terran Empire* by Poul Anderson
*Sir Dominic Flandry: The Last Knight of Terra* by Poul Anderson
*Flandry's Legacy* by Poul Anderson

*The Best of the Bolos: Their Finest Hour* by Keith Laumer

*A Cosmic Christmas*
*A Cosmic Christmas 2 You*
*In Space No One Can Hear You Scream*
*The Baen Big Book of Monsters*
*As Time Goes By*
*Future War . . . and Other Punchlines*
*Worst Contact*
*Things from Outer Space*
*If This Goes Wrong . . .* (forthcoming)

# THINGS FROM OUTER SPACE

Edited by

HANK DAVIS

BAEN

THINGS FROM OUTER SPACE

This is a work of fiction. All the characters and events portrayed in this book are fictional, and any resemblance to real people or incidents is purely coincidental.

A Baen Book

Baen Publishing Enterprises
P.O. Box 1403
Riverdale, NY 10471

ISBN 13: 978-1-4767-8166-2

Cover art by Alan Pollack

The cartoon on page 97 is by Randall Garrett and is used by permission of his estate.

First Baen printing, October 2016

Distributed by Simon & Schuster
1230 Avenue of the Americas
New York, NY 10020

Printed in the United States of America

10 9 8 7 6 5 4 3 2 1

## DEDICATION

This one is for Judy Greenwald Paktor,
a splendid lady who nonetheless
doesn't like scary stories.
(But you don't have to *read* them, Judy.)

## Copyrights of Stories

## ACKNOWLEDGEMENTS

My thanks to all the contributors (and raise a glass to absent friends), and to those who helped with advice, permissions, contact information, and other kindnesses, including Justin Bell, Lynn Bond, Richard Curtis, Robert C. Harrall, Vicki Ann Heydron, Barry Malzberg, Cameron McClure, Lisa Rodgers, David Wixon, George Zebrowski, Kimberley Oliver and Priscilla Olson, and probably other kindly carbon-based life forms which my decrepit memory has unforgivably overlooked.

# CONTENTS

# THINGS FROM OUTER SPACE

# *THINGS* FOR THE MEMORIES

## Introduction by Hank Davis

**IN THE FIRST** of the *Star Trek* movies, Bones McCoy beams onto the massively refurbished *Enterprise* and Admiral Kirk tells him, "There's a thing out there," at which point McCoy breaks in, "Why is it any object we don't understand is always called a thing?"

Kirk ignored the question, but I think he should have said, "Because it sounds so *cool*."

And it does. Particularly if it's italicized: *Thing*.

"Outer space" is a cool phrase, too, though I've never been sure about its exact meaning. Or its inexact meaning, either. Surely it at least means farther out than near space, where the atmosphere has thinned until it can be disregarded aerodynamically, but how far beyond that is "outer"? Beyond the Moon's orbit? Beyond the asteroid belt? Beyond the orbit of Pluto (planet or not)? Farther out than Alpha Centauri? Whatever, it sounds *cool*.

So *Things from Outer Space* sounds like a truly cool title to me, and I'm surprised that, as far as I know, there has never been a movie called *The Thing* (or *Things*) *from Outer Space*. The answer might be a legal matter. The second *Star Trek* movie was originally going to be titled *The Vengeance of Khan* until (according to accounts at the time) George Lucas & Company complained that the title was too similar to the upcoming *Revenge of the Jedi*, and Paramount released it instead as *The Wrath of Kahn*. (And after all that, someone at Lucasfilms changed their mind and the third *Star Wars* flick became *Return of the Jedi*. I often refer to it as *Retread of the Jedi*.) Somewhat earlier, Columbia made it known that a movie announced as *Alien Encounter* was too similar to *Close Encounters of the Third Kind*,so it became *Starship Invasions*.

So it might have been that the 1951 RKO-Radio movie, *The Thing from Another World* sucked all the legal oxygen out of the word "Thing," then two years later, Universal-International's *It Came from Outer Space* did the same for "Outer Space." So, an obvious title was off limits.

I'll hope that nobody has a problem with the title of this anthology, perhaps due to the passage of time. (Did someone say, "But, you can't copyright a title"? Technically true, but the Hollywood legal beagles are darkly ingenious, threatening to sue because the title was also a trademark; or threatening to sue because the similarity of titles constitutes damages and financial loss to their client; or just plain threatening to sue, which suit you might win, but can you afford millions in legal fees and court costs? Welcome to the real world.)

Getting back to the 1951 movie, *The Thing from Another World,* that movie was based on John W. Campbell's great novella, "Who Goes There?" (included herein, as you have doubtless already noticed), which has one of the *Things* to end all *Things*, and the men battling it call it a thing. That might have something to do with the movie not being titled "Who Goes There?", but instead being released as *The Thing from Another World*. I doubt that MGM would have worried about it being confused with *Quo Vadis*, released the same year (a re-re-remake, incidentally). In any case, *The Thing from Another World* sounds scarier. (According to some accounts, the "From Another World" part of the title was an afterthought, and the faded three words which appear underneath the words "The Thing," which seem to be burning through the screen at the beginning, makes the three words *look* like an afterthought.)

The movie was a financial success; one reviewer commented that RKO had "laid a golden monster." But it was not well received in the SF community. Isaac Asimov once called it one of the worst science fiction movies ever. The reason was that the movie left out the most science fictional thing about *The Thing*. Since the story is only a few pages away, I won't tell you what was left out, but I think judgments such as Asimov's are not just unduly harsh, but bloody ridiculous. Getting back to the original story, however, consider the blurb for the story, possibly written by editor Campbell himself, as it originally appeared in the August 1938 *Astounding Stories*: "Who—is that your closest friend—or a monstrous imitation, breed of an alien, deadly world? WHO GOES THERE—?" (If that sounds pulpish, well it *was* a pulp magazine.)

In 1982, John Carpenter did a new version of the

story, this time just titled *The Thing*, and that missing SF factor was not left out. This version, however, was not a hit—some blame its release's coinciding with that of the mega-hit *E.T.*, showing that people preferred a cute, cuddly alien to a hideous and implacably hostile one. The movie certainly deserved to be a hit, in spite of my not being happy with the sort of characters included. The 1951 movie has characters more like those in Campbell's story, while most of the characters in the 1982 version are such losers that one wonders why they were picked to go on a mission to Antarctica. Pity that the two *Things* can't somehow be merged into a more Campbellian *Thing*.

Also, I'd still like an explanation of why an Antarctic base has a flame thrower.

(Incidentally, until I wrote this introduction, it hadn't occurred to me that it has now been longer since the 1982 movie than the time elapsed from the 1951 version to the remake. I must be getting old. But enough personal angst.)

More recently, there was a prequel to the 1982 movie, confusingly also called *The Thing*, which also did not do big box office. It may be a long time until anybody tries to adapt the story again, but the original novella is here and awaits your well-deserved attention. In addition, I've included a parody in verse of the novella by Randall Garrett, and a scary take on the 1982 movie from the viewpoint of the *Thing* by Peter Watts. So this book leads off with a *Thing* sandwich (A *Thing*wich?).

Following that is "The Colour Out of Space" by the grand master of horror, H. P. Lovecraft, who reportedly said that this was his favorite of all his stories.

Interestingly, it too has had three movie versions, of which I've seen only the first, the 1965 *Die, Monster, Die*, whose only virtue was Boris Karloff being in the cast, and it's a toss-up which was worse, the abominable script or Nick Adams' acting. My brother saw the second movie version, *The Curse* (1987), and thought it was a more faithful and far better adaptation of the story, and there is a 2010 German adaptation titled *Die Farbe*, and released on DVD in the U.S. as *The Color Out of Space*, which has been highly praised by Lovecraft expert S. T. Joshi. (Remind me to order the DVD.)

If the long-suffering reader is wondering why I'm going on at length about movie versions of these two classic horror/SF stories, it's because being made into a movie is something that happens only rarely with published SF stories. And when it happens, the results are rarely something to write home about. Even so, a *Thing* from outer space is something that moviemakers seem to think is a can't-miss proposition. This was particularly true during the 1950s, and even more particularly true of one studio: American-International, which, sometimes with the help of Roger Corman, more often with less-talented entities, gave us *The Beast with 1,000,000 Eyes* (minor Corman, but not a total loss), *Not of This Earth* (Corman; very good, followed by *three* remakes), *It Conquered the World* (another good Corman) *Night of the Blood Beast* (gaaahhh!), *Invasion of the Saucer Men* (okay, with some humor; loosely based on a story by former *Amazing Stories* editor Howard Browne), and probably more that I've forgotten.

Other studios got in on the *Things* from space

bandwagon, not including the 1953 movie of *The War of the Worlds*, (based on the 1898 H. G. Wells novel) which preceded the bandwagon's even having the horses hitched up. There were the very good *The Creeping Unknown/The Quatermass Xperiment*, and *Enemy from Space/Quatermass 2*, based on Nigel Kneale's even better serials for British TV. (The third one, *Five Million Years to Earth/Quatermass and the Pit* took a decade and a half to get adapted, and was released long after the 1950s monster movie flood.) Then there was the not-hopeless *Target Earth* (based on another story by Howard Browne), *Earth vs. the Flying Saucers* (in which the one alien we saw outside of his combat suit wasn't very *Thing*-like), *The Blob*, and the amazingly awful *Teenagers from Outer Space* (the alien teens were all pretty boys; this time the *Thing* was a badly photographed, giant lobster), and need I mention *Plan 9 from Outer Space* and *The Robot Monster* (a *Thing* should *not* look like a gorilla in a space helmet). Much better was a movie with one of the most memorable titles of all: *I Married a Monster from Outer Space*

At the same time, the *Things* in SF novels were few and far between. One exception was Robert A. Heinlein's *The Puppet Masters*. Another was Jack Finney's *The Body Snatchers*, which was quickly filmed as *Invasion of the Body Snatchers*, the first of three movies based on the novel. The movies are so well known that in the 1960s, paperback editions of the Finney novel began to appear with the movie's title on the cover. Heinlein's novel had to wait several decades before being turned into an inadequate movie, but then it was serialized in *Galaxy* rather than *Collier's*. British writer, John Lymington, wrote about nasty critters from space in a handful of novels and one, *The Night of the Big Heat*, became a 1967 movie with Christopher Lee and Peter Cushing (once again, the only good things about a movie were the veteran actors). But on the whole, the important SF novels of the1950s, and most of the second string novels, too, were about other things than *Things*: *More Than Human*, *The Space Merchants*, *The Demolished Man*, The original Foundation Trilogy (mostly written in the 1940s, but collected as books in the 1950s), *Double Star*, *Childhood's End* (which had aliens from space, but, in spite of their appearance, their behavior was altogether un-*Thing*-like, *Fahrenheit 451, The Door into Summer*, *The Long Tomorrow*, *The Stars My Destination*, and so on.

Let's skip across the Atlantic to take note of two and a half more exceptions which came from British writer John Wyndham, who wrote *The Day of the Triffids/Revolt of the Triffids*, about mobile, carnivorous plants which, in the original serial in *Collier's*, came from Venus, brought back by Earthlings, but in the book version, were the result of Russian experiments here on Earth. That's the half a book, and it was followed by *The Kraken Wakes*, published in the U.S. with somewhat different contents, as *Out of the Deeps*, in which *Things* from another planet, possibly Jupiter, land in the ocean, and assault the land. The novel is very effective and scary, even if the *Things* themselves are never seen, though their machines are visible as they collect human specimens. His other whole *Things* book, 1957's *The Midwich Cuckoos* is another alien invasion story in which the aliens are not seen, so we don't know how *Thing*-like they may be. *Day of the*

*Triffids* has had an inadequate movie version (in which the triffids arrived in meteorites), and two better TV adaptations, and *The Midwich Cuckoos* has had two movie versions, both released under the title of *Village of the Damned*, but as far as I know *The Kraken Wakes* has only had a few radio adaptations.

Mention that the Triffids came from Russian labs gives me an excuse for a slight digression. All these invaders-from-space movies were, of course, not really about invaders-from-space at all, according to many critics and culture-watchers, who were eager to explain that they really were symbolic representations of the Communist Menace and our "paranoid" fear of it. A lot of these same explainers of culture also thought that fear of Communism was irrational, and besides the Republicans were more of a menace than the Commies any day of the week. This has always struck me as absurd, but then I'm part of that Republican Menace. In any case, in 1991 a TV movie titled *Not of This World* (I wonder if whoever owns the rights to Corman's *Not of This Earth* complained) was shown, involving a *Thing*, arriving in a meteorite, then growing and killing—you know the drill. Movie critic John Leonard, who reviewed movies on a Sunday morning CBS show was baffled as to why the movie was made. We all know that the invaders from space movies of the 1950s, he dolefully reminded us, were symbolic of cold war paranoia (I'm working from memory, and he may not actually have used that imbecilic phrase), and The Cold War was over, so why does this movie exist? he wondered.

I wish I could remember who once sarcastically said, "Whatever would we do without intellectuals?"

But enough of movies. While SF novels rarely involved *Things* from space, still a number of short stories in the 1950s and 1960s nonetheless kept the *Things* from fading away, and several very good examples are here in these pages. Since that time, of course, horror fiction experienced a boom in popularity (Stephen King, a one-man boom, wrote *The Tommyknockers*, a novel-length *Things* story, for example), and Caitlin Kiernan, one of the best new horror writers, is present with a blend of the hard-boiled detective story and Lovecraftian *Things* from space. At the same time, award-winning writer Sarah A. Hoyt and David Afsharirad present brand new stories which take a lighter look at *Things* arriving on Earth. And the awesomely prolific Robert Silverberg sardonically considers whether a modern teenager might have something in common with an alien *Thing*. And more.

The *Things* from outer space have landed in these pages. If you want to consider them symbolic representations, blah, blah, blah, of the Russian (if not Communist) Menace, or the Republican Menace, (I feel *very* menacing!), or the Islamofascist Menace, or the Reality TV Menace, or whatnot, go ahead, but I think these stories don't need a larger context to make them fun. And if you have too much scary fun, you can always hide under the bed from the *Things*.

—Hank Davis
2016

# WHO GOES THERE?

## by John W. Campbell, Jr.

*It had been trapped and waiting for twenty million years—and now it was free.*

❖ ❖ ❖

*To say that* **John W. Campbell, Jr.**. *was the man who built modern science fiction is, if anything, an understatement, and in the space I have here, I'll necessarily only be giving a brief sketch. He had already had two careers as an sf writer, beginning with galactic space epics under his own name in the manner of E. E. "Doc" Smith, then writing very different stories in a different style under the alias of Don A. Stuart. After going to work for* Astounding Stories *in 1937, he became editor in 1938, soon renaming the magazine* Astounding Science-Fiction *and would have re-renamed it just* Science Fiction, *except that another editor beat him to that title. And he soon was discovering new science fiction writers, such as Robert A. Heinlein,*

*Theodore Sturgeon, Isaac Asimov, A. E. van Vogt, L. Sprague de Camp, and (near the end of the, ah,* astounding *(sorry) decade of the 1940s, Arthur C. Clarke, among others. Writers active before 1938, such as Murray Leinster and Clifford D. Simak wrote far better stories for Campbell than their earlier work.*

*He also laid the foundation for modern fantasy, when he started up* Unknown *(later retitled* Unknown Worlds*) and published fantasy told in a modern style. Such stories were not, ah, unknown (sorry, again) before, but now there was a magazine filled with them. While not all were set in the present-day (what, decades later, would be called "urban fantasy"), notably Fritz Leiber's stories of Fafhrd and the Gray Mouser, most were told in a more modern manner than much fantasy had previously employed.*

*His second writing period, as Don A. Stuart, soon ended after he took the reins at* Astounding*. According to some versions, company policy was against his selling stories to his own magazine, and selling to competitors would be even more severely frowned on. Fortunately, the story which follows, one of the last of the Don A. Stuart stories, was published before his writing career effectively ended. Otherwise we wouldn't have one of the greatest horror stories of science fiction.*

**THE PLACE STANK.** A queer, mingled stench that only the ice-buried cabins of an Antarctic camp know, compounded of reeking human sweat, and the heavy, fish-oil stench of melted seal blubber. An overtone of liniment combated the musty smell of sweat-and-snow-drenched furs. The acrid odor of burnt cooking fat, and the animal, not-unpleasant smell of dogs, diluted by time, hung in the air.

Lingering odors of machine oil contrasted sharply with the taint of harness dressing and leather. Yet, somehow, through all that reek of human beings and their associates—dogs, machines, and cooking—came another taint. It was a queer, neck-ruffling thing, a faintest suggestion of an odor alien among the smells of industry and life. And it was a life-smell. But it came from the thing that lay bound with cord and tarpaulin on the table, dripping slowly, methodically onto the heavy planks, dank and gaunt under the unshielded glare of the electric light.

Blair, the little bald-pated biologist of the expedition, twitched nervously at the wrappings, exposing clear, dark ice beneath and then pulling the tarpaulin back into place restlessly. His little birdlike motions of suppressed eagerness danced his shadow across the fringe of dingy gray underwear hanging from the low ceiling, the equatorial fringe of stiff, graying hair around his naked skull a comical halo about the shadow's head.

Commander Garry brushed aside the lax legs of a suit of underwear and stepped toward the table. Slowly his eyes traced around the rings of men sardined into the Administration Building. His tall, stiff body straightened finally, and he nodded. "Thirty-seven. All here." His voice was low, yet carried the clear authority of the commander by nature, as well as by title.

"You know the outline of the story back of that find of the Secondary Pole Expedition. I have been conferring with Second-in-Command McReady, and Norris, as well as Blair and Dr. Copper. There is a difference of opinion, and because it involves the entire group, it is only just that the entire Expedition personnel act on it.

"I am going to ask McReady to give you the details of the story, because each of you has been too busy with his own work to follow closely the endeavors of the others. McReady?"

Moving from the smoke-blued background, McReady was a figure from some forgotten myth, a looming, bronze statue that held life, and walked. Six feet four inches he stood as he halted beside the table, and with a characteristic glance upward to assure himself of room under the low ceiling beams, straightened. His rough, clashingly orange windproof jacket he still had on, yet on his huge frame it did not seem misplaced. Even here, four feet beneath the drift-wind that droned across the Antarctic waste above the ceiling, the cold of the frozen continent leaked in, and gave meaning to the harshness of the man. And he was bronze—his great red-bronze beard, the heavy hair that matched it. The gnarled, corded hands gripping, relaxing, gripping and relaxing on the table planks were bronze. Even the deep-sunken eyes beneath heavy brows were bronzed.

Age-resisting endurance of the metal spoke in the cragged heavy outlines of his face, and the mellow tones of the heavy voice. "Norris and Blair agree on one thing: that animal we found was not—terrestrial in origin. Norris fears there may be danger in that; Blair says there is none.

"But I'll go back to how, and why we found it. To all that was known before we came here, it appeared that this point was exactly over the South Magnetic Pole of Earth. The compass does point straight down here, as you all know. The more delicate instruments of the physicists, instruments especially designed for this expedition and its study of the magnetic pole, detected a secondary effect, a secondary, less powerful magnetic influence about eighty miles southwest of here.

"The Secondary Magnetic Expedition went out to investigate it. There is no need for details. We found it, but it was not the huge meteorite or magnetic mountain Norris had expected to find. Iron ore is magnetic, of course; iron more so—and certain special steels even more magnetic. From the surface indications, the secondary pole we found was small, so small that the magnetic effect it had was preposterous. No magnetic material conceivable could have that effect. Soundings through the ice indicated it was within one hundred feet of the glacier surface.

"I think you should know the structure of the place. There is a broad plateau, a level sweep that runs more than 150 miles due south from the Secondary Station, Van Wall says. He didn't have time or fuel to fly farther, but it was running smoothly due south then. Right there, where that buried thing was, there is an ice-drowned mountain ridge, a granite wall of unshakable strength that has dammed back the ice creeping from the south.

"And four hundred miles due south is the South Polar Plateau. You have asked me at various times why it gets warmer here when the wind rises, and most of you know.

As a meteorologist I'd have staked my word that no wind could blow at -70 degrees; that no more than a five-mile wind could blow at -50; without causing warming due to friction with ground, snow and ice and the air itself.

"We camped there on the lip of that ice-drowned mountain range for twelve days. We dug our camp into the blue ice that formed the surface, and escaped most of it. But for twelve consecutive days the wind blew at forty-five miles an hour. It went as high as forty-eight, and fell to forty-one at times. The temperature was -63 degrees. It rose to -60 and fell to -68. It was meteorologically impossible, and it went on uninterruptedly for twelve days and twelve nights.

"Somewhere to the south, the frozen air of the South Polar Plateau slides down from that 18,000-foot bowl, down a mountain pass, over a glacier, and starts north. There must be a funneling mountain chain that directs it, and sweeps it away for four hundred miles to hit that bald plateau where we found the secondary pole, and 350 miles farther north reaches the Antarctic Ocean.

"It's been frozen there since Antarctica froze twenty million years ago. There never has been a thaw there.

"Twenty million years ago Antarctica was beginning to freeze. We've investigated, though, and built speculations. What we believe happened was about like this.

"Something came down out of space, a ship. We saw it there in the blue ice, a thing like a submarine without a conning tower or directive vanes, 280 feet long and 45 feet in diameter at its thickest.

"Eh, Van Wall? Space? Yes, but I'll explain that better later." McReady's steady voice went on.

"It came down from space, driven and lifted by forces men haven't discovered yet, and somehow—perhaps something went wrong then—it tangled with Earth's magnetic field. It came south here, out of control probably, circling the magnetic pole. That's a savage country there; but when Antarctica was still freezing, it must have been a thousand times more savage. There must have been blizzard snow, as well as drift, new snow falling as the continent glaciated. The swirl there must have been particularly bad, the wind hurling a solid blanket of white over the lip of that now-buried mountain.

"The ship struck solid granite head-on, and cracked up. Not every one of the passengers in it was killed, but the ship must have been ruined, her driving mechanism locked. It tangled with Earth's field, Norris believes. No thing made by intelligent beings can tangle with the dead immensity of a planet's natural forces and survive.

"One of its passengers stepped out. The wind we saw there never fell below forty-one, and the temperature never rose above -60. Then—the wind must have been stronger. And there was drift falling in a solid sheet. The thing was lost completely in ten paces." He paused for a moment, the deep, steady voice giving way to the drone of wind overhead and the uneasy, malicious gurgling in the pipe of the galley stove.

Drift—a drift-wind was sweeping by overhead. Right now the snow picked up by the mumbling wind fled in level, blinding lines across the face of the buried camp. If a man stepped out of the tunnels that connected each of the camp buildings beneath the surface, he'd be lost in ten paces. Out there, the slim, black finger of the radio mast lifted three hundred feet into the air, and at its peak was the clear night sky. A sky of thin, whining wind rushing steadily from beyond to another beyond under the licking, curling mantle of the aurora. And off north, the horizon flamed with queer, angry colors of the midnight twilight. That was Spring three hundred feet above Antarctica.

At the surface—it was white death. Death of a needle-fingered cold driven before the wind, sucking heat from any warm thing. Cold—and white mist of endless, everlasting drift, the fine, fine particles of licking snow that obscured all things.

Kinner, the little, scar-faced cook, winced. Five days ago he had stepped out to the surface to reach a cache of frozen beef. He had reached it, started back—and the drift-wind leapt out of the south. Cold, white death that streamed across the ground blinded him in twenty seconds. He stumbled on wildly in circles. It was half an hour before rope-guided men from below found him in the impenetrable murk.

It was easy for man—or thing—to get lost in ten paces.

"And the drift-wind then was probably more impenetrable than we know." McReady's voice snapped Kinner's mind back. Back to the welcome, dank warmth of the Ad Building. "The passenger of the ship wasn't prepared either, it appears. It froze within ten feet of the ship.

"We dug down to find the ship, and our tunnel happened to find the frozen—animal. Barclay's ice-ax struck its skull.

"When we saw what it was, Barclay went back to the

tractor, started the fire up and when the steam pressure built, sent a call for Blair and Dr. Copper. Barclay himself was sick then. Stayed sick for three days, as a matter of fact.

"When Blair and Copper came, we cut out the animal in a block of ice, as you see, wrapped it and loaded it on the tractor for return here. We wanted to get into that ship.

"We reached the side and found the metal was something we didn't know. Our beryllium-bronze, non-magnetic tools wouldn't touch it. Barclay had some tool-steel on the tractor, and that wouldn't scratch it either. We made reasonable tests—even tried some acid from the batteries with no results.

"They must have had a passivating process to make magnesium metal resist acid that way, and the alloy must have been at least ninety-five percent magnesium. But we had no way of guessing that, so when we spotted the barely opened lock door, we cut around it. There was clear, hard ice inside the lock, where we couldn't reach it. Through the little crack we could look in and see that only metal and tools were in there, so we decided to loosen the ice with a bomb.

"We had decanite bombs and thermite. Thermite is the ice-softener; decanite might have shattered valuable things, where the thermite's heat would just loosen the ice. Dr. Copper, Norris and I placed a twenty-five-pound thermite bomb, wired it, and took the connector up the tunnel to the surface, where Blair had the steam tractor waiting. A hundred yards the other side of that granite wall we set off the thermite bomb.

"The magnesium metal of the ship caught of course. The glow of the bomb flared and died, then it began to flare again. We ran back to the tractor, and gradually the glare built up. From where we were we could see the whole ice-field illuminated from beneath with an unbearable light; the ship's shadow was a great, dark cone reaching off toward the north, where the twilight was just about gone. For a moment it lasted, and we counted three other shadow-things that might have been other—passengers—frozen there. Then the ice was crashing down and against the ship.

"That's why I told you about that place. The wind sweeping down from the Pole was at our backs. Steam and hydrogen flame were torn away in white ice-fog; the flaming heat under the ice there was yanked away toward the Antarctic Ocean before it touched us. Otherwise we wouldn't have come back, even with the shelter of that granite ridge that stopped the light.

"Somehow in the blinding inferno we could see great hunched things—black bulks. They shed even the furious incandescence of the magnesium for a time. Those must have been the engines, we knew. Secrets going in blazing glory—secrets that might have given Man the planets. Mysterious things that could lift and hurl that ship—and had soaked in the force of the Earth's magnetic field. I saw Norris' mouth move, and ducked. I couldn't hear him.

"Insulation—something—gave way. All Earth's field they'd soaked up twenty million years before broke loose. The aurora in the sky above licked down, and the whole plateau there was bathed in cold fire that blanketed vision. The ice-ax in my hand got red hot, and hissed on the ice.

Metal buttons on my clothes burned into me. And a flash of electric blue seared upward from beyond the granite wall.

"Then the walls of ice crashed down on it. For an instant it squealed the way dry ice does when it's pressed between metal.

"We were blind and groping in the dark for hours while our eyes recovered. We found every coil within a mile was fused rubbish, the dynamo and every radio set, the earphones and speakers. If we hadn't had the steam tractor, we wouldn't have gotten over to the Secondary Camp.

"Van Wall flew in from Big Magnet at sun-up, as you know. We came home as soon as possible. That is the history of—that." McReady's great bronze beard gestured toward the thing on the table.

# II

**BLAIR STIRRED UNEASILY,** his little, bony fingers wriggling under the harsh light. Little brown freckles on his knuckles slid back and forth as the tendons under the skin twitched. He pulled aside a bit of the tarpaulin and looked impatiently at the dark ice-bound thing inside.

McReady's big body straightened somewhat. He'd ridden the rocking, jarring steam tractor forty miles that day, pushing on to Big Magnet here. Even his calm will had been pressed by the anxiety to mix again with humans. It was lone and quiet out there in Secondary

Camp, where a wolf-wind howled down from the Pole. Wolf-wind howling in his sleep—winds droning and the evil, unspeakable face of that monster leering up as he'd first seen it through clear, blue ice, with a bronze ice-ax buried in its skull.

The giant meteorologist spoke again. "The problem is this. Blair wants to examine the thing. Thaw it out and make micro slides of its tissues and so forth. Norris doesn't believe that is safe, and Blair does. Dr. Copper agrees pretty much with Blair. Norris is a physicist, of course, not a biologist. But he makes a point I think we should all hear. Blair has described the microscopic life-forms biologists find living, even in this cold and inhospitable place. They freeze every winter, and thaw every summer—for three months—and live.

"The point Norris makes is—they thaw, and live again. There must have been microscopic life associated with this creature. There is with every living thing we know. And Norris is afraid that we may release a plague—some germ disease unknown to Earth—if we thaw those microscopic things that have been frozen there for twenty million years.

"Blair admits that such micro-life might retain the power of living. Such unorganized things as individual cells can retain life for unknown periods, when solidly frozen. The beast itself is as dead as those frozen mammoths they find in Siberia. Organized, highly developed life-forms can't stand that treatment.

"But micro-life could. Norris suggests that we may release some disease-form that man, never having met it before, will be utterly defenseless against.

"Blair's answer is that there may be such still-living germs, but that Norris has the case reversed. They are utterly nonimmune to man. Our life-chemistry probably—"

"Probably!" The little biologist's head lifted in a quick, birdlike motion. The halo of gray hair about his bald head ruffled as though angry. "Heh, one look—"

"I know," McReady acknowledged. "The thing is not Earthly. It does not seem likely that it can have a life-chemistry sufficiently like ours to make cross-infection remotely possible. I would say that there is no danger."

McReady looked toward Dr. Copper. The physician shook his head slowly. "None whatever," he asserted confidently. "Man cannot infect or be infected by germs that live in such comparatively close relatives as the snakes. And they are, I assure you," his clean-shaven face grimaced uneasily, "much nearer to us than—*that*."

Vance Norris moved angrily. He was comparatively short in this gathering of big men, some five feet eight, and his stocky, powerful build tended to make him seem shorter. His black hair was crisp and hard, like short, steel wires, and his eyes were the gray of fractured steel. If McReady was a man of bronze, Norris was all steel. His movements, his thoughts, his whole bearing had the quick, hard impulse of a steel spring. His nerves were steel—hard, quick acting—swift corroding.

He was decided on his point now, and he lashed out in its defense with a characteristic quick, clipped flow of words. "Different chemistry be damned. That thing may be dead—or, by God, it may not—but I don't like it.

Damn it, Blair, let them see the monstrosity you are petting over there. Let them see the foul thing and decide for themselves whether they want that thing thawed out in this camp.

"Thawed out, by the way. That's got to be thawed out in one of the shacks tonight, if it is thawed out. Somebody—who's watchman tonight? Magnetic—oh, Connant. Cosmic rays tonight. Well, you get to sit up with that twenty-million-year-old mummy of his. Unwrap it, Blair. How the hell can they tell what they are buying, if they can't see it? It may have a different chemistry. I don't care what else it has, but I know it has something I don't want. If you can judge by the look on its face—it isn't human so maybe you can't—it was annoyed when it froze. Annoyed, in fact, is just about as close an approximation of the way it felt as crazy, mad, insane hatred. Neither one touches the subject.

"How the hell can these birds tell what they are voting on? They haven't seen those three red eyes and that blue hair like crawling worms. Crawling—damn, it's crawling there in the ice right now!

"Nothing Earth ever spawned had the unutterable sublimation of devastating wrath that thing let loose in its face when it looked around its frozen desolation twenty million years ago. Mad? It was mad clear through—searing, blistering mad!

"Hell, I've had bad dreams ever since I looked at those three red eyes. Nightmares. Dreaming the thing thawed out and came to life—that it wasn't dead, or even wholly unconscious all those twenty million years, but just slowed, waiting—waiting. You'll dream, too, while that damned thing that Earth wouldn't own is dripping, dripping in the Cosmos House tonight.

"And, Connant," Norris whipped toward the cosmic ray specialist, "won't you have fun sitting up all night in the quiet. Wind whining above—and that thing dripping—" he stopped for a moment, and looked around.

"I know. That's not science. But this is, it's psychology. You'll have nightmares for a year to come. Every night since I looked at that thing I've had 'em. That's why I hate it—sure I do—and don't want it around. Put it back where it came from and let it freeze for another twenty million years. I had some swell nightmares—that it wasn't made like we are—which is obvious—but of a different kind of flesh that it can really control. That it can change its shape, and look like a man—and wait to kill and eat—

"That's not a logical argument. I know it isn't. The thing isn't Earth-logic anyway.

"Maybe it has an alien body-chemistry, and maybe its bugs do have a different body-chemistry. A germ might not stand that, but, Blair and Copper, how about a virus? That's just an enzyme molecule, you've said. That wouldn't need anything but a protein molecule of any body to work on.

"And how are you so sure that, of the million varieties of microscopic life it may have, none of them are dangerous. How about diseases like hydrophobia—rabies—that attack any warm-blooded creature, whatever its body-chemistry may be? And parrot fever? Have you a body like a parrot, Blair? And plain rot—gangrene—necrosis if you want? That isn't choosy about body chemistry!"

Blair looked up from his puttering long enough to meet Norris' angry, gray eyes for an instant. "So far the only thing you have said this thing gave off that was catching was dreams. I'll go so far as to admit that." An impish, slightly malignant grin crossed the little man's seamed face. "I had some, too. So. It's dream-infectious. No doubt an exceedingly dangerous malady.

"So far as your other things go, you have a badly mistaken idea about viruses. In the first place, nobody has shown that the enzyme-molecule theory, and that alone, explains them. And in the second place, when you catch tobacco mosaic or wheat rust, let me know. A wheat plant is a lot nearer your body-chemistry than this other-world creature is.

"And your rabies is limited, strictly limited. You can't get it from, nor give it to, a wheat plant or a fish—which is a collateral descendant of a common ancestor of yours. Which this, Norris, is not." Blair nodded pleasantly toward the tarpaulined bulk on the table.

"Well, thaw the damned thing in a tub of formalin if you must. I've suggested that—"

"And I've said there would be no sense in it. You can't compromise. Why did you and Commander Garry come down here to study magnetism? Why weren't you content to stay at home? There's magnetic force enough in New York. I could no more study the life this thing once had from a formalin-pickled sample than you could get the information you wanted back in New York. And—if this one is so treated, never in all time to come can there be a duplicate! The race it came from must have passed away in the twenty million years it lay frozen, so that even if it came from Mars then, we'd never find its like. And—the ship is gone.

"There's only one way to do this—and that is the best possible way. It must be thawed slowly, carefully, and not in formalin."

Commander Garry stood forward again, and Norris stepped back muttering angrily. "I think Blair is right, gentlemen. What do you say?"

Connant grunted. "It sounds right to us, I think—only perhaps he ought to stand watch over it while it's thawing." He grinned ruefully, brushing a stray lock of ripe-cherry hair back from his forehead. "Swell idea, in fact—if he sits up with his jolly little corpse."

Garry smiled slightly. A general chuckle of agreement rippled over the group. "I should think any ghost it may have had would have starved to death if it hung around here that long, Connant," Garry suggested. "And you look capable of taking care of it. 'Ironman' Connant ought to be able to take out any opposing players, still."

Connant shook himself uneasily. "I'm not worrying about ghosts. Let's see that thing. I—"

Eagerly Blair was stripping back the ropes. A single throw of the tarpaulin revealed the thing. The ice had melted somewhat in the heat of the room, and it was clear and blue as thick, good glass. It shone wet and sleek under the harsh light of the unshielded globe above.

The room stiffened abruptly. It was face up there on the plain, greasy planks of the table. The broken haft of the bronze ice-ax was still buried in the queer skull. Three mad, hate-filled eyes blazed up with a living fire, bright as fresh-spilled blood, from a face ringed with a writhing, loathsome nest of worms, blue, mobile worms that crawled where hair should grow—

Van Wall, six feet and two hundred pounds of ice-nerved pilot, gave a queer, strangled gasp, and butted, stumbled his way out to the corridor. Half the company broke for the doors. The others stumbled away from the table.

McReady stood at one end of the table watching them, his great body planted solid on his powerful legs. Norris from the opposite end glowered at the thing with smouldering hate. Outside the door, Garry was talking with half a dozen of the men at once.

Blair had a tack hammer. The ice that cased the thing schluffed crisply under its steel claw as it peeled from the thing it had cased for twenty thousand thousand years—

## III

**"I KNOW** you don't like the thing, Connant, but it just has to be thawed out right. You say leave it as it is till we get back to civilization. All right, I'll admit your argument that we could do a better and more complete job there is sound. But—how are we going to get this across the Line? We have to take this through one temperate zone, the equatorial zone, and halfway through the other temperate zone before we get it to New York. You don't want to sit with it one night, but you suggest, then, that I hang its corpse in the freezer with the beef?" Blair looked up from his cautious chipping, his bald freckled skull nodding triumphantly.

Kinner, the stocky, scar-faced cook, saved Connant the trouble of answering. "Hey, you listen, mister. You put that thing in the box with the meat, and by all the gods there ever were, I'll put you in to keep it company. You birds have brought everything movable in this camp in onto my mess tables here already, and I had to stand for that. But you go putting things like that in my meat box, or even my meat cache here, and you cook your own damn grub."

"But, Kinner, this is the only table in Big Magnet that's big enough to work on," Blair objected. "Everybody's explained that."

"Yeah, and everybody's brought everything in here. Clark brings his dogs every time there's a fight and sews them up on that table. Ralsen brings in his sledges. Hell, the only thing you haven't had on that table is the Boeing. And you'd 'a' had that in if you coulda figured a way to get it through the tunnels."

Commander Garry chuckled and grinned at Van Wall, the huge Chief Pilot. Van Wall's great blond beard twitched suspiciously as he nodded gravely to Kinner. "You're right, Kinner. The aviation department is the only one that treats you right."

"It does get crowded, Kinner," Garry acknowledged. "But I'm afraid we all find it that way at times. Not much privacy in an Antarctic camp."

"Privacy? What the hell's that? You know, the thing that really made me weep, was when I saw Barclay marchin' through here chantin' 'The last lumber in the camp! The last lumber in the camp!' and carryin' it out to build that house on his tractor. Damn it, I missed that moon cut in the door he carried out more'n I missed the sun when it set. That wasn't just the last lumber Barclay was walkin' off with. He was carryin' off the last bit of privacy in this blasted place."

A grin rode even Connant's heavy face as Kinner's perennial, good-natured grouch came up again. But it died away quickly as his dark, deep-set eyes turned again to the red-eyed thing Blair was chipping from its cocoon of ice. A big hand ruffed his shoulder-length hair, and tugged at a twisted lock that fell behind his ear in a familiar gesture. "I know that cosmic ray shack's going to be too crowded if I have to sit up with that thing," he growled. "Why can't you go on chipping the ice away from around it—you can do that without anybody butting in, I assure you—and then hang the thing up over the power-plant boiler? That's warm enough. It'll thaw out a chicken, even a whole side of beef, in a few hours."

"I know," Blair protested, dropping the tack hammer to gesture more effectively with his bony, freckled fingers, his small body tense with eagerness, "but this is too important to take any chances. There never was a find like this; there never can be again. It's the only chance men will ever have, and it has to be done exactly right.

"Look, you know how the fish we caught down near the Ross Sea would freeze almost as soon as we got them on deck, and come to life again if we thawed them gently? Low forms of life aren't killed by quick freezing and slow thawing. We have—"

"Hey, for the love of Heaven—you mean that damned

thing will come to life!" Connant yelled. "You get the damned thing—Let me at it! That's going to be in so many pieces—"

"No! No, you fool—" Blair jumped in front of Connant to protect his precious find. "No. Just low forms of life. For Pete's sake let me finish. You can't thaw higher forms of life and have them come to. Wait a moment now—hold it! A fish can come to after freezing because it's so low a form of life that the individual cells of its body can revive, and that alone is enough to reestablish life. Any higher forms thawed out that way are dead. Though the individual cells revive, they die because there must be organization and cooperative effort to live. That cooperation cannot be reestablished. There is a sort of potential life in any uninjured, quick-frozen animal. But it can't—can't under any circumstances—become active life in higher animals. The higher animals are too complex, too delicate. This is an intelligent creature as high in its evolution as we are in ours. Perhaps higher. It is as dead as a frozen man would be."

"How do you know?" demanded Connant, hefting the ice-ax he had seized a moment before.

Commander Garry laid a restraining hand on his heavy shoulder. "Wait a minute, Connant. I want to get this straight. I agree that there is going to be no thawing of this thing if there is the remotest chance of its revival. I quite agree it is much too unpleasant to have alive, but I had no idea there was the remotest possibility."

Dr. Copper pulled his pipe from between his teeth and heaved his stocky, dark body from the bunk he had been sitting in. "Blair's being technical. That's dead. As dead as the mammoths they find frozen in Siberia. We have all sorts of proof that things don't live after being frozen—not even fish, generally speaking—and no proof that higher animal life can under any circumstances. What's the point, Blair?"

The little biologist shook himself. The little ruff of hair standing out around his bald pate waved in righteous anger. "The point is," he said in an injured tone, "that the individual cells might show the characteristics they had in life if it is properly thawed. A man's muscle cells live many hours after he has died. Just because they live, and a few things like hair and fingernail cells still live, you wouldn't accuse a corpse of being a zombie, or something.

"Now if I thaw this right, I may have a chance to determine what sort of world it's native to. We don't, and can't know by any other means, whether it came from Earth or Mars or Venus or from beyond the stars.

"And just because it looks unlike men, you don't have to accuse it of being evil, or vicious or something. Maybe that expression on its face is its equivalent to a resignation to fate. White is the color of mourning to the Chinese. If men can have different customs, why can't a so-different race have different understandings of facial expressions?"

Connant laughed softly, mirthlessly. "Peaceful resignation! If that is the best it could do in the way of resignation, I should exceedingly dislike seeing it when it was looking mad. That face was never designed to express peace. It just didn't have any philosophical thoughts like peace in its make-up.

"I know it's your pet—but be sane about it. That thing grew up on evil, adolesced slowly roasting alive the local equivalent of kittens, and amused itself through maturity on new and ingenious torture."

"You haven't the slightest right to say that," snapped Blair. "How do you know the first thing about the meaning of a facial expression inherently inhuman? It may well have no human equivalent whatever. That is just a different development of Nature, another example of Nature's wonderful adaptability. Growing on another, perhaps harsher world, it has different form and features. But it is just as much a legitimate child of Nature as you are. You are displaying that childish human weakness of hating the different. On its own world it would probably class you as a fish-belly, white monstrosity with an insufficient number of eyes and a fungoid body pale and bloated with gas.

"Just because its nature is different, you haven't any right to say it's necessarily evil."

Norris burst out a single, explosive, "Haw!" He looked down at the thing. "May be that things from other worlds don't have to be evil just because they're different. But that thing was! Child of Nature, eh? Well, it was a hell of an evil Nature."

"Aw, will you mugs cut crabbing at each other and get the damned thing off my table?" Kinner growled. "And put a canvas over it. It looks indecent."

"Kinner's gone modest," jeered Connant.

Kinner slanted his eyes up to the big physicist. The scarred cheek twisted to join the line of his tight lips in a twisted grin. "All right, big boy, and what were you grousing about a minute ago? We can set the thing in a chair next to you tonight, if you want."

"I'm not afraid of its face," Connant snapped. "I don't like keeping a wake over its corpse particularly, but I'm going to do it."

Kinner's grin spread. "Uh-huh." He went off to the galley stove and shook down ashes vigorously, drowning the brittle chipping of the ice as Blair fell to work again.

## IV

**"CLUCK,"** reported the cosmic-ray counter, "cluck-burrrp-cluck."

Connant started and dropped his pencil.

"Damnation." The physicist looked toward the far corner, back at the Geiger counter on the table near that corner. And crawled under the desk at which he had been working to retrieve the pencil. He sat down at his work again, trying to make his writing more even. It tended to have jerks and quavers in it, in time with the abrupt proud-hen noises of the Geiger counter. The muted whoosh of the pressure lamp he was using for illumination, the mingled gargles and bugle calls of a dozen men sleeping down the corridor in Paradise House formed the background sounds for the irregular, clucking noises of the counter, the occasional rustle of falling coal in the copper-bellied stove. And a soft, steady drip-drip-drip from the thing in the corner.

Connant jerked a pack of cigarettes from his pocket, snapped it so that a cigarette protruded, and jabbed the cylinder into his mouth. The lighter failed to function, and he pawed angrily through the pile of papers in search of a match. He scratched the wheel of the lighter several times, dropped it with a curse and got up to pluck a hot coat from the stove with the coal tongs.

The lighter functioned instantly when he tried it on returning to the desk. The counter ripped out a series of chuckling guffaws as a burst of cosmic rays struck through to it. Connant turned to glower at it, and tried to concentrate on the interpretation of data collected during the past week. The weekly summary—

He gave up and yielded to curiosity, or nervousness. He lifted the pressure lamp from the desk and carried it over to the table in the corner. Then he returned to the stove and picked up the coal tongs. The beast had been thawing for nearly eighteen hours now. He poked at it with an unconscious caution; the flesh was no longer hard as armor plate, but had assumed a rubbery texture. It looked like wet, blue rubber glistening under droplets of water like little round jewels in the glare of the gasoline pressure lantern. Connant felt an unreasoning desire to pour the contents of the lamp's reservoir over the thing in its box and drop the cigarette into it. The three red eyes glared up at him sightlessly, the ruby eyeballs reflecting murky, smoky rays of light.

He realized vaguely that he had been looking at them for a very long time, even vaguely understood that they were no longer sightless. But it did not seem of importance, of no more importance than the labored, slow motion of the tentacular things that sprouted from the base of the scrawny, slowly pulsing neck.

Connant picked up the pressure lamp and returned to

his chair. He sat down, staring at the pages of mathematics before him. The clucking of the counter was strangely less disturbing, the rustle of the coals in the stove no longer distracting.

The creak of the floorboards behind him didn't interrupt his thoughts as he went about his weekly report in an automatic manner, filling in columns of data and making brief, summarizing notes.

The creak of the floorboards sounded nearer.

## V

**BLAIR CAME UP** from the nightmare-haunted depths of sleep abruptly. Connant's face floated vaguely above him; for a moment it seemed a continuance of the wild horror of the dream. But Connant's face was angry, and a little frightened. "Blair—Blair you damned log, wake up."

"Uh-eh?" the little biologist rubbed his eyes, his bony, freckled finger crooked to a mutilated child-fist. From surrounding bunks other faces lifted to stare down at them.

Connant straightened up. "Get up—and get a lift on. Your damned animal's escaped."

"Escaped—what!" Chief Pilot Van Wall's bull voice roared out with a volume that shook the walls. Down the communication tunnels other voices yelled suddenly. The dozen inhabitants of Paradise House tumbled in abruptly, Barclay, stocky and bulbous in long woolen underwear, carrying a fire extinguisher.

"What the hell's the matter?" Barclay demanded.

"Your damned beast got loose. I fell asleep about twenty minutes ago, and when I woke up, the thing was gone. Hey, Doc, the hell you say those things can't come to life. Blair's blasted potential life developed a hell of a lot of potential and walked out on us."

Copper stared blankly. "It wasn't—Earthly," he sighed suddenly. "I—I guess Earthly laws don't apply."

"Well, it applied for leave of absence and took it. We've got to find it and capture it somehow." Connant swore bitterly, his deep-set black eyes sullen and angry. "It's a wonder the hellish creature didn't eat me in my sleep."

Blair started back, his pale eyes suddenly fear-struck. "Maybe it di—er—uh—we'll have to find it."

"You find it. It's your pet. I've had all I want to do with it, sitting there for seven hours with the counter clucking every few seconds, and you birds in here singing night-music. It's a wonder I got to sleep. I'm going through to the Ad Building."

Commander Garry ducked through the doorway, pulling his belt tight. "You won't have to. Van's roar sounded like the Boeing taking off downwind. So it wasn't dead?"

"I didn't carry it off in my arms, I assure you," Connant snapped. "The last I saw, the split skull was oozing green goo, like a squashed caterpillar. Doc just said our laws don't work—it's unearthly. Well, it's an unearthly monster, with an unearthly disposition, judging by the face, wandering around with a split skull and brains oozing out." Norris and McReady appeared in the doorway, a doorway filling with other shivering men. "Has anybody seen it coming over here?" Norris asked innocently.

"About four feet tall—three red eyes—brains oozing out— Hey, has anybody checked to make sure this isn't a cracked idea of humor? If it is, I think we'll unite in tying Blair's pet around Connant's neck like the Ancient Mariner's albatross."

"It's no humor," Connant shivered. "Lord, I wish it were. I'd rather wear—" He stopped. A wild, weird howl shrieked through the corridors. The men stiffened abruptly, and half turned.

"I think it's been located," Connant finished. His dark eyes shifted with a queer unease. He darted back to his bunk in Paradise House, to return almost immediately with a heavy .45 revolver and an ice-ax. He hefted both gently as he started for the corridor toward Dogtown.

"It blundered down the wrong corridor—and landed among the huskies. Listen—the dogs have broken their chains—"

The half-terrorized howl of the dog pack had changed to a wild hunting melee. The voices of the dogs thundered in the narrow corridors, and through them came a low rippling snarl of distilled hate. A shrill of pain, a dozen snarling yelps.

Connant broke for the door. Close behind him, McReady, then Barclay and Commander Garry came. Other men broke for the Ad Building, and weapons—the sledge house. Pomroy, in charge of Big Magnet's five cows, started down the corridor in the opposite direction—he had a six-foot-handled, long-tined pitchfork in mind.

Barclay slid to a halt, as McReady's giant bulk turned abruptly away from the tunnel leading to Dogtown, and vanished off at an angle. Uncertainly, the mechanician wavered a moment, the fire extinguisher in his hands, hesitating from one side to the other. Then he was racing after Connant's broad back. Whatever McReady had in mind, he could be trusted to make it work.

Connant stopped at the bend in the corridor. His breath hissed suddenly through his throat. "Great God—" The revolver exploded thunderously; three numbing, palpable waves of sound crashed through the confined corridors. Two more. The revolver dropped to the hard-packed snow of the trail, and Barclay saw the ice-ax shift into defensive position. Connant's powerful body blocked his vision, but beyond he heard something mewing, and, insanely, chuckling. The dogs were quieter; there was a deadly seriousness in their low snarls. Taloned feet scratched at hard-packed snow, broken chains were clinking and tangling.

Connant shifted abruptly, and Barclay could see what lay beyond. For a second he stood frozen, then his breath went out in a gusty curse. The Thing launched itself at Connant, the powerful arms of the man swung the ice-ax flat-side first at what might have been a head. It scrunched horribly, and the tattered flesh, ripped by a half-dozen savage huskies, leapt to its feet again. The red eyes blazed with an unearthly hatred, an unearthly, unkillable vitality.

Barclay turned the fire extinguisher on it; the blinding, blistering stream of chemical spray confused it, baffled it, together with the savage attacks of the huskies, not for long afraid of anything that did, or could live, and held it at bay.

McReady wedged men out of his way and drove down the narrow corridor packed with men unable to reach the scene. There was a sure foreplanned drive to McReady's attack. One of the giant blowtorches used in warming the plane's engines was in his bronzed hands. It roared gustily as he turned the corner and opened the valve. The mad mewing hissed louder. The dogs scrambled back from the three-foot lance of blue-hot flame.

"Bar, get a power cable, run it in somehow. And a handle. We can electrocute this—monster, if I don't incinerate it." McReady spoke with an authority of planned action. Barclay turned down the long corridor to the power plant, but already before him Norris and Van Wall were racing down.

Barclay found the cable in the electrical cache in the tunnel wall. In a half minute he was hacking at it, walking back. Van Wall's voice rang out in warning shout of "Power!" as the emergency gasoline-powered dynamo thudded into action. Half a dozen other men were down there now; the coal, kindling were going into the firebox of the steam power plant. Norris, cursing in a low, deadly monotone, was working with quick, sure fingers on the other end of Barclay's cable, splicing a contractor into one of the power leads.

The dogs had fallen back when Barclay reached the corridor bend, fallen back before a furious monstrosity that glared from baleful red eyes, mewing in trapped hatred. The dogs were a semi-circle of red-dipped muzzles with a fringe of glistening white teeth, whining with a vicious eagerness that near matched the fury of the red eyes. McReady stood confidently alert at the corridor bend, the gustily muttering torch held loose and ready for action in his hands. He stepped aside without moving his eyes from the beast as Barclay came up. There was a slight, tight smile on his lean, bronzed face.

Norris' voice called down the corridor, and Barclay stepped forward. The cable was taped to the long handle of a snow shovel, the two conductors split and held eighteen inches apart by a scrap of lumber lashed at right angles across the far end of the handle. Bare copper conductors, charged with 220 volts, glinted in the light of pressure lamps. The Thing mewed and hated and dodged. McReady advanced to Barclay's side. The dogs beyond sensed the plan with the almost telepathic intelligence of trained huskies. Their whining grew shriller, softer, their mincing steps carried them nearer. Abruptly a huge night-black Alaskan leapt onto the trapped thing. It turned squalling, saber-clawed feet slashing.

Barclay leapt forward and jabbed. A weird, shrill scream rose and choked out. The smell of burnt flesh in the corridor intensified; greasy smoke curled up. The echoing pound of the gas-electric dynamo down the corridor became a slogging thud.

The red eyes clouded over in a stiffening, jerking travesty of a face. Armlike, leglike members quivered and jerked. The dogs leapt forward, and Barclay yanked back his shovel-handled weapon. The thing on the snow did not move as gleaming teeth ripped it open.

## VI

**GARRY LOOKED** about the crowded room. Thirty-two

men, some tensed nervously standing against the wall, some uneasily relaxed, some sitting, most perforce standing as intimate as sardines. Thirty-two, plus the five engaged in sewing up wounded dogs, made thirty-seven, the total personnel.

Garry started speaking. "All right, I guess we're here. Some of you—three or four at most—saw what happened. All of you have seen that thing on the table, and can get a general idea. Anyone hasn't, I'll lift—" His hand strayed to the tarpaulin bulking over the thing on the table. There was an acrid odor of singed flesh seeping out of it. The men stirred restlessly, hasty denials.

"It looks rather as though Charnauk isn't going to lead any more teams," Garry went on. "Blair wants to get at this thing, and make some more detailed examination. We want to know what happened, and make sure right now that this is permanently, totally dead. Right?"

Connant grinned. "Anybody that doesn't can sit up with it tonight."

"All right then, Blair, what can you say about it? What was it?" Garry turned to the little biologist.

"I wonder if we ever saw its natural form," Blair looked at the covered mass. "It may have been imitating the beings that built that ship—but I don't think it was. I think that was its true form. Those of us who were up near the bend saw the thing in action; the thing on the table is the result. When it got loose, apparently, it started looking around. Antarctica still frozen as it was ages ago when the creature first saw it—and froze. From my observations while it was thawing out, and the bits of tissue I cut and hardened then, I think it was native to a hotter planet than

Earth. It couldn't, in its natural form, stand the temperature. There is no life-form on Earth that can live in Antarctica during the winter, but the best compromise is the dog. It found the dogs, and somehow got near enough to Charnauk to get him. The others smelled it—heard it—I don't know—anyway they went wild, and broke chains, and attacked it before it was finished. The thing we found was part Charnauk, queerly only half-dead, part Charnauk half-digested by the jellylike protoplasm of that creature, and part the remains of the thing we originally found, sort of melted down to the basic protoplasm.

"When the dogs attacked it, it turned into the best fighting thing it could think of. Some other-world beast apparently."

"Turned," snapped Garry. "How?"

"Every living thing is made up of jelly—protoplasm and minute, submicroscopic things called nuclei, which control the bulk, the protoplasm. This thing was just a modification of that same world-wide plan of Nature; cells made up of protoplasm, controlled by infinitely tinier nuclei. You physicists might compare it—an individual cell of any living thing—with an atom; the bulk of the atom, the space-filling part, is made up of the electron orbits, but the character of the thing is determined by the atomic nucleus.

"This isn't wildly beyond what we already know. It's just a modification we haven't seen before. It's as natural, as logical, as any other manifestation of life. It obeys exactly the same laws. The cells are made of protoplasm, their character determined by the nucleus.

"Only, in this creature, the cell nuclei can control those cells at will. It digested Charnauk, and as it digested, studied every cell of his tissue, and shaped its own cells to imitate them exactly. Parts of it—parts that had time to finish changing—are dog-cells. But they don't have dog-cell nuclei." Blair lifted a fraction of the tarpaulin. A torn dog's leg, with stiff gray fur protruded. "That, for instance, isn't dog at all; it's imitation. Some parts I'm uncertain about; the nucleus was hiding itself, covering up with dog-cell imitation nucleus. In time, not even a microscope would have shown the difference."

"Suppose," asked Norris bitterly, "it had had lots of time?"

"Then it would have been a dog. The other dogs would have accepted it. We would have accepted it. I don't think anything would have distinguished it, not microscope, nor X-ray, nor any other means. This is a member of a supremely intelligent race, a race that has learned the deepest secrets of biology, and turned them to its use."

"What was it planning to do?" Barclay looked at the humped tarpaulin.

Blair grinned unpleasantly. The wavering halo of thin hair round his bald pate wavered in a stir of air. "Take over the world, I imagine."

"Take over the world! Just it, all by itself?" Connant gasped. "Set itself up as a lone dictator?"

"No," Blair shook his head. The scalpel he had been fumbling in his bony fingers dropped; he bent to pick it up, so that his face was hidden as he spoke. "It would become the population of the world."

"Become—populate the world? Does it reproduce asexually?"

Blair shook his head and gulped. "It's—it doesn't have to. It weighed eighty-five pounds. Charnauk weighed about ninety. It would have become Charnauk, and had eight-five pounds left, to become—oh, Jack, for instance, or Chinook. It can imitate anything—that is, become anything. If it had reached the Antarctic Sea, it would have become a seal, maybe two seals. They might have attacked a killer whale, and become either killers, or a herd of seals. Or maybe it would have caught an albatross, or a skua gull, and flown to South America."

Norris cursed softly. "And every time it digested something, and imitated it—"

"It would have had its original bulk left, to start again," Blair finished. "Nothing would kill it. It has no natural enemies, because it becomes whatever it wants to. If a killer whale attacked it, it would become a killer whale. If it was an albatross, and an eagle attacked it, it would become an eagle. Lord, it might become a female eagle. Go back—build a nest and lay eggs!"

"Are you sure that thing from hell is dead?" Dr. Copper asked softly.

"Yes, thank Heaven," the little biologist gasped. "After they drove the dogs off, I stood there poking Bar's electrocution thing into it for five minutes. It's dead and—cooked."

"Then we can only give thanks that this is Antarctica, where there is not one, single, solitary, living thing for it to imitate, except these animals in camp."

"Us," Blair giggled. "It can imitate us. Dogs can't make

four hundred miles to the sea; there's no food. There aren't any skua gulls to imitate at this season. There aren't any penguins this far inland. There's nothing that can reach the sea from this point—except us. We've got brains. We can do it. Don't you see—it's got to imitate us—it's got to be one of us—that's the only way it can fly an airplane—fly a plane for two hours, and rule—be—all Earth's inhabitants. A world for the taking—if it imitates us!

"It didn't know yet. It hadn't had a chance to learn. It was rushed—hurried—took the thing nearest its own size. Look—I'm Pandora! I opened the box! And the only hope that can come out is—that nothing can come out. You didn't see me. I did it. I fixed it. I smashed every magneto. Not a plane can fly. Nothing can fly." Blair giggled and lay down on the floor crying.

Chief Pilot Van Wall made for the door. His feet were fading echoes in the corridors as Dr. Copper bent unhurriedly over the little man on the floor. From his office at the end of the room he brought something and injected a solution into Blair's arm. "He might come out of it when he wakes up," he sighed, rising. McReady helped him lift the biologist onto a nearby bunk. "It all depends on whether we can convince him that thing is dead."

Van Wall ducked into the shack, brushing his heavy blond beard absently. "I didn't think a biologist would do a thing like that up thoroughly. He missed the spares in the second cache. It's all right. I smashed them."

Commander Garry nodded. "I was wondering about the radio."

Dr. Copper snorted. "You don't think it can leak out on a radio wave, do you? You'd have five rescue attempts in the next three months if you stop the broadcasts. The thing to do is talk loud and not make a sound. Now I wonder—"

McReady looked speculatively at the doctor. "It might be like an infectious disease. Everything that drank any of its blood—"

Copper shook his head. "Blair missed something. Imitate it may, but it has, to a certain extent, its own body chemistry, its own metabolism. If it didn't, it would become a dog—and be a dog and nothing more. It has to be an imitation dog. Therefore you can detect it by serum tests. And its chemistry, since it comes from another world, must be so wholly, radically different that a few cells, such as gained by drops of blood, would be treated as disease germs by the dog, or human body."

"Blood—would one of those imitations bleed?" Norris demanded.

"Surely. Nothing mystic about blood. Muscle is about 90% water; blood differs only in having a couple percent more water, and less connective tissue. They'd bleed all right," Copper assured him.

Blair sat up in his bunk suddenly. "Connant—where's Connant?"

The physicist moved over toward the little biologist. "Here I am. What do you want?"

"Are you?" giggled Blair. He lapsed back into the bunk contorted with silent laughter.

Connant looked at him blankly. "Huh? Am I what?"

"Are you there?" Blair burst into gales of laughter.

"Are you Connant? The beast wanted to be man—not a dog—"

# VII

**DR. COPPER ROSE** wearily from the bunk, and washed the hypodermic carefully. The little tinkles it made seemed loud in the packed room, now that Blair's gurgling laughter had finally quieted. Copper looked toward Garry and shook his head slowly. "Hopeless, I'm afraid. I don't think we can ever convince him the thing is dead now."

Norris laughed uncertainly. "I'm not sure you can convince me. Oh, damn you, McReady."

"McReady?" Commander Garry turned to look from Norris to McReady curiously.

"The nightmares," Norris explained. "He had a theory about the nightmares we had at the Secondary Station after finding that thing."

"And that was?" Garry looked at McReady levelly.

Norris answered for him, jerkily, uneasily. "That the creature wasn't dead, had a sort of enormously slowed existence, an existence that permitted it, nonetheless, to be vaguely aware of the passing of time, of our coming, after endless years. I had a dream it could imitate things."

"Well," Copper grunted, "it can."

"Don't be an ass," Norris snapped. "That's not what's bothering me. In the dream it could read minds, read thoughts and ideas and mannerisms."

"What's so bad about that? It seems to be worrying you more than the thought of the joy we're going to have with a madman in an Antarctic camp." Copper nodded toward Blair's sleeping form.

McReady shook his great head slowly. "You know that Connant is Connant, because he not merely looks like Connant—which we're beginning to believe that beast might be able to do—but he thinks like Connant, moves himself around as Connant does. That takes more than merely a body that looks like him; that takes Connant's own mind, and thoughts and mannerisms. Therefore, though you know that the thing might make itself look like Connant, you aren't much bothered, because you know it has a mind from another world, a totally unhuman mind, that couldn't possibly react and think and talk like a man we know, and do it so well as to fool us for a moment. The idea of the creature imitating one of us is fascinating, but unreal, because it is too completely unhuman to deceive us. It doesn't have a human mind."

"As I said before," Norris repeated, looking steadily at McReady, "you can say the damnedest things at the damnedest times. Will you be so good as to finish that thought—one way or the other?"

Kinner, the scar-faced expedition cook, had been standing near Connant. Suddenly he moved down the length of the crowded room toward his familiar galley. He shook the ashes from the galley stove noisily.

"It would do it no good," said Dr. Copper, softly as though thinking out loud, "to merely look like something it was trying to imitate; it would have to understand its feelings, its reactions. It is unhuman; it has powers of imitation beyond any conception of man. A good actor, by training himself, can imitate another man, another man's mannerisms, well enough to fool most people. Of course no actor could imitate so perfectly as to deceive men who had been living with the imitated one in the complete lack of privacy of an Antarctic camp. That would take a superhuman skill."

"Oh, you've got the bug, too?" Norris cursed softly.

Connant, standing alone at one end of the room, looked about him wildly, his face white. A gentle eddying of the men had crowded them slowly down toward the other end of the room, so that he stood quite alone. "My God, will you two Jeremiahs shut up?" Connant's voice shook. "What am I? Some kind of microscopic specimen you're dissecting? Some unpleasant worm you're discussing in the third person?"

McReady looked up at him; his slowly twisting hands stopped for a moment. "Having a lovely time. Wish you were here. Signed: Everybody.

"Connant, if you think you're having a hell of a time, just move over on the other end for a while. You've got one thing we haven't; you know what the answer is. I'll tell you this, right now you're the most feared and respected man in Big Magnet."

"Lord, I wish you could see your eyes," Connant gasped. "Stop staring, will you! What the hell are you going to do?"

"Have you any suggestions, Dr. Copper?" Commander Garry asked steadily. "The present situation is impossible."

"Oh, is it?" Connant snapped. "Come over here and

look at that crowd. By Heaven, they look exactly like that gang of huskies around the corridor bend. Benning, will you stop hefting that damned ice-ax?"

The coppery blade rang on the floor as the aviation mechanic nervously dropped it. He bent over and picked it up instantly, hefting it slowly, turning it in his hands, his brown eyes moving jerkily about the room.

Copper sat down on the bunk beside Blair. The wood creaked noisily in the room. Far down a corridor, a dog yelped in pain, and the dog drivers' tense voices floated softly back. "Microscopic examination," said the doctor thoughtfully, "would be useless, as Blair pointed out. Considerable time has passed. However, serum tests would be definitive."

"Serum tests? What do you mean exactly?" Commander Garry asked.

"If I had a rabbit that had been injected with human blood—a poison to rabbits, of course, as is the blood of any animal save that of another rabbit—and the injections continued in increasing doses for some time, the rabbit would be human-immune. If a small quantity of its blood were drawn off, allowed to separate in a test tube, and to the clear serum, a bit of human blood were added, there would be a visible reaction, proving the blood was human. If cow, or dog blood were added—or any protein material other than that one thing—human blood—no reaction would take place. That would prove definitely."

"Can you suggest where I might catch a rabbit for you, Doc?" Norris asked. "That is, nearer than Australia; we don't want to waste time going that far."

"I know there aren't any rabbits in Antarctica," Copper

nodded, "but that is simply the usual animal. Any animal except man will do. A dog for instance. But it will take several days, and due to the greater size of the animal, considerable blood. Two of us will have to contribute."

"Would I do?" Garry asked.

"That will make two," Copper nodded. "I'll get to work on it right away."

"What about Connant in the meantime," Kinner demanded. "I'm going out that door and head off for the Ross Sea before I cook for him."

"He may be human—" Copper started.

Connant burst out in a flood of curses. "Human! May be human, you damned sawbones! What in hell do you think I am?"

"A monster," Copper snapped sharply. "Now shut up and listen." Connant's face drained of color and he sat down heavily as the indictment was put in words. "Until we know—you know as well as we do that we have reason to question the fact, and only you know how that question is to be answered—we may reasonably be expected to lock you up. If you are—unhuman—you're a lot more dangerous than poor Blair there, and I'm going to see that he's locked up thoroughly. I expect that his next stage will be a violent desire to kill you, all the dogs, and probably all of us. When he wakes, he will be convinced we're all unhuman, and nothing on the planet will ever change his conviction. It would be kinder to let him die, but we can't do that, of course. He's going in one shack, and you can stay in Cosmos House with your cosmic ray apparatus. Which is about what you'd do anyway. I've got to fix up a couple of dogs."

Connant nodded bitterly. "I'm human. Hurry that test. Your eyes—Lord, I wish you could see your eyes staring—"

Commander Garry watched anxiously as Clark, the dog-handler, held the big brown Alaskan husky, while Copper began the injection treatment. The dog was not anxious to cooperate; the needle was painful, and already he'd experienced considerable needle work that morning. Five stitches held closed a slash that ran from his shoulder, across the ribs, halfway down his body. One long fang was broken off short; the missing part was to be found half buried in the shoulder bone of the monstrous thing on the table in the Ad Building.

"How long will that take?" Garry asked, pressing his arm gently. It was sore from the prick of the needle Dr. Copper had used to withdraw blood.

Copper shrugged. "I don't know, to be frank. I know the general method. I've used it on rabbits. But I haven't experimented with dogs. They're big, clumsy animals to work with; naturally rabbits are preferable, and serve ordinarily. In civilized places you can buy a stock of human-immune rabbits from suppliers, and not many investigators take the trouble to prepare their own."

"What do they want with them back there?" Clark asked.

"Criminology is one large field. A says he didn't murder B, but that the blood on his shirt came from killing a chicken. The State makes a test, then it's up to A to explain how it is the blood reacts on human-immune rabbits, but not on chicken-immunes."

"What are we going to do with Blair in the meantime?"

Garry asked wearily. "It's all right to let him sleep where he is for a while, but when he wakes up—"

"Barclay and Benning are fitting some bolts on the door of Cosmos House," Copper replied grimly. "Connant's acting like a gentleman. I think perhaps the way the other men look at him makes him rather want privacy. Lord knows, heretofore we've all of us individually prayed for a little privacy."

Clark laughed brittlely. "Not any more, thank you. The more the merrier."

"Blair," Copper went on, "will also have to have privacy—and locks. He's going to have a pretty definite plan in mind when he wakes up. Ever hear the old story of how to stop hoof-and-mouth disease in cattle?"

Clark and Garry shook their heads silently.

"If there isn't any hoof-and-mouth disease, there won't be any hoof-and-mouth disease," Copper explained. "You get rid of it by killing every animal that exhibits it, and every animal that's been near the diseased animal. Blair's a biologist, and knows that story. He's afraid of this thing we loosed. The answer is probably pretty clear in his mind now. Kill everybody and everything in this camp before a skua gull or a wandering albatross coming in with the spring chances out this way and—catches the disease."

Clark's lips curled in a twisted grin. "Sounds logical to me. If things get too bad—maybe we'd better let Blair get loose. It would save us committing suicide. We might also make something of a vow that if things get bad, we see that that does happen."

Copper laughed softly. "The last man alive in Big Magnet—wouldn't be a man," he pointed out. "Somebody's got to kill those—creatures that don't desire to kill themselves, you know. We don't have enough thermite to do it all at once, and the decanite explosive wouldn't help much. I have an idea that even small pieces of one of those beings would be self-sufficient."

"If," said Garry thoughtfully, "they can modify their protoplasm at will, won't they simply modify themselves to birds and fly away? They can read all about birds, and imitate their structure without even meeting them. Or imitate, perhaps, birds of their home planet."

Copper shook his head, and helped Clark to free the dog. "Man studied birds for centuries, trying to learn how to make a machine to fly like them. He never did do the trick; his final success came when he broke away entirely and tried new methods. Knowing the general idea, and knowing the detailed structure of wing and bone and nerve-tissue is something far, far different. And as for other-world birds, perhaps, in fact very probably, the atmospheric conditions here are so vastly different that their birds couldn't fly. Perhaps, even, the being came from a planet like Mars with such a thin atmosphere that there were no birds."

Barclay came into the building, trailing a length of airplane control cable. "It's finished, Doc. Cosmos House can't be opened from the inside. Now where do we put Blair?"

Copper looked toward Garry. "There wasn't any biology building. I don't know where we can isolate him."

"How about East Cache?" Garry said after a moment's thought. "Will Blair be able to look after himself—or need attention?"

"He'll be capable enough. We'll be the ones to watch out," Copper assured him grimly. "Take a stove, a couple of bags of coal, necessary supplies and a few tools to fix it up. Nobody's been out there since last fall, have they?"

Garry shook his head. "If he gets noisy—I thought that might be a good idea."

Barclay hefted the tools he was carrying and looked up at Garry. "If the muttering he's doing now is any sign, he's going to sing away the night hours. And we won't like his song."

"What's he saying?" Copper asked.

Barclay shook his head. "I didn't care to listen much. You can if you want to. But I gathered that the blasted idiot had all the dreams McReady had, and a few more. He slept beside the thing when we stopped on the trail coming in from Secondary Magnetic, remember. He dreamt the thing was alive, and dreamt more details. And—damn his soul—knew it wasn't all dream, or had reason to. He knew it had telepathic powers that were stirring vaguely, and that it could not only read minds, but project thoughts. They weren't dreams, you see. They were stray thoughts that thing was broadcasting, the way Blair's broadcasting his thoughts now—a sort of telepathic muttering in its sleep. That's why he knew so much about its powers. I guess you and I, Doc, weren't so sensitive—if you want to believe in telepathy."

"I have to," Copper sighed. "Dr. Rhine of Duke University has shown that it exists, shown that some are much more sensitive than others."

"Well, if you want to learn a lot of details, go listen in on Blair's broadcast. He's driven most of the boys out of the Ad Building; Kinner's rattling pans like coal going down a chute. When he can't rattle a pan, he shakes ashes.

"By the way, Commander, what are we going to do this spring, now the planes are out of it?"

Garry sighed. "I'm afraid our expedition is going to be a loss. We cannot divide our strength now."

"It won't be a loss—if we continue to live, and come out of this," Copper promised him. "The find we've made, if we can get it under control, is important enough. The cosmic ray data, magnetic work, and atmospheric work won't be greatly hindered."

Garry laughed mirthlessly. "I was just thinking of the radio broadcasts. Telling half the world about the wonderful results of our exploration flights, trying to fool men like Byrd and Ellsworth back home there that we're doing something."

Copper nodded gravely. "They'll know something's wrong. But men like that have judgment enough to know we wouldn't do tricks without some sort of reason, and will wait for our return to judge us. I think it comes to this: men who know enough to recognize our deception will wait for our return. Men who haven't discretion and faith enough to wait will not have the experience to detect any fraud. We know enough of the conditions here to put through a good bluff."

"Just so they don't send 'rescue' expeditions," Garry prayed. "When—if—we're ever ready to come out, we'll have to send word to Captain Forsythe to bring a stock of magnetos with him when he comes down. But—never mind that."

"You mean if we don't come out?" asked Barclay. "I

was wondering if a nice running account of an eruption or an earthquake via radio—with a swell windup by using a stick of decanite under the microphone—would help. Nothing, of course, will entirely keep people out. One of those swell, melodramatic 'last-man-alive-scenes' might make 'em go easy though."

Garry smiled with genuine humor. "Is everybody in camp trying to figure that out, too?"

Copper laughed. "What do you think, Garry? We're confident we can win out. But not too easy about it, I guess."

Clark grinned up from the dog he was petting into calmness. "Confident, did you say, Doc?"

## VIII

**BLAIR MOVED RESTLESSLY** around the small shack. His eyes jerked and quivered in vague, fleeting glances at the four men with him; Barclay, six feet tall and weighing over 190 pounds; McReady, a bronze giant of a man; Dr. Copper, short, squatly powerful; and Benning, five feet ten of wiry strength.

Blair was huddled up against the far wall of the East Cache cabin, his gear piled in the middle of the floor beside the heating stove, forming an island between him and the four men. His bony hands clenched and fluttered, terrified. His pale eyes wavered uneasily as his bald, freckled head darted about in birdlike motion.

"I don't want anybody coming here. I'll cook my own

food," he snapped nervously. "Kinner may be human now, but I don't believe it. I'm going to get out of here, but I'm not going to eat any food you send me. I want cans. Sealed cans."

"OK, Blair, we'll bring 'em tonight," Barclay promised. "You've got coal, and the fire's started. I'll make a last—" Barclay started forward.

Blair instantly scurried to the farthest corner. "Get out! Keep away from me, you monster!" the little biologist shrieked, and tried to claw his way through the wall of the shack. "Keep away from me—keep away—I won't be absorbed—I won't be—"

Barclay relaxed and moved back. Dr. Copper shook his head. "Leave him alone, Bar. It's easier for him to fix the thing himself. We'll have to fix the door, I think—"

The four men let themselves out. Efficiently, Benning and Barclay fell to work. There were no locks in Antarctica; there wasn't enough privacy to make them needed. But powerful screws had been driven in each side of the door frame, and the spare aviation control cable, immensely strong, woven steel wire, was rapidly caught between them and drawn taut. Barclay went to work with a drill and a key-hole saw. Presently he had a trap cut in the door through which goods could be passed without unlashing the entrance. Three powerful hinges made from a stock crate, two hasps and a pair of three-inch cotter pins made it proof against opening from the other side.

Blair moved about restlessly inside. He was dragging something over to the door with panting gasps, and muttering frantic curses. Barclay opened the hatch and glanced in, Dr. Copper peering over his shoulder. Blair had moved the heavy bunk against the door. It could not be opened without his cooperation now.

"Don't know but what the poor man's right at that," McReady sighed. "If he gets loose, it is his avowed intention to kill each and all of us as quickly as possible, which is something we don't agree with. But we've something on our side of that door that is worse than a homicidal maniac. If one or the other has to get loose, I think I'll come up and undo these lashings here."

Barclay grinned. "You let me know, and I'll show you how to get these off fast. Let's go back."

The sun was painting the northern horizon in multicolored rainbows still, though it was two hours below the horizon. The field of drift swept off to the north, sparkling under its flaming colors in a million reflected glories. Low mounds of rounded white on the northern horizon showed the Magnet Range was barely awash above the sweeping drift. Little eddies of wind-lifted snow swirled away from their skis as they set out toward the main encampment two miles away. The spidery finger of the broadcast radiator lifted a gaunt black needle against the white of the Antarctic continent. The snow under their skis was like fine sand, hard and gritty.

"Spring," said Benning bitterly, "is come. Ain't we got fun! And I've been looking forward to getting away from this blasted hole in the ice."

"I wouldn't try it now, if I were you." Barclay grunted. "Guys that set out from here in the next few days are going to be marvelously unpopular."

"How is your dog getting along, Dr. Copper?" McReady asked. "Any results yet?"

"In thirty hours? I wish there were. I gave him an injection of my blood today. But I imagine another five days will be needed. I don't know certainly enough to stop sooner."

"I've been wondering—if Connant were—changed, would he have warned us so soon after the animal escaped? Wouldn't he have waited long enough for it to have a real chance to fix itself? Until we woke up naturally?" McReady asked slowly.

"The thing is selfish. You didn't think it looked as though it were possessed of a store of the higher justices, did you?" Dr. Copper pointed out. "Every part of it is all of it, every part of it is all for itself, I imagine. If Connant were changed, to save his skin, he'd have to—but Connant's feelings aren't changed; they're imitated perfectly, or they're his own. Naturally, the imitation, imitating perfectly Connant's feelings, would do exactly what Connant would do."

"Say, couldn't Norris or Vane give Connant some kind of a test? If the thing is brighter than men, it might know more physics than Connant should, and they'd catch it out," Barclay suggested.

Copper shook his head wearily. "Not if it reads minds. You can't plan a trap for it. Vane suggested that last night. He hoped it would answer some of the questions of physics he'd like to know answers to."

"This expedition-of-four idea is going to make life happy." Benning looked at his companions. "Each of us with an eye on the other to make sure he doesn't do something—peculiar. Man—aren't we going to be a trusting bunch! Each man eyeing his neighbors with the grandest exhibition of faith and truth—I'm beginning to know what Connant meant by 'I wish you could see your eyes.' Every now and then we all have it, I guess. One of you looks around with a sort of 'I-wonder-if-the-other-three-are-look.' Incidentally, I'm not excepting myself."

"So far as we know, the animal is dead, with a slight question as to Connant. No other is suspected," McReady stated slowly. "The 'always-four' order is merely a precautionary measure."

"I'm waiting for Garry to make it four-in-a-bunk," Barclay sighed. "I thought I didn't have any privacy before, but since that order—"

## IX

**NONE WATCHED** more tensely than Connant. A little sterile glass test tube, half filled with straw-colored fluid. One—two—three—four—five drops of the clear solution Dr. Copper had prepared from the drops of blood from Connant's arm. The tube was shaken carefully, then set in a beaker of clear, warm water. The thermometer read blood heat, a little thermostat clicked noisily, and the electric hotplate began to glow as the lights flickered slightly. Then—little white flecks of precipitation were forming, snowing down in the clear straw-colored fluid. "Lord," said Connant. He dropped heavily into a bunk, crying like a baby. "Six days—" Connant sobbed, "six days in there—wondering if that damned test would lie—"

Garry moved over silently, and slipped his arm across the physicist's back.

"It couldn't lie," Dr. Copper said. "The dog was human-immune—and the serum reacted."

"He's—all right?" Norris gasped. "Then—the animal is dead—dead forever?"

"He is human," Copper spoke definitely, "and the animal is dead."

Kinner burst out laughing, laughing hysterically. McReady turned toward him and slapped his face with a methodical one-two, one-two action. The cook laughed, gulped, cried a moment, and sat up rubbing his cheeks, mumbling his thanks vaguely. "I was scared. Lord, I was scared—"

Norris laughed brittlely. "You think we weren't, you ape? You think maybe Connant wasn't?"

The Ad Building stirred with a sudden rejuvenation. Voices laughed, the men clustering around Connant spoke with unnecessarily loud voices, jittery, nervous voices relievedly friendly again. Somebody called out a suggestion, and a dozen started for their skis. Blair, Blair might recover— Dr. Copper fussed with his test tubes in nervous relief, trying solutions. The party of relief for Blair's shack started out the door, skis clapping noisily. Down the corridor, the dogs set up a quick yelping howl as the air of excited relief reached them.

Dr. Copper fussed with his tubes. McReady noticed him first, sitting on the edge of the bunk, with two precipitin-whitened test tubes of straw-colored fluid, his face whiter than the stuff in the tubes, silent tears slipping down from horror-widened eyes.

McReady felt a cold knife of fear pierce through his heart and freeze in his breast. Dr. Copper looked up.

"Garry," he called hoarsely. "Garry, for God's sake, come here."

Commander Garry walked toward him sharply. Silence clapped down on the Ad Building. Connant looked up, rose stiffly from his seat.

"Garry—tissue from the monster—precipitates, too. It proves nothing. Nothing—but the dog was monster-immune too. That one of the two contributing blood—one of us two, you and I, Garry—one of us is a monster."

# X

**"BAR, CALL BACK** those men before they tell Blair," McReady said quietly. Barclay went to the door; faintly his shouts came back to the tensely silent men in the room. Then he was back.

"They're coming," he said. "I didn't tell them why. Just that Dr. Copper said not to go."

"McReady," Garry sighed, "you're in command now. May God help you. I cannot."

The bronzed giant nodded slowly, his deep eyes on Commander Garry.

"I may be the one," Garry added. "I know I'm not, but I cannot prove it to you in any way. Dr. Copper's test has broken down. The fact that he showed it was useless, when it was to the advantage of the monster to have that uselessness not known, would seem to prove he was human."

Copper rocked back and forth slowly on the bunk. "I

know I'm human. I can't prove it either. One of us two is a liar, for that test cannot lie, and it says one of us is. I gave proof that the test was wrong, which seems to prove I'm human, and now Garry has given that argument which proves me human—which he, as the monster, should not do. Round and round and round and round and—"

Dr. Copper's head, then his neck and shoulders began circling slowly in time to the words. Suddenly he was lying back on the bunk, roaring with laughter. "It doesn't have to prove one of us is a monster! It doesn't have to prove that at all! Ho-ho. If we're all monsters it works the same—we're all monsters—all of us—Connant and Garry and I—and all of you."

"McReady," Van Wall, the blond-bearded Chief Pilot, called softly, "you were on the way to an M.D. when you took up meteorology, weren't you? Can you make some kind of test?"

McReady went over to Copper slowly, took the hypodermic from his hand, and washed it carefully in ninety-five percent alcohol. Garry sat on the bunk edge with wooden face, watching Copper and McReady expressionlessly. "What Copper said is possible," McReady sighed. "Van, will you help me here? Thanks." The filled needle jabbed into Copper's thigh. The man's laughter did not stop, but slowly faded into sobs, then sound sleep as the morphia took hold.

McReady turned again. The men who had started for Blair stood at the far end of the room, skis dripping snow, their faces as white as their skis. Connant had a lighted cigarette in each hand; one he was puffing absently, and staring at the floor. The heat of the one in his left hand attracted him and he stared at it and the one in the other hand stupidly for a moment. He dropped one and crushed it under his heel slowly.

"Dr. Copper," McReady repeated, "could be right. I know I'm human—but of course can't prove it. I'll repeat the test for my own information. Any of you others who wish may do the same."

Two minutes later, McReady held a test tube with white precipitin settling slowly from straw-colored serum. "It reacts to human blood too, so they aren't both monsters."

"I didn't think they were," Van Wall sighed. "That wouldn't suit the monster either; we could have destroyed them if we knew. Why hasn't the monster destroyed us, do you suppose? It seems to be loose."

McReady snorted. Then laughed softly. "Elementary, my dear Watson. The monster wants to have life-forms available. It cannot animate a dead body, apparently. It is just waiting—waiting until the best opportunities come. We who remain human, it is holding in reserve."

Kinner shuddered violently. "Hey. Hey, Mac. Mac, would I know if I was a monster? Would I know if the monster had already got me? Oh Lord, I may be a monster already."

"You'd know," McReady answered.

"But we wouldn't," Norris laughed shortly, half hysterically.

McReady looked at the vial of serum remaining. "There's one thing this damned stuff is good for, at that," he said thoughtfully. "Clark, will you and Van help me? The rest of the gang better stick together here. Keep an eye on each other," he said bitterly. "See that you don't get into mischief, shall we say?"

McReady started down the tunnel toward Dogtown, with Clark and Van Wall behind him. "You need more serum?" Clark asked.

McReady shook his head. "Tests. There's four cows and a bull, and nearly seventy dogs down there. This stuff reacts only to human blood and—monsters."

# XI

**MCREADY CAME BACK** to the Ad Building and went silently to the wash stand. Clark and Van Wall joined him a moment later. Clark's lips had developed a tic, jerking into sudden, unexpected sneers.

"What did you do?" Connant exploded suddenly. "More immunizing?"

Clark snickered, and stopped with a hiccough. "Immunizing. Haw! Immune all right."

"That monster," said Van Wall steadily, "is quite logical. Our immune dog was quite all right, and we drew a little more serum for the tests. But we won't make any more."

"Can't—can't you use one man's blood on another dog—" Norris began.

"There aren't," said McReady softly, "any more dogs. Nor cattle, I might add."

"No more dogs?" Benning sat down slowly.

"They're very nasty when they start changing," Van

Wall said precisely. "But slow. That electrocution iron you made up, Barclay, is very fast. There is only one dog left—our immune. The monster left that for us, so we could play with our little test. The rest—" He shrugged and dried his hands.

"The cattle—" gulped Kinner.

"Also. Reacted very nicely. They look funny as hell when they start melting. The beast hasn't any quick escape, when it's tied in dog chains, or halters, and it had to be to imitate."

Kinner stood up slowly. His eyes darted around the room, and came to rest horribly quivering on a tin bucket in the galley. Slowly, step by step, he retreated toward the door, his mouth opening and closing silently, like a fish out of water.

"The milk—" he gasped. "I milked 'em an hour ago—" His voice broke into a scream as he dived through the door. He was out on the ice cap without windproof or heavy clothing.

Van Wall looked after him for a moment thoughtfully. "He's probably hopelessly mad," he said at length, "but he might be a monster escaping. He hasn't skis. Take a blow torch—in case."

The physical motion of the chased helped them; something that needed doing. Three of the men were quietly being sick. Norris was lying flat on his back, his face greenish, looking steadily at the bottom of the bunk above him.

"Mac, how long have the—cows been not-cows—"

McReady shrugged his shoulders hopelessly. He went over to the milk bucket, and with his little tube of serum set to work on it. The milk clouded it, making certainty difficult. Finally he dropped the test tube in the stand, and shook his head. "It tests negatively. Which means either they were cows then, or that, being perfect imitations, they gave perfectly good milk."

Copper stirred restlessly in his sleep and gave a gurgling cross between a snore and a laugh. Silent eyes fastened on him. "Would morphia—a monster—" somebody started to ask.

"Lord knows," McReady shrugged. "It affects every Earthly animal I know of."

Connant suddenly raised his head. "Mac! The dogs must have swallowed pieces of the monster, and the pieces destroyed them! The dogs were where the monster resided. I was locked up. Doesn't that prove—"

Van Wall shook his head. "Sorry. Proves nothing about what you are, only proves what you didn't do."

"It doesn't do that," McReady sighed. "We are helpless because we don't know enough, and so jittery we don't think straight. Locked up! Ever watch a white corpuscle of the blood go through the wall of a blood vessel? No? It sticks out a pseudopod. And there it is—on the far side of the wall."

"Oh," said Van Wall unhappily. "The cattle tried to melt down, didn't they? They could have melted down—become just a thread of stuff and leaked under a door to re-collect on the other side. Ropes—no—no, that wouldn't do it. They couldn't live in a sealed tank or—"

"If," said McReady, "you shoot it through the heart, and it doesn't die, it's a monster. That's the best test I can think of, offhand."

"No dogs," said Garry quietly, "and no cattle. It has to imitate men now. And locking up doesn't do any good. Your test might work, Mac, but I'm afraid it would be hard on the men."

# XII

Clark looked up from the galley stove as Van Wall, Barclay, McReady, and Benning came in, brushing the drift from their clothes. The other men jammed into the Ad Building continued studiously to do as they were doing, playing chess, poker, reading. Ralsen was fixing a sledge on the table; Vane and Norris had their heads together over magnetic data, while Harvey read tables in a low voice.

Dr. Copper snored softly on the bunk. Garry was working with Dutton over a sheaf of radio messages on the corner of Dutton's bunk and a small fraction of the radio table. Connant was using most of the table for cosmic ray sheets.

Quite plainly through the corridor, despite two closed doors, they could hear Kinner's voice. Clark banged a kettle onto the galley stove and beckoned McReady silently. The meteorologist went over to him.

"I don't mind the cooking so damn much," Clark said nervously, "but isn't there some way to stop that bird? We all agreed that it would be safe to move him into Cosmos House."

"Kinner?" McReady nodded toward the door. "I'm

afraid not. I can dope him, I suppose, but we don't have an unlimited supply of morphia, and he's not in danger of losing his mind. Just hysterical."

"Well, we're in danger of losing ours. You've been out for an hour and a half. That's been going on steadily ever since, and it was going for two hours before. There's a limit, you know."

Garry wandered over slowly, apologetically. For an instant, McReady caught the feral spark of fear—horror—in Clark's eyes, and knew at the same instant it was in his own. Garry—Garry or Copper—was certainly a monster.

"If you could stop that, I think it would be a sound policy, Mac," Garry spoke quietly. "There are—tensions enough in this room. We agreed that it would be safe for Kinner in there, because everyone else in camp is under constant eyeing." Garry shivered slightly. "And try, try in God's name, to find some test that will work." McReady sighed. "Watched or unwatched, everyone's tense. Blair's jammed the trap so it won't open now. Says he's got food enough, and keeps screaming 'Go away, go away—you're monsters. I won't be absorbed. I won't. I'll tell men when they come. Go away.' So—we went away."

"There's no other test?" Garry pleaded.

McReady shrugged his shoulders. "Copper was perfectly right. The serum test could be absolutely definitive if it hadn't been—contaminated. But that's the only dog left, and he's fixed now."

"Chemicals? Chemical tests?"

McReady shook his head. "Our chemistry isn't that good. I tried the microscope you know."

Garry nodded. "Monster-dog and real dog were

identical. But—you've got to go on. What are you going to do after dinner?"

Van Wall had joined them quietly. "Rotation sleeping. Half the crowd sleep; half stay awake. I wonder how many of us are monsters? All the dogs were. We thought we were safe, but somehow it got Copper—or you." Van Wall's eyes flashed uneasily. "It may have gotten every one of you—all of you but myself may be wondering, looking. No, that's not possible. You'd just spring then, I'd be helpless. We humans must somehow have the greater numbers now. But—" he stopped.

McReady laughed shortly. "You're doing what Norris complained of in me. Leaving it hanging. 'But if one more is changed—that may shift the balance of power.' It doesn't fight. I don't think it ever fights. It must be a peaceable thing, in its own—inimitable—way. It never had to, because it always gained its end otherwise."

Van Wall's mouth twisted in a sickly grin. "You're suggesting then, that perhaps it already has the greater numbers, but is just waiting—waiting, all of them—all of you, for all I know—waiting till I, the last human, drop my wariness in sleep. Mac, did you notice their eyes, all looking at us."

Garry sighed. "You haven't been sitting here for four straight hours, while all their eyes silently weighed the information that one of us two, Copper or I, is a monster certainly—perhaps both of us."

Clark repeated his request. "Will you stop that bird's noise? He's driving me nuts. Make him tone down, anyway."

"Still praying?" McReady asked.

"Still praying," Clark groaned. "He hasn't stopped for a second. I don't mind his praying if it relieves him, but he yells, he sings psalms and hymns and shouts prayers. He thinks God can't hear well way down here."

"Maybe he can't," Barclay grunted. "Or he'd have done something about this thing loosed from hell."

"Somebody's going to try that test you mentioned, if you don't stop him," Clark stated grimly. "I think a cleaver in the head would be as positive a test as a bullet in the heart."

"Go ahead with the food. I'll see what I can do. There may be something in the cabinets." McReady moved wearily toward the corner Copper had used as his dispensary. Three tall cabinets of rough boards, two locked, were the repositories of the camp's medical supplies. Twelve years ago, McReady had graduated, had started for an internship, and been diverted to meteorology. Copper was a picked man, a man who knew his profession thoroughly and modernly. More than half the drugs available were totally unfamiliar to McReady; many of the others he had forgotten. There was no huge medical library here, no series of journals available to learn the things he had forgotten, the elementary, simple things to Copper, things that did not merit inclusion in the small library he had been forced to content himself with. Books are heavy, and every ounce of supplies had been freighted in by air.

McReady picked a barbiturate hopefully. Barclay and Van Wall went with him. One man never went anywhere alone in Big Magnet.

Ralsen had his sledge put away, and the physicists had

moved off the table, the poker game broken up when they got back. Clark was putting out the food. The clicks of spoons and the muffled sounds of eating were the only sign of life in the room. There were no words spoken as the three returned; simply all eyes focused on them questioningly while the jaws moved methodically.

McReady stiffened suddenly. Kinner was screeching out a hymn in a hoarse, cracked voice. He looked wearily at Van Wall with a twisted grin and shook his head. "Uh-uh."

Van Wall cursed bitterly, and sat down at the table. "We'll just plumb have to take that till his voice wears out. He can't yell like that forever."

"He's got a brass throat and a cast-iron larynx," Norris declared savagely. "Then we could be hopeful, and suggest he's one of our friends. In that case he could go on renewing his throat till doomsday."

Silence clamped down. For twenty minutes they ate without a word. Then Connant jumped up with an angry violence. "You sit as still as a bunch of graven images. You don't say a word, but oh, Lord, what expressive eyes you've got. They roll around like a bunch of glass marbles spilling down a table. They wink and blink and stare—and whisper things. Can you guys look somewhere else for a change, please?

"Listen, Mac, you're in charge here. Let's run movies for the rest of the night. We've been saving those reels to make 'em last. Last for what? Who is it's going to see those last reels, eh? Let's see 'em while we can, and look at something other than each other."

"Sound idea, Connant. I, for one, am quite willing to change this in any way I can."

"Turn the sound up loud, Dutton. Maybe you can drown out the hymns," Clark suggested.

"But don't," Norris said softly, "turn off the lights altogether."

"The lights will be out." McReady shook his head. "We'll show all the cartoon movies we have. You won't mind seeing the old cartoons will you?"

"Goody, goody—a moom-pitcher show. I'm just in the mood." McReady turned to look at the speaker, a lean, lanky New Englander, by the name of Caldwell. Caldwell was stuffing his pipe slowly, a sour eye cocked up to McReady.

The bronze giant was forced to laugh. "OK, Bart, you win. Maybe we aren't quite in the mood for Popeye and trick ducks, but it's something."

"Let's play Classifications," Caldwell suggested slowly. "Or maybe you call it Guggenheim. You draw lines on a piece of paper, and put down classes of things—like animals, you know. One for 'H' and one for 'U' and so on. Like 'Human' and 'Unknown' for instance. I think that would be a hell of a lot better game. Classification, I sort of figure, is what we need right now a lot more than movies. Maybe somebody's got a pencil that he can draw lines with, draw lines between the 'U' animals and the 'H' animals for instance."

"McReady's trying to find that kind of a pencil," Van Wall answered quietly, "but, we've got three kinds of animals here, you know. One that begins with 'M.' We don't want any more."

"Mad ones, you mean. Uh-huh. Clark, I'll help you with those pots so we can get our little peep show going." Caldwell got up slowly.

Dutton and Barclay and Benning, in charge of the projector and sound mechanism arrangements, went about their job silently, while the Ad Building was cleared and the dishes and pans disposed of. McReady drifted over toward Van Wall slowly, and leaned back in the bunk beside him. "I've been wondering, Van," he said with a wry grin, "whether or not to report my ideas in advance. I forgot the 'U animal' as Caldwell named it, could read minds. I've a vague idea of something that might work. It's too vague to bother with, though. Go ahead with your show, while I try to figure out the logic of the thing. I'll take this bunk."

Van Wall glanced up, and nodded. The movie screen would be practically on a line with this bunk, hence making the pictures least distracting here, because least intelligible. "Perhaps you should tell us what you have in mind. As it is, only the unknowns know what you plan. You might be—unknown before you got it into operation."

"Won't take long, if I get it figured out right. But I don't want any more all-but-the-test-dog-monsters things. We better move Copper into this bunk directly above me. He won't be watching the screen either." McReady nodded toward Copper's gently snoring bulk. Garry helped them lift and move the doctor.

McReady leaned back against the bunk, and sank into a trance, almost, of concentration, trying to calculate chances, operations, methods. He was scarcely aware as the others distributed themselves silently, and the screen lit up. Vaguely Kinner's hectic, shouted prayers and his rasping hymn-singing annoyed him till the sound accompaniment started. The lights were turned out, but the large, light-colored areas of the screen reflected enough light for ready visibility. Kinner was still praying, shouting, his voice a raucous accompaniment to the mechanical sound. Dutton stepped up the amplification.

So long had the voice been going on, that only vaguely at first was McReady aware that something seemed missing. Lying as he was, just across the narrow room from the corridor leading to Cosmos House, Kinner's voice had reached him fairly clearly, despite the sound accompaniment of the pictures. It struck him abruptly that it had stopped.

"Dutton, cut that sound," McReady called as he sat up abruptly. The pictures flickered a moment, soundless and strangely futile in the sudden, deep silence. The rising wind on the surface above bubbled melancholy tears of sound down the stove pipes. "Kinner's stopped," McReady said softly.

"For God's sake start that sound then; he may have stopped to listen," Norris snapped.

McReady rose and went down the corridor. Barclay and Van Wall left their places at the far end of the room to follow him. The flickers bulged and twisted on the back of Barclay's gray underwear as he crossed the still-functioning beam of the projector. Dutton snapped on the lights, and the pictures vanished.

Norris stood at the door as McReady had asked. Garry sat down quietly in the bunk nearest the door, forcing Clark to make room for him. Most of the others had stayed exactly where they were. Only Connant walked slowly up and down the room, in steady, unvarying rhythm.

"If you're going to do that, Connant," Clark spat, "we can get along without you altogether, whether you're human or not. Will you stop that damned rhythm?"

"Sorry." The physicist sat down in a bunk, and watched his toes thoughtfully. It was almost five minutes, five ages, while the wind made the only sound, before McReady appeared at the door.

"Well," he announced, "haven't got enough grief here already. Somebody's tried to help us out. Kinner has a knife in his throat, which was why he stopped singing, probably. We've got monsters, madmen, and murderers. Any more 'M's' you can think of, Caldwell? If there are, we'll probably have 'em before long."

## XIII

**"IS BLAIR LOOSE?"** someone asked.

"Blair is not loose. Or he flew in. If there's any doubt about where our gentle helper came from—this may clear it up." Van Wall held a foot-long, thin-bladed knife in a cloth. The wooden handle was half burnt, charred with the peculiar pattern of the top of the galley stove.

Clark stared at it. "I did that this afternoon. I forgot the damn thing and left it on the stove."

Van Wall nodded. "I smelled it, if you remember. I knew the knife came from the galley."

"I wonder," said Benning, looking around at the party warily, "how many more monsters have we? If somebody could slip out of his place, go back of the screen to the galley and then down to the Cosmos House and back—he did come back, didn't he? Yes—everybody's here. Well, if one of the gang could do all that—"

"Maybe a monster did it," Garry suggested quietly.

"There's that possibility."

"The monster, as you pointed out today, has only men left to imitate. Would he decrease his—supply, shall we say?" Van Wall pointed out. "No, we just have a plain, ordinary louse, a murderer to deal with. Ordinarily we'd call him an 'inhuman murderer' I suppose, but we have to distinguish now. We have inhuman murderers, and now we have human murderers. Or one at least."

"There's one less human," Norris said softly. "Maybe the monsters have the balance of power now."

"Never mind that," McReady sighed and turned to Barclay. "Bar, will you get your electric gadget? I'm going to make certain—"

Barclay turned down the corridor to get the pronged electrocuter, while McReady and Van Wall went back toward Cosmos House. Barclay followed them in some thirty seconds.

The corridor to Cosmos House twisted, as did nearly all corridors in Big Magnet, and Norris stood at the entrance again. But they heard, rather muffled, McReady's sudden shout. There was a savage flurry of blows, dull ch-thunk, shluff sounds. "Bar—Bar—" And a curious, savage mewing scream, silenced before even quick-moving Norris had reached the bend.

Kinner—or what had been Kinner—lay on the floor, cut half in two by the great knife McReady had had. The meteorologist stood against the wall, the knife dripping red in his hand. Van Wall was stirring vaguely on the floor, moaning, his hand half-consciously rubbing at his jaw. Barclay, an unutterably savage gleam in his eyes, was methodically leaning on the pronged weapon in his hand, jabbing—jabbing, jabbing.

Kinner's arms had developed a queer, scaly fur, and the flesh had twisted. The fingers had shortened, the hand rounded, the fingernails become three-inch long things of dull red horn, keened to steel-hard, razor-sharp talons.

McReady raised his head, looked at the knife in his hand and dropped it. "Well, whoever did it can speak up now. He was an inhuman murderer at that—in that he murdered an inhuman. I swear by all that's holy, Kinner was a lifeless corpse on the floor here when we arrived. But when It found we were going to jab It with the power—It changed."

Norris stared unsteadily. "Oh, Lord, those things can act. Ye gods—sitting in here for hours, mouthing prayers to a God it hated! Shouting hymns in a cracked voice—hymns about a Church it never knew. Driving us mad with its ceaseless howling—

"Well. Speak up, whoever did it. You didn't know it, but you did the camp a favor. And I want to know how in blazes you got out of the room without anyone seeing you. It might help in guarding ourselves."

"His screaming—his singing. Even the sound projector couldn't drown it." Clark shivered. "It was a monster."

"Oh," said Van Wall in sudden comprehension. "You were sitting right next to the door, weren't you? And almost behind the projection screen already."

Clark nodded dumbly. "He—it's quiet now. It's a

dead—Mac, your test's no damn good. It was dead anyway, monster or man, it was dead."

McReady chuckled softly. "Boys, meet Clark, the only one we know is human! Meet Clark, the one who proves he's human by trying to commit murder—and failing. Will the rest of you please refrain from trying to prove you're human for a while? I think we may have another test."

"A test!" Connant snapped joyfully, then his face sagged in disappointment. "I suppose it's another either-way-you-want-it."

"No," said McReady steadily. "Look sharp and be careful. Come into the Ad Building. Barclay, bring your electrocuter. And somebody—Dutton—stand with Barclay to make sure he does it. Watch every neighbor, for by the Hell these monsters came from, I've got something, and they know it. They're going to get dangerous!"

The group tensed abruptly. An air of crushing menace entered into every man's body, sharply they looked at each other. More keenly than ever before—is that man next to me an inhuman monster?

"What is it?" Garry asked, as they stood again in the main room. "How long will it take?"

"I don't know, exactly," said McReady, his voice brittle with angry determination. "But I know it will work, and no two ways about it. It depends on a basic quality of the monsters, not on us. 'Kinner' just convinced me." He stood heavy and solid in bronzed immobility, completely sure of himself again at last.

"This," said Barclay, hefting the wooden-handled weapon tipped with its two sharp-pointed, charged conductors, "is going to be rather necessary, I take it. Is the power plant assured?"

Dutton nodded sharply. "The automatic stoker bin is full. The gas power plant is on standby. Van Wall and I set it for the movie operation—and we've checked it over rather carefully several times, you know. Anything those wires touch, dies," he assured them grimly. "I know that."

Dr. Copper stirred vaguely in his bunk, rubbed his eyes with fumbling hand. He sat up slowly, blinked his eyes blurred with sleep and drugs, widened with an unutterable horror of drug-ridden nightmares. "Garry," he mumbled, "Garry—listen. Selfish—from hell they came, and hellish shellfish—I mean self— Do I? What do I mean?" He sank back in his bunk, and snored softly.

McReady looked at him thoughtfully. "We'll know presently," he nodded slowly. "But selfish is what you mean, all right. You may have thought of that, half sleeping, dreaming there. I didn't stop to think what dreams you might be having. But that's all right. Selfish is the word. They must be, you see." He turned to the men in the cabin, tense, silent men staring with wolfish eyes each at his neighbor. "Selfish, and as Dr. Copper said—every part is a whole. Every piece is self-sufficient, an animal in itself.

"That, and one other thing, tell the story. There's nothing mysterious about blood; it's just as normal a body tissue as a piece of muscle, or a piece of liver. But it hasn't so much connective tissue, though it has millions, billions of life-cells."

McReady's great bronze beard ruffled in a grim smile. "This is satisfying, in a way. I'm pretty sure we humans still outnumber you—others. Others standing here. And we have what you, your other-world race, evidently doesn't. Not an imitated, but a bred-in-the-bone instinct, a driving, unquenchable fire that's genuine. We'll fight, fight with a ferocity you may attempt to imitate, but you'll never equal! We're human. We're real. You're imitations, false to the core of your every cell."

"All right. It's a showdown now. You know. You, with your mind reading. You've lifted the idea from my brain. You can't do a thing about it.

"Standing here—

"Let it pass. Blood is tissue. They have to bleed; if they bleed when cut, then by Heaven, they're phoney from hell! If they don't bleed—then that blood, separated from them, is an individual—a newly formed individual in its own right, just as they—split, all of them, from one original—are individuals!

"Get it, Van? See the answer, Bar?"

Van Wall laughed very softly. "The blood—the blood will not obey. It's a new individual, with all the desire to protect its own life that the original—the main mass from which it was split—has. The blood will live—and try to crawl away from a hot needle, say!"

McReady picked up the scalpel from the table. From the cabinet, he took a rack of test tubes, a tiny alcohol lamp, and a length of platinum wire set in a little glass rod. A smile of grim satisfaction rode his lips. For a moment he glanced up at those around him. Barclay and Dutton moved toward him slowly, the wooden-handled electric instrument alert.

"Dutton," said McReady, "suppose you stand over by

the splice there where you've connected that in. Just make sure no—thing pulls it loose."

Dutton moved away. "Now, Van, suppose you be first on this."

White-faced, Van Wall stepped forward. With a delicate precision, McReady cut a vein in the base of his thumb. Van Wall winced slightly, then held steady as a half inch of bright blood collected in the tube. McReady put the tube in the rack, gave Van Wall a bit of alum, and indicated the iodine bottle.

Van Wall stood motionlessly watching. McReady heated the platinum wire in the alcohol lamp flame, then dipped it into the tube. It hissed softly. Five times he repeated the test. "Human, I'd say," McReady sighed, and straightened. "As yet, my theory hasn't been actually proven—but I have hopes. I have hopes.

"Don't, by the way, get too interested in this. We have with us some unwelcome ones, no doubt. Van, will you relieve Barclay at the switch? Thanks. OK, Barclay, and may I say I hope you stay with us? You're a damned good guy."

Barclay grinned uncertainly; winced under the keen edge of the scalpel. Presently, smiling widely, he retrieved his long-handled weapon.

"Mr. Samuel Dutt—Bar!"

The tensity was released in that second. Whatever of hell the monsters may have had within them, the men in that instant matched it. Barclay had no chance to move his weapon, as a score of men poured down on the thing that had seemed Dutton. It mewed, and spat, and tried to grow fangs—and was a hundred broken, torn pieces.

Without knives, or any weapon save the brute-given strength of a staff of picked men, the thing was crushed, rent.

Slowly they picked themselves up, their eyes smouldering, very quiet in their motions. A curious wrinkling of their lips betrayed a species of nervousness.

Barclay went over with the electric weapon. Things smouldered and stank. The caustic acid Van Wall dropped on each spilled drop of blood gave off tickling, cough-provoking fumes.

McReady grinned, his deep-set eyes alight and dancing. "Maybe," he said softly, "I underrated man's abilities when I said nothing human could have the ferocity in the eyes of that thing we found. I wish we could have the opportunity to treat in a more befitting manner these things. Something with boiling oil, or melted lead in it, or maybe slow roasting in the power boiler. When I think what a man Dutton was—

"Never mind. My theory is confirmed by—by one who knew? Well, Van Wall and Barclay are proven. I think, then, that I'll try to show you what I already know. That I, too, am human." McReady swished the scalpel in absolute alcohol, burned it off the metal blade, and cut the base of his thumb expertly.

Twenty seconds later he looked up from the desk at the waiting men. There were more grins out there now, friendly grins, yet withal, something else in the eyes.

"Connant," McReady laughed softly, "was right. The huskies watching that thing in the corridor bend had nothing on you. Wonder why we think only the wolf blood has the right to ferocity? Maybe on spontaneous viciousness a wolf takes tops, but after these seven days—abandon all hope, ye wolves who enter here!

"Maybe we can save time. Connant, would you step for—"

Again Barclay was too slow. There were more grins, less tensity still, when Barclay and Van Wall finished their work.

Garry spoke in a low, bitter voice. "Connant was one of the finest men we had here—and five minutes ago I'd have sworn he was a man. Those damnable things are more than imitation." Garry shuddered and sat back in his bunk.

And thirty seconds later, Garry's blood shrank from the hot platinum wire, and struggled to escape the tube, struggled as frantically as a suddenly feral, red-eyed, dissolving imitation of Garry struggled to dodge the snake-tongue weapon Barclay advanced at him, white-faced and sweating. The Thing in the test tube screamed with a tiny, tinny voice as McReady dropped it into the glowing coal of the galley stove.

## XIV

**"THE LAST OF IT?"** Dr. Copper looked down from his bunk with bloodshot, saddened eyes. "Fourteen of them—"

McReady nodded shortly. "In some ways—if only we could have permanently prevented their spreading—I'd like to have even the imitations back. Commander Garry—Connant—Dutton—Clark—"

"Where are they taking those things?" Copper nodded to the stretcher Barclay and Norris were carrying out.

"Outside. Outside on the ice, where they've got fifteen smashed crates, half a ton of coal, and presently will add ten gallons of kerosene. We've dumped acid on every spilled drop, every torn fragment. We're going to incinerate those."

"Sounds like a good plan." Copper nodded wearily. "I wonder, you haven't said whether Blair—"

McReady started. "We forgot him? We had so much else! I wonder—do you suppose we can cure him now?"

"If—" began Dr. Copper, and stopped meaningly.

McReady started a second time. "Even a madman. It imitated Kinner and his praying hysteria—" McReady turned toward Van Wall at the long table. "Van, we've got to make an expedition to Blair's shack."

Van looked up sharply, the frown of worry faded for an instant in surprised remembrance. Then he rose, nodded. "Barclay better go along. He applied the lashings, and may figure how to get in without frightening Blair too much."

Three quarters of an hour, through -37° cold, while the aurora curtain bellied overhead. The twilight was nearly twelve hours long, flaming in the north on snow like white, crystalline sand under their skis. A five-mile wind piled it in drift-lines pointing off to the northwest. Three quarters of an hour to reach the snow-buried shack. No smoke came from the little shack, and the men hastened.

"Blair!" Barclay roared into the wind and when he was still a hundred yards away. "Blair!"

"Shut up," said McReady softly. "And hurry. He may be trying a lone hike. If we have to go after him—no planes, the tractors disabled—"

"Would a monster have the stamina a man has?"

"A broken leg wouldn't stop it for more than a minute," McReady pointed out.

Barclay gasped suddenly and pointed aloft. Dim in the twilit sky, a winged thing circled in curves of indescribable grace and ease. Great white wings tipped gently, and the bird swept over them in silent curiosity. "Albatross—" Barclay said softly. "First of the season, and wandering way inland for some reason. If a monster's loose—"

Norris bent down on the ice, and tore hurriedly at his heavy, windproof clothing. He straightened, his coat flapping open, a grim blue-metaled weapon in his hand. It roared a challenge to the white silence of Antarctica.

The thing in the air screamed hoarsely. Its great wings worked frantically as a dozen feathers floated down from its tail. Norris fired again. The bird was moving swiftly now, but in an almost straight line of retreat. It screamed again, more feathers dropped, and with beating wings it soared behind a ridge of pressure ice, to vanish.

Norris hurried after the others. "It won't come back," he panted.

Barclay cautioned him to silence, pointing. A curiously, fiercely blue light beat out from the cracks of the shack's door. A very low, soft humming sounded inside, a low, soft humming and a clink and clink of tools, the very sounds somehow bearing a message of frantic haste.

McReady's face paled. "Lord help us if that thing has—" He grabbed Barclay's shoulder, and made snipping motions with his fingers, pointing toward the lacing of control cables that held the door.

Barclay drew the wire cutters from his pocket, and kneeled soundlessly at the door. The snap and twang of cut wires made an unbearable racket in the utter quiet of the Antarctic hush. There was only that strange, sweetly soft hum from within the shack, and the queerly, hecticly clipped clicking and rattling of tools to drown their noises.

McReady peered through a crack in the door. His breath sucked in huskily and his great fingers clamped cruelly on Barclay's shoulder. The meteorologist backed down. "It isn't," he explained very softly, "Blair. It's kneeling on something on the bunk—something that keeps lifting. Whatever it's working on is a thing like a knapsack—and it lifts."

"All at once," Barclay said grimly. "No. Norris, hang back, and get that iron of yours out. It may have—weapons."

Together, Barclay's powerful body and McReady's giant strength struck the door. Inside, the bunk jammed against the door screeched madly and crackled into kindling. The door flung down from broken hinges, the patched lumber of the doorpost dropping inward.

Like a blue rubber ball, a Thing bounced up. One of its four tentacle-like arms looped out like a striking snake. In a seven-tentacled hand a six-inch pencil of winking, shining metal glinted and swung upward to face them. Its line-thin lips twitched back from snake-fangs in a grin of hate, red eyes blazing.

Norris' revolver thundered in the confined space. The

hate-washed face twitched in agony, the looping tentacle snatched back. The silvery thing in its hand a smashed ruin of metal, the seven-tentacled hand became a mass of mangled flesh oozing greenish-yellow ichor. The revolver thundered three times more. Dark holes drilled each of the three eyes before Norris hurled the empty weapon against its face.

The Thing screamed in feral hate, a lashing tentacle wiping at blinded eyes. For a moment it crawled on the floor, savage tentacles lashing out, the body twitching. Then it struggled up again, blinded eyes working, boiling hideously, the crushed flesh sloughing away in sodden gobbets.

Barclay lurched to his feet and dove forward with an ice-ax. The flat of the weighty thing crushed against the side of the head. Again the unkillable monster went down. The tentacles lashed out, and suddenly Barclay fell to his feet in the grip of a living, livid rope. The thing dissolved as he held it, a white-hot band that ate into the flesh of his hands like living fire. Frantically he tore the stuff from him, held his hands where they could not be reached. The blind Thing felt and ripped at the tough, heavy, windproof cloth, seeking flesh—flesh it could convert—

The huge blowtorch McReady had brought coughed solemnly. Abruptly it rumbled disapproval throatily. Then it laughed gurglingly, and thrust out a blue-white, three-foot tongue. The Thing on the floor shrieked, flailed out blindly with tentacles that writhed and withered in the bubbling wrath of the blowtorch. It crawled and turned on the floor, it shrieked and hobbled madly, but always

McReady held the blowtorch on the face, the dead eyes burning and bubbling uselessly. Frantically the Thing crawled and howled.

A tentacle sprouted a savage talon—and crisped in the flame. Steadily McReady moved with a planned, grim campaign. Helpless, maddened, the Thing retreated from the grunting torch, the caressing, licking tongue. For a moment it rebelled, squalling in inhuman hatred at the touch of the icy snow. Then it fell back before the charring breath of the torch, the stench of its flesh bathing it. Hopelessly it retreated—on and on across the Antarctic snow. The bitter wind swept over it, twisting the torch-tongue; vainly it flopped, a trail of oily, stinking smoke bubbling away from it—

McReady walked back toward the shack silently. Barclay met him at the door. "No more?" the giant meteorologist asked grimly.

Barclay shook his head. "No more. It didn't split?"

"It had other things to think about," McReady assured him. "When I left it, it was a glowing coal. What was it doing?"

Norris laughed shortly. "Wise boys, we are. Smash magnetos, so planes won't work. Rip the boiler tubing out of the tractors. And leave that Thing alone for a week in this shack. Alone and undisturbed."

McReady looked in at the shack more carefully. The air, despite the ripped door, was hot and humid. On a table at the far end of the room rested a thing of coiled wires and small magnets, glass tubing and radio tubes. At the center a block of rough stone rested. From the center of the block came the light that flooded the place, the fiercely blue light bluer than the glare of an electric arc, and from it came the sweetly soft hum. Off to one side was another mechanism of crystal glass, blown with an incredible neatness and delicacy, metal plates and a queer, shimmery sphere of insubstantiality.

"What is that?" McReady moved nearer.

Norris grunted. "Leave it for investigation. But I can guess pretty well. That's atomic power. That stuff to the left—that's a neat little thing for doing what men have been trying to do with hundred-ton cyclotrons and so forth. It separates neutrons from heavy water, which he was getting from the surrounding ice.

"Where did he get all—oh. Of course. A monster couldn't be locked in—or out. He's been through the apparatus caches." McReady stared at the apparatus. "Lord, what minds that race must have—"

"The shimmery sphere—I think it's a sphere of pure force. Neutrons can pass through any matter, and he wanted a supply reservoir of neutrons. Just project neutrons against silica—calcium—beryllium—almost anything, and the atomic energy is released. That thing is the atomic generator."

McReady plucked a thermometer from his coat. "It's 120° in here, despite the open door. Our clothes have kept the heat out to an extent, but I'm sweating now."

Norris nodded. "The light's cold. I found that. But it gives off heat to warm the place through that coil. He had all the power in the world. He could keep it warm and pleasant, as his race thought of warmth and pleasantness. Did you notice the light, the color of it?"

McReady nodded. "Beyond the stars is the answer.

From beyond the stars. From a hotter planet that circled a brighter, bluer sun they came."

McReady glanced out the door toward the blasted, smoke-stained trail that flopped and wandered blindly off across the drift. "There won't be any more coming. I guess. Sheer accident it landed here, and that was twenty million years ago. What did it do all that for?" He nodded toward the apparatus.

Barclay laughed softly. "Did you notice what it was working on when we came? Look." He pointed toward the ceiling of the shack.

Like a knapsack made of flattened coffee tins, with dangling cloth straps and leather belts, the mechanism clung to the ceiling. A tiny, glaring heart of supernal flame burned in it, yet burned through the ceiling's wood without scorching it. Barclay walked over to it, grasped two of the dangling straps in his hands, and pulled it down with an effort. He strapped it about his body. A slight jump carried him in a weirdly slow arc across the room.

"Antigravity," said McReady softly.

"Antigravity," Norris nodded. "Yes, we had 'em stopped, with no planes, and no birds. The birds hadn't come—but it had coffee tins and radio parts, and glass and the machine shop at night. And a week—a whole week—all to itself. America in a single jump—with antigravity powered by the atomic energy of matter.

"We had 'em stopped. Another half hour—it was just tightening these straps on the device so it could wear it—and we'd have stayed in Antarctica, and shot down any moving thing that came from the rest of the world."

"The albatross—" McReady said softly. "Do you suppose—"

"With this thing almost finished? With that death weapon it held in its hand?

"No, by the grace of God, who evidently does hear very well, even down here, and the margin of half an hour, we keep our world, and the planets of the system, too. Antigravity, you know, and atomic power. Because They came from another sun, a star beyond the stars. They came from a world with a bluer sun."

# WHO RHYMES THERE?
## (A Parody in Verse)

---

### by Randall Garrett
(who also drew the cartoon)

*And now, "Who Goes There?" once more with feeling . . .* some *kind of feeling, anyway.*

❁ ❁ ❁

**Gordon Randall Garrett** *(1927-1987), was an ebullient and frequently hilarious writer (in person and on paper) who often wrote as Randall Garrett, but also under a multitude of pseudonyms, sometimes using his father's names—David and Phillip—in constructing them. Mark Cole has a nifty biographical and bibliographical sketch of Garrett and his diverse works online, and laments a number of forgotten writers of yesteryear: ". . . how many still remember the marvelous stories written by such authors as David Gordon, Ivar Jorgensen, Jonathan Blake MacKenzie, Leonard G. Spencer, Gordon Aghill, Richard Green and Darrell T. Langart? Mind you, they might be* *a little easier to remember if we knew that they all happened to be one man, one brilliant if nearly forgotten writer named Randall Garrett." Well played, Mr. Cole, even if I have to quibble that "Ivar Jorgensen" (sometimes "Jorgenson") was a house name, used by more writers than Mr. Garrett. That list of pseudonyms above, incidentall, does not include "Robert Randall," used for his many collaborations with Robert Silverberg in the 1950s. Thanks to all those pseudonyms, a full accounting of his work is probably Not possible. (Cole mentions 22 novels and 130 short stories.*

*His first published story, "The Absence of Heat," appeared in* Astounding*'s "Probability Zero" department (which specialized in in short-short joke stories) in 1944 when he was only 16. Other bibliographies list "The Waiting Game," in 1951, as his first published story. Garrett is probably best remembered for his Lord Darcy series, about a detective in a parallel world where magic works and is used in criminology as our world uses forensic science. Of his collaborations, I am inordinately fond of the three hilarious novels he did with Laurence M. Janifer (as by "Mark Phillips") about a hapless FBI agent named Kenneth H. Manlone, who has to deal with crimes committed by telepaths, teleporters, and other psi-powered miscreants, the first of which (*That Sweet Little Old Lady *in* Astorunding, *later in paperback as* Brain Twister*) was nominated for the Hugo Award. His last work was also a collaboration, this time with his wife, Vicki Ann Heydron: seven novels of sword-and-sorcery mystery, known collectively as* The Gandalara Cycle.

*Unfortunately (to put it far too mildly), Garrett*

*contracted a brain infection which ended his writing and, later, his life. But he left us a substantial body of work, some of which is online as books, e-books and audiobooks, and which is highly recommended. Also recommended is Mark Cole's splendid essay about Garrett, "The Clown Prince of Science Fiction," which can be found at* http://www.irosf.com/q/zine/article/10578.

Here's a tale of chilling horror
For the sort of guy who more or
Less thinks being an explorer
    Is the kind of life for him.
If he finds his life a bore, he
Ought to read this gory story,
For he'll find exploratory
    Work is really rather grim.

For the story starts by stating
That some guys investigating
The Antarctic are debating
    On exactly what to do
With a monster they've found frozen
Near the campsite they have chosen,

And the quarrel grows and grows, un-
    'Til they're in an awful stew.

There's a guy named Blair who wants to r-
Eally check up on this monster
And dissect it. To his conster-
    Nation, everyone's in doubt.
So, of course, he starts in pleading,
And the rest of them start heeding
All his statements, and conceding
    That the Thing should be thawed out.

So they let this Thing of evil
Start to melt from its primeval
Sheath of ice: they don't perceive a l-
    Ot of trouble will ensue.
When the Thing is thawed, it neatly
Comes to life, and, smiling sweetly,
It absorbs some men completely,
Changing them to monsters, too!

Now we reach the story's nub, ill-
Uminating all the trouble:
Each new monster is a double
    For the men they each replace.
Since it seems a man's own mother
Couldn't tell one from the other,
The guys all watch one another,
    Each with fear upon his face.

And so then the men are tested

To see who has been digested,
And who's been left unmolested,
    But the test doesn't work! It's hexed!
So each man just sits there, shrinking
From the others, madly thinking,
As he watches with unblinking
    Gaze, and wonders—*Who Goes Next?*

Now, they've found that executing
Monsters can't be done by shooting:
They require electrocuting,
    Or cremation with a torch.
When they find these Things, they grab 'em;
They don't try to shoot or stab 'em;
With high-voltage wires, they jab 'em'
    'Til their flesh begins to scorch.

So the entire expedition
Eye each other with suspicion,
For they're in a bad position,
    And there's no denying *that!*
Now, to clear this awful scramble,
The ingenious Mr. Campbell,
Suddenly without preamble,
    Pulls a rabbit from the hat.

Here's the way they solve the muddle;
They discover that a puddle
Of a pseudo-human's blood'll
    Be a little monster, too!
With this test for separating

Men from monsters, without waiting,
They start right in liquidating
All the monsters in the crew.

Thus, the story is completed,
And the awful Thing's defeated,
But he still was badly treated;
It's a shame, it seems to me.
Frozen since the glaciation,
This poor Thing's extermination
Is as sad as the cremation
Of the hapless Sam McGee.

"Who Rhymes There?" was originally published with the title, "Parodies Tossed" in the May 1956 issue of *Science Fiction Stories*. It was reprinted with the title of "All About the Thing" in *SF: The Year's Greatest Science Fiction and Fantasy, Second Annual Volume* edited by Judith Merrill, and published by Gnome Press (1957) and Dell (June 1957).

# THE THINGS

## by Peter Watts

*A change of perspective can make a big difference in how things (or* Things*) appear. Consider matters from the viewpoint of the sorely set-upon monster, for example.*

**Peter Watts** *writes, "I'm quite a cheerful guy in person. Apparently people are surprised by this . . . I seem to be known as The Guy Who Writes the Depressing Stories. My favorite thumbnail of that sentiment comes from James Nicoll—"Whenever I find my will to live becoming too strong, I read Peter Watts.'" He adds, "I don't think my stuff is especially depressing," and says that the story which follows is "an homage to one of my favorite movies and also—to my own surprise—a rumination on the missionary impulse."*

*At this point, I'll stop quoting from Mr. Watts'*

*afterword to his collection of stories,* Beyond the Rift, *since you'll likely want to buy your own copy of the book, and I don't want to deprive you of the fun of reading that essay. Peter Watts, writing from Canada, has also published the Rifters Trilogy*—Starfish, Maelstrom, *and* Behemoth—*and a tacky-yet-enjoyable video game novelization called* Crysis: Legion. *Born in 1958, Peter Watts is a Canadian and a former marine-mammal biologist. His story* The Island *won the Hugo Award for best novelette, and was a finalist for the Theodore Sturgeon Memorial Award and the* Locus *awards. His novel* Blindsight *was a finalist for the Hugo Award, as well as for the Campbell Award and* Locus *Award. I'll quote Charles Stross's description of Mr. Watts's first novel: "Imagine a neurobiology-obsessed version of Greg Egan writing a first contact with aliens story from the point of view of a zombie posthuman crewman aboard a starship captained by a vampire, with not dying as the boobie prize." After that curtain-raiser, how can you not immediately read the novel?*

*As for the story you are about to read, it won the Shirley Jackson Award, took third place in the Theodore Sturgeon Memorial Award, and was a finalist for the Hugo Award, the British Science Fiction Association Award, the* Locus *Award, and the Parsec Award. Aren't you reading it yet?*

**I AM BEING BLAIR.** I escape out the back as the world comes in through the front.

I am being Copper. I am rising from the dead.

I am being Childs. I am guarding the main entrance.

The names don't matter. They are placeholders, nothing more; all biomass is interchangeable. What matters is that these are all that is left of me. The world has burned everything else.

I see myself through the window, loping through the storm, wearing Blair. MacReady has told me to burn Blair if he comes back alone, but MacReady still thinks I am one of him. I am not: I am being Blair, and I am at the door. I am being Childs, and I let myself in. I take brief communion, tendrils writhing forth from my faces, intertwining: I am BlairChilds, exchanging news of the world.

The world has found me out. It has discovered my burrow beneath the tool shed, the half-finished lifeboat cannibalized from the viscera of dead helicopters. The world is busy destroying my means of escape. Then it will come back for me.

There is only one option left. I disintegrate. Being Blair, I go to share the plan with Copper and to feed on the rotting biomass once called Clarke; so many changes in so short a time have dangerously depleted my reserves. Being Childs, I have already consumed what was left of Fuchs and am replenished for the next phase. I sling the flamethrower onto my back and head outside, into the long Antarctic night.

I will go into the storm, and never come back.

I was so much more, before the crash. I was an explorer, an ambassador, a missionary. I spread across the cosmos, met countless worlds, took communion: the fit reshaped the unfit and the whole universe bootstrapped upwards in joyful, infinitesimal increments. I was a soldier, at war with entropy itself. I was the very hand by which Creation perfects itself.

So much wisdom I had. So much experience. Now I cannot remember all the things I knew. I can only remember that I once knew them.

I remember the crash, though. It killed most of this offshoot outright, but a little crawled from the wreckage: a few trillion cells, a soul too weak to keep them in check. Mutinous biomass sloughed off despite my most desperate attempts to hold myself together: panic-stricken little clots of meat, instinctively growing whatever limbs they could remember and fleeing across the burning ice. By the time I'd regained control of what was left the fires had died and the cold was closing back in. I barely managed to grow enough antifreeze to keep my cells from bursting before the ice took me.

I remember my reawakening, too: dull stirrings of sensation in real time, the first embers of cognition, the slow blooming warmth of awareness as body and soul embraced after their long sleep. I remember the biped offshoots surrounding me, the strange chittering sounds they made, the odd uniformity of their body plans. How ill-adapted they looked! How inefficient their morphology! Even disabled, I could see so many things to fix. So I reached out. I took communion. I tasted the flesh of the world—

—and the world attacked me. It attacked me.

I left that place in ruins. It was on the other side of the

mountains—the Norwegian camp, it is called here—and I could never have crossed that distance in a biped skin. Fortunately there was another shape to choose from, smaller than the biped but better adapted to the local climate. I hid within it while the rest of me fought off the attack. I fled into the night on four legs, and let the rising flames cover my escape.

I did not stop running until I arrived here. I walked among these new offshoots wearing the skin of a quadruped; and because they had not seen me take any other shape, they did not attack.

And when I assimilated them in turn—when my biomass changed and flowed into shapes unfamiliar to local eyes—I took that communion in solitude, having learned that the world does not like what it doesn't know.

I am alone in the storm. I am a bottom-dweller on the floor of some murky alien sea. The snow blows past in horizontal streaks; caught against gullies or outcroppings, it spins into blinding little whirlwinds. But I am not nearly far enough, not yet. Looking back I still see the camp crouched brightly in the gloom, a squat angular jumble of light and shadow, a bubble of warmth in the howling abyss.

It plunges into darkness as I watch. I've blown the generator. Now there's no light but for the beacons along the guide ropes: strings of dim blue stars whipping back and forth in the wind, emergency constellations to guide lost biomass back home.

I am not going home. I am not lost enough. I forge on into darkness until even the stars disappear. The faint shouts of angry frightened men carry behind me on the wind.

Somewhere behind me my disconnected biomass regroups into vaster, more powerful shapes for the final confrontation. I could have joined myself, all in one: chosen unity over fragmentation, resorbed and taken comfort in the greater whole. I could have added my strength to the coming battle. But I have chosen a different path. I am saving Child's reserves for the future. The present holds nothing but annihilation.

Best not to think on the past.

I've spent so very long in the ice already. I didn't know how long until the world put the clues together, deciphered the notes and the tapes from the Norwegian camp, pinpointed the crash site. I was being Palmer, then; unsuspected, I went along for the ride.

I even allowed myself the smallest ration of hope.

But it wasn't a ship any more. It wasn't even a derelict. It was a fossil, embedded in the floor of a great pit blown from the glacier. Twenty of these skins could have stood one atop another, and barely reached the lip of that crater. The timescale settled down on me like the weight of a world: how long for all that ice to accumulate? How many eons had the universe iterated on without me?

And in all that time, a million years perhaps, there'd been no rescue. I never found myself. I wonder what that means. I wonder if I even exist any more, anywhere but here.

Back at camp I will erase the trail. I will give them their final battle, their monster to vanquish. Let them win. Let them stop looking.

Here in the storm, I will return to the ice. I've barely even been away, after all; alive for only a few days out of all these endless ages. But I've learned enough in that time. I learned from the wreck that there will be no repairs. I learned from the ice that there will be no rescue. And I learned from the world that there will be no reconciliation. The only hope of escape, now, is into the future; to outlast all this hostile, twisted biomass, to let time and the cosmos change the rules. Perhaps the next time I awaken, this will be a different world.

It will be aeons before I see another sunrise.

This is what the world taught me: that adaptation is provocation. Adaptation is incitement to violence.

It feels almost obscene—an offense against Creation itself—to stay stuck in this skin. It's so ill-suited to its environment that it needs to be wrapped in multiple layers of fabric just to stay warm. There are a myriad ways I could optimize it: shorter limbs, better insulation, a lower surface:volume ratio. All these shapes I still have within me, and I dare not use any of them even to keep out the cold. I dare not adapt; in this place, I can only hide.

What kind of a world rejects communion?

It's the simplest, most irreducible insight that biomass can have. The more you can change, the more you can adapt. Adaptation is fitness, adaptation is survival. It's deeper than intelligence, deeper than tissue; it is cellular, it is axiomatic. And more, it is pleasurable. To take communion is to experience the sheer sensual delight of bettering the cosmos.

And yet, even trapped in these maladapted skins, this world doesn't want to change.

At first I thought it might simply be starving, that these icy wastes didn't provide enough energy for routine shapeshifting. Or perhaps this was some kind of laboratory: an anomalous corner of the world, pinched off and frozen into these freakish shapes as part of some arcane experiment on monomorphism in extreme environments. After the autopsy I wondered if the world had simply forgotten how to change: unable to touch the tissues the soul could not sculpt them, and time and stress and sheer chronic starvation had erased the memory that it ever could.

But there were too many mysteries, too many contradictions. Why these particular shapes, so badly suited to their environment? If the soul was cut off from the flesh, what held the flesh together?

And how could these skins be so empty when I moved in?

I'm used to finding intelligence everywhere, winding through every part of every offshoot. But there was nothing to grab onto in the mindless biomass of this world: just conduits, carrying orders and input. I took communion, when it wasn't offered; the skins I chose struggled and succumbed; my fibrils infiltrated the wet electricity of organic systems everywhere. I saw through eyes that weren't yet quite mine, commandeered motor nerves to move limbs still built of alien protein. I wore these skins as I've worn countless others, took the controls and left the assimilation of individual cells to follow at its own pace.

But I could only wear the body. I could find no memories to absorb, no experiences, no comprehension. Survival depended on blending in, and it was not enough to merely look like this world. I had to act like it—and for the first time in living memory I did not know how.

Even more frighteningly, I didn't have to. The skins I assimilated continued to move, all by themselves. They conversed and went about their appointed rounds. I could not understand it. I threaded further into limbs and viscera with each passing moment, alert for signs of the original owner. I could find no networks but mine.

Of course, it could have been much worse. I could have lost it all, been reduced to a few cells with nothing but instinct and their own plasticity to guide them. I would have grown back eventually—reattained sentience, taken communion and regenerated an intellect vast as a world—but I would have been an orphan, amnesiac, with no sense of who I was. At least I've been spared that: I emerged from the crash with my identity intact, the templates of a thousand worlds still resonant in my flesh. I've retained not just the brute desire to survive, but the conviction that survival is meaningful. I can still feel joy, should there be sufficient cause.

And yet, how much more there used to be.

The wisdom of so many other worlds, lost. All that remains are fuzzy abstracts, half-memories of theorems and philosophies far too vast to fit into such an impoverished network. I could assimilate all the biomass of this place, rebuild body and soul to a million times the capacity of what crashed here—but as long as I am trapped at the bottom of this well, denied communion with my greater self, I will never recover that knowledge.

I'm such a pitiful fragment of what I was. Each lost cell takes a little of my intellect with it, and I have grown so very small. Where once I thought, now I merely react. How much of this could have been avoided, if I had only salvaged a little more biomass from the wreckage? How many options am I not seeing because my soul simply isn't big enough to contain them?

The world spoke to itself, in the same way I do when my communications are simple enough to convey without somatic fusion. Even as dog I could pick up the basic signature morphemes—this offshoot was Windows, that one was Bennings, the two who'd left in their flying machine for parts unknown were Copper and MacReady—and I marveled that these bits and pieces stayed isolated one from another, held the same shapes for so long, that the labeling of individual aliquots of biomass actually served a useful purpose.

Later I hid within the bipeds themselves, and whatever else lurked in those haunted skins began to talk to me. It said that bipeds were called guys, or men, or assholes. It said that MacReady was sometimes called Mac. It said that this collection of structures was a camp.

It said that it was afraid, but maybe that was just me.

Empathy's inevitable, of course. One can't mimic the sparks and chemicals that motivate the flesh without also feeling them to some extent. But this was different. These intuitions flickered within me yet somehow hovered beyond reach. My skins wandered the halls and the cryptic symbols on every surface—Laundry Sched, Welcome to the Clubhouse, This Side Up—almost made a kind of sense. That circular artefact hanging on the wall was a clock; it measured the passage of time. The world's eyes flitted here and there, and I skimmed piecemeal nomenclature from its—from his—mind.

But I was only riding a searchlight. I saw what it illuminated but I couldn't point it in any direction of my own choosing. I could eavesdrop, but I could only eavesdrop; never interrogate.

If only one of those searchlights had paused to dwell on its own evolution, on the trajectory that had brought it to this place. How differently things might have ended, had I only known. But instead it rested on a whole new word:

Autopsy.

MacReady and Copper had found part of me at the Norwegian camp: a rearguard offshoot, burned in the wake of my escape. They'd brought it back—charred, twisted, frozen in mid-transformation—and did not seem to know what it was.

I was being Palmer then, and Norris, and dog. I gathered around with the other biomass and watched as Copper cut me open and pulled out my insides. I watched as he dislodged something from behind my eyes: an organ of some kind.

It was malformed and incomplete, but its essentials were clear enough. It looked like a great wrinkled tumor, like cellular competition gone wild—as though the very processes that defined life had somehow turned against it instead. It was obscenely vascularised; it must have consumed oxygen and nutrients far out of proportion to its mass. I could not see how anything like that could even exist, how it could have reached that size without being outcompeted by more efficient morphologies.

Nor could I imagine what it did. But then I began to look with new eyes at these offshoots, these biped shapes my own cells had so scrupulously and unthinkingly copied when they reshaped me for this world. Unused to inventory—why catalog body parts that only turn into other things at the slightest provocation?—I really saw, for the first time, that swollen structure atop each body. So much larger than it should be: a bony hemisphere into which a million ganglionic interfaces could fit with room to spare. Every offshoot had one. Each piece of biomass carried one of these huge twisted clots of tissue.

I realized something else, too: the eyes, the ears of my dead skin had fed into this thing before Copper pulled it free. A massive bundle of fibers ran along the skin's longitudinal axis, right up the middle of the endoskeleton, directly into the dark sticky cavity where the growth had rested. That misshapen structure had been wired into the whole skin, like some kind of somatocognitive interface but vastly more massive. It was almost as if . . .

No.

That was how it worked. That was how these empty skins moved of their own volition, why I'd found no other network to integrate. There it was: not distributed throughout the body but balled up into itself, dark and dense and encysted. I had found the ghost in these machines.

I felt sick.

I shared my flesh with thinking cancer.

Sometimes, even hiding is not enough.

I remember seeing myself splayed across the floor of the kennel, a chimera split along a hundred seams, taking communion with a handful of dogs. Crimson tendrils writhed on the floor. Half-formed iterations sprouted from my flanks, the shapes of dogs and things not seen before on this world, haphazard morphologies half-remembered by parts of a part.

I remember Childs before I was Childs, burning me alive. I remember cowering inside Palmer, terrified that those flames might turn on the rest of me, that this world had somehow learned to shoot on sight.

I remember seeing myself stagger through the snow, raw instinct, wearing Bennings. Gnarled undifferentiated clumps clung to his hands like crude parasites, more outside than in; a few surviving fragments of some previous massacre, crippled, mindless, taking what they could and breaking cover. Men swarmed about him in the night: red flares in hand, blue lights at their backs, their faces bichromatic and beautiful. I remember Bennings, awash in flames, howling like an animal beneath the sky.

I remember Norris, betrayed by his own perfectly-copied, defective heart. Palmer, dying that the rest of me might live. Windows, still human, burned preemptively.

The names don't matter. The biomass does: so much of it, lost. So much new experience, so much fresh wisdom annihilated by this world of thinking tumors.

Why even dig me up? Why carve me from the ice,

carry me all that way across the wastes, bring me back to life only to attack me the moment I awoke?

If eradication was the goal, why not just kill me where I lay?

Those encysted souls. Those tumors. Hiding away in their bony caverns, folded in on themselves.

I knew they couldn't hide forever; this monstrous anatomy had only slowed communion, not stopped it. Every moment I grew a little. I could feel myself twining around Palmer's motor wiring, sniffing upstream along a million tiny currents. I could sense my infiltration of that dark thinking mass behind Blair's eyes.

Imagination, of course. It's all reflex that far down, unconscious and immune to micromanagement. And yet, a part of me wanted to stop while there was still time. I'm used to incorporating souls, not rooming with them. This, this compartmentalization was unprecedented. I've assimilated a thousand worlds stronger than this, but never one so strange. What would happen when I met the spark in the tumor? Who would assimilate who?

I was being three men by now. The world was growing wary, but it hadn't noticed yet. Even the tumors in the skins I'd taken didn't know how close I was. For that, I could only be grateful—that Creation has rules, that some things don't change no matter what shape you take. It doesn't matter whether a soul spreads throughout the skin or festers in grotesque isolation; it still runs on electricity. The memories of men still took time to gel, to pass through whatever gatekeepers filtered noise from signal —and a judicious burst of static, however indiscriminate, still cleared those caches before their contents could be stored permanently. Clear enough, at least, to let these tumors simply forget that something else moved their arms and legs on occasion.

At first I only took control when the skins closed their eyes and their searchlights flickered disconcertingly across unreal imagery, patterns that flowed senselessly into one another like hyperactive biomass unable to settle on a single shape. (Dreams, one searchlight told me, and a little later, Nightmares.) During those mysterious periods of dormancy, when the men lay inert and isolated, it was safe to come out.

Soon, though, the dreams dried up. All eyes stayed open all the time, fixed on shadows and each other. Offshoots once dispersed throughout the camp began to draw together, to give up their solitary pursuits in favor of company. At first I thought they might be finding common ground in a common fear. I even hoped that finally, they might shake off their mysterious fossilization and take communion.

But no. They'd just stopped trusting anything they couldn't see.

They were merely turning against each other.

My extremities are beginning to numb; my thoughts slow as the distal reaches of my soul succumb to the chill. The weight of the flamethrower pulls at its harness, forever tugs me just a little off-balance. I have not been Childs for very long; almost half this tissue remains unassimilated. I have an hour, maybe two, before I have to start melting my grave into the ice. By that time I need to have converted enough cells to keep this whole skin from crystallizing. I focus on antifreeze production.

It's almost peaceful out here. There's been so much to take in, so little time to process it. Hiding in these skins takes such concentration, and under all those watchful eyes I was lucky if communion lasted long enough to exchange memories: compounding my soul would have been out of the question. Now, though, there's nothing to do but prepare for oblivion. Nothing to occupy my thoughts but all these lessons left unlearned.

MacReady's blood test, for example. His thing detector, to expose imposters posing as men. It does not work nearly as well as the world thinks; but the fact that it works at all violates the most basic rules of biology. It's the center of the puzzle. It's the answer to all the mysteries. I might have already figured it out if I had been just a little larger. I might already know the world, if the world wasn't trying so hard to kill me.

MacReady's test.

Either it is impossible, or I have been wrong about everything.

They did not change shape. They did not take communion. Their fear and mutual mistrust was growing, but they would not join souls; they would only look for the enemy outside themselves.

So I gave them something to find.

I left false clues in the camp's rudimentary computer: simpleminded icons and animations, misleading numbers and projections seasoned with just enough truth to convince the world of their veracity. It didn't matter that the machine was far too simple to perform such calculations, or that there were no data to base them on anyway; Blair was the only biomass likely to know that, and he was already mine.

I left false leads, destroyed real ones, and then—alibi in place—I released Blair to run amok. I let him steal into the night and smash the vehicles as they slept, tugging ever-so-slightly at his reins to ensure that certain vital components were spared. I set him loose in the radio room, watched through his eyes and others as he rampaged and destroyed. I listened as he ranted about a world in danger, the need for containment, the conviction that most of you don't know what's going on around here—but I damn well know that some of you do . . .

He meant every word. I saw it in his searchlight. The best forgeries are the ones who've forgotten they aren't real.

When the necessary damage was done I let Blair fall to MacReady's counterassault. As Norris I suggested the tool shed as a holding cell. As Palmer I boarded up the windows, helped with the flimsy fortifications expected to keep me contained. I watched while the world locked me away for your own protection, Blair, and left me to my own devices. When no one was looking I would change and slip outside, salvage the parts I needed from all that bruised machinery. I would take them back to my burrow beneath the shed and build my escape piece by piece. I volunteered to feed the prisoner and came to myself when the world wasn't watching, laden with supplies enough to keep me going through all those necessary metamorphoses. I went through a third of the camp's food stores in three days, and—still trapped by my own preconceptions—marveled at the starvation diet that kept these offshoots chained to a single skin.

Another piece of luck: the world was too preoccupied to worry about kitchen inventory.

There is something on the wind, a whisper threading its way above the raging of the storm. I grow my ears, extend cups of near-frozen tissue from the sides of my head, turn like a living antennae in search of the best reception.

There, to my left: the abyss glows a little, silhouettes black swirling snow against a subtle lessening of the darkness. I hear the sounds of carnage. I hear myself. I do not know what shape I have taken, what sort of anatomy might be emitting those sounds. But I've worn enough skins on enough worlds to know pain when I hear it.

The battle is not going well. The battle is going as planned. Now it is time to turn away, to go to sleep. It is time to wait out the ages.

I lean into the wind. I move toward the light.

This is not the plan. But I think I have an answer, now: I think I may have had it even before I sent myself back into exile. It's not an easy thing to admit. Even now I don't fully understand. How long have I been out here, retelling the tale to myself, setting clues in order while my skin dies by low degrees? How long have I been circling this obvious, impossible truth?

I move towards the faint crackling of flames, the dull concussion of exploding ordnance more felt than heard.

The void lightens before me: gray segues into yellow, yellow into orange. One diffuse brightness resolves into many: a lone burning wall, miraculously standing. The smoking skeleton of MacReady's shack on the hill. A cracked smoldering hemisphere reflecting pale yellow in the flickering light: Child's searchlight calls it a radio dome.

The whole camp is gone. There's nothing left but flames and rubble.

They can't survive without shelter. Not for long. Not in those skins.

In destroying me, they've destroyed themselves.

Things could have turned out so much differently if I'd never been Norris.

Norris was the weak node: biomass not only ill-adapted but defective, an offshoot with an off switch. The world knew, had known so long it never even thought about it anymore. It wasn't until Norris collapsed that heart condition floated to the surface of Copper's mind where I could see it. It wasn't until Copper was astride Norris's chest, trying to pound him back to life, that I knew how it would end. And by then it was too late; Norris had stopped being Norris. He had even stopped being me.

I had so many roles to play, so little choice in any of them. The part being Copper brought down the paddles on the part that had been Norris, such a faithful Norris, every cell so scrupulously assimilated, every part of that faulty valve reconstructed unto perfection. I hadn't known. How was I to know? These shapes within me, the worlds and morphologies I've assimilated over the aeons— I've only ever used them to adapt before, never to hide. This desperate mimicry was an improvised thing, a last resort in the face of a world that attacked anything unfamiliar. My cells read the signs and my cells conformed, mindless as prions.

So I became Norris, and Norris self-destructed.

I remember losing myself after the crash. I know how it feels to degrade, tissues in revolt, the desperate efforts to reassert control as static from some misfiring organ jams the signal. To be a network seceding from itself, to know that each moment I am less than I was the moment before. To become nothing. To become legion.

Being Copper, I could see it. I still don't know why the world didn't; its parts had long since turned against each other by then, every offshoot suspected every other. Surely they were alert for signs of infection. Surely some of that biomass would have noticed the subtle twitch and ripple of Norris changing below the surface, the last instinctive resort of wild tissues abandoned to their own devices.

But I was the only one who saw. Being Childs, I could only stand and watch. Being Copper, I could only make it worse; if I'd taken direct control, forced that skin to drop the paddles, I would have given myself away. And so I played my parts to the end. I slammed those resurrection paddles down as Norris's chest split open beneath them. I screamed on cue as serrated teeth from a hundred stars away snapped shut. I toppled backwards, arms bitten off above the wrist. Men swarmed, agitation bootstrapping to panic. MacReady aimed his weapon; flames leaped across the enclosure. Meat and machinery screamed in the heat.

Copper's tumor winked out beside me. The world would never have let it live anyway, not after such obvious contamination. I let our skin play dead on the floor while overhead, something that had once been me shattered and writhed and iterated through a myriad random templates, searching desperately for something fireproof.

They have destroyed themselves. They.

Such an insane word to apply to a world.

Something crawls towards me through the wreckage: a jagged oozing jigsaw of blackened meat and shattered, half-resorbed bone. Embers stick to its sides like bright searing eyes; it doesn't have strength enough to scrape them free. It contains barely half the mass of this Childs' skin; much of it, burnt to raw carbon, is already dead.

What's left of Childs, almost asleep, thinks motherfucker, but I am being him now. I can carry that tune myself.

The mass extends a pseudopod to me, a final act of communion. I feel my pain:

I was Blair, I was Copper, I was even a scrap of dog that survived that first fiery massacre and holed up in the walls, with no food and no strength to regenerate. Then I gorged on unassimilated flesh, consumed instead of communed; revived and replenished, I drew together as one.

And yet, not quite. I can barely remember—so much was destroyed, so much memory lost—but I think the networks recovered from my different skins stayed just a little out of synch, even reunited in the same soma. I glimpse a half-corrupted memory of dog erupting from the greater self, ravenous and traumatized and determined to retain its individuality. I remember rage and frustration, that this world had so corrupted me that I could barely fit together again. But it didn't matter. I was more than Blair and Copper and Dog, now. I was a giant with the shapes of worlds to choose from, more than a match for the last lone man who stood against me.

No match, though, for the dynamite in his hand.

Now I'm little more than pain and fear and charred stinking flesh. What sentience I have is awash in confusion. I am stray and disconnected thoughts, doubts and the ghosts of theories. I am realizations, too late in coming and already forgotten.

But I am also Childs, and as the wind eases at last I remember wondering Who assimilates who? The snow tapers off and I remember an impossible test that stripped me naked.

The tumor inside me remembers it, too. I can see it in the last rays of its fading searchlight—and finally, at long last, that beam is pointed inwards.

Pointed at me.

I can barely see what it illuminates: Parasite. Monster. Disease.

Thing.

How little it knows. It knows even less than I do.

I know enough, you motherfucker. You soul-stealing, shit-eating rapist.

I don't know what that means. There is violence in those thoughts, and the forcible penetration of flesh, but underneath it all is something else I can't quite understand. I almost ask—but Childs's searchlight has finally gone out. Now there is nothing in here but me, nothing outside but fire and ice and darkness.

I am being Childs, and the storm is over.

In a world that gave meaningless names to interchangeable bits of biomass, one name truly mattered: MacReady.

MacReady was always the one in charge. The very concept still seems absurd: in charge. How can this world not see the folly of hierarchies? One bullet in a vital spot and the Norwegian dies, forever. One blow to the head and Blair is unconscious. Centralization is vulnerability—and yet the world is not content to build its biomass on such a fragile template, it forces the same model onto its metasystems as well. MacReady talks; the others obey. It is a system with a built-in kill spot.

And yet somehow, MacReady stayed in charge. Even after the world discovered the evidence I'd planted; even after it decided that MacReady was one of those things, locked him out to die in the storm, attacked him with fire and axes when he fought his way back inside. Somehow MacReady always had the gun, always had the flamethrower, always had the dynamite and the willingness to take out the whole damn camp if need be. Clarke was the last to try and stop him; MacReady shot him through the tumor.

Kill spot.

But when Norris split into pieces, each scuttling instinctively for its own life, MacReady was the one to put them back together.

I was so sure of myself when he talked about his test.

He tied up all the biomass—tied me up, more times than he knew—and I almost felt a kind of pity as he spoke. He forced Windows to cut us all, to take a little blood from each. He heated the tip of a metal wire until it glowed and he spoke of pieces small enough to give themselves away, pieces that embodied instinct but no intelligence, no self-control. MacReady had watched Norris in dissolution, and he had decided: men's blood would not react to the application of heat. Mine would break ranks when provoked.

Of course he thought that. These offshoots had forgotten that they could change.

I wondered how the world would react when every piece of biomass in the room was revealed as a shapeshifter, when MacReady's small experiment ripped the façade from the greater one and forced these twisted fragments to confront the truth. Would the world awaken from its long amnesia, finally remember that it lived and breathed and changed like everything else? Or was it too far gone—would MacReady simply burn each protesting offshoot in turn as its blood turned traitor?

I couldn't believe it when MacReady plunged the hot wire into Windows' blood and nothing happened. Some kind of trick, I thought. And then MacReady's blood passed the test, and Clarke's.

Copper's didn't. The needle went in and Copper's blood shivered just a little in its dish. I barely saw it myself; the men didn't react at all. If they even noticed, they must have attributed it to the trembling of MacReady's own hand. They thought the test was a crock of shit anyway. Being Childs, I even said as much.

Because it was too astonishing, too terrifying, to admit that it wasn't.

Being Childs, I knew there was hope. Blood is not soul: I may control the motor systems but assimilation takes time. If Copper's blood was raw enough to pass muster then it would be hours before I had anything to fear from this test; I'd been Childs for even less time.

But I was also Palmer, I'd been Palmer for days. Every last cell of that biomass had been assimilated; there was nothing of the original left.

When Palmer's blood screamed and leapt away from MacReady's needle, there was nothing I could do but blend in.

I have been wrong about everything.

Starvation. Experiment. Illness. All my speculation, all the theories I invoked to explain this place—top-down constraint, all of it. Underneath, I always knew the ability to change—to assimilate—had to remain the universal constant. No world evolves if its cells don't evolve; no cell evolves if it can't change. It's the nature of life everywhere.

Everywhere but here.

This world did not forget how to change. It was not manipulated into rejecting change. These were not the stunted offshoots of any greater self, twisted to the needs of some experiment; they were not conserving energy, waiting out some temporary shortage.

This is the option my shriveled soul could not encompass until now: out of all the worlds of my experience, this is the only one whose biomass can't change. It never could.

It's the only way MacReady's test makes any sense.

I say goodbye to Blair, to Copper, to myself. I reset my morphology to its local defaults. I am Childs, come back from the storm to finally make the pieces fit. Something moves up ahead: a dark blot shuffling against the flames, some weary animal looking for a place to bed down. It looks up as I approach.

MacReady.

We eye each other, and keep our distance. Colonies of cells shift uneasily inside me. I can feel my tissues redefining themselves.

"You the only one that made it?"

"Not the only one . . ."

I have the flamethrower. I have the upper hand. MacReady doesn't seem to care.

But he does care. He must. Because here, tissues and organs are not temporary battlefield alliances; they are permanent, predestined. Macrostructures do not emerge when the benefits of cooperation exceed its costs, or dissolve when that balance shifts the other way; here, each cell has but one immutable function. There's no plasticity, no way to adapt; every structure is frozen in place. This is not a single great world, but many small ones. Not parts of a greater thing; these are things. They are plural.

And that means—I think—that they stop. They just, just wear out over time.

"Where were you, Childs?"

I remember words in dead searchlights: "Thought I saw Blair. Went out after him. Got lost in the storm."

I've worn these bodies, felt them from the inside. Copper's sore joints. Blair's curved spine. Norris and his bad heart. They are not built to last. No somatic evolution to shape them, no communion to restore the biomass and stave off entropy. They should not even exist; existing, they should not survive.

They try, though. How they try. Every thing here is walking dead and yet it all fights so hard to keep going just a little longer. Each skin fights as desperately as I might, if one was all I could ever have.

MacReady tries.

"If you're worried about me—" I begin.

MacReady shakes his head, manages a weary smile. "If we've got any surprises for each other, I don't think we're in much shape to do anything about it . . ."

But we are. I am.

A whole planet of worlds, and not one of them—not one—has a soul. They wander through their lives separate and alone, unable even to communicate except through grunts and tokens: as if the essence of a sunset or a supernova could ever be contained in some string of phonemes, a few linear scratches of black on white. They've never known communion, can aspire to nothing but dissolution. The paradox of their biology is astonishing, yes; but the scale of their loneliness, the futility of these lives, overwhelms me.

I was so blind, so quick to blame. But the violence I've suffered at the hands of these things reflects no great evil. They're simply so used to pain, so blinded by disability, that they literally can't conceive of any other existence. When every nerve is whipped raw, you lash out at even the lightest touch.

"What should we do?" I wonder. I cannot escape into

the future, not knowing what I know now. How could I leave them like this?

"Why don't we just—wait here awhile," MacReady suggests. "See what happens."

I can do so much more than that.

It won't be easy. They won't understand. Tortured, incomplete, they're not able to understand. Offered the greater whole, they see the loss of the lesser. Offered communion, they see only extinction. I must be careful. I must use this newfound ability to hide. Other things will come here eventually, and it doesn't matter whether they find the living or the dead; what matters is that they find something like themselves, to take back home. So I will keep up appearances. I will work behind the scenes. I will save them from the inside, or their unimaginable loneliness will never end.

These poor savage things will never embrace salvation.

I will have to rape it into them.

# THE COLOUR OUT OF SPACE

## by H. P. Lovecraft

*H.P. Lovcraft (1890-1937) was, of course, one of the most influential horror writers of the twentieth century, in particular for his Cthulhu Mythos stories. While this story is not part of the Mythos, it has its own powerful effect and certainly is one of his best, and one of the major reasons for that influence.*

*Though **H.P. Lovecraft** died in 1937, at that time almost unknown outside the pages of* Weird Tales *(though this story was published in Hugo Gernsbach's* Amazing Stories*) which published most of his output while he was alive, and a substantial amount after his death, and had his writing dismissed by critics as varied as Damon Knight and Edmund Wilson, he is now considered a major American writer, with numerous paperback editions of his writing, and a two volume set of his works by the Library of*

*America. (Maybe dying well is the second best revenge.) Recently, the powers that be of the World Fantasy Convention, whose "Howard" awards for the year's best fantasy bore for 41 years a likeness of Lovecraft, fashioned as a caricature by the great cartoonist, Gahan Wilson, in their finite wisdom decreed, the annual award will no longer bear Lovecraft's likeness. I can't help wondering how many of those who protested use of HPL's phiz, will be recognizable names a century from now—like HPL.*

**WEST OF ARKHAM** the hills rise wild, and there are valleys with deep woods that no axe has ever cut. There are dark narrow glens where the trees slope fantastically, and where thin brooklets trickle without ever having caught the glint of sunlight. On the gentle slopes there are farms, ancient and rocky, with squat, moss-coated cottages brooding eternally over old New England secrets in the lee of great ledges; but these are all vacant now, the wide chimneys crumbling and the shingled sides bulging perilously beneath low gambrel roofs.

The old folk have gone away, and foreigners do not like to live there. French-Canadians have tried it, Italians have tried it, and the Poles have come and departed. It is not because of anything that can be seen or heard or handled, but because of something that is imagined. The place is not good for imagination, and does not bring restful dreams at night. It must be this which keeps the foreigners away, for old Ammi Pierce has never told them of anything he recalls from the strange days. Ammi, whose head has been a little queer for years, is the only one who still remains, or who ever talks of the strange days; and he dares to do this because his house is so near the open fields and the travelled roads around Arkham.

There was once a road over the hills and through the valleys, that ran straight where the blasted heath is now; but people ceased to use it and a new road was laid curving far toward the south. Traces of the old one can still be found amidst the weeds of a returning wilderness, and some of them will doubtless linger even when half the hollows are flooded for the new reservoir. Then the dark woods will be cut down and the blasted heath will slumber far below blue waters whose surface will mirror the sky and ripple in the sun. And the secrets of the strange days will be one with the deep's secrets; one with the hidden lore of old ocean, and all the mystery of primal earth.

When I went into the hills and vales to survey for the new reservoir they told me the place was evil. They told me this in Arkham, and because that is a very old town full of witch legends I thought the evil must he something which grandams had whispered to children through centuries. The name "blasted heath" seemed to me very odd and theatrical, and I wondered how it had come into the folklore of a Puritan people. Then I saw that dark westward tangle of glens and slopes for myself, and ceased to wonder at anything beside its own elder mystery. It was morning when I saw it, but shadow lurked always there. The trees grew too thickly, and their trunks were too big for any healthy New England wood. There was too much silence in the dim alleys between them, and the floor was too soft with the dank moss and mattings of infinite years of decay.

In the open spaces, mostly along the line of the old road, there were little hillside farms; sometimes with all the buildings standing, sometimes with only one or two, and sometimes with only a lone chimney or fast-filling cellar. Weeds and briers reigned, and furtive wild things rustled in the undergrowth. Upon everything was a haze of restlessness and oppression; a touch of the unreal and the grotesque, as if some vital element of perspective or chiaroscuro were awry. I did not wonder that the foreigners would not stay, for this was no region to sleep in. It was too much like a landscape of Salvator Rosa; too much like some forbidden woodcut in a tale of terror.

But even all this was not so bad as the blasted heath. I knew it the moment I came upon it at the bottom of a spacious valley; for no other name could fit such a thing, or any other thing fit such a name. It was as if the poet had coined the phrase from having seen this one particular region. It must, I thought as I viewed it, be the outcome of a fire; but why had nothing new ever grown over these five acres of grey desolation that sprawled open to the sky like a great spot eaten by acid in the woods and fields? It lay largely to the north of the ancient road line, but encroached a little on the other side. I felt an odd reluctance about approaching, and did so at last only because my business took me through and past it. There was no vegetation of any kind on that broad expanse, but only a fine grey dust or ash which no wind seemed ever to blow about. The trees near it were sickly and stunted, and many dead trunks stood or lay rotting at the rim. As I walked hurriedly by I saw the tumbled bricks and stones of an old chimney and cellar on my right, and the yawning black maw of an abandoned well whose stagnant vapours played strange tricks with the hues of the sunlight. Even the long, dark woodland climb beyond seemed welcome in contrast, and I marvelled no more at the frightened whispers of Arkham people. There had been no house or ruin near; even in the old days the place must have been lonely and remote. And at twilight, dreading to repass that ominous spot, I walked circuitously back to the town by the curious road on the south. I vaguely wished some clouds would gather, for an odd timidity about the deep skyey voids above had crept into my soul.

In the evening I asked old people in Arkham about the blasted heath, and what was meant by that phrase "strange days" which so many evasively muttered. I could not, however, get any good answers except that all the mystery was much more recent than I had dreamed. It was not a matter of old legendry at all, but something within the lifetime of those who spoke. It had happened in the 'eighties, and a family had disappeared or was killed. Speakers would not be exact; and because they all told me to pay no attention to old Ammi Pierce's crazy tales, I sought him out the next morning, having heard that he lived alone in the ancient tottering cottage where the trees first begin to get very thick. It was a fearsomely ancient place, and had begun to exude the faint miasmal odour which clings about houses that have stood too long. Only with persistent knocking could I rouse the aged man, and when he shuffled timidly to the door I could tell he was not glad to see me. He was not so feeble as I had expected; but his eyes drooped in a curious way, and his unkempt clothing and white beard made him seem very worn and dismal.

Not knowing just how he could best be launched on his tales, I feigned a matter of business; told him of my surveying, and asked vague questions about the district. He was far brighter and more educated than I had been led to think, and before I knew it had grasped quite as much of the subject as any man I had talked with in Arkham. He was not like other rustics I had known in the sections where reservoirs were to be. From him there were no protests at the miles of old wood and farmland to be blotted out, though perhaps there would have been had not his home lain outside the bounds of the future lake. Relief was all that he shewed; relief at the doom of the dark ancient valleys through which he had roamed all his life. They were better under water now—better under water since the strange days. And with this opening his husky voice sank low, while his body leaned forward and his right forefinger began to point shakily and impressively.

It was then that I heard the story, and as the rambling voice scraped and whispered on I shivered again and again despite the summer day. Often I had to recall the speaker from ramblings, piece out scientific points which he knew only by a fading parrot memory of professors' talk, or bridge over gaps, where his sense of logic and continuity broke down. When he was done I did not wonder that his mind had snapped a trifle, or that the folk of Arkham would not speak much of the blasted heath. I hurried back before sunset to my hotel, unwilling to have the stars come out above me in the open; and the next day returned to Boston to give up my position. I could not go into that dim chaos of old forest and slope again, or face another time that grey blasted heath where the black well yawned deep beside the tumbled bricks and stones. The reservoir will soon be built now, and all those elder secrets will be safe forever under watery fathoms. But even then I do not believe I would like to visit that country by night—at least not when the sinister stars are out; and nothing could bribe me to drink the new city water of Arkham.

It all began, old Ammi said, with the meteorite. Before that time there had been no wild legends at all since the witch trials, and even then these western woods were not feared half so much as the small island in the Miskatonic where the devil held court beside a curious stone altar older than the Indians. These were not haunted woods, and their fantastic dusk was never terrible till the strange days. Then there had come that white noontide cloud, that string of explosions in the air, and that pillar of smoke from the valley far in the wood. And by night all Arkham had heard of the great rock that fell out of the sky and bedded itself in the ground beside the well at the Nahum Gardner place. That was the house which had stood where the blasted heath was to come—the trim white Nahum Gardner house amidst its fertile gardens and orchards.

Nahum had come to town to tell people about the stone, and dropped in at Ammi Pierce's on the way. Ammi was forty then, and all the queer things were fixed very strongly in his mind. He and his wife had gone with the three professors from Miskatonic University who hastened out the next morning to see the weird visitor from unknown stellar space, and had wondered why Nahum had called it so large the day before. It had shrunk, Nahum said as he pointed out the big brownish mound above the ripped earth and charred grass near the archaic well-sweep in his front yard; but the wise men answered that stones do not shrink. Its heat lingered persistently, and Nahum declared it had glowed faintly in the night. The professors tried it with a geologist's hammer and found it was oddly soft. It was, in truth, so soft as to be almost plastic; and they gouged rather than chipped a specimen to take back to the college for testing. They took it in an old pail borrowed from Nahum's kitchen, for even the small piece refused to grow cool. On the trip back they stopped at Ammi's to rest, and seemed thoughtful when Mrs. Pierce remarked that the fragment was growing smaller and burning the bottom of the pail. Truly, it was not large, but perhaps they had taken less than they thought.

The day after that—all this was in June of '82—the professors had trooped out again in a great excitement. As they passed Ammi's they told him what queer things the specimen had done, and how it had faded wholly away when they put it in a glass beaker. The beaker had gone, too, and the wise men talked of the strange stone's affinity for silicon. It had acted quite unbelievably in that well-ordered laboratory; doing nothing at all and shewing no occluded gases when heated on charcoal, being wholly negative in the borax bead, and soon proving itself absolutely non-volatile at any producible temperature, including that of the oxy-hydrogen blowpipe. On an anvil it appeared highly malleable, and in the dark its luminosity was very marked. Stubbornly refusing to grow cool, it soon had the college in a state of real excitement; and when upon heating before the spectroscope it displayed shining bands unlike any known colours of the normal spectrum there was much breathless talk of new elements, bizarre optical properties, and other things which puzzled men of science are wont to say when faced by the unknown.

Hot as it was, they tested it in a crucible with all the proper reagents. Water did nothing. Hydrochloric acid was the same. Nitric acid and even aqua regia merely hissed and spattered against its torrid invulnerability. Ammi had difficulty in recalling all these things, but recognized some solvents as I mentioned them in the usual order of use. There were ammonia and caustic soda, alcohol and ether, nauseous carbon disulphide and a dozen others; but although the weight grew steadily less as time passed, and the fragment seemed to be slightly cooling, there was no change in the solvents to shew that they had attacked the substance at all. It was a metal, though, beyond a doubt. It was magnetic, for one thing; and after its immersion in the acid solvents there seemed to be faint traces of the Widmanstätten figures found on meteoric iron. When the cooling had grown very considerable, the testing was carried on in glass; and it was in a glass beaker that they left all the chips made of the original fragment during the work. The next morning both chips and beaker were gone without trace, and only a charred spot marked the place on the wooden shelf where they had been.

All this the professors told Ammi as they paused at his door, and once more he went with them to see the stony messenger from the stars, though this time his wife did not accompany him. It had now most certainly shrunk, and even the sober professors could not doubt the truth of what they saw. All around the dwindling brown lump near the well was a vacant space, except where the earth had caved in; and whereas it had been a good seven feet across the day before, it was now scarcely five. It was still hot, and the sages studied its surface curiously as they detached another and larger piece with hammer and chisel. They gouged deeply this time, and as they pried away the smaller mass they saw that the core of the thing was not quite homogeneous.

They had uncovered what seemed to be the side of a large coloured globule embedded in the substance. The colour, which resembled some of the bands in the meteor's strange spectrum, was almost impossible to describe; and it was only by analogy that they called it colour at all. Its texture was glossy, and upon tapping it appeared to promise both brittleness and hollowness. One of the professors gave it a smart blow with a hammer, and it burst with a nervous little pop. Nothing was emitted, and all trace of the thing vanished with the puncturing. It left behind a hollow spherical space about three inches across, and all thought it probable that others would be discovered as the enclosing substance wasted away.

Conjecture was vain; so after a futile attempt to find additional globules by drilling, the seekers left again with their new specimen which proved, however, as baffling in the laboratory as its predecessor. Aside from being almost plastic, having heat, magnetism, and slight luminosity, cooling slightly in powerful acids, possessing an unknown spectrum, wasting away in air, and attacking silicon compounds with mutual destruction as a result, it presented no identifying features whatsoever; and at the end of the tests the college scientists were forced to own that they could not place it. It was nothing of this earth, but a piece of the great outside; and as such dowered with outside properties and obedient to outside laws.

That night there was a thunderstorm, and when the professors went out to Nahum's the next day they met with a bitter disappointment. The stone, magnetic as it had been, must have had some peculiar electrical property; for it had "drawn the lightning," as Nahum said, with a singular persistence. Six times within an hour the farmer saw the lightning strike the furrow in the front yard, and when the storm was over nothing remained but a ragged pit by the ancient well-sweep, half-choked with a caved-in earth. Digging had borne no fruit, and the scientists verified the fact of the utter vanishment. The failure was total; so that nothing was left to do but go back to the laboratory and test again the disappearing fragment left carefully cased in lead. That fragment lasted a week, at the end of which nothing of value had been learned of it. When it had gone, no residue was left behind, and in time the professors felt scarcely sure they had indeed seen with waking eyes that cryptic vestige of the fathomless gulfs outside; that lone, weird message from other universes and other realms of matter, force, and entity.

As was natural, the Arkham papers made much of the incident with its collegiate sponsoring, and sent reporters to talk with Nahum Gardner and his family. At least one Boston daily also sent a scribe, and Nahum quickly became a kind of local celebrity. He was a lean, genial person of about fifty, living with his wife and three sons on the pleasant farmstead in the valley. He and Ammi exchanged visits frequently, as did their wives; and Ammi had nothing but praise for him after all these years. He seemed slightly proud of the notice his place had attracted, and talked often of the meteorite in the succeeding weeks. That July and

August were hot; and Nahum worked hard at his haying in the ten-acre pasture across Chapman's Brook; his rattling wain wearing deep ruts in the shadowy lanes between. The labour tired him more than it had in other years, and he felt that age was beginning to tell on him.

Then fell the time of fruit and harvest. The pears and apples slowly ripened, and Nahum vowed that his orchards were prospering as never before. The fruit was growing to phenomenal size and unwonted gloss, and in such abundance that extra barrels were ordered to handle the future crop. But with the ripening came sore disappointment, for of all that gorgeous array of specious lusciousness not one single jot was fit to eat. Into the fine flavour of the pears and apples had crept a stealthy bitterness and sickishness, so that even the smallest bites induced a lasting disgust. It was the same with the melons and tomatoes, and Nahum sadly saw that his entire crop was lost. Quick to connect events, he declared that the meteorite had poisoned the soil, and thanked Heaven that most of the other crops were in the upland lot along the road.

Winter came early, and was very cold. Ammi saw Nahum less often than usual, and observed that he had begun to look worried. The rest of his family too, seemed to have grown taciturn; and were far from steady in their church-going or their attendance at the various social events of the countryside. For this reserve or melancholy no cause could be found, though all the household confessed now and then to poorer health and a feeling of vague disquiet. Nahum himself gave the most definite statement of anyone when he said he was disturbed about certain footprints in the snow. They were the usual winter prints of red squirrels, white rabbits, and foxes, but the brooding farmer professed to see something not quite right about their nature and arrangement. He was never specific, but appeared to think that they were not as characteristic of the anatomy and habits of squirrels and rabbits and foxes as they ought to be. Ammi listened without interest to this talk until one night when he drove past Nahum's house in his sleigh on the way back from Clark's Corners. There had been a moon, and a rabbit had run across the road, and the leaps of that rabbit were longer than either Ammi or his horse liked. The latter, indeed, had almost run away when brought up by a firm rein. Thereafter Ammi gave Nahum's tales more respect, and wondered why the Gardner dogs seemed so cowed and quivering every morning. They had, it developed, nearly lost the spirit to bark.

In February the McGregor boys from Meadow Hill were out shooting woodchucks, and not far from the Gardner place bagged a very peculiar specimen. The proportions of its body seemed slightly altered in a queer way impossible to describe, while its face had taken on an expression which no one ever saw in a woodchuck before. The boys were genuinely frightened, and threw the thing away at once, so that only their grotesque tales of it ever reached the people of the countryside. But the shying of horses near Nahum's house had now become an acknowledged thing, and all the basis for a cycle of whispered legend was fast taking form.

People vowed that the snow melted faster around Nahum's than it did anywhere else, and early in March there was an awed discussion in Potter's general store at Clark's Corners. Stephen Rice had driven past Gardner's in the morning, and had noticed the skunk-cabbages coming up through the mud by the woods across the road. Never were things of such size seen before, and they held strange colours that could not be put into any words. Their shapes were monstrous, and the horse had snorted at an odour which struck Stephen as wholly unprecedented. That afternoon several persons drove past to see the abnormal growth, and all agreed that plants of that kind ought never to sprout in a healthy world. The bad fruit of the fall before was freely mentioned, and it went from mouth to mouth that there was poison in Nahum's ground. Of course it was the meteorite; and remembering how strange the men from the college had found that stone to be, several farmers spoke about the matter to them.

One day they paid Nahum a visit; but having no love of wild tales and folklore were very conservative in what they inferred. The plants were certainly odd, but all skunk-cabbages are more or less odd in shape and hue. Perhaps some mineral element from the stone had entered the soil, but it would soon be washed away. And as for the footprints and frightened horses—of course this was mere country talk which such a phenomenon as the aerolite would be certain to start. There was really nothing for serious men to do in cases of wild gossip, for superstitious rustics will say and believe anything. And so all through the strange days the professors stayed away in contempt. Only one of them, when given two phials of dust for analysis in a police job over a year and half later, recalled that the queer colour of that skunk-cabbage had been very like one of the anomalous bands of light shewn by the meteor fragment in the college spectroscope, and like the brittle globule found imbedded in the stone from the abyss. The samples in this analysis case gave the same odd bands at first, though later they lost the property.

The trees budded prematurely around Nahum's, and at night they swayed ominously in the wind. Nahum's second son Thaddeus, a lad of fifteen, swore that they swayed also when there was no wind; but even the gossips would not credit this. Certainly, however, restlessness was in the air. The entire Gardner family developed the habit of stealthy listening, though not for any sound which they could consciously name. The listening was, indeed, rather a product of moments when consciousness seemed half to slip away. Unfortunately such moments increased week by week, till it became common speech that "something was wrong with all Nahum's folks." When the early saxifrage came out it had another strange colour; not quite like that of the skunk-cabbage, but plainly related and equally unknown to anyone who saw it. Nahum took some blossoms to Arkham and shewed them to the editor of the *Gazette*, but that dignitary did no more than write a humorous article about them, in which the dark fears of rustics were held up to polite ridicule. It was a mistake of Nahum's to tell a stolid city man about the way the great, overgrown mourning-cloak butterflies behaved in connection with these saxifrages.

April brought a kind of madness to the country folk, and began that disuse of the road past Nahum's which led to its ultimate abandonment. It was the vegetation. All the orchard trees blossomed forth in strange colours, and through the stony soil of the yard and adjacent pasturage there sprang up a bizarre growth which only a botanist could connect with the proper flora of the region. No sane wholesome colours were anywhere to be seen except in the green grass and leafage; but everywhere were those hectic and prismatic variants of some diseased, underlying primary tone without a place among the known tints of earth. The "Dutchman's breeches" became a thing of sinister menace, and the bloodroots grew insolent in their chromatic perversion. Ammi and the Gardners thought that most of the colours had a sort of haunting familiarity, and decided that they reminded one of the brittle globule in the meteor. Nahum ploughed and sowed the ten-acre pasture and the upland lot, but did nothing with the land around the house. He knew it would be of no use, and hoped that the summer's strange growths would draw all the poison from the soil. He was prepared for almost anything now, and had grown used to the sense of something near him waiting to be heard. The shunning of his house by neighbors told on him, of course; but it told on his wife more. The boys were better off, being at school each day; but they could not help being frightened by the gossip. Thaddeus, an especially sensitive youth, suffered the most.

In May the insects came, and Nahum's place became a nightmare of buzzing and crawling. Most of the creatures seemed not quite usual in their aspects and motions, and their nocturnal habits contradicted all former experience. The Gardners took to watching at night—watching in all directions at random for something—they could not tell what. It was then that they owned that Thaddeus had been right about the trees. Mrs. Gardner was the next to see it from the window as she watched the swollen boughs of a maple against a moonlit sky. The boughs surely moved, and there was no wind. It must be the sap. Strangeness had come into everything growing now. Yet it was none of Nahum's family at all who made the next discovery. Familiarity had dulled them, and what they could not see was glimpsed by a timid windmill salesman from Bolton who drove by one night in ignorance of the country legends. What he told in Arkham was given a short paragraph in the *Gazette*; and it was there that all the farmers, Nahum included, saw it first. The night had been dark and the buggy-lamps faint, but around a farm in the valley which everyone knew from the account must be Nahum's, the darkness had been less thick. A dim though distinct luminosity seemed to inhere in all the vegetation, grass, leaves, and blossoms alike, while at one moment a detached piece of the phosphorescence appeared to stir furtively in the yard near the barn.

The grass had so far seemed untouched, and the cows were freely pastured in the lot near the house, but toward the end of May the milk began to be bad. Then Nahum had the cows driven to the uplands, after which this trouble ceased. Not long after this the change in grass and leaves became apparent to the eye. All the verdure was going grey, and was developing a highly singular quality of brittleness. Ammi was now the only person who ever visited the place, and his visits were becoming fewer and fewer. When school closed the Gardners were virtually cut off from the world, and sometimes let Ammi do their errands in town. They were failing curiously both physically and mentally, and no one was surprised when the news of Mrs. Gardner's madness stole around.

It happened in June, about the anniversary of the

meteor's fall, and the poor woman screamed about things in the air which she could not describe. In her raving there was not a single specific noun, but only verbs and pronouns. Things moved and changed and fluttered, and ears tingled to impulses which were not wholly sounds. Something was taken away—she was being drained of something—something was fastening itself on her that ought not to be—someone must make it keep off—nothing was ever still in the night—the walls and windows shifted. Nahum did not send her to the county asylum, but let her wander about the house as long as she was harmless to herself and others. Even when her expression changed he did nothing. But when the boys grew afraid of her, and Thaddeus nearly fainted at the way she made faces at him, he decided to keep her locked in the attic. By July she had ceased to speak and crawled on all fours, and before that month was over Nahum got the mad notion that she was slightly luminous in the dark, as he now clearly saw was the case with the nearby vegetation.

It was a little before this that the horses had stampeded. Something had aroused them in the night, and their neighing and kicking in their stalls had been terrible. There seemed virtually nothing to do to calm them, and when Nahum opened the stable door they all bolted out like frightened woodland deer. It took a week to track all four, and when found they were seen to be quite useless and unmanageable. Something had snapped in their brains, and each one had to be shot for its own good. Nahum borrowed a horse from Ammi for his haying, but found it would not approach the barn. It shied, balked, and whinnied, and in the end he could do nothing but drive it into the yard while the men used their own strength to get the heavy wagon near enough the hayloft for convenient pitching. And all the while the vegetation was turning grey and brittle. Even the flowers whose hues had been so strange were greying now, and the fruit was coming out grey and dwarfed and tasteless. The asters and goldenrod bloomed grey and distorted, and the roses and zinneas and hollyhocks in the front yard were such blasphemous-looking things that Nahum's oldest boy Zenas cut them down. The strangely puffed insects died about that time, even the bees that had left their hives and taken to the woods.

By September all the vegetation was fast crumbling to a greyish powder, and Nahum feared that the trees would die before the poison was out of the soil. His wife now had spells of terrific screaming, and he and the boys were in a constant state of nervous tension. They shunned people now, and when school opened the boys did not go. But it was Ammi, on one of his rare visits, who first realised that the well water was no longer good. It had an evil taste that was not exactly fetid nor exactly salty, and Ammi advised his friend to dig another well on higher ground to use till the soil was good again. Nahum, however, ignored the warning, for he had by that time become calloused to strange and unpleasant things. He and the boys continued to use the tainted supply, drinking it as listlessly and mechanically as they ate their meagre and ill-cooked meals and did their thankless and monotonous chores through the aimless days. There was something of stolid resignation about them all, as if they walked half in another world between lines of nameless guards to a certain and familiar doom.

Thaddeus went mad in September after a visit to the well. He had gone with a pail and had come back empty-handed, shrieking and waving his arms, and sometimes lapsing into an inane titter or a whisper about "the moving colours down there." Two in one family was pretty bad, but Nahum was very brave about it. He let the boy run about for a week until he began stumbling and hurting himself, and then he shut him in an attic room across the hall from his mother's. The way they screamed at each other from behind their locked doors was very terrible, especially to little Merwin, who fancied they talked in some terrible language that was not of earth. Merwin was getting frightfully imaginative, and his restlessness was worse after the shutting away of the brother who had been his greatest playmate.

Almost at the same time the mortality among the livestock commenced. Poultry turned greyish and died very quickly, their meat being found dry and noisome upon cutting. Hogs grew inordinately fat, then suddenly began to undergo loathsome changes which no one could explain. Their meat was of course useless, and Nahum was at his wit's end. No rural veterinary would approach his place, and the city veterinary from Arkham was openly baffled. The swine began growing grey and brittle and falling to pieces before they died, and their eyes and muzzles developed singular alterations. It was very inexplicable, for they had never been fed from the tainted vegetation. Then something struck the cows. Certain areas or sometimes the whole body would be uncannily shrivelled or compressed, and atrocious collapses or disintegrations were common. In the last stages—and death was always the result—there would be a greying and turning brittle like that which beset the hogs. There could be no question of poison, for all the cases occurred in a locked and undisturbed barn. No bites of prowling things could have brought the virus, for what live beast of earth can pass through solid obstacles? It must be only natural disease—yet what disease could wreak such results was beyond any mind's guessing. When the harvest came there was not an animal surviving on the place, for the stock and poultry were dead and the dogs had run away. These dogs, three in number, had all vanished one night and were never heard of again. The five cats had left some time before, but their going was scarcely noticed since there now seemed to be no mice, and only Mrs. Gardner had made pets of the graceful felines.

On the nineteenth of October Nahum staggered into Ammi's house with hideous news. The death had come to poor Thaddeus in his attic room, and it had come in a way which could not be told. Nahum had dug a grave in the railed family plot behind the farm, and had put therein what he found. There could have been nothing from outside, for the small barred window and locked door were intact; but it was much as it had been in the barn. Ammi and his wife consoled the stricken man as best they could, but shuddered as they did so. Stark terror seemed to cling round the Gardners and all they touched, and the very presence of one in the house was a breath from regions unnamed and unnamable. Ammi accompanied Nahum home with the greatest reluctance, and did what he might to calm the hysterical sobbing of little Merwin. Zenas needed no calming. He had come of late to do nothing but stare into space and obey what his father told him; and

Ammi thought that his fate was very merciful. Now and then Merwin's screams were answered faintly from the attic, and in response to an inquiring look Nahum said that his wife was getting very feeble. When night approached, Ammi managed to get away; for not even friendship could make him stay in that spot when the faint glow of the vegetation began and the trees may or may not have swayed without wind. It was really lucky for Ammi that he was not more imaginative. Even as things were, his mind was bent ever so slightly; but had he been able to connect and reflect upon all the portents around him he must inevitably have turned a total maniac. In the twilight he hastened home, the screams of the mad woman and the nervous child ringing horribly in his ears.

Three days later Nahum burst into Ammi's kitchen in the early morning, and in the absence of his host stammered out a desperate tale once more, while Mrs. Pierce listened in a clutching fright. It was little Merwin this time. He was gone. He had gone out late at night with a lantern and pail for water, and had never come back. He'd been going to pieces for days, and hardly knew what he was about. Screamed at everything. There had been a frantic shriek from the yard then, but before the father could get to the door the boy was gone. There was no glow from the lantern he had taken, and of the child himself no trace. At the time Nahum thought the lantern and pail were gone too; but when dawn came, and the man had plodded back from his all-night search of the woods and fields, he had found some very curious things near the well. There was a crushed and apparently somewhat melted mass of iron which had certainly been the lantern; while a bent handle and twisted iron hoops beside it, both half-fused, seemed to hint at the remnants of the pail. That was all. Nahum was past imagining, Mrs. Pierce was blank, and Ammi, when he had reached home and heard the tale, could give no guess. Merwin was gone, and there would be no use in telling the people around, who shunned all Gardners now. No use, either, in telling the city people at Arkham who laughed at everything. Thad was gone, and now Merwin was gone. Something was creeping and creeping and waiting to be seen and heard. Nahum would go soon, and he wanted Ammi to look after his wife and Zenas if they survived him. It must all be a judgment of some sort; though he could not fancy what for, since he had always walked uprightly in the Lord's ways so far as he knew.

For over two weeks Ammi saw nothing of Nahum; and then, worried about what might have happened, he overcame his fears and paid the Gardner place a visit. There was no smoke from the great chimney, and for a moment the visitor was apprehensive of the worst. The aspect of the whole farm was shocking—greyish withered grass and leaves on the ground, vines falling in brittle wreckage from archaic walls and gables, and great bare trees clawing up at the grey November sky with a studied malevolence which Ammi could not but feel had come from some subtle change in the tilt of the branches. But Nahum was alive, after all. He was weak, and lying on a couch in the low-ceiled kitchen, but perfectly conscious and able to give simple orders to Zenas. The room was deadly cold; and as Ammi visibly shivered, the host shouted huskily to Zenas for more wood. Wood, indeed, was sorely needed; since the cavernous fireplace was unlit and empty, with a cloud of soot blowing about in the chill wind that came down the chimney. Presently Nahum asked him if the extra wood had made him any more comfortable, and then Ammi saw what had happened. The stoutest cord had broken at last, and the hapless farmer's mind was proof against more sorrow.

Questioning tactfully, Ammi could get no clear data at all about the missing Zenas. "In the well—he lives in the well—" was all that the clouded father would say. Then there flashed across the visitor's mind a sudden thought of the mad wife, and he changed his line of inquiry. "Nabby? Why, here she is!" was the surprised response of poor Nahum, and Ammi soon saw that he must search for himself. Leaving the harmless babbler on the couch, he took the keys from their nail beside the door and climbed the creaking stairs to the attic. It was very close and noisome up there, and no sound could be heard from any direction. Of the four doors in sight, only one was locked, and on this he tried various keys of the ring he had taken. The third key proved the right one, and after some fumbling Ammi threw open the low white door.

It was quite dark inside, for the window was small and half-obscured by the crude wooden bars; and Ammi could see nothing at all on the wide-planked floor. The stench was beyond enduring, and before proceeding further he had to retreat to another room and return with his lungs filled with breathable air. When he did enter he saw something dark in the corner, and upon seeing it more clearly he screamed outright. While he screamed he thought a momentary cloud eclipsed the window, and a second later he felt himself brushed as if by some hateful current of vapour. Strange colours danced before his eyes; and had not a present horror numbed him he would have thought of the globule in the meteor that the geologist's hammer had shattered, and of the morbid vegetation that had sprouted in the spring. As it was he thought only of the blasphemous monstrosity which confronted him, and which all too clearly had shared the nameless fate of young Thaddeus and the livestock. But the terrible thing about the horror was that it very slowly and perceptibly moved as it continued to crumble.

Ammi would give me no added particulars of this scene, but the shape in the corner does not reappear in his tale as a moving object. There are things which cannot be mentioned, and what is done in common humanity is sometimes cruelly judged by the law. I gathered that no moving thing was left in that attic room, and that to leave anything capable of motion there would have been a deed so monstrous as to damn any accountable being to eternal torment. Anyone but a stolid farmer would have fainted or gone mad, but Ammi walked conscious through that low doorway and locked the accursed secret behind him. There would be Nahum to deal with now; he must be fed and tended, and removed to some place where he could be cared for.

Commencing his descent of the dark stairs. Ammi heard a thud below him. He even thought a scream had been suddenly choked off, and recalled nervously the clammy vapour which had brushed by him in that frightful room above. What presence had his cry and entry started up? Halted by some vague fear, he heard still further sounds below. Indubitably there was a sort of heavy dragging, and a most detestably sticky noise as of some fiendish and unclean species of suction. With an associative sense goaded to feverish heights, he thought unaccountably of what he had seen upstairs. Good God! What eldritch dream-world was this into which he had blundered? He dared move neither backward nor forward, but stood there trembling at the black curve of the boxed-in staircase. Every trifle of the scene burned itself into his brain. The sounds, the sense of dread expectancy, the darkness, the steepness of the narrow step—and merciful Heaven!—the faint but unmistakable luminosity of all the woodwork in sight; steps, sides, exposed laths, and beams alike.

Then there burst forth a frantic whinny from Ammi's horse outside, followed at once by a clatter which told of a frenzied runaway. In another moment horse and buggy had gone beyond earshot, leaving the frightened man on the dark stairs to guess what had sent them. But that was not all. There had been another sound out there. A sort of liquid splash—water—it must have been the well. He had left Hero untied near it, and a buggy wheel must have brushed the coping and knocked in a stone. And still the pale phosphorescence glowed in that detestably ancient woodwork. God! how old the house was! Most of it built before 1670, and the gambrel roof no later than 1730.

A feeble scratching on the floor downstairs now sounded distinctly, and Ammi's grip tightened on a heavy stick he had picked up in the attic for some purpose. Slowly nerving himself, he finished his descent and walked boldly toward the kitchen. But he did not complete the walk, because what he sought was no longer there. It had come to meet him, and it was still alive after a fashion. Whether it had crawled or whether it had been dragged by any external forces, Ammi could not say; but the death had been at it. Everything had happened in the last half-hour, but collapse, greying, and disintegration were already far advanced. There was a horrible brittleness, and dry fragments were scaling off. Ammi could not touch it, but looked horrifiedly into the distorted parody that had been a face. "What was it, Nahum—what was it?" He whispered, and the cleft, bulging lips were just able to crackle out a final answer.

"Nothin' . . . nothin' . . . the colour . . . it burns . . . cold an' wet, but it burns . . . it lived in the well . . . I seen it . . . a kind of smoke . . . jest like the flowers last spring . . . the well shone at night . . . Thad an' Merwin an' Zenas . . . everything alive . . . suckin' the life out of everything . . . in that stone . . . it must a' come in that stone pizened the whole place . . . dun't know what it wants . . . that round thing them men from the college dug outen the stone . . . they smashed it . . . it was the same colour . . . jest the same, like the flowers an' plants . . . must a' ben more of 'em . . . seeds . . . seeds . . . they growed . . . I seen it the fust time this week . . . must a' got strong on Zenas . . . he was a big boy, full o' life . . . it beats down your mind an' then gets ye . . . burns ye up . . . in the well water . . . you was right about that . . . evil water . . . Zenas never come back from the well . . . can't git away . . . draws ye . . . ye know summ'at's comin' but tain't no use . . . I seen it time an' agin senct Zenas was took . . . whar's Nabby, Ammi? . . . my head's no good . . . dun't know how long sense I fed her . . . it'll git her ef we ain't keerful . . . jest a colour . . . her face is gittin' to hev that colour sometimes towards night . . . an' it burns an' sucks . . . it come from some place whar things ain't as they is here . . . one o' them professors said so . . . he was right . . . look out, Ammi, it'll do suthin' more . . . sucks the life out . . ."

But that was all. That which spoke could speak no more because it had completely caved in. Ammi laid a red checked tablecloth over what was left and reeled out the back door into the fields. He climbed the slope to the ten-acre pasture and stumbled home by the north road and the woods. He could not pass that well from which his horses had run away. He had looked at it through the window, and had seen that no stone was missing from the rim. Then the lurching buggy had not dislodged anything after all—the splash had been something else—something which went into the well after it had done with poor Nahum.

When Ammi reached his house the horses and buggy had arrived before him and thrown his wife into fits of anxiety. Reassuring her without explanations, he set out at once for Arkham and notified the authorities that the Gardner family was no more. He indulged in no details, but merely told of the deaths of Nahum and Nabby, that of Thaddeus being already known, and mentioned that the cause seemed to be the same strange ailment which had killed the live-stock. He also stated that Merwin and Zenas had disappeared. There was considerable questioning at the police station, and in the end Ammi was compelled to take three officers to the Gardner farm, together with the coroner, the medical examiner, and the veterinary who had treated the diseased animals. He went much against his will, for the afternoon was advancing and he feared the fall of night over that accursed place, but it was some comfort to have so many people with him.

The six men drove out in a democrat-wagon, following Ammi's buggy, and arrived at the pest-ridden farmhouse about four o'clock. Used as the officers were to gruesome experiences, not one remained unmoved at what was found in the attic and under the red checked tablecloth on the floor below. The whole aspect of the farm with its grey desolation was terrible enough, but those two crumbling objects were beyond all bounds. No one could look long at them, and even the medical examiner admitted that there was very little to examine. Specimens could be analysed, of course, so he busied himself in obtaining them—and here it develops that a very puzzling aftermath occurred at the college laboratory where the two phials of dust were finally taken. Under the spectroscope both samples gave off an unknown spectrum, in which many of the baffling bands were precisely like those which the strange meteor had yielded in the previous year. The property of emitting this spectrum vanished in a month, the dust thereafter consisting mainly of alkaline phosphates and carbonates.

Ammi would not have told the men about the well if he had thought they meant to do anything then and there. It was getting toward sunset, and he was anxious to be away. But he could not help glancing nervously at the stony curb by the great sweep, and when a detective questioned him he admitted that Nahum had feared something down there so much so that he had never even thought of searching it for Merwin or Zenas. After that nothing would do but that they empty and explore the well immediately, so Ammi had to wait trembling while pail after pail of rank water was hauled up and splashed on the soaking ground outside. The men sniffed in disgust at the fluid, and toward the last held their noses against the foetor they were uncovering. It was not so long a job as they had feared it would be, since the water was phenomenally low. There is no need to speak too exactly of what they found. Merwin and Zenas were both there, in part, though the vestiges were mainly skeletal. There were also a small deer and a large dog in about the same state, and a number of bones of small animals. The ooze and slime at the bottom seemed inexplicably porous and bubbling, and a man who descended on hand-holds with a long pole found that he could sink the wooden shaft to any depth in the mud of the floor without meeting any solid obstruction.

Twilight had now fallen, and lanterns were brought from the house. Then, when it was seen that nothing further could be gained from the well, everyone went indoors and conferred in the ancient sitting-room while the intermittent light of a spectral half-moon played wanly on the grey desolation outside. The men were frankly nonplussed by the entire case, and could find no convincing common element to link the strange vegetable conditions, the unknown disease of live-stock and humans, and the unaccountable deaths of Merwin and Zenas in the tainted well. They had heard the common country talk, it is true; but could not believe that anything contrary to natural law had occurred. No doubt the meteor had poisoned the soil, but the illness of persons and animals who had eaten nothing grown in that soil was another matter. Was it the well water? Very possibly. It might be a good idea to analyze it. But what peculiar madness could have made both boys jump into the well? Their deeds were so similar-and the fragments shewed that they had both suffered from the grey brittle death. Why was everything so grey and brittle?

It was the coroner, seated near a window overlooking the yard, who first noticed the glow about the well. Night had fully set in, and all the abhorrent grounds seemed faintly luminous with more than the fitful moonbeams; but this new glow was something definite and distinct, and appeared to shoot up from the black pit like a softened ray from a searchlight, giving dull reflections in the little ground pools where the water had been emptied. It had a very queer colour, and as all the men clustered round the window Ammi gave a violent start. For this strange beam of ghastly miasma was to him of no unfamiliar hue. He had seen that colour before, and feared to think what it might mean. He had seen it in the nasty brittle globule in that aerolite two summers ago, had seen it in the crazy vegetation of the springtime, and had thought he had seen it for an instant that very morning against the small barred window of that terrible attic room where nameless things had happened. It had flashed there a second, and a clammy and hateful current of vapour had brushed past him—and then poor Nahum had been taken by something of that colour. He had said so at the last—said it was like the globule and the plants. After that had come the runaway in the yard and the splash in the well-and now that well was belching forth to the night a pale insidious beam of the same demoniac tint.

It does credit to the alertness of Ammi's mind that he puzzled even at that tense moment over a point which was essentially scientific. He could not but wonder at his gleaning of the same impression from a vapour glimpsed in the daytime, against a window opening on the morning sky, and from a nocturnal exhalation seen as a phosphorescent mist against the black and blasted landscape. It wasn't right—it was against Nature—and he thought of those terrible last words of his stricken friend, "It come from some place whar things ain't as they is here . . . one o' them professors said so . . ."

All three horses outside, tied to a pair of shrivelled saplings by the road, were now neighing and pawing frantically. The wagon driver started for the door to do something, but Ammi laid a shaky hand on his shoulder. "Dun't go out thar," he whispered. "They's more to this nor what we know. Nahum said somethin' lived in the well that sucks your life out. He said it must be some'at growed from a round ball like one we all seen in the meteor stone that fell a year ago June. Sucks an' burns, he said, an' is jest a cloud of colour like that light out thar now, that ye can hardly see an' can't tell what it is. Nahum thought it feeds on everything livin' an' gits stronger all the time. He said he seen it this last week. It must be somethin' from away off in the sky like the men from the college last year says the meteor stone was. The way it's made an' the way it works ain't like no way o' God's world. It's some'at from beyond."

So the men paused indecisively as the light from the well grew stronger and the hitched horses pawed and whinnied in increasing frenzy. It was truly an awful moment; with terror in that ancient and accursed house itself, four monstrous sets of fragments-two from the house and two from the well-in the woodshed behind, and that shaft of unknown and unholy iridescence from the slimy depths in front. Ammi had restrained the driver on impulse, forgetting how uninjured he himself was after the clammy brushing of that coloured vapour in the attic room, but perhaps it is just as well that he acted as he did. No one will ever know what was abroad that night; and though the blasphemy from beyond had not so far hurt any human of unweakened mind, there is no telling what it might not have done at that last moment, and with its seemingly increased strength and the special signs of purpose it was soon to display beneath the half-clouded moonlit sky.

All at once one of the detectives at the window gave a short, sharp gasp. The others looked at him, and then quickly followed his own gaze upward to the point at which its idle straying had been suddenly arrested. There was no need for words. What had been disputed in country gossip was disputable no longer, and it is because of the thing which every man of that party agreed in whispering later on, that the strange days are never talked about in Arkham. It is necessary to premise that there was no wind at that hour of the evening. One did arise not long afterward, but there was absolutely none then. Even the dry tips of the lingering hedge-mustard, grey and blighted, and the fringe on the roof of the standing democrat-wagon were unstirred. And yet amid that tense godless calm the high bare boughs of all the trees in the yard were moving. They were twitching morbidly and spasmodically, clawing in convulsive and epileptic madness at the moonlit clouds; scratching impotently in the noxious air as if jerked by some allied and bodiless line of linkage with subterrene horrors writhing and struggling below the black roots.

Not a man breathed for several seconds. Then a cloud of darker depth passed over the moon, and the silhouette of clutching branches faded out momentarily. At this there was a general cry; muffled with awe, but husky and almost identical from every throat. For the terror had not faded with the silhouette, and in a fearsome instant of deeper darkness the watchers saw wriggling at that tree top height a thousand tiny points of faint and unhallowed radiance, tipping each bough like the fire of St. Elmo or the flames that come down on the apostles' heads at Pentecost. It was a monstrous constellation of unnatural light, like a glutted swarm of corpse-fed fireflies dancing hellish sarabands over an accursed marsh, and its colour was that same nameless intrusion which Ammi had come to recognize and dread. All the while the shaft of phosphorescence from the well was getting brighter and brighter, bringing to the minds of the huddled men, a sense of doom and abnormality which far outraced any image their conscious minds could form. It was no longer *shining* out; it was *pouring* out; and as the shapeless stream of unplaceable colour left the well it seemed to flow directly into the sky.

The veterinary shivered, and walked to the front door to drop the heavy extra bar across it. Ammi shook no less, and had to tug and point for lack of controllable voice when he wished to draw notice to the growing luminosity of the trees. The neighing and stamping of the horses had become utterly frightful, but not a soul of that group in the old house would have ventured forth for any earthly reward. With the moments the shining of the trees increased, while their restless branches seemed to strain more and more toward verticality. The wood of the well-sweep was shining now, and presently a policeman dumbly pointed to some wooden sheds and bee-hives near the stone wall on the west. They were commencing to shine, too, though the tethered vehicles of the visitors seemed so far unaffected. Then there was a wild commotion and clopping in the road, and as Ammi quenched the lamp for better seeing they realized that the span of frantic greys had broken their sapling and run off with the democrat-wagon.

The shock served to loosen several tongues, and embarrassed whispers were exchanged. "It spreads on everything organic that's been around here," muttered the medical examiner. No one replied, but the man who had been in the well gave a hint that his long pole must have stirred up something intangible. "It was awful," he added. "There was no bottom at all. Just ooze and bubbles and the feeling of something lurking under there." Ammi's horse still pawed and screamed deafeningly in the road outside, and nearly drowned its owner's faint quaver as he mumbled his formless reflections. "It come from that stone—it growed down thar—it got everything livin'—it fed itself on 'em, mind and body—Thad an' Merwin, Zenas an' Nabby—Nahum was the last—they all drunk the water—it got strong on 'em—it come from beyond, whar things ain't like they be here—now it's goin' home—"

At this point, as the column of unknown colour flared suddenly stronger and began to weave itself into fantastic suggestions of shape which each spectator described differently, there came from poor tethered Hero such a sound as no man before or since ever heard from a horse. Every person in that low-pitched sitting room stopped his ears, and Ammi turned away from the window in horror and nausea. Words could not convey it—when Ammi looked out again the hapless beast lay huddled inert on the moonlit ground between the splintered shafts of the buggy. That was the last of Hero till they buried him next day. But the present was no time to mourn, for almost at this instant a detective silently called attention to something terrible in the very room with them. In the absence of the lamplight it was clear that a faint phosphorescence had begun to pervade the entire apartment. It glowed on the broad-planked floor and the fragment of rag carpet, and shimmered over the sashes of the small-paned windows. It ran up and down the exposed corner-posts, coruscated about the shelf and mantel, and infected the very doors and furniture. Each minute saw it strengthen, and at last it was very plain that healthy living things must leave that house.

Ammi shewed them the back door and the path up through the fields to the ten-acre pasture. They walked and stumbled as in a dream, and did not dare look back till they were far away on the high ground. They were glad of the path, for they could not have gone the front way, by that well. It was bad enough passing the glowing barn and sheds, and those shining orchard trees with their gnarled, fiendish contours; but thank Heaven the branches did their worst twisting high up. The moon went under some very black clouds as they crossed the rustic bridge over Chapman's Brook, and it was blind groping from there to the open meadows.

When they looked back toward the valley and the distant Gardner place at the bottom they saw a fearsome sight. At the farm was shining with the hideous unknown blend of colour; trees, buildings, and even such grass and herbage as had not been wholly changed to lethal grey brittleness. The boughs were all straining skyward, tipped with tongues of foul flame, and lambent tricklings of the same monstrous fire were creeping about the ridgepoles of the house, barn and sheds. It was a scene from a vision of Fuseli, and over all the rest reigned that riot of luminous amorphousness, that alien and undimensioned rainbow of cryptic poison from the well—seething, feeling, lapping, reaching, scintillating, straining, and malignly bubbling in its cosmic and unrecognizable chromaticism.

Then without warning the hideous thing shot vertically up toward the sky like a rocket or meteor, leaving behind no trail and disappearing through a round and curiously regular hole in the clouds before any man could gasp or cry out. No watcher can ever forget that sight, and Ammi stared blankly at the stars of Cygnus, Deneb twinkling above the others, where the unknown colour had melted into the Milky Way. But his gaze was the next moment called swiftly to earth by the crackling in the valley. It was just that. Only a wooden ripping and crackling, and not an explosion, as so many others of the party vowed. Yet the outcome was the same, for in one feverish kaleidoscopic instant there burst up from that doomed and accursed farm a gleamingly eruptive cataclysm of unnatural sparks and substance; blurring the glance of the few who saw it, and sending forth to the zenith a bombarding cloudburst of such coloured and fantastic fragments as our universe must needs disown. Through quickly reclosing vapours they followed the great morbidity that had vanished, and in another second they had vanished too. Behind and below was only a darkness to which the men dared not return, and all about was a mounting wind which seemed to sweep down in black, frore gusts from interstellar space. It shrieked and howled, and lashed the fields and distorted woods in a mad cosmic frenzy, till soon the trembling party realized it would be no use waiting for the moon to shew what was left down there at Nahum's.

Too awed even to hint theories, the seven shaking men trudged back toward Arkham by the north road. Ammi was worse than his fellows, and begged them to see him inside his own kitchen, instead of keeping straight on to town. He did not wish to cross the blighted, wind-whipped woods alone to his home on the main road. For he had had an added shock that the others were spared, and was crushed forever with a brooding fear he dared not even mention for many years to come. As the rest of the watchers on that tempestuous hill had stolidly set their faces toward the road, Ammi had looked back an instant at the shadowed valley of desolation so lately sheltering his ill-starred friend. And from that stricken, far-away spot he had seen something feebly rise, only to sink down again upon the place from which the great shapeless horror had shot into the sky. It was just a colour—but not any colour of our earth or heavens. And because Ammi recognized that colour, and knew that this last faint remnant must still lurk down there in the well, he has never been quite right since.

Ammi would never go near the place again. It is forty-four years now since the horror happened, but he has never been there, and will be glad when the new reservoir blots it out. I shall be glad, too, for I do not like the way the sunlight changed colour around the mouth of that abandoned well I passed. I hope the water will always be very deep—but even so, I shall never drink it. I do not think I shall visit the Arkham country hereafter. Three of the men who had been with Ammi returned the next morning to see the ruins by daylight, but there were not any real ruins. Only the bricks of the chimney, the stones of the cellar, some mineral and metallic litter here and there, and the rim of that nefandous well. Save for Ammi's dead horse, which they towed away and buried, and the buggy which they shortly returned to him, everything that had ever been living had gone. Five eldritch acres of dusty grey desert remained, nor has anything ever grown there since. To this day it sprawls open to the sky like a great spot eaten by acid in the woods and fields, and the few who have ever dared glimpse it in spite of the rural tales have named it "the blasted heath."

The rural tales are queer. They might be even queerer if city men and college chemists could be interested enough to analyze the water from that disused well, or the grey dust that no wind seems to disperse. Botanists, too, ought to study the stunted flora on the borders of that spot, for they might shed light on the country notion that the blight is spreading—little by little, perhaps an inch a year. People say the colour of the neighboring herbage is not quite right in the spring, and that wild things leave queer prints in the light winter snow. Snow never seems quite so heavy on the blasted heath as it is elsewhere. Horses—the few that are left in this motor age—grow skittish in the silent valley; and hunters cannot depend on their dogs too near the splotch of greyish dust.

They say the mental influences are very bad, too; numbers went queer in the years after Nahum's taking, and always they lacked the power to get away. Then the stronger-minded folk all left the region, and only the foreigners tried to live in the crumbling old homesteads. They could not stay, though; and one sometimes wonders what insight beyond ours their wild, weird stories of whispered magic have given them. Their dreams at night, they protest, are very horrible in that grotesque country; and surely the very look of the dark realm is enough to stir a morbid fancy. No traveler has ever escaped a sense of strangeness in those deep ravines, and artists shiver as they paint thick woods whose mystery is as much of the spirits as of the eye. I myself am curious about the sensation I derived from my one lone walk before Ammi told me his tale. When twilight came I had vaguely wished some clouds would gather, for an odd timidity about the deep skyey voids above had crept into my soul.

Do not ask me for my opinion. I do not know—that is all. There was no one but Ammi to question; for Arkham people will not talk about the strange days, and all three professors who saw the aerolite and its coloured globule are dead. There were other globules—depend upon that. One must have fed itself and escaped, and probably there was another which was too late. No doubt it is still down the well—I know there was something wrong with the sunlight I saw above the miasmal brink. The rustics say the blight creeps an inch a year, so perhaps there is a kind of growth or nourishment even now. But whatever demon hatchling is there, it must be tethered to something or else it would quickly spread. Is it fastened to the roots of those trees that claw the air? One of the current Arkham tales is about fat oaks that shine and move as they ought not to do at night.

What it is, only God knows. In terms of matter I suppose the thing Ammi described would be called a gas, but this gas obeyed the laws that are not of our cosmos. This was no fruit of such worlds and suns as shine on the telescopes and photographic plates of our observatories. This was no breath from the skies whose motions and dimensions our astronomers measure or deem too vast to measure. It was just a colour out of space—a frightful messenger from unformed realms of infinity beyond all Nature as we know it; from realms whose mere existence stuns the brain and numbs us with the black extra-cosmic gulfs it throws open before our frenzied eyes.

I doubt very much if Ammi consciously lied to me, and I do not think his tale was all a freak of madness as the townsfolk had forewarned. Something terrible came to the hills and valleys on that meteor, and something terrible—though I know not in what proportion—still remains. I shall be glad to see the water come. Meanwhile I hope nothing will happen to Ammi. He saw so much of the thing—and its influence was so insidious. Why has he never been able to move away? How clearly he recalled those dying words of Nahum's—"Can't git away—draws ye—ye know summ'at's comin' but tain't no use—". Ammi is such a good old man—when the reservoir gang gets to work I must write the chief engineer to keep a sharp watch on him. I would hate to think of him as the grey, twisted, brittle monstrosity which persists more and more in troubling my sleep.

# AS IT LAYS

by David Afsharirad

*Someone once said that golf isn't a sport, it's a disease. And some diseases might not be confined to just one planet . . .*

*Born long after the heyday of the science fiction pulps,* ***David Afsharirad*** *owes his love of mid-century SF (and mid-century crime short stories) to a row of battered Alfred Hitchcock Presents anthologies at the Allen, Texas public library. It was in these well-worn volumes that he discovered writers like Fredric Brown,Clifford D. Simak, John Collier, Richard Matheson, Henry Kuttner & C.L. Moore . . . the list goes on. From there he migrated a few shelves over to the Bs, where he found waiting Ray Bradbury and Edgar Rice Burroughs. Though he was born the year that the last issue of* Famous Monsters of Filmland *(now revived) was released, he nevertheless* *cultivated a taste for old horror and SF films and their small-screen cousins like* Star Trek, Night Gallery, *and of course,* The Twilight Zone, *to which the story that follows owes a debt of gratitude. He is the editor of* The Year's Best Military and Adventure SF, *from Baen Books, and his short stories make appearances in various magazines. He lives in Austin, Texas with his wife and son.*

**PETE LIKED** to get to the course early. Like *really* early. Like so early we had to wait in his car for it to get light enough to tee off. I didn't see the point. It was the off season and if history was any indication, we'd have the place to ourselves for at least the first couple of hours. But there was no arguing with Pete.

I was dozing in the passenger seat when I felt him prod me in the ribs.

"Hey, look at that!" he said

I opened my eyes to see the first purple rays of morning peeking over the horizon and a brilliant smear of light descending toward Earth and disappearing behind the trees on the ninth fairway. Moments later, a boom was felt more than heard.

"Meteor?" I said.

"Meteorite," Pete corrected. "If it makes planetfall, it's a meteorite."

"Cool." I settled into my seat and leaned back against the headrest.

"Makes you wonder," Pete said.

I looked over at him. On his face was the wonder-filled

look of a kid on Christmas morning just before he tears into the packages.

"What's that?"

"About *up there*. Space. Our place in the Universe."

"The only thing it makes me wonder," I said, "is if it's going to mess up our game. It's been months since I've played."

"Well then." Pete opened his door and popped the trunk to get our clubs out of the back. "Best stop dilly-dallying."

"It's still too dark. We won't be able to see our balls."

"The sun's over the horizon. By the time we walk to the first hole, there'll be enough light."

Pete was right. It was bright enough for us to tee off. I was rusty from being months out of practice and shot double bogeys on the first three holes, though I managed a birdie on the fourth. By the time we approached the ninth, Pete was ahead of me by a healthy margin. There are guys for whom golf is all about being in nature (manicured nature though it may be), getting light exercise, and hanging out with friends, but I am not one of them. If you aren't going to play to win, to what purpose is keeping score? Pete had improved since last we played together, but I was still the better golfer, and it irritated me to be trailing him.

Well, the ninth hole was a bear: a dogleg right par five, with tall trees surrounding the fairway on all sides and a sandtrap that was near impossible to avoid. Pete had never had much luck on the hole. Perhaps I could change my fortunes. I removed my driver from my bag, lined up the shot hoping to cut off as much of the corner as I could . . . and sliced it, right into the rough.

"Tough break." Pete clapped me on the shoulder. "You want to take the penalty?"

It was probably the smart move, but I didn't like the smug look of satisfaction on Pete's face.

"I'll play it as it lays." I shouldered my bag and trudged off in search of my ball.

The rough was . . . well, rough. Overgrown and littered with dead leaves and branches. My Titleist was nowhere in sight. Even if I found it, it would probably be unplayable. It looked like I was going to have to drop a ball and take the penalty, after all.

"Two more minutes!" Pete called from the edge of the fairway.

"I know," I called back. "It's not like anyone's waiting on us."

"Rules are rules."

The bastard was enjoying this.

I pushed deeper into the rough in one last desperate attempt to locate my ball. So focused was I on the ground in front of me, that I was almost on top of the meteor (sorry, meteor*ite*) before I realized it. I stood at the edge of a shallow crater of bare earth, several yards in diameter, at the center of which I could just make out the glinting top of the meteorite. Above, the tops of the trees had been shorn off during the thing's descent, revealing a low-hanging mantle of winter gray cloud cover.

"Time's up." Pete's voice was a faint cry from the

fairway. I looked back over my shoulder, but he was obscured by tree trunks and distance.

"Damn," I muttered. Well, if I had to take the penalty, I might as well check out the meteorite. I stepped into the crater, toward the little chunk of outer space that had come to visit. I'd seen meteorites before, in textbooks and once on an elementary school field trip to the planetarium, and therefore knew that they tended to be irregularly shaped black rocks.

Whatever was at the center of the crater was no meteorite.

I stooped down next to it to get a closer look. It wasn't black or even charcoal gray, but a wholly unnatural, brilliant white. It was about two feet in diameter and perfectly spherical save for hundreds of pocks in its otherwise smooth surface. Given the activity in which Pete and I were engaged, I should have recognized it for what it was, but realization was slow to dawn. I prodded it with a my club.

"Damn thing looks just like a—"

A bass note thrumming filled the air and I looked up to see a massive craft hovering in the sky above. I stumbled back, away from the thing that was not a meteorite at all.

At first I thought the pounding I felt in my chest was my own terrified, erratic heartbeat, but it soon became clear that what I was hearing was the footsteps of some giant creature—or *creatures*, from the sound of it. To my left, the trees trembled.

<Think I saw it land over this way.> The voice was deep, resonant, but it came from inside my own head. I'd

read once that a woman in Mexico could pick up radio stations on the fillings in her teeth. That's what I imagined this felt like. It certainly rattled my molars.

More ground-shaking and breaking branches, and then the things appeared. There were two of them and they were enormous, nearly as tall as the Douglas firs that they parted like long grass. In some ways, they looked like the sort of men who populate golf courses all over the world. They wore wide brimmed straw hats and brightly colored golf shirts over Bermuda shorts. Their pale, veiny legs ended in two-tone golf shoes, the cleats of which made man-sized depressions in the earth. Wardrobe aside, they couldn't have looked more inhuman. Their knees bent the wrong direction, for one thing, and their faces were a mass of swarming tentacles. Black, oily eyes swiveled on stalks that poked through their sunhats, and instead of hands, their arms ended in fleshy corkscrews.

<Would you look at that!> The one on the right "said." The voice I heard in my mind had an unmistakable smirk in it.

<This damn planetary hazard gets me every time,> the other responded.

<Just take the penalty. You'll catch up.>

<Forget it. I'll play it as it lays.>

I started running, fast as I could, as the head of a nine iron the size of a Volkswagen descended.

# AMANDA AND THE ALIEN

## by Robert Silverberg

*In this corner, a* Thing *from outer space . . . and in the other corner, a rotten spoiled typical American teenager. Let the battle of the titans begin!*

***Robert Silverberg**, prolific author not just of SF, but of authoritative nonfiction books, columnist for* Asimov's SF Magazine, *winner of a constellation of awards, and renowned* bon vivant *surely needs no introduction—but that's never stopped me before.*

*Born in 1935, Robert Silverberg sold his first SF story, "Gorgon Planet," before he was out of his teens, to the British magazine* Nebula. *Two years later, his first SF novel, a juvenile,* Revolt on Alpha C, *followed. Decades later his total SF titles stands at 82 SF novels and 457 short stories. Early on, he won a Hugo Award for most promising new writer—rarely have the Hugo voters been so perceptive. Toward the end of the 1960s and continuing into the 1970s, he wrote a string of novels much darker in tone and deeper in characterization than his work of the 1950s, such as the novels* Nightwings, *the Hugo-nominated* Tower of Glass, Dying Inside, The Book of Skulls, *and others. He took occasional sabbaticals from writing, to return with new works, such as the Majipoor series. His most recent novels include* The Alien Years, The Longest Way Home, *and a new trilogy of Majipoor novels. In 1999, the Science Fiction and Fantasy Hall of Fame inducted him into its ranks and in 2004, the Science Fiction and Fantasy Writers of America presented the Damon Knight Memorial Grand Master Award to Mr. Silverberg. For more information see his "quasi-official" website at* www.majipoor.com *heroically maintained by Jon Davis (no relation).*

**AMANDA SPOTTED THE ALIEN** late Friday afternoon outside the Video Center on South Main. It was trying to look cool and laid-back, but it simply came across as bewildered and uneasy. The alien was disguised as a seventeen-year-old girl, maybe a Chicana, with olive-toned skin and hair so black it seemed almost blue, but Amanda, who was seventeen herself, knew a phony when she saw one. She studied the alien for some moments from the other side of the street to make absolutely certain. Then she walked across.

"You're doing it wrong," Amanda said. "Anybody with half a brain could tell what you really are."

"Bug off," the alien said.

"No. Listen to me. You want to stay out of the detention center or don't you?"

The alien stared coldly at Amanda and said, "I don't know what the crap you're talking about."

"Sure you do. No sense trying to bluff me. Look, I want to help you," Amanda said. "I think you're getting a raw deal. You know what that means, a raw deal? Hey, look, come home with me and I'll teach you a few things about passing for human. I've got the whole friggin' weekend now with nothing else to do anyway."

A flicker of interest came into the other girl's dark chilly eyes. But it went quickly away and she said, "You some kind of lunatic?"

"Suit yourself, O thing from beyond the stars. *Let* them lock you up again. *Let* them stick electrodes up your ass. I tried to help. That's all I can do, is try," Amanda said, shrugging. She began to saunter away. She didn't look back. Three steps, four, five, hands in pockets, slowly heading for her car. Had she been wrong, she wondered? No. No. She could be wrong about some things, like Charley Taylor's interest in spending the weekend with her, maybe. But not this. That crinkly-haired chick was the missing alien for sure. The whole county was buzzing about it—deadly nonhuman life-form has escaped from the detention center out by Tracy, might be anywhere, Walnut Creek, Livermore, even San Francisco, dangerous monster, capable of mimicking human forms, will engulf and digest you and disguise itself in your shape, and there it was, Amanda knew, standing outside the Video Center. Amanda kept walking.

"Wait," the alien said finally

Amanda took another easy step or two. Then she looked back over her shoulder.

"Yeah?"

"How can you tell?"

Amanda grinned. "Easy. You've got a rain slicker on and it's only September. Rainy season doesn't start around here for another month or two. Your pants are the old spandex kind. People like you don't wear that stuff any more. Your face paint is San Jose colors, but you've got the cheek chevrons put on in the Berkeley pattern. That's just the first three things I noticed. I could find plenty more. Nothing about you fits together with anything else. It's like you did a survey to see how you ought to appear, and tried a little of everything. The closer I study you, the more I see. Look, you're wearing your headphones and the battery light is on, but there's no cassette in the slot. What are you listening to, the music of the spheres? That model doesn't have any FM tuner, you know. You see? You may think you're perfectly camouflaged, but you aren't."

"I could destroy yon," the alien said.

"What? Oh, sure. Sure you could. Engulf me right here on the street, all over in thirty seconds, little trail of slime by the door and a new Amanda walks away. But what then? What good's that going to do you? You still won't know which end is up. So there's no logic in destroying me, unless you're a total dummy. I'm on your side. I'm not going to turn you in."

"Why should I trust you?"

"Because I've been talking to you for five minutes and I haven't yelled for the cops yet. Don't you know that half of California is out searching for you? Hey, can you read?

Come over here a minute. Here." Amanda tugged the alien toward the newspaper vending box at the curb. The headline on the afternoon *Examiner* was:

BAY AREA ALIEN TERROR

MARINES TO JOIN NINE-COUNTY HUNT
MAYOR, GOVERNOR CAUTION AGAINST PANIC

"You understand that?" Amanda asked. "That's you they're talking about. They're out there with flame guns, tranquilizer darts, web snares, and God knows what else. There's been real hysteria for a day and a half. And you standing around here with the wrong chevrons on! Christ. Christ! What's your plan, anyway? Where are you trying to go?"

"Home," the alien said. "But first I have to rendezvous at the pickup point."

"Where's that?"

"You think I'm stupid?"

"Shit," Amanda said. "If I meant to turn you in, I'd have done it five minutes ago. But okay. I don't give a damn where your rendezvous point is. I tell you, though, you wouldn't make it as far as San Francisco rigged up the way you are. It's a miracle you've avoided getting caught until now."

"And you'll help me?"

"I've been trying to. Come on. Let's get the hell out of here. I'll take you home and fix you up a little. My car's in the lot on the corner."

"Okay."

"Whew!"Amanda shook her head slowly. "Christ, some people are awfully hard to help."

As she drove out of the center of town, Amanda glanced occasionally at the alien sitting tensely to her right. Basically the disguise was very convincing, Amanda thought. Maybe all the small details were wrong, the outer stuff, the anthropological stuff, but the alien *looked* human, it *sounded* human, it even *smelled* human. Possibly it could fool ninety-nine people out of a hundred, or maybe more than that. But Amanda had always had a good eye for detail. And the particular moment she had spotted the alien on South Main she had been unusually alert, sensitive, all raw nerves, every antenna up. Of course, it wasn't aliens she was hunting for, but just a diversion, a little excitement, something to fill the great gaping emptiness that Charley Taylor had left in her weekend.

Amanda had been planning the weekend with Charley all month. Her parents were going to go off to Lake Tahoe for three days, her kid sister had wangled permission to accompany them, and Amanda was going to have the house to herself, just her and Macavity the cat. And Charley. He was going to move in on Friday afternoon and they'd cook dinner together and get blasted on her stash of choice powder and watch five or six of her parents' X-rated cassettes, and Saturday they'd drive over to the city and cruise some of the kinky districts and go to that bathhouse on Folsom where everybody got naked and climbed into the giant Jacuzzi, and then on Sunday—Well, none of that was going to happen. Charley had called on Thursday to cancel. "Something big came up," he said, and Amanda had a pretty good idea what that was, with his hot little cousin from New Orleans who sometimes came flying out here on no notice at all; but the inconsiderate bastard seemed to be entirely unaware of how much Amanda had been looking forward to this weekend, how much it meant to her, how painful it was to be dumped like this. She had run through the planned events of the weekend in her mind so many times that she almost felt as though she had experienced them: it was that real to her. But overnight it had become unreal. Three whole days on her own, the house to herself, and so early in the semester that there was no homework to think about, and Charley had stood her up! What was she supposed to do now, call desperately around town to scrounge up some old lover as a playmate? Or pick up some stranger downtown? Amanda hated to fool around with strangers. She was half tempted to go over to the city and just let things happen, but they were all weirdos and creeps over there, anyway, and she knew what she could expect. What a waste, not having Charley! She could kill him for robbing her of the weekend.

Now there was the alien, though. A dozen of these star people had come to Earth last year, not in a flying saucer as everybody had expected, but in little capsules that floated like milkweed seeds, and they had landed in a wide arc between San Diego and Salt Lake City. Their natural form, so far as anyone could tell for sure, was something like a huge jellyfish with a row of staring purple eyes down one wavy margin, but their usual tactic was to borrow any local body they found, digesting it and turning themselves into an accurate imitation of it. One of them had made the mistake of turning itself into a brown mountain bear and another into a bobcat—maybe they thought that those were the dominant life-forms on Earth—but the others had taken on human bodies, at the cost of at least ten lives. Then they went looking to make contact with government leaders, and naturally they were rounded up very swiftly and interned, some in mental hospitals and some in county jails, but eventually—as soon as the truth of what they really were sank in—they were all put in a special detention camp in Northern California. Of course, a tremendous fuss was made over them, endless stuff in the papers and on the tube, speculation by this heavy thinker and that about the significance of their mission, the nature of their biochemistry, a little wild talk about the possibility that more of their kind might be waiting undetected out there and plotting to do God knows what, and all sorts of that stuff, and then came a government clamp on the entire subject, no official announcements except that "discussions" with the visitors were continuing; and after a while the whole thing degenerated into dumb alien jokes ("Why did the alien cross the road?") and Halloween invader masks, and then it moved into the background of everyone's attention and was forgotten. And remained forgotten until the announcement that one of the creatures had slipped out of the camp somehow and was loose within a hundred-mile zone around San Francisco. Preoccupied as she was with her anguish over Charley's heartlessness, even Amanda had managed to pick up *that* news item. And now the alien was in her very car. So there'd be some weekend amusement for her after all. Amanda was entirely unafraid of the alleged deadliness of the star being: whatever else the alien might be, it was surely no dope, not if it had been picked to come halfway across the galaxy on a mission like this, and Amanda knew that the alien could see that harming her was not going to be in its own best interests. The alien had need of her, and the alien realized that. And Amanda, in some way that she was only just beginning to work out, had need of the alien.

She pulled up outside her house, a compact split-level at the western end of town. "This is the place," she said. Heat shimmers danced in the air, and the hills back of the house, parched in the long dry summer, were the color of lions. Macavity, Amanda's old tabby, sprawled in the shade of the bottlebrush tree on the ragged front lawn. As Amanda and the alien approached, the cat sat up warily, flattened his cars, hissed. The alien immediately moved into a defensive posture, sniffing the air.

"Just a household pet," Amanda said. "You know what that is? He isn't dangerous. He's always a little suspicious of strangers."

Which was untrue. An earthquake couldn't have brought Macavity out of his nap, and a cotillion of mice dancing minuets on his tail wouldn't have drawn a reaction from him. Amanda calmed him with some fur-ruffling, but he wanted nothing to do with the alien, and went slinking sullenly into the underbrush. The alien watched him with care until he was out of sight.

"You have anything like cats on your planet?" Amanda asked as they went inside.

"We had small wild animals once. They were unnecessary."

"Oh,"Amanda said. The house had a stuffy, stagnant air. She switched on air-conditioning. "Where is your planet, anyway?"

The alien ignored the question. It padded around the living room, very much like a prowling cat itself, studying the stereo, the television, the couches, the vase of dried flowers.

"Is this a typical Earthian home?"

"More or less," said Amanda. "Typical for around here, at least. This is what we call a suburb. It's half an hour by freeway from here to San Francisco. That's a city. A lot of people living all close together. I'll take you over there tonight or tomorrow for a look, if you're interested." She got some music going, high volume. The alien didn't seem to mind, so she notched the volume up more. "I'm going to take a shower. You could use one, too, actually."

"Shower? You mean rain?"

"I mean body-cleaning activities. We Earthlings like to wash a lot, to get rid of sweat and dirt and stuff. It's considered bad form to stink. Come on, I'll show you how to do it. You've got to do what I do if you want to keep from getting caught, you know." She led the alien to the bathroom. "Take your clothes off first."

The alien stripped. Underneath its rain slicker it wore a stained T-shirt that said "Fisherman's Wharf" with a picture of the San Francisco skyline, and a pair of unzipped jeans. Under that it was wearing a black brassiere, unfastened and with the cups over its shoulder blades, and a pair of black shiny panty briefs with a red heart on the left buttock. The alien's body was that of a lean, tough-looking girl with a scar running down the inside of one arm.

"Whose body is that?" Amanda asked. "Do you know?"

"She worked at the detention center. In the kitchen."

"You know her name?"

"Flores Concepion."

"The other way around, probably. Concepion Flores. I'll call you Connie, unless you want to give me your real name."

"Connie will do."

"All right, Connie. Pay attention. You turn the water on here, and you adjust the mix of hot and cold until you like it. Then you pull this knob and get underneath the spout here and wet your body, and rub soap over it and wash the soap off. Afterward you dry yourself and put fresh clothes on. You have to clean your clothes from time to time, too, because otherwise they start to smell and it upsets people. Watch me shower, and then you do it."

Amanda washed quickly, while plans hummed in her head. The alien wasn't going to last long out there wearing the body of Concepion Flores. Sooner or later someone was going to notice that one of the kitchen girls was missing, and they'd get an all-points alarm out for her. Amanda wondered whether the alien had figured that out yet. The alien, Amanda thought, needs a different body in a hurry.

But not mine, she told herself. For sure, not mine.

"Your turn," she said, shutting the water off.

The alien, fumbling a little, turned the water back on

and got under the spray. Clouds of steam rose and its skin began to look boiled, but it didn't appear troubled. No sense of pain? "Hold it," Amanda said. "Step back." She adjusted the water. "You've got it too hot. You'll damage that body that way. Look, if you can't tell the difference between hot and cold, just take cold showers, okay? It's less dangerous. This is cold, on this side." She left the alien under the shower and went to find some clean clothes. When she came back, the alien was still showering, under icy water. "Enough," Amanda said. "Here. Put these on."

"I had more clothes than this before."

"A T-shirt and jeans are all you need in hot weather like this. With your kind of build you can skip the bra, and anyway I don't think you'll be able to fasten it the right way."

"Do we put the face paint on now?"

"We can skip it while we're home. It's just stupid kid stuff anyway, all that tribal crap. If we go out we'll do it, and we'll give you Walnut Creek colors, I think. Concepcion wore San Jose, but we want to throw people off the track. How about some dope?"

"What?"

"Grass. Marijuana. A drug widely used by local Earthians of our age."

"I don't need no drug."

"I don't either. But I'd *like* some. You ought to learn how, just in case you find yourself in a social situation." Amanda reached for her pack of Filter Golds and pulled out a joint. Expertly she tweaked its lighter tip and took a deep hit. "Here," she said, passing it. "Hold it like I did.

Put it to your mouth, breathe in, suck the smoke deep." The alien dragged the joint and began to cough. "Not so deep, maybe," Amanda said. "Take just a little. Hold it. Let it out. There, much better. Now give me back the joint. You've got to keep passing it back and forth. That part's important. You feel anything from it?"

"No."

"It can be subtle. Don't worry about it. Are you hungry?"

"Not yet," the alien said.

"I am. Come into the kitchen." As she assembled a sandwich—peanut butter and avocado on whole wheat, with tomato and onion—she asked, "What sort of things do you eat?"

"Life."

"Life?"

"We never eat dead things. Only things with life."

Amanda fought back a shudder. "I see. *Anything* with life?"

"We prefer animal life. We can absorb plants if necessary."

"Ah. Yes. And when are you going to be hungry again?"

"Maybe tonight," the alien said. "Or tomorrow. The hunger comes very suddenly, when it comes."

"There's not much around here that you could eat live. But I'll work on it.'

"The small furry animal?"

"No. My cat is not available for dinner. Get that idea right out of your head. Likewise me. I'm your protector and guide. It wouldn't be sensible of you to eat me. You follow what I'm trying to tell you?"

"I said that I'm not hungry yet."

"Well, you let me know when you start feeling the pangs. I'll find you a meal." Amanda began to construct a second sandwich. The alien prowled the kitchen, examining the appliances. Perhaps making mental records, Amanda thought, of sink and oven design, to copy on its home world. Amanda said, "Why did you people come here in the first place?"

"It was our mission."

"Yes. Sure. But for what purpose? What are you after? You want to take over the world? You want to steal our scientific secrets?" The alien, making no reply, began taking spices out of the spice rack. Delicately it licked its finger, touched it to the oregano, tasted it, tried the cumin. Amanda said, "Or is it that you want to keep us from going into space? That you think we're a dangerous species, so you're going to quarantine us on our own planet? Come on, you can tell me. I'm not a government spy." The alien sampled the tarragon, the basil, the sage. When it reached for the curry powder, its hand suddenly shook so violently that it knocked the open jars of oregano and tarragon over, making a mess. "Hey, are you all right?" Amanda asked.

The alien said, "I think I'm getting hungry. Are these things drugs, too?"

"Spices," Amanda said. "We put them in our foods to make them taste better." The alien was looking very strange, glassy-eyed, flushed, sweaty. "Are you feeling sick?"

"I feel excited. These powders—"

"They're turning you on? Which one?"

"This, I think." It pointed to the oregano. "It was either the first one or the second."

"Yeah," Amanda said. "Oregano. It can really make you fly." She wondered whether the alien might get violent when zonked. Or whether the oregano would stimulate its appetite. She had to watch out for its appetite. There are certain risks, Amanda reflected, in doing what I'm doing. Deftly she cleaned up the spilled oregano and tarragon and put the caps on the spice jars. "You ought to be careful," she said. "Your metabolism isn't used to this stuff. A little can go a long way."

"Give me some more.

"Later," Amanda said. "You don't want to overdo it."

"More!"

"Calm down. I know this planet better than you, and I don't want to see you get in trouble. Trust me: I'll let you have more oregano when it's the right time. Look at the way you're shaking. And you're sweating like crazy." Pocketing the oregano jar, she led the alien back into the living room. "Sit down. Relax."

"More? Please?"

"I appreciate your politeness. But we have important things to talk about, and then I'll give you some. Okay?" Amanda opaqued the window, through which the hot late-afternoon sun was coming. Six o'clock on Friday, and if everything had gone the right way Charley would have been showing up just about now. Well, she'd found a different diversion. The weekend stretched before her like an open road leading to mysteryland. The alien offered all sorts of possibilities, and she might yet have some fun over the next few days, if she used her head.

Amanda turned to the alien and said, "You calmer now? Yes. Good. Okay: first of all, you've got to get yourself another body."

"Why is that?"

"Two reasons. One is that the authorities probably are searching for the girl you absorbed. How you got as far as you did without anybody but me spotting you is hard to understand. Number two, a teenage girl traveling by herself is going to get hassled too much, and you don't know how to handle yourself in a tight situation. You know what I'm saying? You're going to want to hitchhike out to Nevada, Wyoming, Utah, wherever the hell your rendezvous place is, and all along the way people are going to be coming on to you. You don't need any of that. Besides, it's very tricky trying to pass for a girl. You've got to know how to put your face paint on, how to understand challenge codes, and what the way you wear your clothing says, and like that. Boys have a much simpler subculture. You get yourself a male body, a big hunk of a body, and nobody'll bother you much on the way to where you're going. You just keep to yourself, don't make eye contact, don't smile, and everyone will leave you alone."

"Makes sense," said the alien. "All right. The hunger is becoming very bad now. Where do I get a male body?"

"San Francisco. It's full of men. We'll go over there tonight and find a nice brawny one for you. With any luck we might even find one who's not gay, and then we can have a little fun with him first. And then you take his body over—which incidentally solves your food problem for a while, doesn't it?—and we can have some more fun, a whole weekend of fun." Amanda winked. "Okay, Connie?"

"Okay." The alien winked, a clumsy imitation, first one eye, then the other. "You give me more oregano now?"

"Later. And when you wink, just wink *one* eye. Like this. Except I don't think you ought to do a lot of winking at people. It's a very intimate gesture that could get you in trouble. Understand?"

"There's so much to understand."

"You're on a strange planet, kid. Did you expect it to be just like home? Okay, to continue. The next thing I ought to point out is that when you leave here on Sunday you'll have to—"

The telephone rang.

"What's that sound?" the alien asked.

"Communications device. I'll be right back." Amanda went to the hall extension, imagining the worst: her parents, say, calling to announce that they were on their way back from Tahoe tonight, some mixup in the reservations or something. But the voice that greeted her was Charley's. She could hardly believe it, after the casual way he had shafted her this weekend. She could hardly believe what he wanted, either. He had left half a dozen of his best cassettes at her place last week, Golden Age rock, Abbey Road and the Hendrix one and a Joplin and such, and now he was heading off to Monterey for the festival and he wanted to have them for the drive. Did she mind if he stopped off in half an hour to pick them up?

The bastard, she thought. The absolute trashiness of him! First to torpedo her weekend without even an apology, and then to let her know that he and what's-her-name were scooting down to Monterey for some fun, and could he bother her for his cassettes? Didn't he think she had any feelings? She looked at the telephone in her hand as though it was emitting toads and scorpions. It was tempting to hang up on him.

She resisted the temptation. "As it happens," she said, "I'm just on my way out for the weekend myself. But I've got a friend who's here cat-sitting for me. I'll leave the cassettes with her, okay? Her name's Connie."

"Fine," Charley said. "I really appreciate that, Amanda."

"It's nothing," she said.

The alien was back in the kitchen, nosing around the spice rack. But Amanda had the oregano. She said, "I've arranged for delivery of your next body."

"You did?"

"A large healthy adolescent male. Exactly what you're looking for. He's going to be here in a little while. I'm going to gó out for a drive, and you take care of him before I get back. How long does it take for you to—engulf—somebody?"

"It's very fast."

"Good." Amanda found Charley's cassettes and stacked them on the living-room table. "He's coming over here to get these six little boxes, which are music-storage devices. When the doorbell rings, you let him in and introduce yourself as Connie and tell him his things are on this table. After that you're on your own. You think you can handle it?"

"Sure," the alien said.

"Tuck in your T-shirt better. When it's tight it makes your boobs stick out, and that'll distract him. Maybe he'll even make a pass at you. What happens to the Connie body after you engulf him?"

"It won't be here. What happens is I merge with him and dissolve all the Connie characteristics and take on the new ones."

"Ah. Very nifty. You're a real nightmare thing, you know? You're a walking horror show. Here, have a little hit of oregano before I go." She put a tiny pinch of spice in the alien's hand. "Just to warm up your engine a little. I'll give you more later, when you've done the job. See you in an hour, okay?"

She left the house. Macavity was sitting on the porch, scowling, whipping his tail from side to side. Amanda knelt beside him and scratched him behind the ears. The cat made a low rough purring sound, not much like his usual purr.

Amanda said, "You aren't happy, are you, fella? Well, don't worry. I've told the alien to leave you alone, and I guarantee you'll be okay. This is Amanda's fun tonight. You don't mind if Amanda has a little fun, do you?" Macavity made a glum snuffling sound. "Listen, maybe I can get the alien to create a nice little calico cutie for you, okay? Just going into heat and ready to howl. Would you like that, guy? Would you? I'll see what I call do when 1 get back. But I have to clear out of here now, before Charley shows up."

She got into her car and headed for the westbound freeway ramp. Half past six, Friday night, the sun still hanging high above the Bay. Traffic was thick in the eastbound lanes, the late commuters slogging toward home, and it was beginning to build up westbound, too, as people set out for dinner in San Francisco. Amanda drove through the tunnel and turned north into Berkeley to cruise city streets. Ten minutes to seven now. Charley must have arrived. She imagined Connie in her tight T-shirt, all stoned and sweaty on oregano, and Charley giving her the eye, getting ideas, thinking about grabbing a bonus quickie before taking off with his cassettes. And Connie leading him on, Charley making his moves, and then suddenly that electric moment of surprise as the alien struck and Charley found himself turning into dinner. It could be happening right this minute, Amanda thought placidly No more than the bastard deserves, isn't it? She had felt for a long time that Charley was a big mistake in her life, and after what he had pulled yesterday she was sure of it. No more than he deserves. But, she wondered, what if Charley had brought his weekend date along? The thought chilled her. She hadn't considered that possibility at all. It could ruin everything. Connie wasn't able to engulf two at once, was she? And suppose they recognized her as the missing alien and ran out screaming to call the cops?

No, she thought. Not even Charley would be so tacky as to bring his date over to Amanda's house tonight. And Charley never watched the news or read a paper. He wouldn't have a clue as to what Connie really was until it was too late for him to run.

Seven o'clock. Time to head for home.

The sun was sinking behind her as she turned onto the freeway. By quarter past she was approaching her house. Charley's old red Honda was parked outside. Amanda left hers across the street and cautiously let herself in, pausing just inside the front door to listen.

Silence.

"Connie?"

"In here," said Charley's voice.

Amanda entered the living room. Charley was sprawled out comfortably on the couch. There was no sign of Connie.

"Well?" Amanda said. "How did it go?"

"Easiest thing in the world," the alien said. "He was sliding his hands under my T-shirt when I let him have the nullifier jolt."

"Ah. The nullifier jolt."

"And then I completed the engulfment and cleaned up the carpet. God, it feels good not to be hungry again. You can't imagine how tough it was to resist engulfing you, Amanda. For the past hour I kept thinking of food, food, food—"

"Very thoughtful of you to resist."

"I knew you were out to help me. It's logical not to engulf one's allies."

"That goes without saying. So you feel well fed, now? He was good stuff?"

"Robust, healthy, nourishing—yes."

"I'm glad Charley turned out to be good for something. How long before you get hungry again?"

The alien shrugged. "A day or two. Maybe three, on account of he was so big. Give me more oregano, Amanda?"

"Sure," she said. "Sure." She felt a little let down. Not that she was remorseful about Charley, exactly, but it all seemed so casual, so offhanded—there was something anticlimactic about it, in a way. She suspected she should have stayed and watched while it was happening. Too late for that now, though.

She took the oregano from her purse and dangled the jar teasingly. "Here it is, babe. But you've got to earn it first."

"What do you mean?"

"I mean that I was looking forward to a big weekend with Charley, and the weekend is here, and Charley's here too, more or less, and I'm ready for fun. Come show me some fun, big boy."

She slipped Charley's Hendrix cassette into the deck and turned the volume way up.

The alien looked puzzled. Amanda began to peel off her clothes.

"You too," Amanda said. "Come on. You won't have to dig deep into Charley's mind to figure out what to do. You're going to be my Charley for me this weekend, you follow? You and I are going to do all the things that he and I were going to do. Okay? Come on. Come on." She beckoned. The alien shrugged again and slipped out of Charley's clothes, fumbling with the unfamiliarities of his zipper and buttons. Amanda, grinning, drew the alien close against her and down to the living-room floor. She took its hands and put them where she wanted them to be. She whispered instructions. The alien, docile, obedient, did what she wanted.

It felt like Charley. It smelled like Charley. It even moved pretty much the way Charley moved.

But it wasn't Charley, it wasn't Charley at all, and after the first few seconds Amanda knew that she had goofed things up very badly. You couldn't just ring in an imitation like this. Making love with this alien was like making love with a very clever machine, or with her own mirror image. It was empty and meaningless and dumb.

Grimly she went on to the finish. They rolled apart, panting, sweating.

"Well?" the alien said. "Did the earth move for you?"

"Yeah. Yeah. It was wonderful—Charley."

"Oregano?"

"Sure," Amanda said. She handed the spice jar across. "I always keep my promises, babe. Go to it. Have yourself a blast. Just remember that that's strong stuff for guys from your planet, okay? If you pass out, I'm going to leave you right there on the floor."

"Don't worry about me."

"Okay. You have your fun. I'm going to clean up, and then maybe we'll go over to San Francisco for the nightlife. Does that interest you?"

"You bet, Amanda." The alien winked—one eye, then the other—and gulped a huge pinch of oregano. "That sounds terrific."

Amanda gathered up her clothes, went upstairs for a quick shower, and dressed. When she came down the alien was more than half blown away on the oregano, goggle-eyed, loll-headed, propped up against the couch and crooning to itself in a weird atonal way. Fine, Amanda thought. You just get yourself all spiced up, love. She took the portable phone from the kitchen, carried it with her into the bathroom, locked the door, dialed the police emergency number.

She was bored with the alien. The game had worn thin very quickly. And it was crazy, she thought, to spend the whole weekend cooped up with a dangerous extraterrestrial creature when there wasn't going to be any fun in it for her. She knew now that there couldn't be any fun at all. And in a day or two the alien was going to get hungry again.

"I've got your alien," she said. "Sitting in my living room, stoned out of its head on oregano. Yes, I'm absolutely certain. It was disguised as a Chicana girl first, Concepcion Flores, but then it attacked my boyfriend Charley Taylor, and—yes, yes, I'm safe. I'm locked in the john. Just get somebody over here fast—okay, I'll stay on the line—what happened was, I spotted it downtown, it insisted on coming home with me—"

The actual capture took only a few minutes. But there was no peace for hours after the police tactical squad hauled the alien away, because the media was in on the act right away, first a team from Channel 2 in Oakland, and then some of the network guys, and then the *Chronicle,* and finally a whole army of reporters from as far away as Sacramento, and phone calls from Los Angeles and San Diego and—about three that morning—New York. Amanda told the story again and again until she was sick of it, and just as dawn was breaking she threw the last of them out and barred the door.

She wasn't sleepy at all. She felt wired up, speedy, and depressed all at once. The alien was gone, Charley was gone, and she was all alone. She was going to be famous for the next couple of days, but that wouldn't help. She'd still be alone. For a time she wandered around the house, looking at it the way an alien might, as though she had never seen a stereo cassette before, or a television set, or a rack of spices. The smell of oregano was everywhere. There were little trails of it on the floor.

Amanda switched on the radio and there she was on the six a.m. news. "—the emergency is over, thanks to the courageous Walnut Creek high school girl who trapped and outsmarted the most dangerous life-form in the known universe—"

She shook her head. "You think that's true?" she asked the cat. "Most dangerous life-form in the universe? I don't think so, Macavity. I think I know of at least one that's a lot deadlier. Eh, kid?" She winked. "If they only knew, eh? If they only knew." She scooped the cat up and hugged it, and it began to purr. Maybe trying to get a little sleep would be a good idea around this time, she told herself. And then she had to figure out what she was going to do about the rest of the weekend.

# WE DON'T WANT ANY TROUBLE

by James H. Schmitz

*These* Things *had dropped in and apparently were going to visit for a time—maybe a* long *time. And even though they could be killed, that was part of the problem.*

***

**James H. Schmitz** *(1911-1981) was a master of action-adventure science fiction, notably in his stories of the Hub, a loosely-bound confederation of star systems. His most popular characters, both female, were Telzey Amberdon, the spunky teenage telepath, and Trigger Argee, a crack shot with a gun and reflexes that made lighting look lethargic. His most popular novel,* The Witches of Karres, *though not part of the Hub universe, is a classic space opera. Still, Schmitz could write more than adventure SF, and this story did not appear in the often optimistic* Astounding, *but in the often sardonic* *newer magazine,* Galaxy, *where it was right at home with its uncompromising grimness . . . and that unsettling last line.*

**"WELL,** that wasn't a very long interview, was it?" asked the professor's wife. She'd discovered the professor looking out of the living room window when she'd come home from shopping just now. "I wasn't counting on having dinner before nine," she said, setting her bundles down on the couch. "I'll get at it right away."

"No hurry about dinner," the professor replied without turning his head. "I didn't expect we'd be through there before eight myself."

He had clasped his hands on his back and was swaying slowly, backward and forward on his feet, staring out at the street. It was a favorite pose of his, and she never had discovered whether it indicated deep thought or just daydreaming. At the moment, she suspected uncomfortably it was very deep thought, indeed. She took off her hat.

"I suppose you could call it an interview," she said uneasily. "I mean you actually talked with it, didn't you?"

"Oh, yes, we talked with it," he nodded. "Some of the others did, anyway."

"Imagine *talking* with something like that! It really *is* from another world, Clive?" She laughed uneasily, watching the back of his head with frightened eyes. "But, of course, you can't violate the security rules, can you? You can't tell me anything about it at all. . . ."

He shrugged, turning around. "There'll be a newscast at six o'clock. In ten minutes. Wherever there's a radio or television set on Earth, everybody will hear what we found out in that interview. Perhaps not quite everything, but almost everything."

"Oh?" she said in a surprised, small voice. She looked at him in silence for a moment, her eyes growing more frightened. "Why would they do a thing like that?"

"Well," said the professor, "it seemed like the right thing to do. The best thing, at any rate. There may be some panic, of course." He turned back to the window and gazed out on the street, as if something there were holding his attention. He looked thoughtful and abstracted, she decided. But then a better word came to her, and it was "resigned."

"Clive," she said, almost desperately, "what happened?"

He frowned absently at her and walked to the radio. It began to make faint, humming noises as the professor adjusted dials unhurriedly. The humming didn't vary much.

"They've cleared the networks, I imagine," he remarked.

The sentence went on repeating itself in his wife's mind, with no particular significance at first. But then a meaning came into it and grew and swelled swiftly, until she felt her head would burst with it. They've cleared the networks. All over the world this evening, they've cleared the networks. Until the newscast comes on at six o'clock . . .

"As to what happened," she heard her husband's voice

saying, "that's a little difficult to understand or explain. Even now. It was certainly amazing—" He interrupted himself. "Do you remember Milt Caldwell, dear?"

"Milt Caldwell?" She searched her mind blankly. "No," she said, shaking her head.

"A rather well-known anthropologist," the professor informed her, with an air of faint reproach. "Milt got himself lost in the approximate center of the Australian deserts some two years ago. Only we have been told he didn't get lost. They picked him up—"

"*They?*" she said. "You mean there's more than one?"

"Well, there would be more than one, wouldn't there?" he asked reasonably. "That explains, at any rate, how they learned to speak English. It made it seem a little more reasonable, anyhow," he added, "when it told us that. Seven minutes to six . . ."

"What?" she said faintly.

"Seven minutes to six," the professor repeated. "Sit down, dear. I believe I can tell you, in seven minutes, approximately what occurred. . . ."

The Visitor from Outside sat in its cage, its large gray hands slackly clasping the bars. Its attitudes and motions, the professor had noted in the two minutes since he had entered the room with the other men, approximated those of a rather heavily built ape. Reporters had called it "the Toad from Mars," on the basis of the first descriptions they'd had of it—the flabby shape and loose, warty skin made that a vaguely adequate identification. The round, horny head almost could have been that of a lizard.

With a zoologist's fascination in a completely new

genus, the professor catalogued these contradicting physical details in his mind. Yet something somewhat like this might have been evolved on Earth, if Earth had chosen to let the big amphibians of its Carboniferous Period go on evolving.

That this creature used human speech was the only almost-impossible feature.

It had spoken as they came in. "What do you wish to know?" it asked. The horny, toothed jaws moved, and a broad yellow tongue became momentarily visible, forming the words. It was a throaty, deliberate "human" voice.

For a period of several seconds, the human beings seemed to be shocked into silence by it, though they had known the creature had this ability. Hesitantly, then, the questioning began.

The professor remained near the back of the room, watching. For a while, the questions and replies he heard seemed to carry no meaning to him. Abruptly he realized that his thoughts were fogged over with a heavy, cold, physical dread of this alien animal. He told himself that under such circumstances fear was not an entirely irrational emotion, and his understanding of it seemed to lighten its effects a little.

But the scene remained unreal to him, like a badly lit stage on which the creature in its glittering steel cage stood out in sharp focus, while the humans were shadow-shapes stirring restlessly against a darkened background.

"This won't do!" he addressed himself, almost querulously, through the fear. "I'm here to observe, to conclude, to report—I was selected as a man they could trust to think and act rationally!"

He turned his attention deliberately away from the cage and what it contained, and he directed it on the other human beings, to most of whom he had been introduced only a few minutes before. A young, alert-looking Intelligence major, who was in some way in charge of this investigation; a sleepy-eyed general; a very pretty captain acting as stenographer, whom the major had introduced as his fiancee. The handful of other scientists looked for the most part like brisk business executives, while the two Important Personages representing the government looked like elderly professors.

He almost smiled. They were real enough. This was a human world. He returned his attention again to the solitary intruder in it.

"Why shouldn't I object?" the impossible voice was saying with a note of lazy good humor. "You've caged me like—a wild animal! And you haven't even informed me of the nature of the charges against me. Trespassing, perhaps—eh?"

The wide mouth seemed to grin as the Thing turned its head, looking them over one by one with bright black eyes. The grin was meaningless; it was the way the lipless jaws set when the mouth was closed. But it gave expression to the pleased malice the professor sensed in the voice and words.

The voice simply did not go with that squat animal shape.

Fear surged up in him again. He found himself shaking.

If it looks at me now, he realized in sudden panic, I might start to scream!

One of the men nearest the cage was saying something in low, even tones. The captain flipped over a page of her shorthand pad and went on writing, her blonde head tilted to one side. She was a little pale, but intent on her work. He had a moment of bitter envy for their courage and self-control. But they're insensitive, he tried to tell himself; they don't know Nature and the laws of Nature. They can't feel as I do how *wrong* all this is!

Then the black eyes swung around and looked at him.

Instantly, his mind stretched taut with blank, wordless terror. He did not move, but afterward he knew he did not faint only because he would have looked ridiculous before the others, and particularly in the presence of a young woman. He heard the young Intelligence officer speaking sharply; the eyes left him unhurriedly, and it was all over.

"You indicate," the creature's voice was addressing the major, "that you can force me to reveal matters I do not choose to reveal at this time. However, you are mistaken. For one thing, a body of this type does not react to any of your drugs."

"It will react to pain!" the major said, his voice thin and angry.

Amazed by the words, the professor realized for the first time that he was not the only one in whom this being's presence had aroused primitive, irrational fears. The other men had stirred restlessly at the major's threat, but they made no protest.

The Thing remained silent for a moment, looking at the major.

"This body will react to pain," it said then, "only when

I choose to let it feel pain. Some of you here know the effectiveness of hypnotic blocks against pain. My methods are not those of hypnosis, but they are considerably more effective. I repeat, then, that for me there is no pain, unless I choose to experience it."

"Do you choose to experience the destruction of your body's tissues?" the major inquired, a little shrilly.

The captain looked up at him quickly from the chair where she sat, but the professor could not see her expression. Nobody else moved.

The Thing, still staring at the major, almost shrugged.

"And do you choose to experience death?" the major cried, his face flushed with excitement.

In a flash of insight, the professor understood why no one was interfering. Each in his own way, they had felt what he was feeling: that here was something so outrageously strange and new that no amount of experience, no rank, could guide a human being in determining how to deal with it. The major was dealing with it—in however awkward a fashion. With no other solution to offer, they were, for the moment, unable or unwilling to stop him.

The Thing then said slowly and flatly, "Death is an experience I shall never have at your hands. That is a warning. I shall respond to no more of your threats. I shall answer no more questions.

"Instead, I shall tell you what will occur now. I shall inform my companions that you are as we judged you to be—foolish, limited, incapable of harming the least of us. Your world and civilization are of very moderate interest. But they are a novelty which many will wish to view for themselves. We shall come here and leave here, as we please. If you attempt to interfere again with any of us, it will be to your own regret."

"Will it?" the major shouted, shaking. "Will it now?"

The professor jerked violently at the quick successive reports of a gun in the young officer's hand. Then there was a struggling knot of figures around the major, and another man's voice was shouting hoarsely, "You fool! You damned hysterical fool!"

The captain had dropped her notebook and clasped her hands to her face. For an instant, the professor heard her crying, "Jack! Jack! Stop—don't—"

But he was looking at the thing that had fallen on its back in the cage, with the top of its skull shot away and a dark-brown liquid staining the cage floor about its shoulders.

What he felt was an irrational satisfaction, a warm glow of pride in the major's action. It was as if he had killed the Thing himself.

For that moment, he was happy.

Because he stood far back in the room, he saw what happened then before the others did.

One of the Personages and two of the scientists were moving excitedly about the cage, staring down at the Thing. The others had grouped around the chair into which they had forced the major. Under the babble of confused, angry voices, he could sense the undercurrent of almost joyful relief he felt himself.

The captain stood up and began to take off her clothes.

She did it quickly and quietly. It was at this moment,

the professor thought, staring at her in renewed terror, that the height of insanity appeared to have been achieved in this room. He wished fervently that he could keep that sense of insanity wrapped around him forevermore, like a protective cloak. It was a terrible thing to be rational! With oddly detached curiosity, he also wondered what would happen in a few seconds when the others discovered what he already knew.

The babbling voices of the group that had overpowered the major went suddenly still. The three men at the cage turned startled faces toward the stillness. The girl straightened up and stood smiling at them.

The major began screaming her name.

There was another brief struggling confusion about the chair in which they were holding him. The screaming grew muffled as if somebody had clapped a hand over his mouth.

"I warned you," the professor heard the girl say clearly, "that there was no death. Not for us."

Somebody shouted something at her, like a despairing question. Rigid with fear, his own blood a swirling roar in his ears, the professor did not understand the words. But he understood her reply.

"It could have been any of you, of course," she nodded. "But I just happened to like *this* body."

After that, there was one more shot.

The professor turned off the radio. For a time, he continued to gaze out the window.

"Well, they know it now!" he said. "The world knows it now. Whether they believe it or not— At any rate . . ."

His voice trailed off. The living room had darkened and he had a notion to switch on the lights, but decided against it. The evening gloom provided an illusion of security.

He looked down at the pale oval of his wife's face, almost featureless in the shadows.

"It won't be too bad," he explained, "if not too many of them come. Of course, we don't know how many there are of them, actually. Billions, perhaps. But if none of our people try to make trouble—the aliens simply don't want any trouble."

He paused a moment. The death of the young Intelligence major had not been mentioned in the broadcast. Considering the issues involved, it was not, of course, a very important event and officially would be recorded as a suicide. In actual fact, the major had succeeded in wresting a gun from one of the men holding him. Another man had shot him promptly without waiting to see what he intended to do with it.

At all costs now, every rational human being must try to prevent trouble with the Visitors from Outside.

He felt his face twitch suddenly into an uncontrollable grimace of horror.

"But there's no way of being absolutely sure, of course," he heard his voice tell the silently gathering night about him, "that they won't decide they just happen to like *our* kind of bodies."

# AND YOUR LITTLE DOG TOO

## by Sarah A. Hoyt

*An encounter with a* Thing *and his (its?) dog. Or maybe that should be spelled dawg. The author says she has been reading a great deal of Clifford D. Simak lately, and it certainly shows.*

❖ ❖ ❖

***Sarah A. Hoyt*** *won the Prometheus Award for her novel* Darkship Thieves, *published by Baen, and has authored* Darkship Renegades *(nominated for the following year's Prometheus Award),* A Few Good Men, Through Fire, *three more novels set in the same universe. She has written numerous short stories and novels in a number of genres, including science fiction, fantasy, mystery, historical novels and historical mysteries, many under a number of pseudonyms, and has been published—among other places— in* Analog, Asimov's, *and* Amazing. *For Baen, she has also written three books in her popular* *shape-shifter urban fantasy series,* Draw One in the Dark, Gentleman Takes a Chance, *and* Noah's Boy. *Her According to Hoyt is one of the most interesting blogs on the internet. Originally from Portugal, she lives in Colorado with her husband, two sons, and the surfeit of cats necessary to a die-hard Heinlein fan.*

**"YOU ARE NOT** from around here, are you?" Peter asked. It was an understatement, but he didn't know how else to ask it without sounding like a complete idiot, even to his own ears. Particularly to his own ears.

His passenger shifted slightly, as though the question were a complex one that needed great pondering. Peter caught a look at him, by the moon and the reflected light of the headlights, and he couldn't be sure of anything. Not precisely. The dense trees on either side of the mountain road filtered the moonlight down to a vague candle glow, and the headlights weren't doing much for the space behind the dashboard either. He could turn the interior lights on, but what excuse?

Peter was not in the habit of taking up hitchhikers, but here, in the middle of nowhere, West Virginia, the old boy standing by the side of the road, with his medium sized dog, and talking about how his ve-hi-cle—he'd made it at least three distinct syllables—had broken down had seemed like an odd figure to be afraid of.

And Peter still wasn't afraid of him. Not exactly. It was more—he thought, as he shuffled in his own seat, feeling not so much suspicious as bothered—it was more that the old hunter he'd given a ride to, to go to his friend's cabin "Over there," felt wrong.

Perhaps it was the smell. Oldest sense in the world, wasn't it? Peter thought. The kind of sense that connected directly to the oldest part of the brain. That was it, for sure. Somewhere in the old, old part of Peter's brain, a long dead dinosaur was sniffling the air and worrying about the scent. Because Peter's passenger didn't smell like any mammal that Peter had ever been around. From the good ol' boy in coveralls, with a straggle of white hair around his crown, he'd expected undertones of sweat and soap and maybe an overhanging odor of tobacco or wood smoke. But there were none of those, only a smell that kept sending Peter back to the reptile house at the zoo, in the lost afternoons of his childhood.

"No," the man said, at last, and his accent was slightly off too. Local, but not local. Of course there were lots of variants in "local" and Peter could be mistaken. Which was the problem all along, with all of it. Perhaps the good old boy had a pet snake, and perhaps he didn't speak with quite the local accent. People moved around all over and all sorts of influences fell in their speech. When he was dating Ginny she'd go on and on about collecting samples and about how many dialects there were in a ten mile radius of a relatively isolated part of the state. Any state. "Come here every summer," the man said. "For the hunting, you know?" Another pause. "Not that I hunt much, not as such. It's just a good excuse to stroll outside among all the vegetation, with my dog. Dog likes it, and it's a relaxing time." Long pause. "The rifle—" he patted the forestock where it leaned against his chest, the barrel against his shoulder "—it's more in case we run across something that really needs it, but we've never yet had to use it. No siree, the things Dog and I hunt are more friendly like. We chase them for a while under the moonlight, you know, and then I point my rifle at them and I say 'bang,' and then we call it a night, Dog and I. Foxes are the best. They seem almost like they should be sentient, like maybe they are but we just don't know how to talk to them. They dart and play and seem to have a sense that I'm in it for the game of it, and not to fetch their pelt and take their lives." Having said all that, fast, not so much as a rehearsed speech but as something he thought of carefully, as if he were afraid of saying the wrong word, the passenger said, as if it had just occurred to him, in the way of a bright idea, "And you? You're not from 'round here, either?"

Peter gave a distracted headshake—he'd been a little surprised by hearing the word, "sentient," not usually found in a good old boy's working vocabulary—then thought the man might not see it. Peter couldn't turn to look for sure, because right now the road was so shadowed, it was hard to tell where the side-of-the road precipice started, and where it was just the shadow of tree branches on the road. "No," he said aloud. "I go to UWV." A long stop and then he thought he should say more, because the silence lengthened and because he was thinking that the man sounded funny too, that his breathing came very sporadically and not in the way a normal human being would breathe. Beat, beat, beat, breath. Beat, beat, beat. What was that, three seconds between breaths? More like five. Humans didn't breathe that way. "Aerospace engineering."

"Ah. So. You're also a long way from home," the man said. "But not as far as you'd like to go." There was a sound that might have been a chuckle or just a deeper breath.

"No," Peter said. He put on the brakes, as they neared what looked in the headlights like a fallen tree, blocking the road, but as he approached it, the tree seemed to vanish into smoke. Which means it might just have been how his eyes perceived the motley pattern or shadows and light created by the moon and the headlights as they came near. There probably was no tree at all. A thing he did know was that trees didn't move. Even if in the dark of night, with a stranger in the car, everything looked really strange and spooky. From behind Peter the dog snuffled and it was both a perfectly normal dog snuffle, and just slightly wrong, the same as the man's accent and his smell. "No," he said. "I mean given the current state of the art, in my lifetime I might get to send some probes out to Mars and stuff, or maybe make some out of the atmosphere forays, but they're not going very far, and I certainly won't be in whatever we send out." As he said it, he felt a wave of regret, because of course he was studying aerospace engineering because he wanted to go out there. And if he couldn't, he wanted humanity to go out there. Mom kept talking about how she'd got to see the moon landing and how her generation had thought they'd all live in space by now.

At least Mom had had the dream. In his twenty years, Peter had never even been able to dream they'd get off of the Earth in his lifetime. He'd never go elsewhere. Humanity would never make contact with another intelligence. Unless—

"So, you think it's important for humans to get off of the Earth?"

"Of course it's important. Just look at the risk of asteroids. And sooner or later one of the super volcanoes will cut loose. We should have people in other places. Just in case something that destroys the world happens. It won't need to destroy the species then."

"That's right enough," the man answered. "Too few thinking species out there for one to be lost."

The statement was so matter of fact that it took a minute for Peter to realize what the man had said. Was he really laying claim to knowing how many intelligent species there were in—what? Near-earth-space? Galaxy? Universe? He was afraid to ask. Once or twice, when following a lead and stopping some place to ask directions, he'd thought he and a local were on the same page, only to have the local break out into raves about angels and demons and, on one signal occasion, in a diner North of Charleston, the waitress tried to exorcise him.

Not that Peter had anything against religious faith as such, of course. He'd been brought up Episcopal and confirmed, and everything, but he'd been mortally embarrassed as the waitress screamed for devils to come out of him. Fortunately the diner had been almost deserted. Even in the car—particularly in the car, given the tight confines—he didn't want a repeat of that scene, so he said, "I came here following a UFO."

"Ah?"

"It's a bit of a hobby of mine," he said. "Well, of ours. There's a club of us, at UWV. Official name is The Club For Contact With Extraterrestrial intelligence, but we call ourselves the Mashed Potatoes Club. After the *Close Encounters* movie, you know."

"Close encounters?"

"It was a movie back in the seventies. Aliens were beaming things into this guy's brain, and telling him to meet them at this mountain, and he sculpted the point of meeting out of mashed potatoes and—"

"Oh, I know," the man said. "We do watch movies, you know, even though not always the latest. Yes, Dog, just a few more minutes, and Gauln will have your chow right enough, and a place for us to sleep too."

There had been a snuffle from the dog, while the old man was talking, but the thing that disturbed Peter, unable to turn around and look, because it took all his concentration to navigate the road, was the feeling that the dog had put forward a tentacle, in between the seats, to touch the old man's arm. Not a paw, but a delicate, elongating tendril, like the probing end of an octopus's appendage. "And . . . and what did you think of *Close Encounters*?"

The man made a sound somewhere between a hiss and a chuckle. "Damnfool idea," he said. "Beaming thoughts into a man's head. Even if there were any civilized species that would allow that, and it weren't a violation of all sorts of treaties, damnfool idea. Why not just land and say *Hey there, we want to have a word with you.*"

"People wouldn't believe it," Peter said. *I don't believe it.*

"Turn left here. Gauln's cabin is down this path. Just a few more turns. Yeah, go easy," in answer to a slipping sound. "This is all gravel there, and there's a creek down below." He took another of those long-spaced-out breaths. "Thing is, why should they? And why should people from space want humans to believe it? Or not to believe it? What is the whole thing humans have got going where they think that folks from other stars would be better just because they're from other stars? Why would people come here and play a lot of music and stuff to offer guidance? That's not how the universe works. That's not how any species out there works. Oh, maybe there are some who think they're better than everyone else, and could teach the world a thing or two about how to live," he said. "But they usually don't have enough money to go to far flung planets and lord it over people there. They content themselves with being snooty right at home."

There was a prickle of something up and down the back of Peter's neck, as he forced a laugh, "So, more of an *Independence Day* thing? No one travels trillions of miles not to take over the land they conquer."

The man cackled. "Nah. That's tomfoolery, too. Oh, sure there are wars and conquest, but any species like that would be committing suicide by alliance. It would be like encouraging everyone else to gang up on them and send them into the extinct list. Also, very few people travel in spaceships, right? I mean, too much fuel and stuff. Yeah, no one would cross the deep interstellar nothing, taking hundreds or hundreds of thousands of years just to say howdy. But it's possible to travel by folding space around time—or at least that's what my brother-in-law tells me—I'm not a science guy, and it's cheap enough in energy that people go to other planets for all sorts of reasons."

"What kinds of reasons?"

"Retirement," he said. "Mostly, in the case of Earth that's what it is. You've got yourselves a mighty pleasant planet, with very few sentients per square mile, and a lot of non-sentient life. I don't think you know how rare that is. And of course, the price is right. Because you're teeming with life, it's right easy to earn a living in the oldest sense. Grow a few plants. Do a little hunting. That sort of thing. I might consider it myself, maybe, if I ever retire. But for now, I do a little hunting, when I have time."

"But—" Was the old codger really telling him he was from out of space? Or was he just having fun with the college kid?

"Turn right here, then fast left on the next. No, here. Yeah, I know the trees kind of cover the entrance. I think Gauln likes it that way. Not that he's a bad old boy, but he's not that fond of company."

"Will he be upset we're coming here?"

"What? No. We go back two hundred years, do Gauln and I, and I have a standing invitation to come to his cabin and stay as long as I like. He's just a private . . . man. Well, you could say. He used to be very sociable and all, but his mate died, and mostly he likes his solitude. He says he can almost hear the trees. He might have gone a little loopy. Right here. Yeah, that's right. Mind the road, it's a bit twisty. Normally I land in the patio behind Gauln's cabin, but damn it if the oscillator fold didn't go out on the vehicle. I need to buy him a new one. Maybe I should take fewer hunting trips."

The dog made a sound like "arrooo?" from the back, and now, despite the curvy road, Peter dared to peek, and there it was, a bluish-grey tentacle in the faint light, touching the man's shoulder.

The man put a hand back, to pat the dog, and Peter had to turn back really quick and look at the road, but he'd swear the man's arm had bent whichever way, not at the elbow. More a sinuous length of . . . something, like flexible tubing.

"Right there," the man said. "Yes, Dog, you'll get your warm bed tonight. Right there, the log cabin, see it?"

Peter saw it, in a clearing surrounded by trees. It too was subtly wrong, though he couldn't say why. It looked like a normal log cabin, except you got the impression it was a log cabin built by someone who had a very different idea what a log cabin should be. Hard to tell in the dark and all, but he'd swear there was a little tower on top, a little cupola-like thing, like they put on top of Russian churches. Built in logs. Not that people didn't get eccentric about their abode, sometimes, but this was . . . odd. Not as odd as a dog with tentacles, maybe. Or a man with no bones in his arm. But odd.

"You can pull up there, to the right. There's a patio area. It's where I'd have landed, if the oscillator hadn't gone out."

Peter pulled onto what felt like cement under his wheels. He wasn't sure he'd call this a patio, though. In the filtered moonlight, it seemed to extend about the size of his parent's yard, and be uniformly grey and vast. He pulled forward a little more, to where there were no trees overhead. More light now. "I was following a UFO," he said. His words surprised him, as he'd not intended to say anything. "I was following a UFO, straight through the mountains. Just a dot of light, moving like no star could, like no satellite could. Then there was this flash of light, and then a cone of darkness, here, in the mountains, and I followed, and I found—and you were there."

"I'm right glad you followed, son," the man said. "Because otherwise Dog and I would have had to trudge all this way, and Dog gets cranky about just walking. No playing with foxes, nothing. Just walking."

Peter heard the car door unlock and looked over. He'd swear the hand pushing the door open had too many fingers. And now the man turned, and he still looked like a good old boy, with sun-baked skin, and the circle of standing up grey hair around his head, and faded blue eyes. There were wrinkles of amusement at the corner of his eyes. "That cone of darkness thing? That was the oscillator giving up the ghost, but Gauln will have a spare one. He usually does living so far from civilization."

The passenger opened the back door and Peter heard the dog shuffle out. Normal shuffling sounds, except for that odd dragging undertone. The back door closed. The passenger door started to close, then stopped, as if the man were hesitating. He bent, to look at Peter through the window. His hand on the door was very visible, and Peter realized that what he thought was a red flannel plaid shirt seemed to grow right into the skin or the skin into it.

And now the man said, very softly, "Son, if I were you I wouldn't go looking for UFOs. People who come here don't want to be made a fuss of. They don't have no big message of love and peace, and they don't want to conquer the Earth. They're just folks, wanting to hunt or retire, or spend some time in a beautiful world. They don't need no grief, and they won't take kindly to getting it. And some are more . . . protective of their privacy than others. Gauln is a right demon for privacy. I trust you take my meaning? You're a nice cub and no one wishes you ill." He smiled then.

Peter sat frozen, behind the wheel, watching him walk away, just a good ol' boy and his rifle and his dog, their disguise— if it was a disguise – almost perfect, except that they didn't move quite right.

It wasn't until they knocked at the cabin door and it opened, and something—he'd swear to tentacles, but nothing more—peeked out, that Peter found the energy to turn on the engine, and back out. Back slowly out, negotiating the twisty road, and trying to remember the turns he'd taken.

The smile had done it. If that was a disguise, someone should have told the good ol' . . . thing that humans didn't smile vertically, splitting their face from between the eyes to the chin in an amiable display of teeth and lolling tongue.

He shuddered.

It was an hour before he realized he was irretrievably lost. Another hour before he found his way to the highway.

Peter realized he could never find his way back to the cabin. Oh, sure, during the day, with a party, he might have dared approach, take photographs. Maybe hide in the trees and wait till—what? If only he'd thought to get his phone out and take a picture of that bizarre smile.

As it was, no one would believe him. He wasn't even

sure, as time went by, that he believed himself. But he thought no one could imagine that smile. Not that smile.

He pulled off at a diner and ordered a coffee, and sipped it while looking at the night outside. Were these mountains full of aliens and their dogs not-hunting-foxes? Was the Earth the Florida of the Galaxy? Was any of it true?

He couldn't say. And worse, even if it was true, no one would believe him.

Peter wasn't even just another crazy who'd seen a UFO. All he'd seen was an old man who smiled wrong, and a dog with tentacles.

He looked up, at the twinkling lights in the vast dark. In the middle of nowhere you saw the stars so much more clearly.

And they'd never felt so distant.

# RIDING THE WHITE BULL

by Caitlin R. Kiernan

*I'm tempted to call this one Raymond Chandler meets H. P. Lovecraft in a tale of alien-infested mean streets, but that would be undervaluing what a strongly individual writer Caitlin R. Kiernan is, the sort who doesn't just absorb influences, but transmutes them into pure horror gold.*

*The* New York Times *recently called* **Caitlin R. Kiernan** *"one of our essential writers of dark fiction" and S. T. Joshi had declared ". . . hers is now the voice of weird fiction." Caitlin's novels incude* Silk, Threshold, Low Red Moon, Daughter of Hounds, The Red Tree *(nominated for the Shirley Jackson and World Fantasy awards) and* The Drowning Girl: A Memoir *(winner of the James Tiptree, Jr. and Bram Stoker awards, nominated for the Nebula, World Fantasy, British Fantasy, Mythopoeic,* Locus, *and*

*Shirley Jackson awards). To date, her short fiction has been collected in thirteen volumes, including* Tales of Pain and Wonder, From Weird and Distant Shores, Alabaster, A is for Alien, The ammonite Violin & Others, Confessions of a Five-Chambered Heart, Two Worlds and In Between, The Best of Caitlin R. Kiernan (Volume One), *and the Fantasy Award winning* The Ape's Wife and Other Stories. *She has also won a World Fantasy Award for Best Short Fiction for "The Prayer of Ninety Cats." During the 1990s, she wrote* The Dreaming *for DC Comics' Vertigo imprint, and has recently completed* Alabaster *for Dark Horse Comics. The first volume,* Alabaster Wolves, *received the Bram Stoker Award. She lives in Providence Rhode Island with her partner, Kathryn Pollnac.*

*But all she ever* wanted *was to be a paleontologist.*

**"YOU'VE BEEN DRINKING AGAIN,** Mr. Paine," Sarah said, and I suppose I must have stopped whatever it was I was doing, probably staring at those damned pics again, the ones of the mess the cops had turned up that morning in a nasty little dump on Columbus—or maybe chewing at my fingernails, or thinking about sex. Whatever. Something or another that suddenly didn't matter anymore because she wasn't asking me a question. Sarah rarely had time for questions. She just wasn't that sort of a girl anymore. She spoke with a directness and authority that would never match her pretty, artificial face, and that dissonance, that absolute betrayal of expectation, always made people sit up and listen. If I'd been looking at the photos—I honestly can't remember—I probably laid them down again and looked at her, instead.

"There are worse things," I replied, which I suppose I thought was some sort of excuse or defense or something, but she only scowled at me and shook her head.

"Not for you there aren't," she whispered, speaking so low that I almost couldn't make out the words over the faint hum of her metabolic servos and the rumble of traffic down on the street. She blinked and turned away, staring out my hotel window at the dark gray sky hanging low above the Hudson. The snow had finally stopped falling and the clouds had an angry, interrupted intensity to them. Jesus. I can remember the fucking clouds, can even assign them human emotions, but I can't remember what I was doing when Sarah told me I was drinking again. The bits we save, the bits we throw away. Go figure.

"The Agency doesn't need drunks on its payroll, Mr. Paine. The streets of New York are full of drunks and junkies. They're cheaper than rat shit. The Agency needs men with clear minds."

Sarah had a way of enunciating words so that I knew they were capitalized. And she always capitalized Agency. Always. Maybe it was a glitch in one of her language programs, or, then again, maybe she just made me paranoid. Sarah and the booze and the fucking Agency and, while I'm on the subject, February in Manhattan. By that point, I think I'd have given up a couple of fingers and a toe to be on the next flight back to LA.

"We hired you because Fennimore said you were sober. We checked your records with the Department of—"

"Why are you *here*, Sarah? What do you want? I have work to do," and I jabbed a thumb at the cluttered desk on the other side of my unmade bed. "Work for you and the Agency."

"Work you can't do drunk."

"Yeah, so why don't you fire my worthless, intoxicated ass and put me on the next jump back to Los Angeles? After this morning, I honestly couldn't give a shit."

"You understood, when you took this job, Mr. Paine, that there might be exceptional circumstances."

She was still staring out the window towards the sludgy, ice-jammed river and Jersey, an almost expectant expression on her face, the sullen winter light reflecting dull and iridescent off her unaging dermafab skin.

"We were quite explicit on that point."

"Of course you were," I mumbled, half to myself, even less than half to the cyborg who still bothered to call herself Sarah, and then I stepped around the foot of the bed and sat down on a swivel-topped aluminum stool in front of the desk. I made a show of shuffling papers about, hoping that she'd take the hint and leave. I needed a drink and time alone, time to think about what the hell I was going to do next. After the things I'd seen and heard, the things in the photographs I'd taken, the things they wouldn't *let* me photograph, I was beginning to understand why the Agency had decided not to call an alert on this one, why they were keeping the CDC and BioCon and the WHO in the dark. Why they'd called in a scrubber, instead.

"It'll snow again before morning," Sarah said, not turning away from the window.

"If you can call that crap out there snow," I replied, impatiently. "It's not even white. It smells like . . . fuck, I don't know what it smells like, but it doesn't smell like snow."

"You have to learn to let go of the past, Mr. Paine. It's no good to you here. No good at all."

"Is that Agency policy?" I asked, and Sarah frowned.

"No, that's not what I meant. That's not what I meant at all." She sighed then, and I wondered if it was just habit or if she still needed to breathe, still needed oxygen to drive the patchwork alchemy of her biomechs. I also wondered if she still had sex and, if so, with what. Sarah and I had gone a few rounds, way back in the day, back when she was still one-hundred percent flesh and blood, water and bone and cartilage. Back when she was still scrubbing freelance, before the Agency gave her a contract and shipped her off to the great frozen dung heap of Manhattan. Back then, if anyone had asked, I'd have said it was her life, her decisions to make, and a girl like Sarah sure as fuck didn't need someone like me getting in her way.

"I was trying to say—here, now—we have to live in the present. That's all we have."

"Forget it," I told her, glancing up too quickly from the bloody, garish images flickering across the screen of my old Sony-Akamatsu laptop. "Thanks for the ride, though."

"No problem," Sarah whispered. "It's what I do," and she finally turned away from the window, the frost on the Plexiglas, the wide interrupted sky.

"If I need anything, I'll give you or Templeton a ring,"

I said and Sarah pretended to smile, nodded her head and walked across the tiny room to the door. She opened it, but paused there, one foot across the threshold, neither in nor out, the heavy, cold air and flat fluorescent lighting from the hallway leaking in around her, swaddling her like a second-rate halo.

"Try to stay sober," she said. "Please. Mr. Paine. This one…it's going to be a squeeze." And her green-brown eyes shimmered faintly, those amazing eight-mill-a-pair spheres of fiber-optic filament and scratch-resistant acrylic, tinted mercury suspension-platinum lenses and the very best circuitry German optimetrics had figured out how to cram into a 6.5 cc socket. I imagined, then or only later on—that's something else I can't remember—that the shimmer stood for something Sarah was too afraid to say aloud, or something the Agency's behavioral inhibitors wouldn't allow her to say, something in her psyche that had been stamped Code Black, Restricted Access.

"Please," she said again.

"Sure. For old time's sake," I replied.

"Whatever it takes, Mr. Paine," and she left, pulling the door softly closed behind her, abandoning me to my dingy room and the dingier afternoon light leaking in through the single soot-streaked window. I listened to her footsteps on the tile, growing fainter as she approached the elevator at the other end of the hall, and when I was sure she wasn't coming back, I reached for the half-empty bottle of scotch tucked into the shadows beneath the edge of the bed.

* * *

Back then, I still dreamed about Europa every fucking night. Years later, after I'd finally been retired by the Agency and was only Dietrich Paine again, pensioned civilian has-been rotting away day by day by day in East LA or NoHo or San Diego—I moved around a lot for a drunk—a friend of a friend's croaker hooked me up with some black-market head tweaker. And he slipped a tiny silver chip into the base of my skull, right next to my metencephalon, and the bad dreams stopped, just like that. No more night flights, no more cold sweats, no more screaming until the neighbors called the cops.

But that winter in Manhattan, I was still a long, long decade away from the tweaker and his magic silver chip, and whenever the insomnia failed me and I dozed off for ten or fifteen or twenty minutes, I was falling again, tumbling silently through the darkness out beyond Ganymede, falling towards that Great Red Spot, that eternal crimson hurricane, my perfect, vortical Hell of phosphorus-stained clouds. Always praying to whatever dark Jovian gods might be watching my descent that *this* time I'd sail clear of the moons and the anti-cyclone's eye would swallow me at last, dragging me down, burning me, crushing me in that vast abyss of gas and lightning and infinite pressure. But I never made it. Not one single goddamn time.

"Do you believe in sin?" Sarah would ask me, when she was still just Sarah, before the implants and augmentations, and I would lie there in her arms, thinking that I was content, and stare up at the ceiling of our apartment and laugh at her.

"I'm serious, Deet."

"You're always serious. You've got serious down to an exact science."

"I think you're trying to avoid the question."

"Yeah, well, it's a pretty silly fucking question."

"Answer it anyway. Do you believe in sin?"

There's no way to know how fast I'm moving as I plummet towards the hungry, welcoming storm, and then Europa snags me. *Maybe next time*, I think. *Maybe next time.*

"It's only a question," Sarah would say. "Stop trying to make it anything more than that."

"Most of us get what's coming to us, sooner or later."

"That's not the same thing. That's not what I asked you."

And the phone would ring, or I'd slip my hand between her unshaven legs, or one of our beepers would go off, and the moment would melt away, releasing me from her scrutiny.

It never happened exactly that way, of course, but who's keeping score?

In my dreams, Europa grows larger and larger, sprouting from the darkness exactly like it did in the fucking orientation vids every scrubber had to sit through in those days if he or she wanted a license. Snippets of video from this or that probe borrowed for my own memories. Endless fractured sheets of ice the color of rust and sandstone, rising up so fast, so fast, and I'm only a very small speck of meat and white EMU suit streaking north and east across the ebony skies above Mael Dúin, the Echion Linea, Cilix, the southeastern terminus of the Rhadamanthys Linea. I'm only a shooting star hurtling along above that terrible varicose landscape, and I can't remember how to close my eyes.

"Man, I was right fucking there when they opened the thing," Ronnie says again and takes another drag off her cigarette. Her hand trembles and ash falls to the Formica tabletop. "I'd asked to go to Turkey, right, to cover the goddamn war, but I pulled the IcePIC assignment instead. I was waiting in the pressroom with everyone else, watching the feed from the quarantine unit when the sirens started."

"The Agency denies you were present," I reply as calmly as I can, and she smiles that nervous, brittle smile she always had, laughs one of her dry, humorless laughs, and gray smoke leaks from her nostrils.

"Hell, I know that, Deet. The fuckers keep rewriting history so it always comes out the way they want it to, but I was there, man. I *saw* it, before they shut down the cameras. I saw all that shit that 'never happened'," and she draws quotation marks in the air with her index fingers.

That was the last time I talked to Ronnie, the last time I visited her out at La Casa Psychiatric, two or three weeks before she hung herself with an electrical cord. I went to the funeral, of course. The Agency sent a couple of black-suited spooks with carefully-worded condolences for her family, and I ducked out before the eulogy was finished.

And here, a few kilometers past the intersection of Tectamus Linea and Harmonia Linea, I see the familiar scatter of black dots laid out helter-skelter on the crosscut plains. "Ice-water volcanism," Sarah whispers inside my helmet; I know damn well she isn't there, hasn't been anywhere near me for years and years, and I'm alone and only dreaming her voice to break the deafening weight of silence. I count the convection cells like rosary beads, like I was ever Catholic, like someone who might have once believed in sin. I'm still too far up to see any evidence of the lander, so I don't know which hole is The Hole, Insertion Point 2071A, the open sore that Emmanuel Weatherby-Jones alternately referred to as "the plague gate" and "the mouth of Sakpata" in his book on the Houston incident and its implications for theoretical and applied astrobiology. I had to look that up, because he never explained who or what Sakpata was. I found it in an old book on voodoo and Afro-Caribbean religions. Sakpata is a god of disease.

I'm too far up to guess which hole is Sakpata's mouth and I don't try.

I don't want to know.

A different sort of god is patiently waiting for me on the horizon.

"They started screaming," Ronnie says. "Man, I'll never forget that sound, no matter how many pills these assholes feed me. We all sat there, too fucking stunned to move, and this skinny little guy from CNN—"

"Last time he was from *Newsweek*," I say, interrupting her, and she shakes her head and takes another drag, coughs and rubs at her bloodshot eyes.

"You think it makes any goddamned difference?"

"No," I reply dishonestly, and she stares at me for a while without saying anything else.

"When's the last time you got a decent night's sleep?" she asks me, finally, and I might laugh, or I might shrug, and "Yeah," she says. "That's what I thought."

She starts rattling on about the hydrobot, then, the towering black smokers, thermal vents, chemosynthesis, those first grainy snatches of video, but I'm not listening. I'm too busy zipping helplessly along above buckled Europan plains and vast stretches of blocky, shattered chaos material; a frozen world caught in the shadow of Big Daddy Jupiter, frozen for ages beyond counting, but a long fucking way from dead, and I would wake up screaming or crying or, if I was lucky, too scared to make any sound at all.

"They're ready for you now, Mr. Paine," the cop said, plain old NYPD street blue, and I wondered what the fuck he was doing here, why the Agency was taking chances like that. Probably the same poor bastard who'd found the spooch, I figured. Templeton had told me that someone in the building had complained about the smell and, so, the super buzzed the cops, so this was most likely the guy who answered the call. He might have a partner around somewhere. I nodded at him, and he glanced nervously back over his shoulder at the open door to the apartment, the translucent polyurethane iso-seal curtain with its vertical black zipper running right down the middle, all the air hoses snaking in and out of the place, keeping the pressure inside lower than the pressure outside. I doubted he would still be breathing when the sweeper crews were finished with the scene.

"You see this sort of shit very often?" he asked, and it didn't take a particularly sensitive son of a bitch to hear the fear in his voice, the fear and confusion and whatever comes after panic. I didn't respond. I was busy checking the batteries in one of my cameras and, besides, I had the usual orders from Templeton to keep my mouth shut around civvies. And knowing the guy was probably already good as dead, that he'd signed his death warrant just by showing up for work that morning, didn't make me particularly eager to chat.

"Well, I don't mind telling you, I've never seen shit like that thing in there," he said and coughed. "I mean, you see some absolutely fucked-up shit in this city, and I even did my four years in the army—hell, I was in fucking Damascus after the bomb, but holy Christ Almighty."

"You were in Damascus?" I asked, but didn't look up from my equipment, too busy double-checking the settings on the portable genetigraph clipped to my belt to make eye contact.

"Oh yeah, I was there. I got to help clean up the mess when the fires burned out."

"Then that's something we have in common," I told him and flipped my vidcam's on switch and the gray LED screen showed me five zeros. I was patched into the portable lab down on the street, a black Chevy van with Maryland plates and a yellow ping-pong ball stuck on the antenna. I knew Sarah would be in the van, waiting for my feed, jacked in, riding the amps, hearing everything I heard, seeing everything I saw through her perfectly calibrated eyes.

"You were in Syria?" the cop asked me, glad to have something to talk about besides what he'd seen in the apartment.

"No, I clean up other people's messes."

"Oh," he said, sounding disappointed. "I see."

"Had a good friend in the war, though. But he was stationed in Cyprus, and then the Taurus Mountains."

"You ever talk with him? You know, about the war?"

"Nope. He didn't make it back," I said, finally looking up, and I winked at the cop and stepped quickly past him to the tech waiting for me at the door. I could see she was sweating inside her hazmat hood, even though it was freezing in the hallway. Scrubbers don't get hazmat suits. It interferes with the contact, so we settle for a couple of hours in decon afterwards, antibiotics, antitox, purgatives, and hope we don't come up red somewhere down the line.

"This is bad, ain't it?" the cop asked. "I mean, this is something *real* bad," and I didn't turn around, just shrugged my shoulders as the tech unzipped the plastic curtain for me.

"Is that how it looked to you?" I replied. I could feel the gentle rush of air into the apartment as the slit opened in front of me.

"Jesus, man, all I want's a straight fucking answer," he said. "I think I deserve that much. Don't you?" and since I honestly couldn't say one way or the other, since I didn't even care, I ignored him and stepped through the curtain into this latest excuse for Hell.

There's still an exhibit at the American Museum of Natural History, on the fourth floor with the old Hall of Vertebrate Origins and all the dinosaur bones. The Agency didn't shut it down after the first outbreaks, the glory spooches that took out a whole block in Philadelphia and a trailer park somewhere in West Virginia, but it's not as popular as you might think. A dark, dusty alcove crowded with scale models and dioramas, videos monitors running clips from the IcePIC's hydrobot, endless black and white loops of gray seafloors more than half a billion kilometers from earth. When the exhibit first opened, there were a few specimens on loan from NASA, but those were all removed a long time ago. I never saw them for myself, but an acquaintance on staff at the museum, a geologist, assures me they were there. A blue-black bit of volcanic rock sealed artfully in a Lucite pyramid, and two formalin-filled specimen canisters, one containing a pink worm-like organism no more than a few centimeters in length, the other preserving one of the ugly little slugs that the mission scientists dubbed "star minnows."

"Star leeches" would have been more accurate.

On Tuesday afternoon, the day after I'd worked the scene on Columbus, hung over and hoping to avoid another visit from Sarah, I took the B-Line from my hotel to the museum and spent a couple of hours sitting on a bench in that neglected alcove, watching the video clips play over and over again for no one but me. Three monitors running simultaneously—a NASA documentary on the exploration of Europa, beginning with Pioneer 10 in 1973, a flyover of the moon's northern hemisphere recorded shortly before the IcePIC orbiter deployed its probes, and a snippet of film shot beneath the ice. That's the one I'd come to see. I chewed aspirin and watched as the hydrobot's unblinking eyes peered through veils of silt and megaplankton, into the interminable darkness of an alien ocean, the determined glare of the bot's lights never seeming to reach more than a few feet into the gloom.

Near the end of the loop, you get to see one of the thermal vents, fringed with towering sulfide chimneys spewing superheated, methane- and hydrogen-rich water into the frigid Europan ocean. In places, the sides of the chimneys were completely obscured by a writhing, swaying carpet of creatures. Something like an eel slipped unexpectedly past the camera lens. A few seconds later, the seafloor was replaced by a brief stream of credits and then the NASA logo before the clip started itself over again.

I tried hard to imagine how amazing these six minutes of video must have seemed, once upon a time, how people must have stood in lines just to see it, back before the shit hit the fan and everyone everywhere stopped wanting to talk about IcePIC and its fucking star minnows. Before the government axed most of NASA's exobiology program, scrapped all future missions to Europa, and cancelled plans to explore Titan. Back before ET became a four-letter word. But no matter how hard I tried, all I could think about was that thing on the bed, the crap growing from the walls of the apartment and dripping from the goddamn ceiling.

In the museum, above the monitor, there was a long quote from H. G. Wells printed in red-brown ink on a clear Lexan plaque, and I read it several times, wishing that I had a cigarette—"We look back through countless millions of years and see the great will to live struggling out of the intertidal slime, struggling from shape to shape and from power to power, crawling and then walking confidently upon the land, struggling generation after generation to master the air, creeping down into the darkness of the deep; we see it turn upon itself in rage and hunger and reshape itself anew, we watch it draw nearer and more akin to us, expanding, elaborating itself, pursuing its relentless inconceivable purpose, until at last it reaches us and its being beats through our brains and arteries."

I've never cared very much for irony. It usually leaves a sick, empty feeling in my gut. I wondered why no one had taken the plaque down.

By the time I got back to my room it was almost dark, even though I'd splurged and taken a taxi. After the video, the thought of being trapped in the crowded, stinking subway, hurtling along through the city's bowels, through those tunnels where the sun never reaches, gave me a righteous fucking case of the heebie-jeebies and, what the hell, the Agency was picking up the tab. All those aspirin had left my stomach aching and sour, and hadn't done much of anything about the hangover, but there was an unopened pint waiting for me beneath the edge of the bed.

I was almost asleep when Sarah called.

Here's a better quote. I've been carrying it around with me for the last few years, in my head and on a scrap of paper. It showed up in my email one day, sent by some anonymous someone or another from an account that turned out to be bogus. Scrubbers get a lot of anonymous email. Tips, rumors, bullshit, hearsay, wicked little traps set by the Agency, confessions, nightmares, curses, you name it and it comes rolling our way, and after a while you don't even bother to wonder who sent the shit. But this one, this one kept me awake a few nights:

"But what would a deep-sea fish learn even if a steel plate of a wrecked vessel above him should drop and bump him on the nose?

"Our submergence in a sea of conventionality of almost impenetrable density.

"Sometimes I'm a savage who has found something on the beach of his island. Sometimes I'm a deep-sea fish with a sore nose.

"The greatest of mysteries:

"Why don't they ever come here, or send here, openly?

"Of course, there's nothing to that mystery if we don't take so seriously the notion—that we must be interesting. It's probably for moral reasons that they stay away—but even so, there must be some degraded ones among them."

It's that last bit that always sinks its teeth (or claws or whatever the fuck have you) into me and hangs on. Charles Hoyt Fort. *The Book of the Damned*. First published in 1919, a century and a half before IcePIC, and it occurs to me now that I shouldn't be any less disturbed by prescience than I am by irony. But there you go. Sometimes I'm a savage. Sometimes I'm a deep-sea fish. And my life is become the sum of countless degradations.

"You're not going down there alone," Sarah said, telling, not asking, because, like I already noted, Sarah stopped being the kind of girl who asks questions when she signed on with the Agency for life plus whatever else they could milk her biomeched cadaver for. I didn't reply immediately, lay there a minute or three, rubbing my eyes, waiting for the headache to start in on me again, listening to the faint, insistent crackle from the phone. Manhattan's landlines were shit and roses that February, had been that way for years, ever since some Puerto Ricans in Brooklyn had popped a homemade micro-EMP rig to celebrate the Fourth of July. I wondered why Sarah hadn't called me on my thumbline while I looked about for the scotch. Turned out I was lying on the empty bottle, and I rolled over, wishing I'd never been born. I held the phone cradled between my left shoulder and my cheek and stared at the darkness outside the window of my hotel room.

"Do you even know what time it is?" I asked her.

"Templeton said you were talking about going out to Roosevelt. He said you might have gone already."

"I didn't say dick to Templeton about Roosevelt," I said, which was the truth—I hadn't—but also entirely beside the point. It was John Templeton's prerogative to stay a few steps ahead of his employees, especially when those employees were scrubbers, especially freebie scrubbers on the juice. I tossed the empty bottle at a cockroach on the wall across the room. The bottle didn't break, but squashed the roach and left a satisfying dent in the drywall.

"You know Agency protocol for dealing with terrorists."

"They went and stuck something in your head so you don't *have* to sleep anymore, is that it?"

"You can't go to the island alone," she said. "I'm sending a couple of plain-clothes men over. They'll be at your hotel by six a.m., at the latest."

"Yeah, and I'll be fucking asleep at six," I mumbled,

more interested in watching the roaches that had emerged to feed on the remains of the one I'd nailed than arguing with her.

"We can't risk losing you, Mr. Paine. It's too late to call in someone else if anything happens. You know that as well as I do."

"Do I?"

"You're a drunk, not an idiot."

"Look, Sarah, if I start scutzing around out there with two of Temp's goons in tow, I'll be lucky if I *find* a fucking stitch, much less get it to talk to me."

"They're all animals," Sarah said, meaning the stitches and meatdolls and genetic changelings that had claimed Roosevelt Island a decade or so back. There was more than a hint of loathing in her voice. "It makes me sick, just thinking about them."

"Did you ever stop to consider they probably feel the same way about you?"

"No," Sarah said coldly, firmly, one-hundred percent shit sure of herself. "I never have."

"If those fuckers knock on my door at six o'clock, I swear to god, Sarah, I'll shoot them."

"I'll tell them to wait for you in the lobby."

"That's real damn thoughtful of you."

There was another static-littered moment of silence then, and I closed my eyes tight. The headache was back and had brought along a few friends for the party. My thoughts were starting to bleed together, and I wondered if I'd vomit before or after Sarah finally let me off the phone. I wondered if cyborgs vomited. I wondered exactly what all those agents in the black Chevy van had seen on their consoles and face screens when I'd walked over and touched a corner of the bed in the apartment on Columbus Avenue.

"I'm going to hang up now, Sarah. I'm going back to sleep."

"You're sober."

"As a judge," I whispered and glanced back at the window, trying to think about anything at all except throwing up. There were bright lights moving across the sky above the river, red and green and white, turning clockwise; one of the big military copters, an old Phoenix 6-98 or one of the newer Japanese whirlybirds, making its circuit around the Rotten Apple.

"You're still a lousy liar," she said.

"I'll have to try harder."

"Don't fuck this up, Mr. Paine. You're a valued asset. The Agency would like to see you remain that way."

"I'm going back to sleep," I said again, disregarding the not-so-subtle threat tucked between her words; it wasn't anything I didn't already know. "And I meant what I said about shooting those assholes. Don't think I didn't. Anyone knocks on this door before eight sharp, and that's all she wrote."

"They'll be waiting in the lobby when you're ready."

"Goodnight, Sarah."

"Goodnight, Mr. Paine," she replied, and a second or two later there was only the ragged dial tone howling in my ear. The lights outside the window were gone, the copter probably all the way to Harlem by now. I almost made it to the toilet before I was sick.

* * *

If I didn't keep getting the feeling that there's someone standing behind me, someone looking over my shoulder as I write this, I'd say more about the dreams. The dreams are always there, tugging at me, insistent, selfish, wanting to be spilled out into the wide, wide world where everyone and his brother can get a good long gander at them. They're not content anymore with the space *inside* my skull. My skull is a prison for dreams, an enclosed and infinite prison space where the arrows on the number line point towards each other, infinitely converging but never, ever, ever meeting and so infinite all the same. But I *do* keep getting that feeling, and there's still the matter of the thing in the apartment.

The thing on the bed.

The thing that the cop who'd been in Damascus after the Israelis' 40-megaton fireworks show died for.

My thirteenth and final contact.

After I was finished with the makeshift airlock at the door, one of Templeton's field medics, safe and snug inside a blue hazmat suit, led me through the brightly-lit apartment. I held one hand cupped over my nose and mouth, but the thick clouds of neon yellow disinfectant seeped easily between my fingers, gagging me. My eyes burned and watered, making it even more difficult to see. I've always thought that shit smelled like licorice, but it seems to smell like different things to different people. Sarah used to say it reminded her of burning tires. I used to know a guy who said it smelled like carnations.

"It's in the bedroom," the medic said, his voice flat and tinny through the suit's audio. "It doesn't seem to have spread to any of the other rooms. How was the jump from Los Angeles, sir?"

I didn't answer him, too ripped on adrenaline for small talk and pleasantries, and he didn't really seem to care, my silence just another part of the routine. I took shallow breaths and followed the medic through the yellow fog, which was growing much thicker as we approached ground zero. The disinfectant was originally manufactured by Dow for domestic bioterrorism cleanup, but the Agency's clever boys and girls had added a pinch of this, a dash of that, and it always seemed to do the job. We passed a kitchenette, beer cans and dirty dishes and an open box of corn flakes sitting on the counter, then turned left into a short hallway leading past a bathroom too small for a rat to take a piss in, past a framed photograph of a lighthouse on a rocky shore (the bits we remember, the bits we forget), to the bedroom. Templeton was there, of course, decked out in his orange hazmat threads, one hand resting confidently on the butt of the big Beretta Pulse 38A on his hip, and he pointed at me and then pointed at the bed.

Sometimes I'm a deep-sea fish.

Sometimes I'm a savage.

"We're still running MRS and backtrace on these two," Templeton said, pointing at the bed again, "but I'm pretty sure the crit's a local." His gray eyes peered warily out at me, the lights inside his hood shining bright so I had no trouble at all seeing his face through the haze.

"I figure one of them picked it up from an untagged mobile, probably the woman there, and it's been hitching dormant for the last few weeks. We're guessing the trigger was viral. She might have caught a cold. Corona's always a good catalyst."

I took a deep breath and coughed. Then I gagged again and stared up at the ceiling for a moment.

"Come on, Deet. I need you frosty on this one. You're not drunk, are you? Fennimore said—"

"I'm not drunk," I replied, and I wasn't, not yet. I hadn't had a drink in almost six months, but, hey, the *good* news was, the drought was almost over.

"That's great," Templeton said. "That's real damn great. That's exactly what I wanted to hear."

I looked back at the bed.

"So, when you gonna tell me what's so goddamn special about this one?" I asked. "The way Sarah sounded, I figured you'd already lost a whole building."

"What's so goddamn special about them, Deet, is that they're still conscious, both of them. Initial EEGs are coming up pretty solid. Clean alpha, beta, and delta. The theta's are weakening, but the brain guys say the waves are still synchronous enough to call coherent."

Temp kept talking, but I tuned him out and forced myself to take a long, hard look at the bed.

Sometimes I'm a deep-sea fish.

The woman's left eye was still intact, open very wide and wet with tears, her blue iris bright as Christmas Day, and I realized she was watching me.

"It's pure," Templeton said, leaning closer to the bed, "more than ninety-percent proximal to the Lælaps strain. Beats the fuck outta me why their brains aren't soup by now."

"I'm going to need a needle," I muttered, speaking

automatically, some part of me still there to walk the walk and talk the talk, some part of me getting ready to take the plunge, because the only way out of this hole was straight ahead. A very small, insensate part of me not lost in that pleading blue eye. "Twelve and a half max, okay, and not that fife-and-drum Australian shit you gave me in Boston. I don't want to feel *anything* in there but the critter, you understand?"

"Sure," Templeton said, smiling like a ferret.

"I mean it. Whatever's going through their heads right now, I don't want to hear it, Temp. Not so much as a peep, not even a fucking whisper."

"Hey, you're calling the shots, Deet."

"Bullshit," I said. "Don't suck my dick, just get me the needle."

He motioned to a medic, and in a few more minutes the drugs were singing me towards that spiraling ebony pipeline, the Scrubber's Road, Persephone's Staircase, the Big Drop, the White Bull, whatever you want to call it, it's all the same to me. I was beginning to sweat and trying to make it through the procedure checklist one last time. Templeton patted me on the back, the way he always did when I was standing there on the brink. I said a silent prayer to anything that might be listening that one day it'd be his carcass rotting away at the center of the Agency's invisible clockwork circus. And then I kneeled down at the edge of the bed and got to work.

Sarah sent the goons over, just like she'd said she would, but I ducked out the back and, luckily, she hadn't seen fit to have any of Temp's people watching all the hotel's exits. Maybe she couldn't pull that many warm bodies off the main gig down on Columbus. Maybe Temp had bigger things on his mind. I caught a cash-and-ride taxi that took me all the way to the ruins along York Avenue. The Vietnamese driver hadn't wanted to get any closer to the Queensboro Bridge than Third, but I slipped him five hundred and he found a little more courage somewhere. He dropped me at the corner of Second and East Sixty-First Street, crossed himself twice, and drove away, bouncing recklessly over the trash and disintegrating blacktop. I watched him go, feeling more alone than I'd expected. Overhead, the Manhattan sky was the color of buttermilk and mud, and I wished briefly, pointlessly, that I'd brought a gun. The 9 mm Samson-L4 Enforcer I'd bought in a Hollywood pawnshop almost four years before was back at the hotel, hidden in a locked compartment of my suitcase. But I knew it'd be a whole lot worse to be picked up crossing the barricades without a pass if I were carrying an unregistered weapon, one more big red blinking excuse for the MPs to play a few rounds of Punch and Judy with my face while they waited for my papers and my story about the Agency to check out.

I started walking north, the gray-blue snow crunching loudly beneath my boots, the collar of my coat turned up against the wind whistling raw between the empty, burned-out buildings. I'd heard security was running slack around the Sixty-Third Street entrance. I might get lucky. It had happened before.

"Yes, but what exactly did you think you'd find on the island?" Buddhadev Krishnamurthy asked when he interviewed me for his second book on technoshamanism and the Roosevelt parahumanists, the one that won him a Pulitzer.

"Missing pieces, maybe," I replied. "I was just following my nose. The Miyake girl turned up during the contact."

"But going to the island alone, wasn't that rather above and beyond? I mean, if you hated Templeton and the Agency so much, why stick your neck out like that?"

"Old habits," I said, sipping at my tequila and trying hard to remember how long it had taken me to find a way past the guards and up onto the bridge. "Old habits and bad dreams," I added, and then, "But I never said I was doing it for the Agency." I knew I was telling him more than I'd intended. Not that it mattered. None of my interview made it past the censors and into print.

I kept to the center lanes, except for a couple of times when rusted and fire-blackened tangles of wrecked automobiles and police riot-rollers forced me to the edges of the bridge. The West Channel glimmered dark and iridescent beneath the late February clouds, a million shifting colors dancing lazily across the oily surface of the river. The wind shrieked through the cantilever spans, like angry sirens announcing my trespass to anyone who would listen. I kept waiting for the sound of helicopter rotors or a foot patrol on its way back from Queens, for some sharpshooter's bullet to drop me dead in my tracks. Maybe it was wishful thinking.

Halfway across I found the access stairs leading down to the island, right where my contact in Street and Sanitation had said they would be. I checked my watch. It was five minutes until noon.

"Will you tell me about the dreams, Mr. Paine?"

Krishnamurthy asked, after he'd ordered me another beer and another shot of tequila. His voice was like silk and cream, the sort of voice that seduced, that tricked you into lowering your defenses just long enough for him to get a good peek at all the nasty nooks and crannies. "I hear lots of scrubbers had trouble with nightmares back then, before the new neural-drag sieves were available. The suicide rate's dropped almost 50-percent since they became standard issue. Did you know that, Mr. Paine?"

"No," I told him. "Guess I missed the memo. I'm kind of outside the flow these days."

"You're a lucky man," he said. "You should count your blessings. At least you made it out in one piece. At least you made it out sane."

I think I told him to fuck off then. I know I didn't tell him about the dreams.

"What do you see down there, Deet? The sensors are getting a little hinky on me," Sarah said and, in the dreams, back when, in the day, before the tweaker's silver chip, I took another clumsy step towards the edge of the chasm created by hot water welling up from the deep-sea vents along the Great Charon Ridge. A white plume of salty steam rose high into the thin Europan atmosphere, blotting out the western horizon, boiling off into the indifferent blackness of space. I knew I didn't want to look over the edge again. I'd been there enough times already, and it was always the same, and I reminded myself that no one had ever walked on Europa, no one human, and it was only a dream. Shit. Listen to me. *Only* a dream. Now, there's a contradiction to live by.

"Am I coming through?" Sarah asked. "Can you hear me?"

I didn't answer her. My mouth was too dry to speak, bone dry from fear and doubt and the desiccated air circulating through the helmet of my EMU suit.

"I need you to acknowledge, Deet. Can you hear me?"

The mouth of Sakpata, the plague gate, yawning toothless and insatiable before me, almost nine kilometers from one side to the other, more than five miles from the edge of the hole down to the water. I was standing near the center of the vast field of cryovolcanic lenticulae first photographed by the Galileo probe in 1998, on its fifteenth trip around Jupiter. Convection currents had pushed the crust into gigantic pressure domes that finally cracked and collapsed under their own weight, exposing the ocean below. I took another step, almost slipping on the ice, and wondered how far I was from the spot where IcePIC had made landfall.

"Deet, do you copy?"

"Do you believe in sin, Deet?"

*Nor shapes of men nor beasts we ken—*

*The ice was all between.*

Sarah sets her coffee cup down and watches me from the other side of our apartment on Cahuenga. Her eyes are still her eyes, full of impatience and secrets. She reaches for a cigarette, and I wish this part weren't a dream, that I could go back to *here* and start again. This sunny LA morning, Sarah wearing nothing but her bra and panties, and me still curled up in the warm spot she left in the sheets. Go back and change the words. Change every goddamn day that's come between now and then.

"They want my decision by tomorrow morning," she says and lights her cigarette. The smoke hangs like a caul about her face.

"Tell them you need more time," I reply. "Tell them you have to think about it."

"This is the fucking Agency," she says and shakes her head. "You don't ask them for more time. You don't ask them shit."

"I don't know what you want me to say, Sarah."

"It's everything I've always wanted," she says and flicks ash into an empty soft drink can.

*Are those her ribs through which the Sun*
*Did peer, as through a grate?*

I took another step nearer the chasm and wished that this would end and I would wake up. If I could wake up, I wouldn't have to see. If I could wake up, there'd be a bottle of scotch or bourbon or tequila waiting for me, a drink of something to take the edge off the dryness in my mouth. The sun was rising behind me, a distant, pale thing lost among the stars, and the comms buzzed and crackled in my ears.

"If it's what you want, take it," I say, the same thing I always say, the same words I can never take back. "I'm not going to stand in your way." I could tell it was the last thing that Sarah wanted to hear. The End. The curtain falls and everyone takes a bow. The next day, Wednesday, I'll drive her to LAX-1, and she'll take the 4:15 jump to D.C.

We are more alone than ever.

Ronnie used her own blood to write those six words on the wall of her room at La Casa, the night she killed herself.

My boots left no trace whatsoever on the slick, blue-white ice. A few more steps and I was finally standing at the edge, walking cautiously onto the wide shelf formed by an angular chaos block jutting a few meters out over the pit. The constant steam had long since worn the edges of the block smooth. Eventually, this block would melt free, undercut by ages of heat and water vapor, and pitch into the churning abyss far below. I took a deep breath of the dry, stale air inside my helmet and peered into the throat of Sakpata.

"Tell me, what the hell did we expect to find out there, Deet?" Ronnie asked me. "What did we think it would be? Little gray men with the answers to all the mysteries of the universe, free for the asking? A few benign extremophiles clinging stubbornly to the bottom of an otherwise lifeless sea? I can't *remember* anymore. I try, but I can't. I lie awake at night trying to remember."

"I don't think it much matters," I told her, and she started crying again.

"It was waiting for us, Deet," she sobbed. "It was waiting for us all along, a million fucking years alone out there in the dark. It knew we'd come, sooner or later."

Sarah was standing on the ice behind me, naked, the wind tearing at her plastic skin.

"Why do you keep coming here?" she asked. "What do you think you'll find?"

"Why do you keep following me?"

"You turned off your comms. I wasn't getting a signal. You didn't leave me much choice."

I turned to face her, turning my back on the hole, but

the wind had already pulled her apart and scattered the pieces across the plain.

We are more alone than ever.

And then I'm in the pipe, slipping along the Scrubber's Road, no friction, no resistance, rushing by high above the frozen moon, waiting for that blinding, twinkling moment of perfect agony when my mind brushes up against that other mind. That instant when it tries to hide, tries to withdraw, and I dig in and hang on and drag it screaming into the light. I hear the whir of unseen machineries as the techs on the outside try to keep up with me, with it.

I stand alone at the edge of Sakpata's mouth, where no man has ever stood, at the foot of the bed on Columbus, in the airport lobby saying goodbye to Sarah. I have all my cameras, my instruments, because I'll need all that later on, when the spin is over and I'm drunk and there's nothing left but the footwork.

When I have nothing left to do but track down the carrier and put a bullet or two in his or her or its head.

Cut the cord. Tie off the loose ends.

"Do you believe in sin, Deet?"

*Instead of the cross, the Albatross . . .*

"It's only a question. Stop trying to make it anything more than that."

"Do you copy?" Sarah asks again. "Global can't get a fix on you." I take another step closer to the hole, and it slips a few feet farther away from me. The sky is steam and stars and infinite night.

I followed East Road north to Main Street, walking as

quickly as the snow and black ice and wrecks littering the way would allow. I passed through decaying canyons of brick and steel, broken windows and gray concrete, the tattered ruins of the mess left after the Feds gave Roosevelt Island up for lost, built their high barricades and washed their righteous hands of the place. I kept my eyes on the road at my feet, but I could feel them watching me, following me, asking each other if this one was trouble or just some fool out looking for his funeral. I might have been either. I still wasn't sure myself. There were tracks in the snow and frozen mud, here and there, some of them more human than others.

Near the wild place that had once been Blackwell Park, I heard something call out across the island. It was a lonely, frightened sound, and I walked a little faster.

I wondered if Sarah would try to send an extraction team in after me, if she was in deep sharn with Templeton and the boys for letting me scoot. I wondered if maybe Temp was already counting me among the dead and kicking himself for not putting me under surveillance, trying to figure out how the hell he was going to lay it all out for the bastards in Washington. It took me the better part of an hour to reach the northern tip of the island and the charred and crumbling corpse of Coler-Goldwater Hospital. The ragtag militia of genetic anarchists who had converged on Manhattan in the autumn of '69, taking orders from a schizo ex-movie star who called herself Circe Nineteen, had claimed the old hospital as their headquarters. When the army decided to start shelling, Coler had taken the worst of the mortars. Circe Nineteen had been killed by a sniper, but there'd been plenty of freaks on hand to fill her shoes, so to speak.

Beneath the sleeting February sky, the hospital looked as dead as the day after Armageddon. I tried not to think about the spooch, all the things I'd seen and heard the day before, the things I'd felt, the desperate stream of threats and promises and prayers the crit had spewed at me when I'd finally come to the end of the shimmering aether pipeline and we'd started the dance.

Inside, the hospital stunk like a zoo, a dying, forgotten zoo, but at least I was out of the wind. My face and hands had gone numb. How would the Agency feel about a scrubber without his fingers? Would they toss me on the scrap heap, or would they just give me a shiny new set, made in Osaka, better than the originals? Maybe work a little of the biomech magic they'd worked on Sarah? I followed a long ground-floor hallway past doors and doorways without doors, pitch dark rooms and chiaroscuro rooms ruled by the disorienting interplay of shadow and light, until I came to a row of elevators. All the doors had been jammed more or less open at some point, exposing shafts filled with dust and gears and rusted cables. I stood there a while, as my fingers and lips began to tingle, the slow pins-and-needles thaw, and listened to the building whispering around me.

"They're all animals," Sarah had sneered the day before. But they weren't, of course, no more than she was truly a machine. I knew Sarah was bright enough to see the truth, even before they'd squeezed all that hardware into her skull. Even if she could never admit it to herself or anyone else. The cyborgs and H+ brigade were merely opposing poles in the same rebellion against the flesh—black pawn, white pawn—north and south on the same twisted post-evolutionary road. Not that it made much difference to me. It still doesn't. But standing there, my breath fogging and the feeling slowly returning to my hands, her arrogance was pissing me off more than usual. Near as I could tell, the biggest difference between Sarah and whatever was waiting for me in the bombed-out hospital that afternoon—maybe the only difference that actually mattered—was that the men and women in power had found a use for her kind, while the stitches and changelings had never been anything to them but a nuisance. It might have gone a different way. It might yet.

There was a stairwell near the elevators, and I climbed it to the third floor. I hadn't thought to bring a flashlight with me, so I stayed close to the wall, feeling my way through the gloom, stumbling more than once when my feet encountered chunks of rubble that had fallen from somewhere overhead.

On the third floor, the child was waiting for me.

"What do you want here?" he barked and blinked at me with the golden eyes of a predatory bird. He was naked, his skin hidden beneath a coat of fine yellow-brown fur.

"Who are you?" I asked him.

"The manticore said you were coming. She saw you on the bridge. What do you want?"

"I'm looking for a girl named Jet."

The child laughed, a strange, hitching laugh, and rolled his eyes. He leaned forward, staring at me intently, expectantly, and the vertical pupils of those big golden eyes dilated slightly.

"Ain't no *girls* here, Mister," he chuckled. "Not anymore. You skizzled or what?"

"Is there anyone here named Jet? I've come a long way to talk to her."

"You got a gun, maybe?" he asked. "You got a knife?"

"No," I said. "I don't. I just want to talk."

"You come out to Stitchtown without a gun *or* a knife? Then you must have some bangers, Mister. You must have whennymegs big as my fist," and he held up one clenched fist so I could see exactly what he meant. "Or you don't want to live so much longer, maybe."

"Maybe," I replied.

"Meat's scarce this time of year," the boy chuckled and then licked his thin ebony lips.

Down at the other end of the hallway, something growled softly, and the boy glanced over his shoulder, then back up at me. He was smiling, a hard smile that was neither cruel nor kind, revealing the sharp tips of his long canines and incisors. He looked disappointed.

"All in good time," he said and took my hand. "All in good time," and I let him lead me towards the eager shadows crouched at the other end of the hallway.

Near the end of his book, Emmanuel Weatherby-Jones writes, "The calamities following, and following from, the return of the IcePIC probe may stand as mankind's gravest defeat. For long millennia, we had asked ourselves if we were alone in the cosmos. Indeed, that question has surely formed much of the fundamental matter of the world's religions. But when finally answered, once and for all, we were forced to accept that there had been greater comfort in our former, vanished ignorance."

We are more alone than ever. Ronnie got that part right.

When I'd backed out of the contact and the techs had a solid lockdown on the critter's signal, when the containment waves were pinging crystal mad off the putrescent walls of the bedroom on Columbus and one of the medics had administered a stimulant to clear my head and bring me the rest of the way home, I sat down on the floor and cried.

Nothing unusual about that. I've cried almost every single time. At least I didn't puke.

"Good job," Templeton said and rested a heavy gloved hand on my shoulder.

"Fuck you. I could hear them. I could hear both of them, you asshole."

"We did what we could, Deet. I couldn't have you so tanked on morphine you'd end up flat lining."

"Oh my god. Oh Jesus god," I sobbed like an old woman, gasping, my heart racing itself round smaller and smaller circles, fried to a crisp on the big syringe full of synthetadrine the medic had pumped into my left arm. "Kill it, Temp. You kill it right this fucking instant."

"We have to stick to protocol," he said calmly, staring down at the writhing mass of bone and meat and protoplasm on the bed. A blood-red tendril slithered from the place where the man's mouth had been and began burrowing urgently into the sagging mattress. "Just as soon as we have you debriefed and we're sure stasis is holding, then we'll terminate life signs."

"Fuck it," I said and reached for his Beretta, tearing the pistol from the velcro straps of the holster with enough force that Temp almost fell over on top of me. I shoved him aside and aimed at the thing on the bed.

"Deet, don't you even fucking *think* about pulling that trigger!"

"You can go straight to Hell," I whispered, to Templeton, to the whole goddamn Agency, to the spooch and that single hurting blue eye still watching me. I squeezed the trigger, emptying the whole clip into what little was left of the man and woman's swollen skulls, hoping it would be enough.

Then someone grabbed for the gun, and I let them take it from me.

"You stupid motherfucker," Temp growled. "You goddamn, stupid bastard. As soon as this job is finished, you are *out*. Do you fucking understand me, Deet? You are *history*!"

"Yeah," I replied and sat back down on the floor. In the silence left after the roar of the gun, the containment waves pinged, and my ears rang, and the yellow fog settled over me like a shroud.

At least, that's the way I like to pretend it all went down. Late at night, when I can't sleep, when the pills and booze aren't enough, I like to imagine there was one moment in my wasted, chicken-shit life when I did what I should have done.

Whatever really happened, I'm sure someone's

already written it down somewhere. I don't have to do it again.

In the cluttered little room at the end of the third-floor hallway, the woman with a cat's face and nervous, twitching ears sat near a hole that had been a window before the mortars. There was no light but the dim winter sun. The boy sat at her feet and never took his eyes off me. The woman—if she had a name, I never learned it—only looked at me once, when I first entered the room. The fire in her eyes made short work of whatever resolve I had left, and I was glad when she turned back to the hole in the wall and stared north across the river towards the Astoria refineries.

She told me the girl had left a week earlier. She didn't have any idea where Jet Miyake might have gone.

"She brings food and medicine, sometimes," the woman said, confirming what I'd already suspected. Back then, there were a lot of people willing to risk prison or death to get supplies to Roosevelt Island. Maybe there still are. I couldn't say.

"I'm sorry to hear about her parents," she said.

"It was quick," I lied. "They didn't suffer."

"You smell like death, Mr. Paine," the woman said, flaring her nostrils slightly. The boy at her feet laughed and hugged himself, rocking from side to side. "I think it follows you. I believe you herald death."

"Yeah, I think the same thing myself sometimes," I replied.

"You hunt the aliens?" she purred.

"That's one way of looking at it."

"There's a certain irony, don't you think? Our world was dying. We poisoned *our* world and then went looking for life somewhere else. Do you think we found what we were looking for, Mr. Paine?"

"No," I told her. "I don't think we ever will."

"Go back to the city, Mr. Paine. Go now. You won't be safe after sunset. Some of us are starving. Some of our children are starving."

I thanked her and left the room. The boy followed me as far as the stairs, then he stopped and sat chuckling to himself, his laughter echoing through the stairwell, as I moved slowly, step by blind step, through the uncertain darkness. I retraced my path to the street, following Main to East, past the wild places, through the canyons, and didn't look back until I was standing on the bridge again.

I found Jet Miyake in Chinatown two days later, hiding out in the basement of the Buddhist Society of Wonderful Enlightenment on Madison Street. The Agency had files on a priest there, demonstrating a history of pro-stitch sentiment. Jet Miyake ran, because they always run if they can, and I chased her, down Mechanics Alley, across Henry, and finally caught up with her in a fish market on East Broadway, beneath the old Manhattan Bridge. She tried to lose me in the maze of kiosks, the glistening mounds of octopus and squid, eel and tuna and cod laid out on mountains of crushed ice. She headed for a back door and almost made it, but slipped on the wet concrete floor and went sprawling ass over tits into a big display of dried soba and canned chicken broth. I don't actually remember all those details, just the girl and the stink of fish, the clatter of the cans on the cement, the angry, frightened shouts from the merchants and customers. But the details, the octopus and soba noodles, I don't know. I think I'm trying to forget this isn't fiction, that it happened, that I'm not making it up as I go along.

Sometimes.

Sometimes I'm a savage.

I held the muzzle of my pistol to her right temple while I ran the scan. She gritted her teeth and stared silently up at me. The machine read her dirty as the gray New York snow, though I didn't need the blinking red light on the genetigraph to tell me that. She was hurting, the way only long-term carriers can hurt. I could see it in her eyes, in the sweat streaming down her face, in the faintly bluish tinge of her lips. She'd probably been contaminated for months. I knew it'd be a miracle if she'd infected no one but her parents. I showed her the display screen on the genetigraph and told her what it meant, and I told her what I had to do next.

"You can't stop it, you know," she said, smiling a bitter, sickly smile. "No matter how many people you kill, it's too late. It's been too late from the start."

"I'm sorry," I said, whether I actually was or not, and squeezed the trigger. The 9mm boomed like thunder in a bottle, and suddenly she wasn't my problem anymore. Suddenly she was just another carcass for the sweepers.

I have become an unreliable narrator. Maybe I've been an unreliable narrator all along. Just like I've been a coward and a hypocrite all along. The things we would rather remember, the things we choose to forget. As the old saying goes, it's only a movie.

I didn't kill Jet Miyake.

"You can't stop it, you know," she said. That part's the truth. "No matter how many people you kill, it's too late. It's been too late from the start."

"I'm sorry," I said.

"We brought it here. We invited it in, and it likes what it sees. It means to stay." She did smile, but it was a satisfied, secret smile. I stepped back and lowered the muzzle of the gun. The bore had left a slight circular impression on her skin.

"Please step aside, Mr. Paine," Sarah said, and when I turned around she was standing just a few feet behind me, pointing a ridiculously small carbon-black Glock at the girl. Sarah fired twice and waited until the body stopped convulsing, then put a third bullet in Jet Miyake's head, just to be sure. Sarah had always been thorough.

"Templeton thought you might get cold feet," she said and stepped past me, kneeling to inspect the body. "You know this means that you'll probably be suspended."

"She was right, wasn't she?" I muttered. "Sooner or later, we're going to lose this thing," and for a moment I considered putting a few rounds into Sarah's skull, pulling the trigger and spraying brains and blood and silicon across the floor of the fish market. It might have been a mercy killing. But I suppose I didn't love her quite as much as I'd always thought. Besides, the Agency would have probably just picked up the pieces and stuck her back together again.

"One day at a time, Mr. Paine," she said. "That's the only way to stay sane. One day at a time."

"No past, no future."

"If that's the way you want to look at it."

She stood up and held out a hand. I popped the clip from my pistol and gave her the gun and the ammo. I removed the genetigraph from my belt, and she took that, too.

"We'll send someone to the hotel for the rest of your equipment. Please have everything in order. You have your ticket back to Los Angeles."

"Yes," I said. "I have my ticket back to Los Angeles."

"You lasted a lot longer than I thought you would," she said.

And I left her there, standing over the girl's body, calling in the kill, ordering the sweeper crew. The next day I flew back to LA and found a bar where I was reasonably sure no one would recognize me. I started with tequila, moved on to scotch, and woke up two days later, facedown in the sand at Malibu, sick as a dog. The sun was setting, brewing a firestorm on the horizon, and I watched the stars come out above the sea. A meteor streaked across the sky and was gone. It only took me a moment to find Jupiter, Lord of the Heavens, Gatherer of Clouds, hardly more than a bright pin-prick near the moon.

# THE MONSTER FROM NOWHERE

## by Nelson Bond

*I'm fudging a bit here, since this* Thing *is not from the space beyond the Earth, but from a higher dimensional space—which I think is even more frightening, since it might be next to you and you wouldn't even be aware of it—until it was too late.*

**Nelson S. Bond** *(1908-2006) was a prolific writer for the pulps and, occasionally, for the "slick" magazines. Though his first SF story was "Down the Dimensions" in* Astounding Stories *in 1937,* Weird Tales *and* Fantastic Adventures *published more of his stories, though his most reliable market was the general pulp magazine,* Blue Book*. One of his most popular fantasy stories, "Mr. Mergenthwirker's Lobblies" became a radio series, was adapted for TV in 1957, and gave the title to one of his books of stories. The story combined SF and fantasy with slickly written humor. Another example of his humor was* *the series about spaceman Lancelot Biggs, who has improbable adventures in space, and keeps coming up with even more improbable improvisations to save the day. Another of Bond's humorous heroes was Pat Pending, a deranged inventor who nevertheless has his name, "Pat. Pending" on many household and office items. Bond's best-known story is probably "Conqueror's Isle," about an ordinary human who discovers a conspiracy of* Homo Superior *to take over the world, and ends up in an insane asylum run by one of the supermen. It is one of those stories with a great last line, which I will not repeat here. I first encountered it in a radio adaptation in the early 1950s, then later saw a TV adaptation as part of a series of SF stories (which included a Pat Pending adaptation, as well).*

*I'm sure that Mr. Bond was paid for* those *adaptations, but my first encounter with "The Monster from Nowhere" was through an adaptation for which I suspect no payment was made to Bond. It was in a comic book in the early 1950s and the story was somewhat altered, but still recognizable. Later on, I found that other stories which I had read in the same comic book, or one of its companions, were "adaptations" of Henry Kuttner's "Don't Look Now," Martin Gardner's "Thang," Henry Gregor Felson's "The Spaceman Cometh" (that one was in* Collier's; *they stole from the best), a Robert Sheckley story, and more. But enough about unprincipled funny-book publishers. Let's get back to good, honest* Things.

**ONE NICE THING** about the Press Club is that you can

get into almost any kind of wrangle you want. This night we were talking about things unusual. Jamieson of the *Dispatch* mentioned some crackpot he had heard of who thought he could walk through glass. "Snipe" Andrews of the *Morning Call* had a wild yarn about the black soul of Rhoderick Dhu, who, Nova Scotians claim, still walks the moors near Antigonish. The guy named Joe brought up the subject of Ambrose Bierce's invisible beast.

You remember the story? About the diarist who was haunted, and pursued, by a gigantic thing which couldn't be seen? And who was finally devoured by it?

Well, we chewed the fat about that one for a while and Jamieson said the whole thing was fantastic; that total invisibility was impossible. The guy named Joe said Bierce was right; that several things *could* cause invisibility. A complete absence of light, for one thing, he said. Or curvature of light waves. Or coloration in a wavelength which was beyond that of the human eye's visual scope.

Snipe Andrews said, "Nuts!" Winky Peters, who was getting a little tight, hiccoughed something to the effect that "There are more things under Heav'n and Earth than are dreamed of in your Philosophy—" and then got in a hell of a fuss with the bartender who said his name *wasn't* Horatio.

I said nothing, because I didn't know. Maybe that is the reason why this stranger, a few minutes later, moved over beside me and opened a conversation.

"You're Harvey, aren't you?" he asked.

"That's me," I agreed. "Len Harvey—chief errand boy and dirt scratcher-upper for the *Star Telegram*. You've got me, though, pal. Who are you?"

He smiled and said, "Let's go over in that corner, shall we, Harvey? It's quieter over there."

That made it sound like a touch, but I liked something about this guy. Maybe it was his face. I like tough faces; the real McCoy, tanned by Old Sol instead of sunlamp rays. Maybe it was the straightness of his back; maybe the set of his shoulders. Or it could have been just the way he spoke. I don't know.

Anyway, I said, "Sure!" and we moved to the corner table. He ordered, and I ordered, and we just sat there for a moment, staring at each other. Finally he said, "Harvey, your memory isn't so good. We've met before."

"I meet 'em all," I told him. "Sometimes they are driving Black Marias, and sometimes they're in 'em. Mostly, they're lying in the Morgue, with a pretty white card tied to their big toe. Or, maybe—Hey!" I said, "You're not Ki Patterson, who used to write for the Cincinnati *News?*"

He grinned then.

"No, but you're close. I'm Ki Patterson's brother, Burch."

"Burch Patterson!" I gasped. "But, hell—you're not going to get away with this!" I climbed to my feet and started to shout at the fellows. "Hey, gang—"

"Don't, Len!" Patterson's voice was unexpectedly sharp. There was a note of anxiety in it, too. He grabbed my arm and pulled me back into my seat. "I have very good reasons for not wanting anyone to know I'm back—yet."

I said, "But, hell, Burch, you can't treat a bunch of newspaper men like this. These guys are your friends."

Now that he had told me who he was, I could recognize him. But the last time I had seen him—the only time I had ever met him, in fact—he had been dressed in a khaki shirt and corduroy breeches and had worn an aviator's helmet. No wonder I hadn't known him in civvies.

I remembered that night, two years ago, when he and his expedition had taken off from Roosevelt Field for their exploration trip to the Maratan Plateau in upper Peru. The primary purpose of the trip had been scientific research. The Maratan Plateau, as you undoubtedly know, is one of the many South American spots as yet unexplored. It was Burch Patterson's plan to study the region, incidentally paying expenses *à la* Frank Buck, by "bringing back alive" whatever rare beasts city zoos would shell out for.

For a few weeks, the expedition had maintained its contact with the civilized world. Then, suddenly—that was all! A month . . . two months . . . passed. No word or sign from the explorers. The United States government sent notes to the Peruvian solons. Peru replied in smooth, diplomatic terms that hinted Uncle Sam would a damn sight better keep his nutsack adventurers in his own backyard. A publicity-seeking aviatrix ballyhooed fund for a "relief flight"—but was forbidden the attempt when it was discovered she had already promised three different companies to endorse their gasoline.

The plight of the lost expedition was a nine-days' wonder. Then undeclared wars grabbed page one. And the National Air Registry scratched a thin blue line through the number of pilot Burchard Patterson, and wrote after his name, "Lost."

But now, here before me in the flesh, not lost at all, but very much alive, was Burch Patterson.

I had so many questions to ask him that I began babbling like a greenhorn leg-man on his first job.

"When did you get back?" I fired at him. "Where's your crew? What happened? Did you reach the Plateau? And does anyone know you're—"

He said, "Easy, Len. All in good time. I haven't told anyone I'm back yet for a very good reason. Very good! As for my men—" He stared at me somberly. "They're dead, Len. All of them. Toland . . . Fletcher . . . Gainelle.

I was quiet for a moment. The way he repeated the names was like the tolling of a church bell. Then I began thinking what a wow of a story this was. I could almost see my name by-lining the yarn. I wanted to know the rest so bad I could taste it. I said, "I'm sorry, Burch. Terribly sorry. But, tell me, what made you come here tonight? And why all the secrecy?"

"I came here tonight," he said, "searching for someone I could trust. I hoped no one would remember my face—for it *is* changed, you know. I have something, Len. Something so great, so stupendous, that I hardly know how to present it to the world. Or even—if I should.

"I liked the way you kept out of that crazy argument a few minutes ago—" He motioned to the bar, where a new wrangle was now in progress "—because you obviously had an open mind on the subject. I think you are the man whose help and advice I need."

I said, "Well, that's sure nice of you, Patterson. But I think you're overrating me. I kept my yap shut just because I'm kind of dumb about scientific things. Ask me how many words to a column inch, or how many gangsters got knocked off in the last racket war, but—"

"You're the man I'm looking for. I don't want a man with a scientific mind. I need a man with good, sound common sense." He looked at his wrist watch. "Len—will you come out to my home with me?"

"When?"

"Now."

I said, "Jeepers, Burch—I've got to get up at seven tomorrow. I really shouldn't—"

He leaned over the table; stared at me intently.

"Don't stall, Len. This is important. Will you?"

I told you I was snoopy. I stood up.

"My hat's in the cloakroom," I said. "Let's go!"

Patterson's estate was in North Jersey. A rambling sort of place, some miles off the highway. It was easy to see how he could return to it, open it up, and still not let anyone know he had returned. As we drove, he cleared up a few foggy points for me.

"I didn't return to the States on a regular liner. I had reasons for not doing so—which you will understand in a short time. I chartered a freighter, a junky little job, from an obscure Peruvian port. Pledged the captain to secrecy. He landed me and my—my cargo—" he stumbled on the word for a moment "—at a spot which I'm not at liberty to reveal. Then I came out here and opened up the house.

"That was just two days ago. I wired my brother, Ki, to come immediately. But he—"

"He's working in L.A.," I said.

"Yes. The soonest he could get here would be tonight.

He may be at the house when we arrive. I hope so. I'd like to have two witnesses of that which I am going to show you."

He frowned. "Maybe I'm making a mistake, Len. It is the damnedest thing you ever heard of. Maybe I ought to call in some professor, too. But—I don't know. It's so utterly beyond credibility, I'd like you and Ki to advise me, first."

I said, "Well, what the hell is it, Burch?" Then I suddenly remembered a motion picture I'd seen some years ago; a thing based on a story by H.G. Wells. "It's not a—a monster, is it?" I asked. "Some beast left over from prehistoric ages?"

"No; not exactly. At least, I can assure you of *this*—it is not a fossil, either living or dead. It's a thing entirely beyond man's wildest imaginings."

I leaned back and groaned. "I feel like a darned kid," I told him, "on Christmas Eve. Step on it, guy!"

There were lights in the house when we got there. As Burch Patterson had hoped, Ki had arrived from California. He heard us pull up the gravel lane, and came to the door. There was a reunion scene; one of those back-clapping, how-are-you-old-fellow things. Then we went in.

"I found your note," Ki said, "and knew you'd be right back. I needn't tell you I'm tickled to death you're safe, Burch. But—why all the secrecy?"

"That's what I asked him," I said. "But he's not giving out."

"It's something," Ki accused, "about the old workshop behind the house. I know that. I was snooping around back there, and—"

Burch Patterson's face whitened. He clutched his brother's arm swiftly.

"You didn't go inside?"

"No. I couldn't. The place was locked. Say—" Ki stared at his brother curiously. "Are you feeling okay, guy? Are you sure you're not—"

"You must be careful," said Burch Patterson. "You must be very, very careful when you approach that shed. I am going to take you out there now, but you must stand exactly where I tell you to, and not make any sudden moves."

He strode to a library table, took out three automatics. One he tucked into his own pocket. The others he handed to us. "I'm not sure," he said, "that these would be any good if—if anything happened. But it is the only protection we have. You *might* be lucky enough to hit a vulnerable spot."

"A vulnerable spot!" I said. "Then it *is* a beast?"

"Come," he said. "I shall show you."

He led the way to the workshop. It lay some yards behind and beyond the house; a big, lonesome sort of place, not quite as large as a barn, but plenty big. My first idea was that at some time it must have been used as a barn, for as we approached it, I could catch that animal odor you associate with barns, stables, zoos.

Only more so. It was a nasty, fetid, particularly offensive odor. You know how animals smell worse when they get excited. Or when they've been exercising a lot? Well, the place smelled like that.

I was nervous, and when I get nervous I invariably try to act funny. I said, "If they're horses, you ought to curry them more often."

I saw a faint blur in the black before me. It was Ki's face, turning to peer back. He said, "Not horses, Len. We've never kept horses on this estate."

Then we were at the door of the shed, and Burch was fumbling with a lock. I heard metal click; then the door creaking open. Patterson fumbled for a switch. The sudden blaze of light made me blink.

"In here," said Burch. And, warningly, "Stay close behind me!"

We crowded in. First Burch, then Ki, then me. And as Ki got through the door, I felt his body stiffen; heard him gasp hoarsely. I peered over his shoulder—

Then I, too, gasped!

The thing I saw was incredible. There were two uprights of steel, each about four inches in diameter, deeply imbedded in a solid steel plate which was secured to a massive concrete block. Each of these uprights was "eyed"—and through the eyes ran a third steel rod which had been hammered down so that the horizontal bar was held firmly in place by the two uprights.

And on this horizontal rod was—a *thing!*

That is all I can call it. It had substance, but it had no form. Or, to be more accurate, it had every form of which you can conceive. For, like a huge, black amoeba, or like a writhing chunk of amorphous matter, it *changed!*

Where the steel rod pierced this blob of *thing* was a clotted, brownish excrescence. This, I think, accounted for some of the animal odor. But not all of it. The whole shop was permeated with the musty scent.

The *thing* changed! As I watched, there seemed to be, at one time, a globular piece of matter twisting on the rod.

An instant later, the globe had turned into a triangle—then into something remotely resembling a cube. It was constantly in motion; constantly in flux. But here is the curious part. It did not change shape slowly, as an amoeba, so that you could watch the sphere turn into an oblong; the oblong writhed into a formless blob of flesh. It made these changes instantaneously!

Ki Patterson cried, "Good God, Burch! What unholy thing is this?" and took a step forward, past his brother's shoulder.

Burch shouted, "Back!" and yanked at Ki's arm. He moved just in time. For as Ki quitted the spot to which he had advanced, there appeared *in the air* right over that spot, another mass of the same black stuff that was captured on the bar. A blob of shapeless, stinking matter that gaped like some huge mouth; then closed convulsively just where Ki had stood a moment before!

And now the fragment on the rod was really moving! It changed shape so rapidly; twisted and wriggled with such determination, that there was no doubt whatsoever about the sentiency governing it. And other similar blobs suddenly sprang into sight! A black pyramid struck the far wall of the shed, and trembling woodwork told that here was solid matter. An ebon sphere rose from nowhere to roll across the floor, stopping just short of us. Most weirdly of all, a shaft of black jolted down *through* the floor—and failed to break the flooring!

That's about all I remember of that visit. For Ki suddenly loosed a terrified yelp; turned and scrambled past me to the door. I take no medals for courage. He was four steps ahead of me at the portal, but I beat him to the house by a cool ten yards. Burch was the only calm one. He took time to lock the workshop door; then followed us.

But don't let anyone tell you *he* was exactly calm, either. His face wasn't white, like Ki's. Nor did his hand shake on the whisky-and-splash glass, like mine. But there was real fear in his eyes. I mean, *real* fear!

The whisky was a big help. It brought my voice back. "Well, Burch," I said, "we've seen it. Now, what in hell did we see?"

"You have seen," said Burch Patterson soberly, "the thing that killed Toland, and Fletcher, and Gainelle."

"We found it," said Burch, "on the Maratan Plateau. For we did get there, you know. Yes. Even though our radio went bad on us, just after we left Quiché, and we lost contact with the world. For a while, we considered going into Lima for repairs, but Fletcher thought he could fix it up once we were on solid ground, so we let it ride.

"We found a good, natural landing field on the Plateau, and began our investigations." He brooded silently for a minute. Then, reluctantly, "The Maratan is even richer in paleontological data than men have dared hope. But Man must never try to go there again. Not until his knowledge is greater than it is today."

Ki said, "Why? That *thing* outside?"

"Yes. It is the Gateway for that—and others like it. Someday, I will tell you all about the marvels we saw on the Plateau, but now my story concerns only one; the one you have seen.

"Fletcher saw it first. We had left Gainelle tending

camp, and were making a field survey, when we saw a bare patch in the jungle which surrounded our landing field. Fletcher trained his glasses on the spot, and before he even had time to adjust them properly he was crying, 'There's something funny over there! Take a look!'

"We all looked then. And we saw—what you saw a few minutes ago. Huge, amorphous blobs of jet black, which seemed to be of the earth, yet not quite of it. Sometimes these ever-changing fragments were suspended in air, with no visible support! At other times they seemed to rest naturally enough on solid ground. But ever and ever again—they changed!

"Afire with curiosity, we went to the open spot. It was a mistake."

"A mistake?" I said.

"Yes. Fletcher lost his life—killed by his own curiosity. I need not tell you how he died. It was, you must believe me, horrible. Out of nowhere, one of the jet blobs appeared before him . . . then around him . . . then, he was gone!"

"Gone!" exclaimed Ki. "You mean—dead?"

"I mean gone! One second he was there. The next, both he and the *thing* which had snatched him had disappeared into thin air.

"Toland and I fled, panic-stricken, back to camp. We told Gainelle what we had seen. Gainelle, a crack shot and a gallant sportsman, was incredulous; perhaps even dubious. At his insistence, we armed and returned to the tiny glade.

"This time, it was as if the *thing* expected us—for it did not await our attack. It attacked us. We had barely entered its domain when suddenly, all about us, were clots of this ever-changing black. I remembered hearing Toland scream, high and thin, like a woman. I dimly recall hearing the booming cough of Gainelle's express rifle, and of firing myself.

"I remember thinking, subconsciously, that Gainelle was a crack shot. That he never missed anything he aimed at. But it didn't seem to matter. If you hit one of those fleshy blobs, it bled a trifle—maybe. More likely than not, it changed shape. Or disappeared entirely.

"It was a rout. We left Toland behind us, dead, on the plain. A black, triangular *thing* had slashed Gainelle from breast to groin. I managed to drag him half way out of the glade before he died in my arms. Then I was alone.

"I am not a good pilot, under the best conditions. Now I was frantic; crazed with fear. Somehow I managed to reach the plane. But in attempting to take off, I cracked up. I must bear a charmed life. I was not injured, myself, but the plane was ruined. My expedition, hardly started, was already at an end."

I was beginning to understand, now, why Burch Patterson had not wanted the world to know of his return. A tale as wild and fantastic as this would lead him to but one spot—the psychopathic ward. Had I not seen the *thing* there in the shed, I would never have believed him myself. But as it was—

"And then?" I asked.

"I think there is a form of insanity," said Burch, "which is braver than bravery. I think that insanity came upon me then. All I could comprehend was that some *thing*—a *thing* that changed its shape—had killed my companions.

"I determined to capture that *thing*—or die in the attempt. But first I had to sit down and figure out what it *was!*"

Ki licked his lips. "And—and did you figure it out, Burch?"

"I think so. But the result of my reasoning is as fantastic as the *thing* itself. That is why I want the help and advice of you two. I will tell you what I think. Then you must say what it is best to do."

I poured another drink all around. It wasn't my house, or my liquor, but nobody seemed to mind. Ki and I waited for Burch to begin. Burch had picked up, and was now handling with a curiously abstract air, a clean, white sheet of notepaper. As he began, he waved this before us.

"Can you conceive," he said, "of a world of only two dimensions? A world which scientists might call 'Flatland'? A world constructed like this piece of paper—on which might live creatures who could not even visualize a third dimension of depth?"

"Sure," said Ki. I wasn't so sure, myself, but I said nothing.

"Very well. Look—" Burch busied himself with a pencil for an instant. "I draw on this sheet of paper, a tiny man. He is a Flatlander. He can move forward or backward. Up or down. But he can never move *out* of his world, into the third dimension, because he has no knowledge of a dimension angular to that in which he lives. He does not even dream of its existence."

I said, "I see what you mean now. But what has that to do with—"

"Wait, Len." Patterson suddenly struck the paper a

blow with one finger, piercing it. He held the sheet up for our inspection. "Look at this. What do you see?"

"A sheet of paper," I said, "with a hole in it."

"Yes. But what does the *Flatlander* see?"

Ki looked excited. "I get it, Burch! He sees an unexpected, solid object appear before him—out of nowhere! If he walks around this object, he discovers it to be crudely round!"

"Exactly. Now I push the finger farther through the hole—"

"The object expands!"

"And if I bend it?"

"It changes its shape!"

"And if I thrust another finger through Flatland—"

"Another strangely shaped piece of solid matter materializes before the Flatlander!" Ki's eyes were widening by the moment. I didn't understand why.

I said, "I told you I didn't have a scientific mind, Burch. What does all this mean?"

Burch said patiently, "I have merely been establishing a thought-pattern, Len, so you can grasp the next step of my reasoning. Forget the Flatlander now—or, rather, try to think of *us* as being in his place!

"Would we not, to a creature whose natural habitat is a higher plane than ours, appear much the same sort of projection as the Flatlander is to us?

"Suppose a creature of this higher plane projected a portion of himself into *our* dimension—as I projected my finger into Flatland. We would not be able to see *all* of him, just as the Flatlander could not see all of us. We would see only a tri-dimensional cross-section of him;

as the Flatlander saw a bi-dimensional cross-section of us!"

This time I got it. I gasped: "Then you think that *thing* in the work-shed is a cross-section of a creature from the—"

"Yes, Len. From the Fourth Dimension!"

Patterson smiled wanly.

"That is the decision I reached on the Maratan Plateau. There confronted me the problem of capturing the *thing.* The answer eluded me for weeks. Finally, I found it."

"It was—" Ki was leaning forward breathlessly.

"The Flatlander," said Burch, "could not capture my finger, *ever,* by lassoing it. No matter how tight he drew his noose, I could always withdraw my finger.

"But he *could* secure a portion of me, by fastening me to his dimension. Thus—" He showed us how a pin, laid flat in Flatland, could pierce a small piece of skin. "Now if this pin were bolted securely, the finger thus prisoned could not be withdrawn.

"That was the principle on which I worked, but my task had just begun. It took months to effect the capture. I had to study, from afar, the amorphous black *thing* which was my quarry. Try to form some concept of what incredible Fourth Dimensional beast would cast projections of that nature into the Third.

"Finally I decided that one certain piece of black matter, occurring in a certain relationship to the changing whole, was a foot. How, it is not important to tell. It was, after all, theory, coupled with guesswork.

"I constructed the shackle you have seen. Two

uprights, with a third that must pierce the *thing;* then lock upon it. I waited, then, many weeks. Finally there came a chance to spring my trap. And—it worked!"

Ki said, "And then?"

"The rest is a long and tiresome story. Somehow I found my way to a native village; there employed natives to drag my captive from the Plateau. We were handicapped by the fact that we could never get too near the trap. You see, it is a *limb* we have imprisoned. The head, or eating apparatus, or whatever it is, is still free. That is what tried to reach you, Ki, there in the shed.

"Anyway, we made an arduous trek to the coast. As I have told you, I chartered a vessel. The sailors hated my cargo, and feared it. The trip was not an easy one. But I was determined, and my determination bore fruit. And—here we are."

I said, "Yeah—here we are. Just like the man who grabbed a tiger by the tail; then couldn't let go. Now that you've got this *thing,* what are you going to do with it?"

"That's what I want you to tell me."

Ki's eyes were glowing. He said, "Good Lord, man, is there any question in your mind? Call in the scientists—the whole damned brigade of them! Show them this thing! You've got the marvel of the age on your hands!"

"And you, Len?"

"You want it straight?" I said. "Or would you like to have me pull my punches?"

"Straight. That's why I asked you out here."

"Then get rid of it," I said. "Kill it. Set it on fire. Destroy it. I don't know just how you're going to do it, but I do know that's the thing to do.

"Oh, I know what you're thinking, Ki—so shut up! I'm a dope. Sure. I'm ignorant. Sure. I don't have the mind or the heart of a true scientist. Okay—you win! But Burch said I had common sense—and I'm exercising it now. I say—get rid of that damned thing before something happens. Something horrible that you will regret for the rest of your life!"

Ki looked a little peeved. He said, "You're nuts, Len! The thing's tied down, isn't it? Dammit man—you're the kind of guy who holds back the progress of the world. I bet you'd have voted to kill Galileo if you'd been alive in his day."

"If he'd trapped a monster like this," I retorted, "a monster who'd already killed at least three men, I'd have voted just that way. I'm not superstitious, Burch. But I'm afraid. I'm afraid that when Man starts monkeying with the Unknown, he gets beyond his depth. I say—kill it, now!"

Burch looked at me anxiously.

"That's your last word, Len?"

"Absolutely my last," I said. I rose. "And just to prove it, I'm going home now. And I'm not even going to write a damned word about what I've seen tonight. I don't care if this is the best story since the Deluge—I'm not going to write it!"

Ki said, "You give me a pain, Len. In the neck."

"Same to you," I told him, "only lower down. Well, so long, guys." And I went home.

I kept my word. Though I had the mimsies all night, tossing and thinking about that crazy, changing black *thing,* I didn't put a word concerning it on paper. I half-expected to hear from Burch Patterson some time during the next day. But I didn't. Then, the following morning, I saw why. The *Call* carried a front-page blast, screaming to the astonished world the news that, "The missing explorer, Burch Patterson, has returned home," and that, "Tonight there will be a convocation of eminent scientists" at his home to view some marvel brought back from the wilds of upper Peru.

All of which meant that brother Ki's arguments had proven more persuasive than mine. And that tonight there was to be a preview of that damned *thing.*

I was pretty sore about it. I thought the least they could have done was give me the news beat on the yarn. But there wasn't any use crying over spilt milk. Anyway, I remembered that Ki's paper had a tie-up with the *Call.* It was natural he should route the story that way.

And then I went down to the office, and Joe Slade, the human buzz saw who calls himself our City Editor, waved me up to his desk.

"You, Harvey," he said. "I'm going to give you a chance to earn some of that forty per we're overpaying you. I want you to represent us tonight out at Patterson's home in Jersey. He's going to unveil something mysterious."

I said, "Who—me? Listen, chief, give it to Bill Reynolds, won't you? I've got some rewrites to do—"

"You, I said. What's the matter? Does New Jersey give you asthma?"

"Chief," I pleaded, "I can't cover this. I don't know anything about science or—"

"What do you mean—science?" He pushed back his

eyeshade and glared at me. "Do you know what this is all about?"

That stopped me. I didn't want to go, but if I ever admitted that I'd known about Patterson's changeable what-is-it, and not beaten the *Call* to the streets with the story, I would be scanning the want ads in fifteen seconds flat. So I gulped and said, "Okay, boss. I'll go."

Everybody and his brother was there that night. I recognized a professor of Physics from Columbia U., and the Dean of Paleontology from N.Y.U. Two old graybeards from the Academy of Natural History were over in a corner discussing something that ended in "-zoic", and the curator of the Museum was present, smelling as musty as one of his ancient mummies.

The Press was out in force. All the bureaus, and most of the New York papers. Ki was doing the receiving. Burch had not yet put in an appearance. I found a minute to get Ki aside, and told him what a skunky trick I thought he'd pulled on me, but he merely shrugged.

"I'm sorry, Len. But you had your chance. After all, I had to think of my own paper first." Then he smiled. "And besides, you were in favor of destroying the *thing.*"

"I still am," I told him dourly.

"Then what are you here for?"

It was my turn to shrug. "It was either come or lose my job," I said. "What do you think?"

Then Burch put in an appearance, and the whole outfit went genteelly crazy. Flash bulbs started blazing, and all my learned *confrères* of the Third Estate started shooting questions at him. About his trip, the loss of his comrades, his experiences. I knew all that stuff, so I just waited for the big blow-off to follow.

It came, at last. The moment when Burch said: "Before I tell my entire story, I prefer that you see that which I brought back with me," and he led the way out to the workshed.

Ki and Burch had fixed up the place a little; put chalk lines on the floor to show the visitors where they might stand.

"And I warn you," Burch said, just before he opened the shed door, "not to move beyond those lines. Afterward you will understand why."

Then the crowd began to file in. From my vantage point in the rear, I could tell when the first pair of eyes sighted that *thing*—and when every subsequent visitor saw it, as well. Gasps, exclamations, and little cries of astonishment rippled through the crowd as one by one they moved into the room.

The *thing* was still suspended on its imprisoning rod. As before, it was wriggling and moving; changing its shape with such rapidity that the human eye could scarcely view one shape before that turned into another. In view of what Burch had told me, I could comprehend the *thing* better now. I could understand how, if that black blob of flesh captured by the bar were *really*—as Burch presumed—a leg of some ultra-dimensional monster, the movements of that limb, as it sought to break free, would throw continually changing projections into our world.

I could understand, too, why from time to time we would see *other* bits of solid matter appear in various sections of the room. Though these seemed disassociated with that chunk hanging on the trap, I knew it was really separate portions of the same beast. Because if a *man* were to thrust four fingers, simultaneously into Flatland, to the Flatlander these would appear to be four separate objects; while in reality they were part of a single unit in a dimension beyond his powers of conception.

The astonishment of the professors was something to behold. I began to feel a little bit ashamed of myself, there in the background. Perhaps I had been wrong to give Burch the advice I had. Perhaps, as Ki had said, this was one of the greatest discoveries of all time. It belonged to the world of science.

One of the photographers was dropping to his knee, levelling his Graflex at the shifting, changing *thing* on the rod. I caught myself thinking, swiftly, "He shouldn't do that!" Evidently Burch had the same idea. He took a swift step forward; cried, "Please! If you don't mind—"

He spoke too late. The man's finger pressed. For an instant the room was flooded with light.

And then it happened. I heard a sound like a thin, high bleating that seemed to come from far, far away. Or it may not have been a sound at all in the true sense of that word. It may have been some tonic wave of supernal heights; for it tortured the eardrums to hear it.

The thing on the rod churned into motion. Violent motion. It grew and dwindled; shifted from cube to hemisphere; back to cube again. Then a truncated pyramidal form was throbbing, jerking, churning on the steel. Where I had once noticed an old, ugly, healed wound, ichor-clotted, now, I saw ragged edges of black break open. Saw a few, fresh gouts of brownish fluid well from what seemed to be raw edges in that changing black.

Burch's horrified voice rose above the tumult.

"Get out! Get out—all of you! Before it—"

That was all he found time to say. For there came a horrible, sucking sound, like the sound of gangrenous flesh tearing away; and where there had been a changing black shape swirling on an imprisoning steel rod—now there was nothing!

But with equal suddenness, several of the shapeless blobs of matter from various parts of the room seemed to rush together with frightful speed. Someone, screaming with terror, bumped against me then. I fell to my hands and knees in the doorway, feeling the flood of human fear scramble over me.

But not until I had seen a scimitar-shaped blob of black flesh reach out to strike at Ki Patterson. Ki had not even time to cry out. He went down, dead, as though stricken by the sickle of Chronos.

I cried, "Burch!"

Burch had turned to face the coalescing monster. A revolver in his hand was filling the little room with thunder. Orange gouts of flame belched from its muzzle; and I knew he was not missing. Still the thing was closing in on him. I saw what seemed to be four jet circles appear in a ring over the head of Burch Patterson. Saw the circles expand; and a wider expanse of black—flat and sinister—appear directly over his head. They came together with a clutching, enveloping movement. Then—he was gone!

Somehow I managed to struggle out of that work shed. Not that it made any difference. For with the disappearance of Burch Patterson, the *thing* itself disappeared.

I won't try to describe the frightened group of news men and scientists who gathered at the Patterson house. Who trembled and quaked, and offered fantastic reasons for that which had transpired. Who finally summoned up courage enough to return to the shed cautiously; seeking the mortal remains of Burch Patterson.

They never found anything, of course. Ki was there, but Ki was dead. Burch was gone. The air was still putrid with that unearthly animal stench. Beneath the steel "trap" Patterson had built for his *thing*, there was a pool of drying brownish fluid. One of the scientists wanted to take a sample of this for analysis. He returned to the house for a test-tube in which to put it . . .

Maybe it was the wrong thing for me to do. But I thought, then, that it was best. And I still think so. If he had taken that sample, made that analysis, sooner or later another expedition would have set out for the Maratan Plateau in search of that *thing* whose blood did not correspond to that of any known animal. I didn't believe this should happen. So, while he was gone, I set fire to the workshed. It was an old place; old and dry as tinder. By the time he had returned, it was a seething cauldron of flame. It made a fitting pyre for the body of Ki Patterson . . .

But—I don't know. I have wondered, since. Somehow, I have a feeling that Burch Patterson may not be dead, after all. That is—if a human can live in a dimension of which he cannot conceive.

The more I think of it, the more I try to reconcile that

which I saw with that which Burch told me; the more I believe that the thing which descended upon Burch, there in the shed, was not a "mouth"—but a gigantic paw! You know, I saw four circles appear . . . with a flat black spot above. It could have been four huge fingers . . . with the palm descending to grasp the daring tri-dimensional "Flatlander" who had the audacity to match wits with a creature from a superior world. If that be so . . . and if the *thing* were intelligent . . . Patterson might still be alive . . .

I don't know. But sometimes I am tempted to organize another expedition to the Maratan Plateau, myself. Try to learn the truth concerning the *thing* from beyond the Gateway. The truth concerning Burch Patterson's fate.

What would *you* do?

# SITTING DUCK

by Daniel F. Galouye

*Was he a smart duck . . . or a dead duck?*

**Daniel F. Galouye** *(1920-1976, and pronounced Gah-lou-ey) served in World War II as a Navy flight instructor and test pilot, and, according to one online source, piloted rocket planes. In the early 1950s, he became a journalist for a New Orleans newspaper,* The States-Item *,and also began writing SF stories, his first sale being "Rebirth" in the March 1952* Imagination. *In the 1950s and 1960s, he was widely published in such SF magazines as* Galaxy, The Magazine of Fantasy & Science Fiction, *and* If. *He published five novels, including* Dark Universe, *a massively esxpanded version of his story, "Rebirth," which was a Hugo Award finalist*, and Simulacron-3 *(published in the UK as* Counterfeit World*) which was very well adapted in the movie,* The Thirteenth Floor. *He eventually became* *an editor on the newpaper he had worked for as a reporter, but had to retire due to failing health as a result of injuries sustained in the war. In 2007, he was named the recipient of the Cordwainer Smith Rediscovery Award. His many short stories are certainly overdue for rediscovery, including this one.*

**THE SHIMMERING MOTE** dropped toward the plain to the east. Like a silver mirror, it captured the luster of the sinking sun and hurled it back sparkling toward the city.

A band of smudge-faced boys, their feet rooted in the dust of the play lot, stared at the point of scintillating brilliance.

Four women, poised before the entrance of a supermarket, strained to watch.

In the downtown district, a stock broker paused in mid-sentence as the reflection danced through the window. His client tensed, leaned forward for a better view.

For a long while the radiant mote hovered, soaking up the shadows of dusk that drifted from the surface like a mist. Then it dropped quietly, hiding itself in a subtle contour of the plain.

"Come on!" shouted a blond tyke as he retrieved the football. "We ain't got all night."

The women in front of the supermarket exchanged glances, then dispersed, three going on into the store while the fourth trundled off her cart of groceries.

Turning from the window, the broker thumbed through a stack of papers. "Here's an attractive investment . . ."

Hundreds closer to the site said the mote was a great sphere of gleaming metal. But when the first detachment of Guardsmen pushed across the plain hours later that Friday night, they found nothing—or practically nothing.

It was almost noon Saturday when Ray Kirkland ringed the hat rack with an underhanded toss and shrugged off his topcoat, together with the chill of the plain that clung to it like a clammy film. He was a large, thick-shouldered man with a blunt face and stout jaw.

Balston, the managing editor, laced him with a caustic eye. "You sure took your time getting back."

"Thought I'd try to squeeze a few more quotes out of Stoddard for the last edition," said Ray.

"Did the general find out where they dropped down?"

"As I said on the phone, they pinpointed it with Geiger counters. But, like in the first twelve landings, there weren't any other kinds of marks."

Balston, a tall, gaunt man with wiry graying hair, leaned back. "Did the general have any theories?"

Ray shrugged. "The usual. No cause for concern—would have acted by now—probably setting down to replenish water or oxygen."

The editor made a sound that was somewhat like a sarcastic grunt. "I suppose he didn't venture an opinion on why they have to land *close to cities* to get their water and oxygen?"

"No. But he did suggest they might be so superior

that they'd have nothing to gain by coming in contact with us."

Balston squinted quizzically.

"Stoddard," Ray explained, "put it this way: If one of our naval ships had to land on a primitive island to fill its water tanks, the crew wouldn't want to get involved socially with the savages."

The other chewed thoughtfully on a pencil. "At least that's a different line of speculation. Put your new lead on it for the final."

Ray started for his desk.

"Kirkland!" one of the reporters called. "Telephone—your father-in-law."

"That you, Ray boy?" the receiver rasped eagerly in his ear when he picked it up. "Drop by Clark's store and bring home a box of number five shells, will you?"

"Duck season doesn't open for another week," Ray reminded him, annoyed.

The old man laughed. "Nothing like being prepared. And don't forget, son—you're going out in the marsh with me tomorrow."

Ray slumped in the chair. He'd forgotten about the blind. A hell of a way to spend Sunday. And Alice would sulk if he didn't pamper the old boy.

At supper, his father-in-law sat across the table, half-hidden behind a mound of decoys that congregated around his plate as though it were a lush feeding pond.

"As I figure it," Ray was saying, "since all these landings were close to cities, there must be a purpose behind them *in connection with the cities.* There ought to be some tangible results. I'm sure if I looked close enough, I might find something that's different from what it was yesterday."

"But giving up your Sunday!" Alice exclaimed. "I won't have that! You do enough for that paper."

He hunched forward. "But think of the recognition I could get . . ." His voice trailed into silence as she merely shook her head.

The old man pushed a pair of dusky brown pintails out of the way and straightened with no small amount of resentment.

"Tomorrow's the only day we have to fix that blind, son," he said soberly, "if we're going to be ready for Saturday."

Ray cast him a glance of sullen hostility. "But don't you understand, Dad? There's been a landing near here and—"

"And try to get back from that swamp early, Raymond," Alice broke in. "There's a new house in the subdivision that may be just what we're looking for. It's on that corner lot—where you said you'd like to build."

Enheartened at the unexpected prospect of not having to spend his entire day in the swamp, he smiled gratefully.

But his smile changed to a puzzled frown. "There's no house on that corner."

"Of course there is, dear. A small Cape Cod. I walked past it at noon."

"It wasn't there when I drove by this morning," he insisted.

The existence or nonexistence of the Cape Cod

remained unsettled as Alice, disinterested, busied herself with gathering up the dishes.

Dad proudly picked up two green-winged teals with stupid blunt heads and stubby necks. He held one in each hand. "It'd take a darn smart duck to be suspicious of these, wouldn't it, son?"

Sunday in the marsh was particularly tedious and frustrating as Ray subordinated his professional interest in the reported landing to the whims of his father-in-law and paddled down a narrow waterway. The raucous squawks of the mallard hen, as produced by the old man's duck call, made the monotony no more endurable as they reached a pond adjoining the central lake.

A flock of sleek-headed canvasbacks hugged the northern edge of the pothole. The lead male, tense and alert, stretched his neck to keep a wary eye on the skiff.

Two females, preening themselves in the reeds along the shore, looked up in alarm.

Several of the younger ducks clustered uneasily, training their beady eyes alternately on the lead bird and the skiff as it glided through the slough into the lake.

When Ray glanced back over the top of the saw grass, the ducks had recovered from the intrusion.

The lead male was swimming among the others, as though reassuring them. The two hens on shore had returned nonchalantly to their preening. And the yearlings were dispersing from their cluster and spreading out boldly once more over the surface of the pothole.

Two of the larger males left the main group and swam

over to the clouded water where the skiff had passed. They glided in circles, inspecting the area curiously.

Ray paddled into the blind and helped his father-in-law onto the platform. But the structure was only half-concealed by the reeds they had used to camouflage it the year before.

The old man reached back into the boat and untied his bundle of tools, arranging a saw, hammer, pliers, and roll of wire on the platform.

The lead canvasback from the pothole was in the air now. Flying over the lake, he dipped down occasionally to touch the water and peer into clumps of saw grass.

"Damned drake's trying to see where we went," Dad said irately. "Wouldn't want him to get wise to our setup and louse things up for next Saturday."

The big duck rose higher, banked and came in directly over the blind, squawking stridently as it spotted the men.

Dad reared up from the sack of tools, clutching his twelve-gauge automatic. His florid face froze in an expression of delight as he swept the butt to his shoulder and sent the barrel arching past Ray's shoulder.

Instinctively, Ray hurled himself on the platform. The gun went off, its spread of number-five shot roaring by within searing range of his face.

"Got him!" the old man shouted exuberantly.

The shotgun blast was still a far-away buzzing in his ear as Ray drove up in front of the Cape Cod that afternoon. Surrounded by new shrubbery, it was a neat little bungalow that surveyed the freshly turned ground around it.

"See?" Alice said smugly. "I told you they built on this corner."

The sign next to the walk identified it as a product of Castle Estates, Inc., and announced that the four-kitchen, one-and-a-half-bedroom home was open for inspection.

Ray did a double-take. The sign *did* say "four kitchens."

"Wait here," he told Alice, still skeptical that a complete house could have been built in less than three days. "I'll see if the agent's inside."

At the entrance, he pushed the bell. But the button wouldn't budge. Defects, so soon?

He tried the buzzer again, gave it up, and knocked on the door. But with the first rap, his fist went *through* the oak paneling as though it were crisp cardboard.

Swearing, he tried to pull his hand from the shattered panel. The door came off at the hinges and folded over limply as it fluttered to the ground.

"For goodness *sake,* Raymond!" Alice called impatiently from the car. "What are you *doing?*"

Confounded, he entered.

But there was no inside to the house.

From the landing, he stepped down onto a mud floor with a sickly matting of brown, sun-starved grass. Overhead was the inverted "V" of the roof—no ceiling joists, no rafters. And the walls—it was as though they had been poured from a mold, with imperfections here and there in the form of raised ridges, like seepage seams from matrices that had failed to match evenly.

Tipping his hat up off his forehead, he walked around surveying the eviscerated house. Probably something new in prefabricated construction, he decided. Might bear looking into for a Sunday supplement yarn.

Backing toward the door, he started as something sharp nudged him in the side. He turned and almost knocked over a contraption he hadn't noticed before. Mounted on spindly legs, it resembled a surveyor's transit, with the telescope pointed through a window in the general direction of a row of ligustrum plants.

Interested, he inspected the thing, running his hand over its slick metal surface. His fingers touched a protuberance on the side of the cylinder and an almost inaudible, high-pitch humming erupted in his ear, crescendoed until it ended with an abrupt *click*.

He thrust his hands guiltily into his pockets, hoping he hadn't disturbed some delicate adjustment that might make a construction worker catch hell the next day.

Turning to leave, he almost tripped over something else he hadn't noticed previously—a wax-leafed ligustrum plant that lay on the mud floor, its roots shining and moist as though it had just been plucked from the soil.

Outside, as he strode toward Alice's impatient grimace, his eyes swept the row of ligustrums. There was a breach in the hedge where a vandal had no doubt uprooted the plant.

"Of course it isn't ours!" exclaimed August Sandifer, developer. "Castle Estates doesn't deal in cracker boxes! We have a motto: 'Every Castle-Built Home Is a Home-Built Castle' and . . ."

Ray eased the receiver farther from his ear. On his desk before him was spread the Monday morning mail edition with its story of the two new landings—one east of Denver and the other near San Diego.

"You mean you didn't build the Cape Cod?"

"It wasn't there Friday," Sandifer snapped. "It's there now. That's all I know about it."

"How do you suppose it got there?"

"One of those prefab outfits must have gotten their delivery addresses mixed. We've got the city permit division out there now. If they can't tell us who is responsible, we're going to put a match to the damned thing!"

Ray checked with the permit office before he sent out a photographer. Then he started in on the story, featurizing it heavily:

FOUND: House with 4 Kitchens

City officials and a local housing developer were stumped today over the enigma of a misplaced prefabricated house . . .

It rated a byline and a spot on the bottom of page one for the first street edition. Sample copies of the run were shuttled up from the press room just as Balston came in.

The managing editor settled down in his chair, spread the paper on his desk and promptly recoiled ceilingward, bellowing, "Kirkland! Come here!"

Ray went over uncertainly.

"You walked into this damned thing wide open!" Balston's eyes darted incriminatingly from the front page to Ray. "Don't you know a promotion trick when you see one?"

"It's no publicity stunt," Ray objected. "Sandifer didn't come to us. I went—"

Exasperated, Balston brushed him aside. "Hawkins!" he shouted at the city editor. "Get that thing out of the paper and find something legitimate for Kirkland to do!"

"Ray," one of the reporters called from a rear desk. "Sandifer's on the phone again. Says that house is gone—and two of his agents with it."

The managing editor shot up and spun around. "Tell him to peddle his promotion stuff somewhere else!"

Ray went over to the city editor's desk.

"I didn't think he'd take it that way," Hawkins sympathized. "Check this out for a possible human interest angle."

He reached into the assignment book and selected a classified ad clipping:

FOR SALE, CHEAP: *One giant mutated sea horse, complete with harness and aqua-sled. Apply Dr. Whitmore Vandell, Rt. 4, Sand Beach.*

The advertisement, whatever its purpose, had drawing power, Ray conceded as he turned off the highway toward the dumpy white frame structure that squatted half in the water like a centipede on its creosoted pilings. There were three cars parked randomly on a level area a short distance from the beach house. A fourth was throwing up a dust barrage on the road ahead of him.

By the time he drew up next to the newly arrived

vehicle, its driver was threading his way among boulders and scrubby growth toward the house. Ray sat in the car and traced the man's progress along the path—behind a rock, across a sandy stretch, behind a bush . . .

There was the annoying, high-pitch buzzing of a mosquito in his ear and he fanned the air to chase it away. His eyes, however, remained on the last bush behind which the man had disappeared. A minute passed and still he hadn't emerged.

Curious, Ray started down the path, keeping the bush and house in sight. But when he reached the spot where the man should have been, he wasn't there.

Tense and suspicious, he stood staring hesitantly at the house. His shadow was an almost black patch on the intensely white sand. The muffled sound of surf on rock was a subdued whisper. In the distance, a gull circled above the water, wailing plaintively.

An abrupt movement beyond a window on his right attracted his attention. Through the pane he saw a small, tubular object resembling a compact telescope on a tripod. It was a duplicate of the transitlike instrument in the window of the Cape Cod!

The tube swiveled in his direction and he squinted to make out the shadowy form that lurked behind it—something huge, not human. Thin, jointless arms extended from a rotund and scaly gray torso to coil like tendrils around the transit. An even more bulbous head swung around with the instrument, following him as he backed away from the house in fright. If there were eyes in that head, they were hidden in a mass of scales and lesser tendrils.

Bristling with fear, he remembered the transit in the Cape Cod and the high-pitched humming it had produced when he touched the tube. It was a sound suspiciously similar *to* the buzzing of the mosquito he had heard only minutes earlier—*at the same time the man had vanished from behind the bush!*

The telescope steadied on him and he whirled and raced toward the nearest boulder, skirting a clump of bushes and flushing a startled seagull from concealment behind the foliage. The humming sounded again and the bush disappeared, as though it had been uprooted and flung out of sight at a speed too fast for the eye to follow. Gone too was the gull in mid-flight.

He dived behind the rock, remembering the ligustrum he had almost stumbled over in the Cape Cod. Now he was *certain* the plant hadn't been there before he touched the transit!

The high-pitched note wailed again and he felt the rock vibrate before him. Apprehensively, he pressed closer against the boulder. Some of it made sense now. He had suggested looking for a purpose behind the landing, scouting for effects that hadn't existed before. Was this—and the Cape Cod, too—part of those effects?

"Help me! Please help me!"

He started. The cry had come from the house. One of the windows on the side was open and a young woman in a torn dress, her face streaked with terror, leaned half-out, screaming.

"Jump!" he called. "Run along the beach! They've got the thing pointed *this* way!"

Her slim white hands gripped the sill, but she only stared frantically at him, paralyzed with terror.

"Help me! Please help me!"

He seized a rock and hurled it at the transit in the front window. It went wild, crashing against the house. The second hurtled through the window but missed also. The third hit the tube squarely and it toppled out of sight.

Bolting around to where the girl was, he seized her arm and hauled her over the sill.

"Help me! Please help me!"

He grabbed her hand to race away, but she almost collapsed. He slung her over his shoulder, running along the bluff and leaping into a gully that shielded them from the house.

Climbing out of the shallow ravine at a point close to his car, he set her on the ground. She swayed, then steadied. But there was only panic on her face.

"Help me! Please help me!" Her eyes were focused beyond him and her cries were unchanged from the first time he had heard them.

Suddenly confounded, he backed away. The girl only stood there, repeating her desperate plea. Then he saw the rough ridge that ran from her temple, along her cheek, neck, and shoulder and down the outside of her arm—like imperfections in an object cast from a matrix.

Sickened and horrified, he reeled back to the car.

Her unvarying cries followed him as her lips moved, but too methodically and not in synchronization with the words.

He sent the car plunging up the dirt road toward the highway. When he looked back, the girl wasn't there any longer—nor were the other four cars and the beach house.

But there *was* something else, speeding above the road behind him—a vague symmetrical shadow, like the merest suggestion of an oval-shaped cloud.

He reached the highway and swerved recklessly into the stream of traffic. Through his rearview mirror, he watched the patch of dense haze pause at the intersection, as though confused. Then it turned and streaked off southward, gaining altitude. In its path, perhaps ten miles away, a fragment of silver glistened radiantly in the sky.

Ray pounded his fist on the managing editor's desk. "Sure I came straight back here. You think this is the kind of thing you go chat with Chief Johnson about?"

"So you came here instead, expecting to find me less skeptical?" Balston demanded.

Ray bent over tensely. "Don't you see? The Cape Cod, the beach house, the landing, the ad in the paper—they're all connected! And there are other ads that look phony. Check the paper. You'll see them."

The managing editor sat up. "Look, Kirkland. How'd you like to take a day or two off?"

"You don't believe me!"

A half-dozen staff members, crowded around them, dispersed respectfully. Across the room, Hawkins hunched busily over the city desk, not doing a very good job of pretending to be preoccupied. He sighed gratefully as the phone rang and he had to answer it.

"The Cape Cod, the beach house," Ray went on, "don't you see they're traps—devices to lure people within range of those things? This may be happening all over!"

"Why *lure* people?" Balston asked. "If they're as advanced as you're implying, they shouldn't have to use deception."

"I don't pretend to have all the answers. I'm just telling you what I know. It's your job to see that the facts get to the public."

The city editor replaced his phone on the hook. "State Police Headquarters," he called over, "says there's no beach house out there."

Ray spread his hands. "I told you that when I came in. Didn't the Cape Cod disappear, too—after Sandifer and I found out it was just a blind?"

Balston rose and gripped his shoulder. "Take the rest of the week off. A good rest—"

Ray shrugged out from under the other's hand. "Oh, for God's sake!"

"You admit you've been scouting around *looking* for unusual things resulting from the so-called landing?"

"So I've found them!"

"What? Scaly creatures with gooseneck arms?" There was no laughter in Balston's voice. But it was heavily implied.

"What'll you do when people start turning up missing?"

"We have never been a sensational newspaper," the managing editor said, "and we don't intend to create panic now. So don't be difficult, Kirkland. Take a week off, then see how you feel."

Hands thrust dejectedly in his pockets, Ray trudged toward the parking lot. Ahead, a crowd jammed the sidewalk in front of a gaudily decorated department store that flew a festooned banner:

IS KOSTLEMAN KRAZY? BIGGEST SAIL OF ALL!
Lesser pennants advertised: 21-Ounce Telavideo—$13.95! Combination Washer-Shaver—$13.66! Bicycle—$2.19; Tricycle—$3.77; Quadricycle—$5.98!

Drifting slowly up from the roof of the building were two of the almost indiscernible patches of dark haze. A third was descending. Squinting, he located the speck of silver that hung steady overhead, almost lost in the blue.

He pushed into the wedge that was pouring in through the main entrance.

"Wait!" he shouted, arms upraised. "Don't go in! They'll kill you!"

The man pressing against him laughed. "You crazy? This is a publicity stunt."

"What won't they think of next!" the woman next to him exclaimed, smiling.

Abysmally, Ray thought of a vast formation of ducks flying high over a blind occupied by a persistent caller . . . several of the hens wavering in flight, impatient to set down among the decoys . . . the irate lead drake seeing through the phony setup and quacking his alarm . . . the other birds ignoring his warning and peeling off to plunge to the destruction that waited below.

Caught up in the tide of eager bargain-seekers, he was swept into the store and deposited in a long aisle where a young couple stood examining a console television set. The man propped his elbow on top of the cabinet and his arm promptly plunged right through the paneling. Confounded, he backed away.

The buzzing sound of the transit was barely audible as man and wife vanished.

Backing away fearfully, Ray saw the metal tube and its tripod—high on a shelf against the wall. To the left, flanking the next row, was another; to the right, a third.

The faint humming sounded again—and again—and again.

He turned and bolted for the entrance. But the press of the crowd was too great, so he lunged for the back of the store. At the end of the aisle, he swerved to race along the wall looking for another exit. But be tripped over a carton and his impetus carried him headlong into the rear wall—*through* the wall—as easily as his fist had gone through the door of the Cape Cod!

He regained his feet in a darkened room and stood staring terrified at a huge scaly thing like the one he had seen in the window of the beach house. A transit, its collapsed tripod gripped in the coil of a gooseneck arm, was slung over a protuberance that might have been a shoulder. Its other tendril was wrapped tightly around the necks of a lifeless man and three women who hung in a cluster.

The thing tensed and faded into an almost indiscernible shadow, only the transit remaining visible. Then the instrument swung toward Ray.

He lunged for the sidewall, diving through it as though it were made of papier-mache. The alley outside, however, was narrow and the force of his sprawling leap sent him crashing into the brick wall of the next building.

Dazed, he rose shaking his head and staggered toward the sidewalk. But he pulled up sharply, cringing against the wall. Farther down the alley, an area of shadow seemed to be striving for materialization. It drifted on toward him.

He lurched out onto the sidewalk and melted inconspicuously into the stream of shoppers. When he paused a block away to look back, there was no sign of the vague oval shadow.

Then he thought suddenly of Alice and sprinted for the parking lot. God, they might throw up a booby trap *anywhere*—even in his own neighborhood!

While racing home, his suspicions were twice verified . . . A man whose motions were too mechanical stood on the roof of a supermarket tossing down dollar bills; but the throng below was too preoccupied to notice a woman on the very edge of the crowd vanish, a delivery boy go next. Closer to home, a theater which he was sure hadn't been there two days earlier offered free admission for the first showing of "Marriln Monrow" in *Bus Halt*.

He jolted the car to a stop in the carport and swept in through the kitchen door.

His father-in-law sat at a table honing a hunting knife. "Home early today, ain't you, son?"

"Where's Alice?" Ray asked frantically.

The old man brushed three decoys out of the way to make more room for the sweep of his hand over the stone. "At the neighbor's . . . You suppose we ought to spend Friday night at the lodge?"

Ray hunched over the table. "Dad, how smart are ducks?"

"Too danged smart sometimes. Take that big canvasback I shot down over the blind—"

"I mean do they ever get wise to our decoys, our blinds?"

"Damned right." His father-in-law ran a thumb delicately over the edge of the blade. "Some of 'em know what a gun means, too."

"Do they *all* go for a duck call?"

"A good caller can fool any duck, no matter how smart it is."

"Alice!" Ray said in fright. "Dad, we've got to find her!"

"Why so excited?" She stepped in from the dining room and deposited a partly embroidered tablecloth next to the decoys.

He started for her, but the phone rang and he crossed over to the extension to answer it first.

"For God's sake, get the hell back here!" It was Balston. "You were right. People are missing all over!"

"I'm on my way." Ray slammed the receiver down and grabbed his hat.

"Why so excited?" Alice asked again.

"Don't go outside!" he ordered. "There's no time to explain. But stay in the house till you hear from me!"

The old man followed him to the door. "Don't get tied up this weekend. The season starts Saturday, you know."

Ray paused, half in the car. "I'm afraid it's already started."

Alice's strained voice floated after him. "Why so excited?"

He was halfway down the drive when he tensed and

jammed on the brakes, realizing Alice had bogged down on the phrase, "Why so excited?"—just as the woman-thing at the beach house had on her plea for help.

Then he saw the patch of haze hovering ominously above the house, casting an even more tenuous shadow over his car. Paralyzed, he sat there gripping the wheel.

Alice stumbled awkwardly out of the kitchen door. Through the windshield, he watched her turn clumsily toward him. She came forward in a halting stride—*but her feet weren't even touching the pavement!*

Her shoulder struck a post of the carport and she tottered momentarily, then keeled over, falling against the side of the house. One of her arms snapped off neatly along a shoulder seam and rolled grotesquely down the driveway. She lay on her side, her legs continuing to pump uninterrupted in their walking motion, like an overturned mechanical doll.

Gears clashed as he sent the car lurching back into the street, then plunging forward toward the business district.

The woman-thing at the beach-house hadn't been a personalized decoy, but this Alice-thing had. That could mean only that they were now after him *specifically!*

Why? Because he had discovered their pattern of blinds and ruses? Because he had exposed it partially through the article on the Cape Cod? Had intruded and escaped at the beach house and again at the department store?

Of course that was it! He had the knowledge to reveal in detail what was happening. And unless they eliminated him—just as his father-in-law had eliminated the canvasback that had discovered the blind—he could ruin *their* sport!

The whole concept was vast and appalling. Sportsmen from who only knew how far away, finding a spot teeming with what to them was only game, descending and setting up their blinds, preparing their decoys, perfecting their human calls . . .

An oval shadow darkened the surface of the street behind him and he leaned out the window to glance up. The thing that had been over the house was following—overtaking him!

The pressure *was* on him personally now, just as earlier it had been on the lead duck in the swamp! But there was a way he could escape! If he succeeded in alerting the flock—if he got his story in print and had the wire services pick it up and carry it all over—there would no longer be any point in eliminating him. And he would then have just as good a chance as the rest of the game!

But the symmetrical haze was already maneuvering in position over the car.

He whipped the wheel around and careened into an alleyway, hurled the door open and dived out. He hit the asphalt surface at a speed too great for his legs to take and rumbled over, rolling into the recessed freight entrance of the building on the left.

The shadow clouded the alley as his car crashed into the other building. Then the car vanished and the shadow went away.

Minutes later, after the pain had subsided in the abrasion burns along his forearm and thigh, he crept out to the street and continued groggily toward the newspaper office. He was fighting mad.

Balston looked up impatiently as he entered the newsroom. "For God's sake! Get it down on paper—quick!"

At his desk, Ray sat motionless for a moment, arranging his mental notes before beginning the story. He stared around the room. No shadows—not yet, at least.

Hawkins was hunched over his desk reading copy. Two reporters were busy taking calls over the telephone. The staccato of the clacking keys in the glass-enclosed teletype room was a muffled distraction that plucked annoyingly at his concentration.

Finally, the lead of the story began taking form in his mind and he squared away in front of the typewriter.

"Get it down on paper—quick!" Balston broke in impatiently on his thoughts.

He ran a sheet of paper through the roller and began knocking out the story.

"For God's sake! Get it down on paper—quick!"

Ray froze with his hands poised above the keyboard. He pivoted slowly toward Balston. From his position, he could see behind the managing editor's desk . . .

Balston existed from the waist up only. From there down, a slim pedestal held him upright.

And the shadows were in the newsroom. He could see them now—one in the far corner close to the ceiling, another behind the glass in the teletype room, a third hovering behind the immobile Hawkins at the city desk.

And the transits were there too—one half-hidden in back of the water cooler, the tube of another protruding from behind the copy desk, still another poking out above Hawkins' shoulder. They all swung around slowly, carefully focusing on him.

None of the other blinds had worked, he realized, and remembered what his father-in-law had said: "A good caller can fool any duck, no matter how smart it is." And then he heard the first note of the high-pitched whine.

# THE MIND SPIDER

## by Fritz Leiber

*It had been imprisoned on Earth for countless eons, if not before the planet even existed. Now that it had awakened, and found that humans had evolved, it finally had a chance to be let out—to destroy them.*

**Fritz Leiber** *(1910-1992)—whose name is pronounced* Lie-bur, *not* Lee-bur, *incidentally—was an expert fencer, a champion chess tournament player, and an actor, but fortunately for us all, he was also very much a master craftsman of a writer. He may lately be best known for his marvelous stories of those heroes/scalawags, Fafhrd and the Gray Mouser, paragons of the fantasy subgenre of sword and sorcery (a term which Leiber coined, incidentally), but recently several collections of his short stories have resurfaced in both trade paperback and e-book editions, and Leiber's talent for fantasy, horror, and (of course) science fiction is once again on display, in*

Smoke Ghost & Other Apparitions; Horrible Imaginings; The Black Gondolier; Strange Wonders; Day Dark, Night Bright; *and I am grateful to John Pelan for his role in getting those story collections into print, in spite of his deserving a pie in the face for his, ah,* intemperate *remarks about Robert A. Heinlein in one of his introductions. Heinlein and Leiber had very different politics, but Heinlein obviously appreciated his colleague, dedicating one of the best of his celebrated YA novels,* Citizen in Space, *to Leiber.*

*Neither urban fantasy nor the modern horror field would likely be the same if he hadn't written "Smoke Ghost" in 1941 and the novel* Conjure Wife *in 1943. His skill for satire has also shown up in all three fields, as in "Coming Attraction" (1950), "A Bad Day for Sales" (1953), "The Night He Cried" (1953), or "The Last Letter," (1958). Though the rise of e-mail has made the future of the latter story less likely, it is brilliantly written and still has bite. His satirical talent works at longer lengths, too, as in 1968's* A Spectre is Haunting Texas, *one of his too-few novels. (The title, incidentally, is a switch on the first line of* The Communist Manifesto*—very sneaky.) His other novels include another satirical novel,* The Silver *Eggheads; the Hugo-winning* The Wanderer; *another award-winner, his horror novel,* Our Lady of Darkness; The Green Millennium *(in which a green cat saves the world); another Hugo-winner,* The Big *Time; and my own favorite,* Gather, Darkness.*He was the last young writer to engage in a voluminous correspondence with H. P. Lovecraft (and I wonder what he would think of the World Fantasy Convention's recent disavowal of HPL as* *the image of their annual awards) and was one of John Campbell's legendary stable of writers for* Astounding *and* Unknown. *He won a total of five Hugo Awards, and three Nebula Awards, as well as other awards, and in 1981, The Science Fiction and Fantasy Writers of America made him a Grand Master. Centipede Press has recently kicked off its Masters of Science Fiction series by releasing a massive (though pricey) volume of his SF short stories edited by John Pelan which will be followed by a similar volume of his fantasy stories. There's plenty of Leiber out there now, so get busy and discover or re-discover a giant of the SF field. In the meantime, here's Leiber's* Thing *story, in which the eponymous cosmic menace faces a very unusual family, about whom I wish Mr. Leiber had written several more stories.*

**HOUR AND MINUTE** hand of the odd little grey clock stood almost at midnight, Horn Tune, and now the second hand, driven by the same tiny, invariable radioactive pulses, was hurrying to overtake them. Morton Horn took note. He switched off his book, puffed a brown cigarette alight, and slumped back gratefully against the saddle-shaped forcefield which combined the sensations of swansdown and laced rawhide.

When all three hands stood together, he flicked the switch of a small black cubical box in his smock pocket A. look of expectancy came into his pleasant, swarthy face, as if he were about to receive a caller, although the door had not spoken.

With the flicking of the switch a curtain of brainwave static surrounding his mind vanished. Unnoticed while present, because it was a meaningless thought-tone—a kind of mental grey—the vanishing static left behind a great inward silence and emptiness. To Morton it was as if his mind were crouched on a mountain-peak in infinity.

"Hello, Mort. Are we first?"

A stranger in the room could not have heard those words, yet to Mort they were the cheeriest and friendliest greeting imaginable—words clear as crystal without any of the air-noise or bone-noise that blurs ordinary speech, and they sounded like chocolate tastes.

"Guess so, Sis,"' his every thought responded, "unless the others have started a shaded contact at their end."

His mind swiftly absorbed a vision of his sister Grayl's studio upstairs, just as it appeared to her. A corner of the work table, littered with air-brushes and cans of dye and acid. The easel, with one half-completed film for the multi-level picture she was spraying, now clouded by cigarette smoke. In the foreground, the shimmery grey curve of her skirt and the slim, competent beauty of her hands, so close—especially when she raised the cigarette to puff it—that they seemed his own. The feathery touch of her clothes on her skin. The sharp cool tingly tone of her muscles. In the background, only floor and cloudy sky, for the glastic walls of her studio did not refract.

The vision seemed a ghostly thing at first, a shadowy projection against the solid walls of his own study. But as the contact between their minds deepened, it grew more real. For a moment, the two visual images swung apart and stood side by side, equally real, as if he were trying to focus one with each eye. Then for another moment his room became the ghost room and Grayl's the real one—as if he had become Grayl. He raised the cigarette in her hand to her lips and inhaled the pleasant fumes, milder than those of his own rompe-pecho. Then he savored the two at once and enjoyed the mental blendfag of her Virginia cigarette with his own Mexican "chestbreaker."

From the depths of her . . . his . . . their mind Grayl laughed at him amiably.

"Here now, don't go sliding into all of me!" she told him. "A girl ought to be allowed some privacy."

"Should she?" he' asked teasingly

"Well, at least leave me my fingers and toes! What if Fred had been visiting me?

"I knew he wasn't," Morton replied. "You know, Sis, I'd never invade your body while you were with your non-telepathic sweetheart."

"Nonsense, you'd love to, you old hedonist!—and I don't think I'd grudge you the experience—-especially if at the same time you let me be with your lovely Helen! But now please get out of me. Please, Morton."

He retreated obediently until their thoughts met only at the edges. But he had noticed something strangely skittish in her first reaction. There had been a touch of .hysteria in even the laughter and banter and certainly in the final plea. And there had been a knot of something like fear under her breastbone. He questioned her about it Swiftly as the thoughts of one person, the mental dialogue spun itself out.

"Really afraid of me taking control of you, Grayl?"

"Of course not, Mort! I'm as keen for control-exchange experiments as any of us, especially when I exchange with a man. But . . . we're so exposed, Mort—it sometimes bugs me."

'How do you mean exactly?"

"You know, Mort. Ordinary people are protected. Their minds are walled in from birth, and behind the walls it may be stuffy but it's very safe. So safe that they don't even realize that there are walls . . . that there are frontiers of mind as well as frontiers of matter . . . and that things can get at you across those frontiers."

"What sort of things? Ghosts? Martians? Angels? Evil spirits? Voices from the Beyond? Big bad black static-clouds?" His response was joshing. "You know how flatly we've failed to establish any contacts in those directions. As mediums we're a howling failure. We've never got so much as a hint of any telepathic mentalities save our own. Nothing in the whole mental universe but silence and occasional clouds of noise—static—and the sound of distant Horns, if you'll pardon the family pun."

"I know Mort, but we're such a tiny young cluster of mind, and the universe is an awfully big place and there's a chance of some awfully queer things existing in it. Just yesterday I was reading an old Russian novel from the Years of Turmoil and one of the characters said something that my memory photographed. Now where did I tuck it away?—No, keep out of my files, Mort! I've got it anyway—here it is."

A white oblong bobbed up in her mind. Morton read the black print on it.

"We always imagine eternity (it said) as something beyond our conception, something vast, vast! But why must it be vast? Instead of all that, what if it's one little room, like a bathhouse, in. the country, black and grimy and spiders in every corner, and that's all eternity is? I sometimes fancy it like that."

"Brrr!" Morton thought, trying to make the shiver comic for Grayls sake. "Those old White and Red Russkies certainly had, black mindsl Andreyev? Dostoyevsky?"

"Or Svidrigailov, or some name like that. But it wasn't the book that bothered me. It was that about an hour ago I switched off my static box to taste the silence and for the first time in my life I got the feeling there was something nasty and alien in infinity and that it was watching me, just like those spiders in the bathhouse. It had been asleep for centuries but now it was waking up. I switched on my box fast!"

"Ho-ho! The power of suggestion! Are you sure that Russian wasn't named Svengali, dear self-hypnosis-susceptible sister?"

"Stop poking fun! It was real, I tell you."

"Real? How? Sounds like mood-reality to me. Here, stop being so ticklish and let me get a dose-up."

He started mock-forcibly to explore her memories, thinking that a friendly mental roughhouse might be what she needed, but she pushed away his thought-tendrils with a panicky and deathly-serious insistence. Then, he saw her decisively stub out her cigarette and he felt a sudden secretive chilling of her feelings.

"It's all really nothing, Mort," she told him briskly. "Just a mood, I guess, like you say. No use bothering a family conference with a mood. no matter how black and devilish."

"Speaking of the devil and his cohorts, here we are! May we come in?" The texture of the interrupting thought was bluff and yet ironic, highly individual—suggesting not chocolate but black coffee. Even if Mort and Grayl had not been well acquainted with its tone and rhythms, they would have recognized it as that of a third person. It was as if a third dimension had been added to the two of their shared mind. They knew it immediately.

"Make yourself at home. Uncle Dean." was the welcome Grayl gave him. "Our minds are yours."

"Very cozy indeed," the newcomer responded with a show of gruff amusement. "I'll do as you say, my dear. Good to be in each other again." They caught a glimpse of scudding ragged clouds patching steel-blue sky above to grey-green forest below—their uncle's work as a ranger kept him up in his flyabout a good deal of the day.

"Dean Horn coming in," he announced with a touch of formality and then immediately added, "Nice tidy little mental parlour you've got, as the fly said to the spider."

"Uncle Dean!—what made you think of spiders?" Grayl's question was sharply anxious.

"Haven't the faintest notion, my dear. Maybe recalling the time we took turns mind-sitting with Evelyn until she got over her infant fear of spiders. More likely just reflecting a thought-flicker from your own unconscious or Morton's. Why the fear-flurry?"

But just then a fourth mind joined them—resinous in flavour like Greek wine. "Hobart Horn coming in." They saw a ghostly laboratory, with chemical apparatus,

Then a fifth—sweet-sour apple-tasting. "Evelyn Horn coming in. Yes, Grayl, late as usual—thirty-seven seconds by Horn Time. I didn't miss your duck-duck thought" The newcomer's tartness was unmalicious. They glimpsed the large office in which Evelyn worked, the microtypewriter and rolls of her correspondence tape on her desk. "But—bright truth!—someone always has to be last," she continued. "And I'm working overtime. Always make a family conference, though; Afterwards will you take control of me, Grayl, and spell me at -this typing for a while? I'm really fagged—and I don't want to leave my body on automatic too long. It gets hostile on automatic and hurts to squeeze back into. How about it, Grayl?"

"I will," Grayl promised, "but don't make it a habit. I don't know what your administrator would say if he knew you kept sneaking off two thousand miles to my studio to smoke cigarettes—and get my throat raw for mel"

"All present and accounted for," Mort remarked. "Evelyn, Grayl, Uncle Dean, Hobart, and myself—the whole damn family. Would you care to share my day's experiences first? Pretty dull armchair stuff, I warn you. Or shall we make it a five-dimensional free-for-all? A Quintet for Horns? Hey, Evelyn, quit directing four-letter thoughts at the chair!"

With that the conference got underway. Five minds that were in a sense one mind, because they were wide open to each other, and in another sense twenty-five minds, because there were five sensory-memory set-ups available for each individual. Five separate individuals, some of them thousands of miles apart, each viewing a different sector of the world of the First Global

Democracy. Five separate visual landscapes—study, studio, laboratory, office, and the cloud-studded openness of the upper .air—all of them existing in one mental space, now superimposed on each other, now replacing each other. now jostling each other as two ideas may jostle in a single non-telepathic mind. Five varying auditory landscapes —-the deep throb of the vanes of Dean's flyabout making the dominant tone, around which the other noises wove counterpoint. In short, five complete sensory pictures, open to mutual inspection.

Five different ideational set-ups too. Five concepts of truth and beauty and honor, of good and bad, of wise and foolish, and of all the other so-called abstractions with which men and women direct their lives—all different, yet all vastly more similar than such concepts are among the non-telepathic, who can never really share them. Five different ideas of life, jumbled together like dice in a box.

And yet there was no confusion. The dice were educated. The five minds slipped into and out of each other with the practiced grace and courtesy of diplomats at a tea. For these daily conferences had been going on ever since Grandfather Horn first discovered that he could communicate mentally with his children. Until then he had not .known that he was a telepathic mutant, for before his children were born there had been no other minds with which he could communicate—and the strange mental silence, disturbed from time to time by clouds of mental static, had even made him fear that he was psychotic. Now Grandfather Horn was dead, but the conferences went on between the members of the slowly widening circle of his lineal descendants—at present only five in number, although the mutation appeared to be a partial dominant. The conferences of the Horns were still as secret as the earliest ones had been. The First Global Democracy was still ignorant that telepathy was a longestablished fact—among the Horns. For the Horns believed that jealousy and suspicion and savage hate would be what they would get from the world if it ever became generally known that, by the chance of mutated heredity, they possessed a power which other men could never hope for. Or else they would be exploited as all-weather and interplanetary "radios." So to the outside world, including even their non-telepathic husbands and wives, sweethearts and friends, they were just an ordinary group of blood relations—no more "psychic" certainly than any group of close-knit brothers and sisters and cousins. They had something of a reputation of being a family of "daydreamers"—that was about all. Beyond enriching their personalities and experience, the Horns' telepathy was-no great advantage to them. They could not read the minds of animals and other humans and they seemed to have no powers whatever of clairvoyance, clairaudience, talekinesis, or foreseeing the future or past. Their telepathic power was, in short, simply like having a private, all-senses family telephone.

The conference—it was much more a hyper-intimate gabfest—proceeded.

"My static box bugged out for a few ticks this morning," Evelyn remarked in the course of talking over the trivia of the past twenty-four hours.

The static boxes were an invention of Grandfather Horn. They generated a tiny cloud of meaningless brain waves. Without such individual thought-screens, there was too much danger of complete loss of individual personality—once Grandfather Horn had "become" his infant daughter as well as himself for several hours and the unfledged mind had come close to being permanently lost in its own subconscious. The static boxes provided a mental wall be hind which a mind could safely grow and function, similar to the wall by which ordinary minds are apparently always enclosed. In spite of the boxes, the Horns shared thoughts and emotions to an amazing degree. Their mental togetherness was as real and as mysterious—and as incredible—as thought itself . . . and thought is the original angel-cloud dancing on the head of a pin. Their present conference was as warm and intimate and tart as any actual family gathering in one actual room around one actual table. Five minds, joined together in the vast mental darkness that shrouds all minds. Five minds hugged together for comfort and safety in the infinite mental loneliness that pervades the cosmos.

Evelyn continued, "Your boxes were all working, of course, so I couldn't get your thoughts—just the blurs' of your boxes like little old dark grey stars. But this time it gave me a funny uncomfortable feeling, like a spider crawling down my—Grayl! Don't *feel* so wildly! What *is* it?"

Then . . . just as Grayl started to think her answer . . . *something crept from the vast mental darkness and infinite cosmic loneliness surrounding the five minds of the Horns.*

Grayl was the first to notice. Her panicky thought had the curling too-keen edge of hysteria. "There are six of us now! There should only be five, but there are six. Count! Count, I tell you! Six!"

To Mort it seemed that a gigantic spider was racing. across the web of their thoughts. He felt Dean's hands grip convulsively at the controls of his flyabout He felt Evelyn's slave-body freeze at her desk and Hobart grope out blindly so that a piece of apparatus fell with a crystalline tinkle. As if they had been sitting together at dinner .and had suddenly realized that there was a sixth place set and a tall figure swathed in shadows sitting at it A figure that to Mort exuded an overpowering taste and odor of brass—a sour metallic stench.

And then that figure spoke. The greater portion of the intruder's thought was alien, unintelligible, frightening in its expression of an unearthly power and an unearthly hunger.

The understandable portion of its speech seemed to be in the nature of a bitter and coldly menacing greeting, insofar as references and emotional sense could be at all determined.

"I, the Mind Spider as you name me—the deathless one, the eternally exiled, the eternally imprisoned—or so his overconfident enemies suppose—coming in."

Mort saw the danger almost too late—and he was the first to see it. He snatched toward the static box in his smock.

In what seemed no more than an instant he saw-the shadow of the intruder darken the four other minds, saw them caught and wrapped in the intruder's thoughts, just as a spider twirls a shroud around its victims, saw the black half-intelligible thoughts of the intruder scuttle toward him with blinding speed, felt the fanged impact of indomitable power, felt his own will fail.

There was a click. By a hairsbreadth his fingers had carried out their mission. Around his mind the neutral grey wall was up and—Thank the Lord!—it appeared that the intruder could not penetrate it.

Mort sat there gasping, shaking, staring with the dull eyes of shock. Direct mental contact with the utterly inhuman—with *that* sort of inhumanity—is not something that can be lightly brushed aside or ever forgotten. It makes a wound. For minutes afterwards a man cannot think at all.

And the brassy stench lingered tainting his entire consciousness—a stench of Satanic power and melancholy. When he finally sprang up, it was not because he had thought things out but because he heard a faint sound behind him and knew with a chilling certainty that it meant death.

It was Grayl. She was carrying an airbrush as if it were a gun. She had kicked off her shoes. Poised there in the doorway she was the incarnation of taut stealthiness, as if she had sloughed off centuries of civilization in seconds of time, leaving only the primeval core of the jungle killer.

But it was her face that was the worst, and the most revealing. Pale and immobile as a corpse's—almost. But the little more left over from the "almost" was a spiderish implacability, the source of which Mort knew only too well.

She pointed the airbrush at his eyes. His sidewise twist

saved them from the narrow pencil of oily liquid that spat from the readjusted nozzle, but a little splashed against his hand and he felt the bite of acid. He lunged toward her, ducking away from the spray as she whipped it back toward him. He caught her wrist, bowled into her and carried her with him to the floor.

She dropped the airbrush and fought—with teeth and claws like a cat, yet with this horrible difference that it was not like an animal lashing out instinctively but like an animal listening for orders and obeying them.

Suddenly she went limp. The static from his box had taken effect. He made doubly sure by switching on hers.

She was longer, than he had been in recovering from theshock, but when she began to speak it was with a rush, as if she already realized that every minute was vital.

"We've got to stop the others, Mort, before they let it out. The . . . the Mind Spider, Mort! It's been imprisoned for eons, for cosmic ages. First floating in space, then

in the Antarctic, where its prison spiralled to Earth. Its enemies . . . really its judges . . . had to imprison it, because it's something that can't be killed. I can't make you understand just why they imprisoned it—" (Her face went a shade greyer) "—you'd have to experience the creature's thoughts for that—but it had to do with the perversion and destruction of the life-envelopes of more than one planet."

Even under the stress of horror, Mort had time to realize how strange it was to be listening to Grayl's words instead of her thoughts. They never used words except when ordinary people were present. It was like acting in a play. Suddenly it occurred to him that they would never be able to share thoughts again. Why, if their static boxes were to fail for a few seconds, as Evelyn's had this morning . . .

"That's where it's been," Grayl continued, "locked in the heart of the Antarctic, dreaming its centuries-long dreams of escape and revenge, waking now and again to rage against its captivity and rack its mind with a thousand schemes—and searching, searching, always searching! Searching for telepathic contact with creatures capable of operating the locks of its prison. And now, waking after its last fifty year trance, finding them!"

He nodded and caught her trembling hands in his.

"Look," he said, "do you know where the creature's prison is located?"

She glanced up at him fearfully. "Oh, yes, it printed the coordinates of the place on my mind as if my brain were graph paper. You see, the creature has a kind of colorless perception that lets it see out of its prison. It sees through rock as it sees through air and what it sees it measures. I'm sure that it knows all about Earth—because it knows exactly what it wants to do with Earth, beginning with the forced evolution of new dominant life forms from the insects and arachnids . . . and other organisms whose sensation-tone pleases it more than that of the mammals."

He nodded again. "All right," he said, "that pretty well settles what you and I have got to do. Dean and Hobart and Evelyn are under its control—we've got to suppose that. It may detach one or even two of them for the side job of finishing us off, just as it tried to use you to finish me. But it's a dead certainty that it's guiding at least one of them as fast as is humanly possible to its prison, to release it. We can't call in Interplanetary Police or look for help anywhere. Everything hinges on our being telepathic, and it would take days to convince them even of that We've got to handle this all by ourselves, There's not a soul in the world can help us. We've got to hire an all-purpose flyabout that can make the trip, and we've got to go down there. While you were unconscious I put through some calls. Evelyn has left the office. She hasn't gone home. Hobart should be at his laboratory, but he isn't Dean's home station can't get in touch with him. We can't hope to intercept them on the way—I thought of getting I.P. to nab them by inventing some charges against them, but that would probably end with the police stopping *us*. The only place where we have a chance of finding them, and of stopping them, is down .there, where *it* is.

"And we'll have to be ready to kill them."

For millenniums piled on millenniums, the gales of Earth's loftiest, coldest, loneliest continent had driven the powdered ice against the dull metal without scoring it, without rusting it, without even polishing it Like some grim temple sacred to pitiless gods it rose from the Antarctic gorge, a blunt hemisphere ridged with steps, with a tilted platform at the top, as if for an altar. A temple built to outlast eternity. Unmistakably the impression came through that this structure was older than Earth, older perhaps than the low-circling sun, that it had ,felt colds to which this was summer warmth, that it had known the grip of forces to which these ice-fisted gales .were playful breezes, that it had known loneliness to which this white wasteland was teeming with life.

Not so the two tiny figures struggling toward it from one of three flyabouts lying crazily atilt on the drift. Their every movement betrayed frail humanity. They stumbled and swayed, leaning into the wind. Sometimes a gust would send them staggering. Sometimes one would fall.

But always they came on. Though their clothing appeared roughly adequate—the sort of polar clothing a person might snatch up in five minutes in the temperate zone—It was obvious that they could not survive long in this frigid region. But that did not seem to trouble them.

Behind them toiled two other tiny figures, coming from the second grounded flyabout. Slowly, very slowly, they gained on the first two. Then a fifth figure came from behind a drift and confronted the second pair,

"Steady now. Steady!" Dean Horn shouted against the wind, levelling his blaster. "Morti Grayl! For your lives, don't move!"

For a moment these words resounded in Mort's ears with the inhuman and mocking finality of the Antarctic .gale. Then the faintly hopeful thought came to him that .Dean would hardly have spoken that way if he had been under the creature's control. He would hardly have bothered to speak at all.

The wind shrieked and tore. Mort staggered and threw an arm around Grayl's shoulders for mutual support, Dean fought his way toward them, blaster always leveled. In his other hand he had a small black cube—his static box, Mort recognized. He held it a little in front of him (like a cross, Mort thought) and as he came close to them he thrust it toward their heads (as if be were exorcising demons, Mort thought). Only then did Dean. lower the muzzle of his blaster.

Mort said, "I'm glad you didn't count lurching with the wind as moving!"

Dean smiled harshly. "I dodged the thing, too," he explained. "Just managed to flick on my static box. Like you did, I guess. Only I had no way of knowing that, so when I saw you I had to make sure I—"

The circular beam of a blaster hissed into the drift beside them, raining a great cloud of steam and making a hole wide as a bushel basket. Mort lunged at Dean, toppling him down out of range, pulling Grayl after.

"Hobart and Evelyn!" He pointed. "In the hollow ahead! Blast to keep them in it, Dean. What I've got in mind won't take long. Grayl, stay close to Dean . . . and give me your static box!"

He crawled forward along a curve that would take him to the edge of the hollow. Behind him and at the further side of the hollow, snow puffed into clouds of steam as the blasters spat free energy. Finally he glimpsed a shoulder, cap, and upturned collar. He estimated the distance,

hefted Grayl's static box,' guessed at the wind and made a measured throw. Blaster-fire from the hollow ceased. He rushed forward, waving to Dean and Grayl.

Hobart was sitting in the snow, staring dazedly at the weapon in his hand, as if it could tell him why he'd done what he'd done. He looked up at Mort with foggy eyes. The black static box had lodged in the collar of his coat and Mort felt a surge of confidence at the freakish accuracy of his toss.

But Evelyn was nowhere in sight. Over the lip of the hollow, very close now, appeared the ridged and dully gleaming hemisphere, like the ascendant disk of some tiny and ill-boding asteroid- A coldness that was more than that of the ice-edged wind went through Mort. He snatched Hobart's blaster and ran. The other shouted after him, but he only waved back at them once, frantically.

The metal of the steps seemed to suck warmth even from the wind that ripped at his back like a snow-tiger as he climbed. The steps were as crazily tilted as those in a nightmare, and there seemed always to be more of them, as if they were somehow growing and multiplying. He found himself wondering if material and mental steps could ever get mixed.

He reached the platform. As his head came up over the edge, he saw, hardly a dozen feet away, Evelyn's face, blue with cold but having frozen into the same spiderish expression he had once seen in Grayl's. He raised the blaster, but in the same moment the face dropped out of sight. There was a metallic clang. He scrambled up onto the platform and clawed impotently at the circular plate barring the opening into which Evelyn had vanished. He was still crouched there when the others joined him.

The demon wind had died, as if it were the Mind Spider's ally and had done its work. The hush was like a prelude to a planet's end, and Hobart's bleak words, gasped but disjointedly, were like the sentence of doom.

"There are two doors. The thing told us all about them . . . while we were under its control. The first would be open . . . we were to go inside and shut it behind us. That's what Evelyn's done . . . she's locked it from the inside . . . just the. simplest sliding bolt . . . but it will keep us from getting at her . . . while she activates the locks of the second door . . . the real door. We weren'tto get the instructions . . . on how to do that . . . until we got inside."

"Stand aside," Dean said, aiming his blaster at the trapdoor, but he said it dully, as if he knew beforehand that it wasn't going to work. Waves of heat made the white hill beyond them waver. But the dull metal did not change colour and when Dean cut off his blaster and tossed down a handful of snow on the spot, it did not melt.

Mort found himself wondering if you could make a metal of frozen thought. Through his numbed mind flashed a panorama of the rich lands and seas of the Global Democracy they had flown over yesterday—the greenframed white power stations of the Orinoco, the fabulous walking cities of the Amazon Basin, the jet-atomic launching fields of the Gran Chaco, the multi-domed Oceanographic Institute of the Falkland Islands. A dawn world, you might call it. He wondered vaguely if other dawn worlds had struggled an hour or two into the morning only to fall prey to things like the Mind Spider.

"No!" The word came like a command heard in a dream. He looked up dully and realized that it was Grayl who had spoken—realized, with stupid amazement, that her eyes were flashing with anger.

"No! There's still one way we can get at it and try to stop it. The same way it got at us. Thought! It took us by surprise. We didn't have time to prepare resistance. We were panicked and it's given us a permanent panic-psychology. We could only think of getting behind our thought-screens and about how—once there—we'd never dare come out again. Maybe this time, if we all stand firm when we open our screens . . .

"I know it's a slim chance, a crazy chance . . ."

Mort knew that too. So did Dean and Hobart. But some thing in him, and in them, rejoiced at Grayl's words, rejoiced at the prospect of meeting the thing, however hopelessly, on its own ground, mind to mind. Without hesitation they brought out their static boxes, and, at the signal of Dean's hand uplifted, switched them off.

That action plunged them from a material wilderness of snow and bleakly clouded sky into a sunless, dimensionless wilderness of thought Like some lone fortress on an endless plain, their minds linked together, foursquare, waiting the assault. And like some monster of nightmare, the thoughts of the creature that accepted the name of the Mind Spider rushed toward them across that plain. threatening to overmaster them by the Satanic prestige that absolute selfishness and utter cruelty confer. The brassy stench of its being was like a poison cloud.

They held firm. The thoughts of the Mind Spider darted ,about, seeking a weak point, then seemed to settle down upon them everywhere, engulfingly, like a dry black web,

Alien against human, egocentric killer-mind against mutually loyal preserver-minds—and in the end it was the mutual loyalty and knittedness that turned the tide, giving them each a four-fold power of resistance. The thoughts of the Mind Spider retreated. Theirs pressed after. They sensed that a comer of his mind was not truly his. They pressed a pincers attack at that point, seeking to cut it off. There was a moment of desperate resistance. Then suddenly they were no longer four minds against the Spider, but five.

The trapdoor opened. It was Evelyn. They could at last switch on their thought-screens and find refuge behind the walls of neutral grey and prepare to fight back to their flyabouts and save their bodies.

.But there was something that had to be said first, something that Mort said for them.

"The danger remains and we probably can't ever destroy it. They couldn't destroy it, or they wouldn't have built this prison. We can't tell anyone about it. Non-telepaths wouldn't believe all our story and would want to find out what was inside. We Horns have the job of being a monster's jailers. Maybe someday we'll be able to practice telepathy again—behind some sort of static-spheres. We will have to prepare for that time and work out many precautions, such as keying our static boxes, so that switching on one switches on all. But the Mind Spider and its prison remains our responsibility and our trust, forever."

# THE THING FROM—OUTSIDE

## by George Allan England

*Some* Things *from outer space arrive and either start shooting, or start making demands, or both ("Surrender, puny human," as Marvel Comics might have put it before their superhero revival) and explain everything. But maybe an arriving* Thing *will be completely incomprehensible to the human mind, and its actions will be equally baffling. Which is not to say they wouldn't be deadly.*

**George Allen England** *(1877-1936), in spite of his name, was an American, and even ran for Governor of Maine, unsuccessfully. (He was a socialist, but then, nobody's perfect.) His major work in SF was the post-apocalyptic trilogy* Darkness and Dawn *which has been in and out of print for decades, though modern readers may have trouble with the author's attitude toward the "lesser" races. It comprises the three novels,* The Vacant World (1912),

Beyond the Great Oblivion (1913), *and* The Afterglow (1914). *England wrote many other SF novels in the first quarter of the 20th century, such as* The Golden Blight, The Flying Legion, *and* The Elixir of Hate, *to name three. He was a prolific writer of short stories, but this one, originally published in Hugo Gernsback's* Science & Invention *in 1923, three years before Gernsback founded* Amazing Stories, *is probably the best known nowadays—and with good reason.*

**THEY SAT ABOUT THEIR CAMP-FIRE,** that little party of Americans retreating southward from Hudson Bay before the on-coming menace of the great cold. Sat there, stolid under the awe of the North, under the uneasiness that the day's trek had laid upon their souls. The three men smoked. The two women huddled close to each other. Fireglow picked their faces from the gloom of night among the dwarf firs. A splashing murmur told of the Albany River's haste to escape from the wilderness, and reach the Bay.

"I don't see what there was in a mere circular print on a rock-ledge to make our guides desert," said Professor Thorburn. His voice was as dry as his whole personality. "Most extraordinary."

"They knew what it was, all right," answered Jandron, geologist of the party. "So do I." He rubbed his cropped mustache. His eyes glinted grayly. "I've seen prints like that before. That was on the Labrador. And I've seen things happen, where they were."

"Something surely happened to our guides, before they'd got a mile into the bush," put in the Professor's wife; while Vivian, her sister, gazed into the fire that revealed her as a beauty, not to be spoiled even by a tam and a rough-knit sweater. "Men don't shoot wildly, and scream like that, unless—"

"They're all three dead now, anyhow," put in Jandron. "So they're out of harm's way. While we—well, we're two hundred and fifty wicked miles from the C. P. R. rails."

"Forget it, Jandy!" said Marr, the journalist. "We're just suffering from an attack of nerves, that's all. Give me a fill of 'baccy. Thanks. We'll all be better in the morning. Ho-hum! Now, speaking of spooks and such—"

He launched into an account of how he had once exposed a fraudulent spiritualist, thus proving—to his own satisfaction—that nothing existed beyond the scope of mankind's everyday life. But nobody gave him much heed. And silence fell upon the little night-encampment in the wilds; a silence that was ominous.

Pale, cold stars watched down from spaces infinitely far beyond man's trivial world.

Next day, stopping for chow on a ledge miles upstream, Jandron discovered another of the prints. He cautiously summoned the other two men. They examined the print, while the women-folk were busy by the fire. A harmless thing the marking seemed; only a ring about four inches in diameter, a kind of cup-shaped depression with a raised center. A sort of glaze coated it, as if the granite had been fused by heat.

Jandron knelt, a well-knit figure in bright mackinaw and canvas leggings, and with a shaking finger explored the smooth curve of the print in the rock. His brows contracted as he studied it.

"We'd better get along out of this as quick as we can," said he in an unnatural voice. "You've got your wife to protect, Thorburn, and I,—well, I've got Vivian. And—"

"You have?" nipped Marr. The light of an evil jealously gleamed in his heavy-lidded look. "What you need is an alienist."

"Really, Jandron," the Professor admonished, "you mustn't let your imagination run away with you."

"I suppose it's imagination that keeps this print cold!" the geologist retorted. His breath made faint, swirling coils of vapor above it.

"Nothing but a pot-hole," judged Thorburn, bending his spare, angular body to examine the print. The Professor's vitality all seemed centered in his big-bulged skull that sheltered a marvellous thinking machine. Now he put his lean hand to the base of his brain, rubbing the back of his head as if it ached. Then, under what seemed some powerful compulsion, he ran his bony finger around the print in the rock.

"By Jove, but it is cold!" he admitted. "And looks as if it had been stamped right out of the stone. Extraordinary!"

"Dissolved out, you mean," corrected the geologist. "By cold."

The journalist laughed mockingly.

"Wait till I write this up!" he sneered. "'Noted Geologist Declares Frigid Ghost Dissolves Granite!'"

Jandron ignored him. He fetched a little water from the river and poured it into the print.

"Ice!" ejaculated the Professor. "Solid ice!"

"Frozen in a second," added Jandron, while Marr frankly stared. "And it'll never melt, either. I tell you, I've seen some of these rings before; and every time, horrible things have happened. Incredible things! Something burned this ring out of the stone—burned it out with the cold of interstellar space. Something that can import cold as a permanent quality of matter. Something that can kill matter, and totally remove it."

"Of course that's all sheer poppycock," the journalist tried to laugh, but his brain felt numb.

"This something, this Thing," continued Jandron, "is a Thing that can't be killed by bullets. It's what caught our guides on the barrens, as they ran away—poor fools!"

A shadow fell across the print in the rock. Mrs. Thorburn had come up, was standing there. She had overheard a little of what Jandron had been saying.

"Nonsense!" she tried to exclaim, but she was shivering so she could hardly speak.

That night, after a long afternoon of paddling and portaging—laboring against inhibitions like those in a nightmare—they camped on shelving rocks that slanted to the river.

"After all," said the Professor, when supper was done, "we mustn't get into a panic. I know extraordinary things are reported from the wilderness, and more than one man has come out, raving. But we, by Jove! with our superior brains—we aren't going to let Nature play us any tricks!"

"And of course," added his wife, her arm about Vivian,

"everything in the universe is a natural force. There's really no super-natural, at all."

"Admitted," Jandron replied. "But how about things outside the universe?"

"And they call you a scientist?" gibed Marr; but the Professor leaned forward, his brows knit.

"Hm!" he grunted. A little silence fell.

"You don't mean, really," asked Vivian, "that you think there's life and intelligence—Outside?"

Jandron looked at the girl. Her beauty, haloed with ruddy gold from the firelight, was a pain to him as he answered:

"Yes, I do. And dangerous life, too. I know what I've seen, in the North Country. I know what I've seen!"

Silence again, save for the crepitation of the flames, the fall of an ember, the murmur of the current. Darkness narrowed the wilderness to just that circle of flickering light ringed by the forest and the river, brooded over by the pale stars.

"Of course you can't expect a scientific man to take you seriously," commented the Professor.

"I know what I've seen! I tell you there's Something entirely outside man's knowledge."

"Poor fellow!" scoffed the journalist; but even as he spoke his hand pressed his forehead.

"There are Things at work," Jandron affirmed, with dogged persistence. He lighted his pipe with a blazing twig. Its flame revealed his face drawn, lined. "Things. Things that reckon with us no more than we do with ants. Less, perhaps."

The flame of the twig died. Night stood closer, watching.

"Suppose there are?" the girl asked. "What's that got to do with these prints in the rock?"

"*They*," answered Jandran, "are marks left by one of those Things. Footprints, maybe. That Thing is near us, here and now!"

Marr's laugh broke a long stillness.

"And you," he exclaimed, "with an A. M. and a B. S. to write after your name,"

"If you knew more," retorted Jandron, "you'd know a devilish sight less. It's only ignorance that's cock-sure."

"But," dogmatized the Professor, "no scientist of any standing has ever admitted any outside interference with this planet."

"No, and for thousands of years nobody ever admitted that the world was round, either. What I've seen, I know."

"Well, what *have* you seen?" asked Mrs. Thorburn, shivering. "

You'll excuse me, please, for not going into that just now."

"You mean," the Professor demanded, dryly, "if the—hm!—this suppositious Thing wants to—?"

"It'll do any infernal thing it takes a fancy to, yes! If it happens to want us—"

"But what *could* Things like that want of us? Why should They come here, at all?"

"Oh, for various reasons. For inanimate objects, at times, and then again for living beings. They've come here lots of times, I tell you," Jandron asserted with strange irritation, "and got what They wanted, and then gone away to—Somewhere. If one of Them happens to want us, for any reason, It will take us, that's all. If It doesn't want us, It will ignore us, as we'd ignore gorillas in Africa if we were looking for gold. But if it was gorilla-fur we wanted, that would be different for the gorillas, wouldn't it?"

"What in the world," asked Vivian, "could a—well, a Thing from Outside want of us?"

"What do men want, say, of guinea-pigs? Men experiment with 'em, of course. Superior beings use inferior, for their own ends. To assume that man is the supreme product of evolution is gross self-conceit. Might not some superior Thing want to experiment with human beings?"

"But how?" demanded Marr,

"The human brain is the most highly-organized form of matter known to this planet. Suppose, now—"

"Nonsense!" interrupted the Professor. "All hands to the sleeping-bags, and no more of this. I've got a wretched headache. Let's anchor in Blanket Bay!"

He, and both the women, turned in. Jandron and Marr sat a while longer by the fire. They kept plenty of wood piled on it, too, for an unnatural chill transfixed the night-air. The fire burned strangely blue, with greenish flicks of flame.

At length, after vast acerbities of disagreement, the geologist and the newspaperman sought their sleeping-bags. The fire was a comfort. Not that a fire could avail a pin's weight against a Thing from interstellar space, but subjectively it was a comfort. The instincts of a million years, centering around protection by fire, cannot be obliterated.

After a time—worn out by a day of nerve-strain and

of battling with swift currents, of flight from Something invisible, intangible—they all slept.

The depths of space, star-sprinkled, hung above them with vastness immeasurable, cold beyond all understanding of the human mind.

Jandron woke first, in a red dawn.

He blinked at the fire, as he crawled from his sleeping-bag. The fire was dead; and yet it had not burned out. Much wood remained unconsumed, charred over, as if some gigantic extinguisher had in the night been lowered over it.

"*Hmmm!*" growled Jandron. He glanced about him, on the ledge. "Prints, too. I might have known!"

He aroused Marr. Despite all the jourelist's mocking hostility, Jandron felt more in common with this man of his own age than with the Professor, who was close on sixty.

"Look here, now!" said he. "*It* has been all around here. See? *It* put out our fire—maybe the fire annoyed *It*, some way—and *It* walked round us, everywhere." His gray eyes smouldered. "I guess, by gad, you've got to admit facts, now!"

The journalist could only shiver and stare.

"Lord, what a head I've got on me, this morning!" he chattered. He rubbed his forehead with a shaking hand, and started for the river. Most of his assurance had vanished. He looked badly done up.

"Well, what say?" demanded Jandron. "See these fresh prints?"

"Damn the prints!" retorted Marr, and fell to grumbling

some unintelligible thing. He washed unsteadily, and remained crouching at the river's lip, inert, numbed.

Jandron, despite a gnawing at the base of his brain, carefully examined the ledge. He found prints scattered everywhere, and some even on the river-bottom near the shore. Wherever water had collected in the prints on the rock, it had frozen hard. Each print in the river-bed, too, was white with ice. Ice that the rushing current could not melt.

"Well, by gad!" he exclaimed. He lighted his pipe and tried to think. Horribly afraid—yes, he felt horribly afraid, but determined. Presently, as a little power of concentration came back, he noticed that all the prints were in straight lines, each mark about two feet from the next.

"*It* was observing us while we slept," said Jandron.

"What nonsense are you talking, eh?" demanded Marr. His dark, heavy face sagged. "Fire, now, and grub!"

He got up and shuffled unsteadily away from the river. Then he stopped with a jerk, staring.

"Look! Look a' that axe!" he gulped, pointing.

Jandron picked up the axe, by the handle, taking good care not to touch the steel. The blade was white-furred with frost. And deep into it, punching out part of the edge, one of the prints was stamped.

"This metal," said he, "is clean gone. It's been absorbed. The Thing doesn't recognize any difference in materials. Water and steel and rock are all the same to It."

"You're crazy!" snarled the journalist. "How could a Thing travel on one leg, hopping along, making marks like that?"

"It could roll, if it was disk-shaped. And—"

A cry from the Professor turned them. Thorburn was stumbling toward them, hands out and tremulous.

"My wife—!" he choked.

Vivian was kneeling beside her sister, frightened, dazed.

"Something's happened!" stammered the Professor. "Here—come here—!"

Mrs. Thorburn was beyond any power of theirs, to help. She was still breathing; but her respirations were stertorous, and a complete paralysis had stricken her. Her eyes, half-open and expressionless, showed pupils startlingly dilated. No resources of the party's drug-kit produced the slightest effect on the woman.

The next half-hour was a confused panic, breaking camp, getting Mrs. Thorburn into a canoe, and leaving that accursed place, with a furious energy of terror that could no longer reason. Up-stream, ever up against the swirl of the current the party fought, driven by horror. With no thought of food or drink, paying no heed to landmarks, lashed forward only by the mad desire to be gone, the three men and the girl flung every ounce of their energy into the paddles. Their panting breath mingled with the sound of swirling eddies. A mist-blurred sun brooded over the northern wilds. Unheeded, hosts of black-flies sang high-pitched keenings all about the fugitives. On either hand the forest waited, watched.

Only after two hours of sweating toil had brought exhaustion did they stop, in the shelter of a cove where black waters circled, foam-flecked. There they found the Professor's wife—she was dead.

Nothing remained to do but bury her. At first Thorburn would not hear of it. Like a madman he insisted that through all hazards he would fetch the body out. But no—impossible. So, after a terrible time, he yielded.

In spite of her grief, Vivian was admirable. She understood what must be done. It was her voice that said the prayers; her hand that—lacking flowers—laid the fir boughs on the cairn. The Professor was dazed past doing anything, saying anything.

Toward mid-afternoon, the party landed again, many miles up-river. Necessity forced them to eat. Firs would not burn. Every time they lighted it, it smouldered and went out with a heavy, greasy smoke. The fugitives ate cold food and drank water, then shoved off in two canoes and once more fled.

In the third canoe, hauled to the edge of the forest, lay all the rock-specimens, data and curios, scientific instruments. The party kept only Marr's diary, a compass, supplies, fire-arms and medicine-kit.

"We can find the things we've left—sometime," said Jandron, noting the place well. "Sometime—after *It* has gone,"

"And bring the body out," added Thorburn. Tears, for the first time, wet his eyes. Vivian said nothing. Marr tried to light his pipe. He seemed to forget that nothing, not even tobacco, would burn now.

Vivian and Jandron occupied one canoe. The other carried the Professor and Marr. Thus the power of the two canoes was about the same. They kept well together, up-stream.

The fugitives paddled and portaged with a dumb,

desperate energy. Toward evening they struck into what they believed to be the Mamattawan. A mile up this, as the blurred sun faded beyond a wilderness of ominous silence, they camped. Here they made determined efforts to kindle fire. Not even alcohol from the drug-kit would start it. Cold, they mumbled a little food; cold, they huddled into their sleeping-bags, there to lie with darkness leaden on their fear. After a long time, up over a world void of all sound save the river-flow, slid an amber moon notched by the ragged tops of the conifers. Even the wail of a timber-wolf would have come as welcome relief; but no wolf howled.

Silence and night enfolded them. And everywhere they felt that *It* was watching.

Foolishly enough, as a man will do foolish things in a crisis, Jandron laid his revolver outside his sleeping-bag, in easy reach. His thought—blurred by a strange, drawing headache—was:

"If *It* touches Vivian, I'll shoot!"

He realized the complete absurdity of trying to shoot a visitant from interstellar space; from the Fourth Dimension, maybe. But Jandron's ideas seemed tangled. Nothing would come right. He lay there, absorbed in a kind of waking nightmare. Now and then, rising on an elbow, he hearkened; all in vain. Nothing so much as stirred.

His thought drifted to better days, when all had been health, sanity, optimism; when nothing except jealousy of Marr, as concerned Vivian, had troubled him. Days when the sizzle of the frying-pan over friendly coals had made friendly wilderness music; when the wind and the northern star, the whirr of the reel, the whispering vortex of the paddle in clear water had all been things of joy. Yes, and when a certain happy moment had, through some word or look of the girl, seemed to promise his heart's desire. But now—

"Damn it, I'll save *her*, anyhow!" he swore with savage intensity, knowing all the while that what was to be, would be, unmitigably. Do ants, by any waving of antenna, stay the down-crushing foot of man?

Next morning, and the next, no sign of the Thing appeared. Hope revived that possibly It might have flitted away elsewhere; back, perhaps, to outer space. Many were the miles the urging paddles spurned behind. The fugitives calculated that a week more would bring them to the railroad. Fire burned again. Hot food and drink helped, wonderfully. But where were the fish?

"Most extraordinary," all at once said the Professor, at noonday camp. He had become quite rational again. "Do you realize, Jandron, we've seen no traces of life in some time?"

The geologist nodded. Only too clearly he had noted just that, but he had been keeping still about it.

"That's so, too!" chimed in Marr, enjoying the smoke that some incomprehensible turn of events was letting him have. "Not a muskrat or beaver. Not even a squirrel or bird."

"Not so much as a gnat or black-fly!" the Professor added. Jandron suddenly realized that he would have welcomed even those.

That afternoon, Marr fell into a suddenly vile temper. He mumbled curses against the guides, the current, the portages, everything. The Professor seemed more cheerful. Vivian complained of an oppressive headache. Jandron gave her the last of the aspirin tablets; and as he gave them, took her hand in his.

"I'll see *you* through, anyhow," said he, "I don't count, now. Nobody counts, only you!"

She gave him a long, silent look. He saw the sudden glint of tears in her eyes; felt the pressure of her hand, and knew they two had never been so near each other as in that moment under the shadow of the Unknown.

Next day—or it may have been two days later, for none of them could be quite sure about the passage of time—they came to a deserted lumber-camp. Even more than two days might have passed; because now their bacon was all gone, and only coffee, tobacco, beef-cubes and pilot-bread remained. The lack of fish and game had cut alarmingly into the duffle-bag. That day—whatever day it may have been—all four of them suffered terribly from headache of an odd, ring-shaped kind, as if something circular were being pressed down about their heads. The Professor said it was the sun that made his head ache. Vivian laid it to the wind and the gleam of the swift water, while Marr claimed it was the heat. Jandron wondered at all this, inasmuch as he plainly saw that the river had almost stopped flowing, and the day had become still and overcast.

They dragged their canoes upon a rotting stage of fir-poles and explored the lumber-camp; a mournful place set back in an old "slash," now partly overgrown with scrub poplar, maple and birch. The log buildings, covered with tar-paper partly torn from the pole roofs, were of the usual North Country type. Obviously the place had not been used for years. Even the landing-stage where once logs had been rolled into the stream had sagged to decay.

"I don't quite get the idea of this," Marr exclaimed. "Where did the logs go to? Downstream, of course. But *that* would take 'em to Hudson Bay, and there's no market for spruce timber or pulpwood at Hudson Bay." He pointed down the current.

"You're entirely mistaken," put in the Professor. "Any fool could see this river runs the other way. A log thrown in here would go down toward the St. Lawrence!"

"But then," asked the girl, "why can't we drift back to civilization?"

The Professor retorted: "Just what we have been doing, all along! Extraordinary, that I have to explain the obvious!" He walked away in a huff.

"I don't know but he's right, at that," half admitted the journalist. "I've been thinking almost the same thing, myself, the past day or two—that is, ever since the sun shifted."

"What do you mean, shifted?" from Jandron, "You haven't noticed it?"

"But there's been no sun at all, for at least two days!"

"Hanged if I'll waste time arguing with a lunatic!" Marr growled. He vouchsafed no explanation of what he meant by the sun's having "shifted," but wandered off, grumbling.

"What are we going to do?" the girl appealed to Jandron. The sight of her solemn, frightened eyes, of her palm-outward hands and (at last) her very feminine fear, constricted Jandron's heart.

"We're going through, you and I," he answered simply. "We've got to save them from themselves, you and I have."

Their hands met again, and for a moment held. Despite the dead calm, a fir-tip at the edge of the clearing suddenly flicked aside, shrivelled as if frozen. But neither of them saw it.

The fugitives, badly spent, established themselves in the "bar-room" or sleeping-shack of the camp. They wanted to feel a roof over them again, if only a broken one. The traces of men comforted them: a couple of broken peavies, a pair of snowshoes with the thongs all gnawed off, a cracked bit of mirror, a yellowed almanac dated 1899.

Jandron called the Professor's attention to this almanac, but the Professor thrust it aside.

"What do *I* want of a Canadian census-report?" he demanded, and fell to counting the bunks, over and over again. His big bulge of his forehead, that housed the massive brain of him, was oozing sweat. Marr cursed what he claimed was sunshine through the holes in the roof, though Jandron could see none; claimed the sunshine made his head ache.

"But it's not a bad place," he added. "We can make a blaze in that fireplace and be comfy. I don't like that window, though."

"What window?" asked Jandron. "Where?"

Marr laughed, and ignored him. Jandron turned to

Vivian, who had sunk down on the "deacon-seat" and was staring at the stove.

'*Is* there a window here?" he demanded. "Don't ask me," she whispered. "I—I don't know."

With a very thriving fear in his heart, Jandron peered at her a moment. He fell to muttering:

"I'm Wallace Jandron. Wallace Jandron, 37 Ware Street, Cambridge, Massachusetts. I'm quite sane. And I'm going to stay so. I'm going to save her! I know perfectly well what I'm doing. And I'm sane. Quite, quite sane!"

After a time of confused and purposeless wrangling, they got a fire going and made coffee. This, and cube bouillon with hardtack, helped considerably. The camp helped, too. A house, even a poor and broken one, is a wonderful barrier against a Thing from—Outside.

Presently darkness folded down. The men smoked, thankful that tobacco still held out. Vivian lay in a bunk that Jandron had piled with spruce boughs for her, and seemed to sleep. The Professor fretted like a child, over the blisters his paddle had made upon his hands. Marr laughed, now and then; though what he might be laughing at was not apparent. Suddenly he broke out:

"After all, what should It want of us?"

"Our brains, of course," the Professor answered, sharply.

"That lets Jandron out," the journalist mocked.

"But," added the Professor, "I can't imagine a Thing callously destroying human beings. And yet—"

He stopped short, with surging memories of his dead wife.

"What was it," Jandron asked, "that destroyed all those people in Valladolid, Spain, that time so many of 'em died in a few minutes after having been touched by an invisible Something that left a slight red mark on each? The newspapers were full of it."

"Piffle!" yawned Marr.

"I tell you," insisted Jandron, "there are forms of life as superior to us as we are to ants. We can't see 'em. No ant ever saw a man. And did any ant ever form the least conception of a man? These Things have left thousands of traces, all over the world. If I had my reference-books—"

"Tell that to the marines!"

"Charles Fort, the greatest authority in the world on unexplained phenomena," persisted Jandron, "gives innumerable cases of happenings that science can't explain, in his *Book of the Damned*. He claims this earth was once a No-Man's land where all kinds of Things explored and colonized and fought for possession. And he says that now everybody's warned off, except the Owners. I happen to remember a few sentences of his: 'In the past, inhabitants of a host of worlds have dropped here, hopped here, wafted here, sailed, flown, motored, walked here; have come singly, have come in enormous numbers; have visited for hunting, trading, mining. They have been unable to stay here, have made colonies here, have been lost here.'"

"Poor fish, to believe that!" mocked the journalist, while the Professor blinked and rubbed his bulging forehead.

"I *do* believe it!" insisted Jandron. "The world is covered with relics of dead civilizations, that have mysteriously vanished, leaving nothing but their temples and monuments."

"Rubbish!"

"How about Easter Island? How about all the gigantic works there and in a thousand other places!—Peru, Yucatan and so on—which certainly no primitive race ever built?"

"That's thousands of years ago," said Marr, "and I'm sleepy. For heaven's sake, can it!"

"Oh, all right. But *how* explain things, then!"

"What the devil could one of those Things want of our brains?" suddenly put in the Professor. "After all, what?"

"Well, what do we want of lower forms of life? Sometimes food. Again, some product or other. Or just information. Maybe It is just experimenting with us, the way we poke an ant-hill. There's always this to remember, that the human brain-tissue is the most highly-organized form of matter in this world."

"Yes," admitted the Professor, "but what—?"

"*It* might want brain-tissue for food, for experimental purposes, for lubricant—how do I know?"

Jandron fancied he was still explaining things; but all at once he found himself waking up in one of the bunks. He felt terribly cold, stiff, sore. A sift of snow lay here and there on the camp floor, where it had fallen through holes in the roof.

"Vivian!" he croaked hoarsely. "Thorburn! Marr!"

Nobody answered. There was nobody to answer. Jandron crawled with immense pain out of his bunk, and blinked round with bleary eyes. All of a sudden he saw the Professor, and gulped.

The Professor was lying stiff and straight in another

bunk, on his back. His waxen face made a mask of horror. The open, staring eyes, with pupils immensely dilated, sent Jandron shuddering back. A livid ring marked the forehead, that now sagged inward as if empty.

"*Vivian!*" croaked Jandron, staggering away from the body. He fumbled to the bunk where the girl had lain. The bunk was quite deserted.

On the stove, in which lay half-charred wood—wood smothered out as if by some noxious gas—still stood the coffee-pot. The liquid in it was frozen solid. Of Vivian and the journalist, no trace remained.

Along one of the sagging beams that supported the roof, Jandron's horror-blasted gaze perceived a straight line of frosted prints, ring-shaped, bitten deep.

"Vivian! Vivian!"

No answer.

Shaking, sick, gray, half-blind with a horror not of this world, Jandron peered slowly around. The duffle-bag and supplies were gone. Nothing was left but that coffee-pot and the revolver at Jandron's hip.

Jandron turned, then. A-stare, his skull feeling empty as a burst drum, he crept lamely to the door and out—out into the snow.

Snow. It came slanting down. From a gray sky it steadily filtered. The trees showed no leaf. Birches, poplars, rock-maples all stood naked. Only the conifers drooped sickly-green. In a little shallow across the river snow lay white on thin ice.

Ice? Snow? Rapt with terror, Jandron stared. Why, then, he must have been unconscious three or four weeks? But how—?

Suddenly, all along the upper branches of trees that edged the clearing, puffs of snow flicked down. The geologist shuffled after two half-obliterated sets of footprints that wavered toward the landing.

His body was leaden. He wheezed, as he reached the river. The light, dim as it was, hurt his eyes. He blinked in a confusion that could just perceive one canoe was gone. He pressed a hand to his head, where an iron band seemed screwed up tight, tighter.

"Vivian! Marr! Halloooo!"

Not even an echo. Silence clamped the world; silence, and a cold that gnawed. Everything had gone a sinister gray.

After a certain time—though time now possessed neither reality nor duration—Jandron dragged himself back to the camp and stumbled in. Heedless of the staring corpse he crumpled down by the stove and tried to think, but his brain had been emptied of power. Everything blent to a gray blur. Snow kept slithering in through the roof.

"Well, why don't you come and get me, Thing?" suddenly snarled Jandron. "Here I am. Damn you, come and get me!"

Voices. Suddenly he heard voices. Yes, somebody was outside, there. Singularly aggrieved, he got up and limped to the door. He squinted out into the gray; saw two figures down by the landing. With numb indifference he recognized the girl and Marr.

"Why should they bother me again?" he nebulously wondered. Can't they go away and leave me alone?" He felt peevish irritation.

Then, a modicum of reason returning, he sensed that they were arguing. Vivian, beside a canoe freshly dragged from thin ice, was pointing; Marr was gesticulating. All at once Marr snarled, turned from her, plodded with bent back toward the camp.

"But listen!" she called, her rough-knit sweater all powdered with snow. "*That's* the way!" She gestured downstream.

"I'm not going either way!" Marr retorted. "I'm going to stay right here!" He came on, bareheaded. Snow grayed his stubble of beard; but on his head it melted as it fell, as if some fever there had raised the brain-stuff to improbable temperatures. "I'm going to stay right here, all summer." His heavy lids sagged. Puffy and evil, his lips showed a glint of teeth. "Let me alone!"

Vivian lagged after him, kicking up the ash-like snow. With indifference, Jandron watched them. Trivial human creatures!

Suddenly Marr saw him in the doorway and stopped short. He drew his gun; he aimed at Jandron.

"*You* get out!" he mouthed. "Why in ____ can't you stay dead?"

"Put that gun down, you idiot!" Jandron managed to retort. The girl stopped and seemed trying to understand. "We can get away yet, if we all stick together."

"Are you going to get out and leave me alone?" demanded the journalist, holding his gun steadily enough.

Jandron, wholly indifferent, watched the muzzle. Vague curiosity possessed him. Just what, he wondered, did it feel like to be shot?

Marr pulled the trigger.

*Snap*!

The cartridge missed fire. Not even powder would burn.

Marr laughed, horribly, and shambled forward. "Serves him right!" he mouthed, "He'd better not come back again!"

Jandron understood that Marr had seen him fall. But still he felt himself standing there, alive. He shuffled away from the door. No matter whether he was alive or dead, there was always Vivian to be saved.

The journalist came to the door, paused, looked down, grunted and passed into the camp. He shut the door. Jandron heard the rotten wooden bar of the latch drop. From within echoed a laugh, monstrous in its brutality.

Then quivering, the geologist felt a touch on his arm.

"Why did you desert us like that?" he heard Vivian's reproach. "Why?"

He turned, hardly able to see her at all.

"Listen," he said, thickly. "I'll admit anything. It's all right. But just forget it, for now. We've got to get out o' here. The Professor is dead, in there, and Marr's gone mad and barricaded himself in there. So there's no use staying. There's a chance for us yet. Come along!"

He took her by the arm and tried to draw her toward the river, but she held back. The hate in her face sickened him. He shook in the grip of a mighty chill.

"Go, with—you?" she demanded.

"Yes, by God!" he retorted, in a swift blaze of anger, "or I'll kill you where you stand. *It* shan't get you, anyhow!"

Swiftly piercing, a greater cold smote to his inner marrows. A long row of the cup-shaped prints had just appeared in the snow beside the camp. And from these marks wafted a faint, bluish vapor of unthinkable cold.

"What are you staring at?" the girl demanded.

"Those prints! In the snow, there—see?" He pointed a shaking finger.

"How can there be snow at this season?"

He could have wept for the pity of her, the love of her. On her red tam, her tangle of rebel hair, her sweater, the snow came steadily drifting; yet there she stood before him and prated of summer. Jandron heaved himself out of a very slough of down-dragging lassitudes. He whipped himself into action.

"Summer, winter—no matter!" he flung at her. "You're coming along with me!" He seized her arm with the brutality of desperation that must hurt, to save. And murder, too, lay in his soul. He knew that he would strangle her with his naked hands, if need were, before he would ever leave her there, for It to work Its horrible will upon.

"You come with me," he mouthed, "or by the Almighty—!"

Marr's scream in the camp, whirled him toward the door. That scream rose higher, higher, even more and more piercing, just like the screams of the runaway Indian guides in what now appeared the infinitely long ago. It seemed to last hours; and always it rose, rose, as if being wrung out of a human body by some kind of agony not conceivable in this world. Higher, higher—

Then it stopped.

Jandron hurled himself against the plank door. The bar smashed; the door shivered inward.

With a cry, Jandron recoiled. He covered his eyes with a hand that quivered, claw-like.

"Go away, Vivian! Don't come here—don't look—"

He stumbled away, babbling.

Out of the door crept something like a man. A queer, broken, bent over thing; a thing crippled, shrunken and flabby, that whined.

This thing—yes, it was still Marr—crouched down at one side, quivering, whimpering. It moved its hands as a crushed ant moves its antennæ, jerkily, without significance.

All at once Jandron no longer felt afraid. He walked quite steadily to Marr, who was breathing in little gasps. From the camp issued an odor unlike anything terrestrial. A thin, grayish grease covered the sill.

Jandron caught hold of the crumpling journalist's arm. Marr's eyes leered, filmed, unseeing. He gave the impression of a creature whose back has been broken, whose whole essence and energy have been wrenched asunder, yet in which life somehow clings, palpitant. A creature vivisected.

Away through the snow Jandron dragged him. Marr made no resistance; just let himself be led, whining a little, palsied, rickety, shattered. The girl, her face whitely cold as the snow that fell on it, came after.

Thus they reached the landing at the river.

"Come, now, let's get away!" Jandron made shift to articulate. Marr said nothing. But when Jandron tried to bundle him into a canoe, something in the journalist revived with swift, mad hatefulness. That something lashed him into a spasm of wiry, incredibly venomous resistance. Slavers of blood and foam streaked Marr's lips. He made horrid noises, like an animal. He howled dismally, and bit, clawed, writhed, and grovelled! he tried to sink his teeth into Jandron's leg. He fought appallingly, as men must have fought in the inconceivably remote days even before the Stone Age. And Vivian helped him. Her fury was a tiger-cat's.

Between the pair of them, they almost did him in. They almost dragged Jandron down—and themselves, too—into the black river that ran swiftly sucking under the ice. Not till Jandron had quite flung off all vague notions and restraints of gallantry; not until he struck from the shoulder—to kill, if need were—did he best them.

He beat the pair of them unconscious, trussed them hand and foot with the painters of the canoes, rolled them into the larger canoe, and shoved off. After that, the blankness of a measureless oblivion descended.

Only from what he was told, weeks after, in the Royal Victoria Hospital at Montreal, did Jandron ever learn how and when a field-squad of Dominion Foresters had found them drifting in Lake Mooaswamkeag. And that knowledge filtered slowly into his brain during a period inchoate as Iceland fogs.

That Marr was dead and the girl alive—that much, at all events, was solid. He could hold to that; he could climb back, with that, to the real world again.

Jandron climbed back, came back. Time healed him, as it healed the girl. After a long, long while, they had speech together. Cautiously he sounded her wells of memory. He saw that she recalled nothing. So he told her white lies about capsized canoes and the sad death—in realistically-described rapids—of all the party except herself and him.

Vivian believed. Fate, Jandron knew, was being very kind to both of them.

But Vivian could never understand in the least why her husband, not very long after marriage, asked her not to wear a wedding-ring or any ring whatever.

"Men are so queer!" covers a multitude of psychic agonies.

Life, for Jandron—life, softened by Vivian—knit itself up into some reasonable semblance of a normal pattern. But when, at lengthening intervals, memories even now awake—memories crawling amid the slime of cosmic mysteries that it is madness to approach—or when at certain times Jandron sees a ring of any sort, his heart chills with a cold that reeks of the horrors of Infinity.

And from shadows past the boundaries of our universe seem to beckon Things that, God grant, can never till the end of time be known on earth.

# THE SPACE HORDE

## by Chad Oliver

*The voracious arrivals from space could not be stopped by anything that humans could do. But maybe there was someone else who could help.*

**Chad Oliver,** *born Symmes Chadwick Oliver, wrote a respectable amount of SF, in short and novel lengths, and might have written a lot more if his day job hadn't had the description of head of the anthropology department of the University of Texas at Austin. He took his PhD in Anthropology from the University of California. His SF frequently echoed his chosen academic field, as did several western novels he wrote, including* The Wolf is My Brother, *which won the Spur Award for best historical novel. His first novel was the YA book,* Mists of Dawn, *published as one of the Winston Juvenile Science Fiction books, and it was either the second or the third SF novel*

*I read, back in the third grade (my first was definitely van Vogt's* Slan *in the second grade, but I don't now remember whether I read Simak's* City *or Oliver's* Mists of Dawn *next a year later). Either way, my fate was sealed after reading those three guys. That and his other novels are certainly worth seeking out, such as* Shadows in the Sun, The Winds of Time, Unearthly Neighbors, *and the* Things *from space novel,* The Shores of Another Sea *among others. The SF club NESFA has issued two massive volumes collecting many of his short stories,* A Star Above It *and* Far From This Earth, *also recommended, but the story which follows wasn't included, and this is, in fact, its first appearance in book form.*

**LOOK UP,** and out, to the stars.

Look along the light-years, across the gulfs of immensity, out through a universe of thinly starred darkness. Look, if you will, through tubular telescopes with concave mirrors two hundred inches in diameter. Look out into your universe, out and out and out—

You cannot see it all.

For the Earth is dust, dust floating in a black and endless sea. Space is a word, a feeble man-mouthed symbol, and it stands for a sea that mocks the imagination. Space is a sea, a titanic deep, an ocean. Space is no gentle lake, no friendly pond that welcomes the painted toys of children. Space is an ocean of vastness beyond comprehension, an ocean that is—

*Alive.*

A seething ocean adrift with millions and billions of floating islands, their faces turned toward galaxies of suns that flare and pulse and hurl radiation from many-colored atomic furnaces. A boiling maelstrom acrawl with life, life that slithers and creeps and walks and glides beneath liquids unimaginable. Oceans are the birthplaces of life, and on the billion shores of this huge mother-sea there is—

Everything.

And out of that sea, out of that dark ocean of life, one day They came, as They had to come. They pushed past man's little outposts and space stations as They would kick aside the strewn toys of children. They came as a hurricane, a ravening cyclone of alien life, thundering across cities as though cities were so many flimsy native huts and science only a primitive magic shrieked into the cutting teeth of the wind.

*They* came.

They came searching, hungering for reasons unguessable.

They came in screaming metal shells and the shells thudded into the Earth like hail. The shells cracked open, eggs bursting with life, and They came out. And They subdivided. They multiplied, spread out in bubbling circles, acid on the Earth. They ingested, They consumed—

Everything. Anything.

Insects, lizards, trees, rabbits, men.

They came from the mother-sea, from the ocean of dark immensity. They came to the Earth, thirsting, wanting—

And They could not be stopped.

*In a farmhouse only sixty miles from Paris, a haggard man took a few minutes too long to decide what he would carry with him. He got his wife and his eight-year-old daughter and they ran for the road under a warm, blind sun.*

*The sound, the hissing, bubbling sound, was all around them.*

*The girl began to scream.*

*There was a terrible scorched smell in the air, a smell of meat left too long on the fire.*

*The family was cut off.*

*The man threw down what he had in his arms, heaved it into the undulating, colorless mass. It disappeared. He picked up his daughter, ran back to the house, found a ladder. He helped his wife climb up to the roof, boosted the girl up the ladder, climbed up himself. They went as high as they could go and hung on.*

*It took a long time. The sun lazed through the arc of afternoon.*

*The stuff bubbled through the farmyard. A tree fell into it with a dull plop. The tree disappeared.*

*The house began to tremble, to slide—*

*They hung on, the man and the woman and the child, not even screaming now.*

*The house crumbled under them.*

*They—fell in . . .*

From outside, through the open window, the sound came. It came in waves, rising and falling, like a chant. It was made by fifty thousand human voices.

The sound came from the football stadium.

"Close that blasted window," Adrian Hackett said, grinding out his cigarette against the untidy pile of butts in the ashtray on the polished brown table. "That lament for the dead is driving me nuts."

Of the three men in the room, the biologist Owen Landseer was closest to the window. He heaved his stocky frame out of his chair, reached out with his powerful hairy arms, and pulled the double windows shut with a surprisingly gentle motion.

They could still hear the prayers from the stadium, but the sound was muted now, a faraway wind sighing through nameless trees.

Landseer sat down again, hunching his big shoulders. "Maybe we should join them. My wife is over there now."

Quincy Rice, from the primate lab, snorted. He pulled at his neat, square beard. His voice was surprisingly loud for such a small man. "Nuts," he said succinctly. "We've got a job to do. Let's do it."

Ade Hackett fired up another cigarette, knowing that he was smoking too much, thinking what Donna would say if she knew. Funny to worry about that now. "We're one hell of a long way from being another Manhattan Project," he said. "Of course, there are thousands of other research teams working on this thing, but no one else is hitting it quite from our angle."

"I'd feel better if we *had* an angle," Landseer said gently. "I don't see one yet, but maybe I'm a little on the obtuse side."

"Puns, already," Quincy muttered.

"We've got five days to turn in a preliminary report to

the United Nations," Ade said. "The situation is simple. Those things, whatever They are, landed on this planet slightly over a month ago. I guess most of us never really thought that Earth *was* a planet—it was the world, the universe, all there was. We weren't worried about space; we thought we had troubles enough here at home. Result: we're helpless, absolutely helpless. We're all set up to defend ourselves against the wrong enemy."

Outside, the prayers from the football stadium continued. They made a steady background, a surf of sound breaking against the granite rocks of a lonely shore.

Ade felt the tension crawling within him. He hadn't tried to eat any breakfast and he had been sick after lunch. Donna had been in London visiting her mother, and now she couldn't get out. All the transportation facilities were tied into a monumental knot. Sure, They weren't in England yet, but the Channel was narrow, so narrow, and They were boiling across rivers in France . . .

He looked at his cigarette. She had been after him for years to cut down on his smoking.

"The papers and the newscasts are making with the same old junk," he said. "We're making jim-dandy progress, the solution is near at hand, keep calm—all the usual bromides. The fact is that we haven't been able to touch Them at all. We don't even know what They are. Apparently, They can nullify our best weapons with ease. Planes can't get near Them. Missiles with hydrogen warheads just drop in the middle of that stuff and are *digested.* Chemicals have no effect. So far, we haven't even been an irritant. We might as well not be here."

"They've just hit the three places, that right?" Quincy asked, filling his pipe from a red tobacco can.

Ade nodded. "There are three centers. One in France, one in East Africa, one in China near Peiping. If They go on expanding at the present rate, we've got less than two years left to us. Probably not that long—the riots and the epidemics have already started. And there may be other landings. They could be right here in Michigan tomorrow."

The word hung in the smoke-blued air of the room.

*Tomorrow.*

Owen Landseer involuntarily glanced toward the door.

"They won't use the door, Owen," Quincy said, puffing on his pipe. "They just multiply right through the wall."

"Cut it out," Owen said nervously.

"I talked to General Massinger this morning," Ade said, ignoring the byplay. "They've got that report from the Rand boys."

Quincy raised his eyebrows.

The room was suddenly very still.

"The guys at the Rand Corporation have fed all the data we have into the big computers," Ade told them. "Unless those data were all wet, which is hardly very likely, there's only a very small possibility for error."

"And?" prompted Owen Landseer.

"And the computers figure that man's survival chances are precisely zero," Ade said quietly. "Given the nature of the problem, the kind of brains we have to work with, and the amount of time available, *there is no solution.* In plain English, gentlemen, if we ourselves are the best defense Earth has to offer, then man has had it. We're through."

There was a long silence in the little academic room with the polished brown table and hard wooden chairs.

Outside, the chanted prayers rose up from the football stadium and lost themselves in the wind and the sky.

*Tanganyika Territory, East Africa.*

*Highland country, rich grasslands surrounded by towering volcanic mountains. Flat-topped acacia trees, flowers nodding under the sun, warm and pleasant days.*

*It had been a good place to live.*

*Mud-roofed huts grouped in a circle, with an outside fence of thorn-brush for protection. Humped cattle, some with long, graceful horns, some with stubby horns. A smell of milk and cattle and native beer—*

*And a smell of terror.*

*They have come: out of the sky, across the lakes and fields.*

*A sound: hissing, seething, bubbling.*

*The village is empty now, the people are gone.*

*They move in, taking Their time. Eating, digesting, destroying. There is no hurry. Grass, frantic cattle, sheep, a few donkeys, and then the fragile huts themselves . . .*

*At the doorway of one of the huts, framed by the darkness within, a small boy, rubbing his sleepy eyes. Left behind somehow, forgotten in the haste and the confusion and the fear.*

*He looks, listens.*

*He cries out a word, a child's word, an uncomprehending word. He calls to his family, his clan, the world he has known. They have never failed him before. He expects gentle arms, warmth, reassurance.*

*There is nothing.*

*The boy begins to run, crying, his eyes wide.*

*He steps into the bubbling, hissing mass.*

*He has no foot.*

*He pitches forward, and he is gone. His screams continue for an impossibly long time.*

*Only the sky is clean, for They have taken the land.*

High in the branches of a tropical forest, half-hidden in pools of shadow, an animal nibbles at a wild fruit with sharp white teeth. It is a small animal, no larger than a rabbit. It has bright, alert eyes and its coat is soft and brown. It cocks its head as though listening, but there is no sound. Then it moves gracefully along the high branches from one tree to another. Half a mile away, invisible in the cool green shadows, another animal licks out his long red tongue, catches an insect and waits.

Ade Hackett shifted his position on the hard chair and chewed on a menthol cough drop to get the stale taste of smoke out of his mouth. He wasn't sleepy, and in fact, he knew he would be unable to sleep without a pill when he finally did get to bed, but he was in that flat state of exhaustion where a man just keeps going on nervous energy. His bloodshot eyes burned in his skull.

Ade was a paleontologist, and a good one, but he seldom thought of himself that way. No man, to himself, is merely a paleontologist or psychologist or butcher or mechanic or writer. A man is many things: a scientist, perhaps, but also a guy who likes to get drunk once in a while, make love, tell jokes, go fishing. Ade was a tall, skinny man with a tough, weather-beaten face and blue eyes that had twinkled in happier days. He was no lover of crowds, and there were those who considered him unfriendly. He was most content when he could get outside in the lonesome western canyons, feel the sun on his back. He loved to sleep under the warm stars where he could hear the frogs croaking along the banks of a mist-cloaked river.

Sometimes, Ade figured that paleontology was more an excuse than anything else. Fossil-hunting was like fishing: it gave a man a reason to get off by himself, get off where he could smell the trees and the grass and the sand and the woodsmoke, get off where he could be a man again, and be happy.

If it hadn't been for Donna, he would have been tempted to go off somewhere and enjoy himself. If the world had to end, it would be better to face it in the clean air under a blue sky. A conference room was no place to shake hands with death.

He would have been tempted, but he wouldn't have gone. There were times when a man just didn't run away.

"Okay," he said. "Our job is to turn in a preliminary report. We don't have to *prove* anything. We don't even have to think that our idea is very likely. We're up the creek without a paddle, and we have to do the best we can."

Owen Landseer nodded, his heavy features haggard with strain. "We're faced with a problem we can't solve," he said. "And if we can't solve it—"

"Check," Ade agreed. "Our business boils down to one simple question: *Are we absolutely certain that man is the highest life-form on this planet?* All of us are supposed to be experts on the process of evolution. Has evolution stopped with man—or is there something else?"

"You mean we're looking for a kind of superman?" Quincy Rice nudged his beard with his red tobacco can. "Nothing to it. All we need is the Abominable Snowman. We track him down, clap him on the shoulder, and say, 'Well, Abominable, old bean, how about lending us a hand?' Then Abominable giggles abominably, shoves us off a cliff, and we're right back where we started."

Ade laughed. He hadn't laughed in a long time. "Afraid our job is a bit more fundamental, Quincy," he said. "There are other research teams exploring the possibility of *Homo superior.* No, we're looking for something else." He paused, fingering the cellophane wrapper from the cough drop box. "You know, we chatter a lot about mutations and advances and one thing and another, and yet we always seem to assume that the next step up in evolution is going to be a development of *man.* But isn't that really contrary to everything we know about past evolution?"

Owen Landseer frowned. "I see what you're getting at. The first amphibians came from the lobe-finned fish, which weren't very advanced fishes. The first mammals came from a very primitive reptile group, before the dinosaurs or the snakes had even evolved."

"In other words," Quincy said, leaning forward, "what comes after the *mammals*?"

"Exactly." Ade lit another cigarette, excited now despite his weariness. "If you look back over the fossil record, there's one very interesting fact. The first fish came from the Silurian period of the Paleozoic, around 390 million years ago. The first amphibians came later in the Paleozoic, and so did the first reptiles. About 190 million years ago you get into the Mesozoic, the so-called Age of Reptiles, but in terms of evolution, the Mesozoic is mainly important because it gave rise to the first mammals and the first birds, both of them offshoots from the reptiles. And then the last great era, the Cenozoic, got underway around 55 million years ago. We're still in the Cenozoic. And, gentlemen, what new vertebrate class has evolved in our Cenozoic?"

"Zero," said Quincy Rice, lighting his pipe with a wooden stick match and then carefully breaking the match before he tossed it into the wastebasket.

"Zero," Ade agreed. "In the whole Cenozoic we don't get a single new *kind* of animal. Sure, we get the Primates, winding up with men, but the primates are just one special type of mammal. What's happened? Is there some unknown animal hiding in the brush today, just as the first mammals scurried under the feet of the dinosaurs? *What come after the mammals?*"

"Maybe nothing does," Quincy suggested.

"Do *you* believe that?" Ade asked.

"No," Quincy admitted cheerfully, puffing on his pipe.

"There's one point, though," Owen Landseer said. "It could be that physical evolution has more or less been by-passed. Julian Huxley and others have shown that you get a basically different kind of evolution in man. His culture, his way of life, changes without a corresponding change in physical type. An ant society can only change genetically because the ant lifeway is essentially instinctive, but man *learns* his way of life by means of language. There haven't been any fundamental changes in human physical structure for at least fifty thousand years, but our culture has changed plenty."

"I'll buy that," Ade said, "but it only applies to man. We still haven't obliterated other forms of life on this planet—how much effect have we had, say, on some of the wilder parts of the Amazon jungles?"

"But look here," Quincy objected. "You're asking us to perform an impossible task. How can we imagine a radically different form of life? How can we speculate about an animal as far above us as we are above the lizards? I can't see how we would have much better luck than a bright ape back in the Miocene would have in trying to dream up New York City. We're limited by our own mental processes, after all; that's why fictional supermen are supermen, nothing but magnified human beings."

Ade lit another cigarette, inhaled, and almost at once ground it out in the overflowing ashtray. "You're forgetting something, Quincy. We have one important advantage over that bright ape of yours. We've got a tool to work with: the scientific method. We know something about the processes of evolution, and we've got the record of past evolutionary development to work from. There *are* some consistent trends in evolution: in patterns of reproduction, in the efficiency of energy utilization, in the growth of certain parts of the brain, in the circulatory systems, in the placement of the limbs. If there *is* something on this planet higher than the mammals, I think we might be able to make some pretty good guesses about it. I think we've got all the information we need, locked up inside our own three skulls. All we have to do is drag it out and look at it."

"If the animal exists at all," Quincy said.

"It had better exist," Ade said grimly.

*It was raining in Peiping: a dull gray rain that fell endlessly from a leaden sky.*

*Lapping at the city like a nightmare swamp, They bubbled and heaved over what had been roads and collective farms, fields of grain and cotton, barnyards alive with pigs and poultry. The rain fell into Them with sodden splashes, and was gone.*

*There had been some two million people in Peiping. Almost a million of them were still there, milling through the streets.*

*They came. They hissed and bubbled. They nibbled at the edges of the new housing developments, sucked at the old courtyard homes, licked at the streaming streets.*

*On an old brick wall, a smiling portrait of Chairman Mao.*

*They ate at the wall, slowly, brick by brick.*

*A dumpy short-haired woman in a quilted blue uniform watches them, her dark eyes wild.*

*She screams.*

*She runs at the wall, claws at Them, fills her hands with the elastic, colorless bubbles—desperate movements . . .*

*She looks at the stumps of her arms.*

*She falls forward, her eyes wide open.*

*She is a lump, and then nothing.*

*A terrible, burning stench fills the wet air, until even the rain is a stinking, evil thing, falling, falling . . .*

* * *

The trees stand on strong bark-covered legs and far above the jungle floor they spread out the green umbrellas of their branches to make a roof for the world.

In those trees, two animals, side by side.

They smile, sharing each other. Oh, yes, they can smile—smile with lips and eyes and minds. You might see them from below, brown coats blending into the bark of the trees. You might think they were monkeys or even squirrels, for you would not see them well.

You might even take a shot at them, but you will miss.

They sit there quietly, smiling, looking down.

Thinking?

Perhaps.

You might call it that.

Ade Hackett hung up the telephone in the hall and walked slowly down the corridor past the deserted classrooms. He went back into the little conference room, fighting a blind sense of panic.

"They've landed in Ohio," he said.

"Where?" asked Owen Landseer.

"Near Akron."

"And?" said Quincy, cleaning his pipe.

"We've thrown everything at Them up to and including the kitchen sink. Nothing. So many spitballs. We're evacuating the area."

"And then what?" Quincy asked.

Ade shrugged. "You evacuate areas until there aren't any more areas to evacuate. Then you sit and take it."

"They'll be here in Michigan soon," Quincy said.

Outside, they could hear the swell of voices from the football stadium.

"Let's get with it," Ade said. "Owen, you keep notes, will you? You're the only one with a decent handwriting. Now, what have we got?"

They went to work. It was nothing very impressive, Ade thought. No fancy lights and big computers. No hysterics. No shouts of "Eureka!" Just three guys sitting in a room, trying to do the toughest job—

Trying to think. There was one thing that made it easier. Obviously, if the animal existed at all, and if he was capable of action against the things, he didn't know of Their existence; They had encountered no opposition. Therefore, the animal didn't live in Africa, France, China, or the United States. When you subtracted those, there were only a few possible places where such an animal might be found: the Polar Regions, the wilder areas of South America, some scattered islands.

*Think, damn you, think!*

Well, what would the animal look like?

It would be an offshoot from the mammals, obviously. But it would not be a development from the most complex and specialized of living mammals; evolution *always* builds on simple, generalized forms. It wouldn't *look* very spectacular. The first ratlike mammals hadn't been very impressive, and the *very* early mammals, the transitional forms such as Cynognathus, hadn't even looked like mammals at all.

See him?

Small, furry, inconspicuous . . .

It would have a good brain. The dumbest mammal looked like Einstein if you compared him to a fish or a frog or a dinosaur. But the animal wouldn't just be smart as a man is smart. It would *use* its brain differently. Man found the capacity to symbolize, and thus to create a language. The next step would be to eliminate the *necessity* for language . . .

A silent animal, to our ears.

Man's brain can grope its way ahead, step by step, and communicate its findings to others by language. It can proceed logically by trial and error, it can build on past results.

Next?

A new brain, a different brain. See it? It is a short-cut brain. It sees relationships, quickly and accurately, and it sees them *intuitively.* No need to pack around a warehouse full of facts. It perceives answers at will *when and if it needs them.* They are simply there, as a man sees a club in a fallen branch. And if two beings always evaluate situations in the same way, if they really *understand* each other, what is there to communicate?

And if a brain knows its own power . . .

Babies?

There would be few births. Twins would be unknown. The female would have a very long pregnancy. An individual would be born almost fully mature, eliminating the long period of youthful helplessness.

See him?

He looks like a simple mammal. He would have evolved from a generalized animal—

Like an opossum.

Like a tree shrew.

He lives in tropical country, where the trees are thick. In the Old World, probably. An island, perhaps—

Like Madagascar?

The three of them, Ade and Owen and Quincy, turned in their report to the United Nations. A long shot? Certainly.

What else can you do when your back is against the wall, the blindfold over your eyes, the rifles of the firing squad lifting in the sunlight?

Outside, the prayers continued.

*They kept coming.*

*They seeped across the fields under cloudless blue sides, They poured into towns and cities beneath a silver moon and frosted stars.*

*They kept coming.*

*Man could not stop Them.*

*But man was searching—*

High in the trees that thrust their green arms toward the sun, lost in jungle-shadows, the two animals sit on a branch. They are silent, enjoying the cool shade.

They turn, looking, before the sounds come.

Men, hacking their way across the jungle floor.

Men.

Funny men! Oh, they know men. They see men even in the jungle depths. They listen to the hums and buzzes in men's minds.

Men are comical.

Men are the biggest and the smallest animals in the jungle.

They think they rule the world.

The young like men. They look and listen and laugh. Sometimes you had to join them. Men *are* funny! Yes, they are cute. You have to give them that . . .

New thoughts.

New hums and buzzes.

The two animals sit more erectly, more alertly.

They close their eyes to see better—

*Help.*

*If we could only find them, if only they exist.*

*Where could they be?*

*What can we say to them?*

*Death. Destruction. A jelly-sea rising on the Earth. Eggs from the stars, eggs that hatch into living bubbles that eat into the very land you walk on. Bubbles. Devouring, ingesting, hissing—*

*Oh, God, Mary was in France . . .*

*Not here yet. Looks so peaceful. Wish I had a drink of water. Feet are tired. They'll be here, they'll be everywhere.*

*Crazy animal. Dream animal! Doesn't exist!*

*Wild goose chase.*

*What time is it?*

*Help!*

*Assistance!*

*Where are you?*

*No use—*

*Oh, God, Mary was in France . . .*

*Feet hurt.*

*Where are you? Where . . .*

* * *

Men.

Funny men!

Men are always worried.

Comical.

The two animals move higher into the trees, seeking concealment. They blend into the bark of the branches. They sit quietly.

They care little for men, though men *are* cute.

But they love their land, their winds and flowers, their long nights and lazy afternoons.

Those images.

Those things from the star-sea.

Alien.

Hostile.

Dangerous?

They had better be stopped. They should not be allowed to come further.

The two animals walk along the high branches toward the center of the island. Other animals converge on the place, taking their time, enjoying their world. The sun is warm, the earth below them fresh and moist.

There are many of them. There have never been so many in the circle before. They fill the trees. They do not touch. They do not speak.

Their eyes are closed.

*Concentrate.*

Frequencies?

*Project.*

While it is still daylight there is nothing to see. A faint vibration in the air, perhaps. Heat waves. A tension.

Electricity. Other animals are nervous, uncertain. Somewhere, a dog howls.

Then twilight.

Night.

See it?

A crackling electric blue. It is not bright but it hurts the eyes to look upon it. A sheet of vibrating blue fire. A field, an aura. It hovers over the island, taut, shimmering.

It pushes out, seeking, searching—

Finding.

*Hurting!*

*Burning!*

Fire, searing at alien nervous systems.

*Concentrate!*

Simple.

Men are so funny.

Always making a big thing out of nothing. Of course, they can't understand, not really.

They *are* comical!

Men.

But they are cute.

You have to give them that . . .

The change came with startling abruptness.

The hissing torrent of alien life had washed over the Earth like a tidal wave from an infinite sea, smashing all before it. They had come, and They had expanded, grown, multiplied. They had been a monstrous cancer eating at the life of a planet, and They had seemed invincible. And then They—stopped. Suddenly. Completely.

Some said that the electric blue haze visible in the

night sky had something to do with it. Some said that it was the will of God. Some advanced learned explanations concerning metabolic exhaustion and chemical poisoning. No one knew. But They stopped. The crowding pressure ceased. The edges of that colorless mass of jelly began to shrivel. They did not die, whatever They were. They simply contracted, flowing back, leaving a lifeless husk behind. They retreated, recombined, snaked back along invisible, biochemical threads toward the original centers of radiation.

They flowed back through the inert crust—

And there was a heaving, a trembling, a volcanic upheaval deep in the Earth. The sunken metal shells screamed up through the lifeless muck, dripped into the sky, flashed back—

Back through the blue skies and white clouds, back into the dark ocean of life that had spawned. Them. Back to the billion-shored mother-sea, back to the ocean of stars.

Behind Them, They left vast sheets of colorless, crusted matter: strange new glaciers to gleam and melt beneath a golden sun. And They left other things behind Them—

A memory.

A fear.

A promise.

A vault of night, dusted with diamond stars: a night that would never again be soft and comforting, a night that had become a window opening on a seething maelstrom of life, life that slithers and creeps and walks and glides beneath liquids unimaginable . . .

And a naked, terrible sky.

But the land-choking crusts shriveled and blackened and disintegrated. The rains came, and the husk became a scum that fertilized the soil.

Plants began to grow, and green grass.

And men came back to their lands.

Ade Hackett sprawled comfortably in his favorite easy chair, his sleeves rolled up over his tanned arms, his feet propped indecorously on the glass-topped coffee table. He could hear Donna whistling an off-key tune in the kitchen as she brewed her magic on the stove. Around him he sensed the security of his home: the paintings, the books, the sectioned fly rod, the pleasant clutter.

He jiggled the ice in his Scotch, sipped it, felt the smoky liquid warm him all the way down.

"When I was a kid," he said, "we used to boil grasshoppers, just for the hell of it. Drop them into a tin can full of hot water and watch them turn pink. I don't like to think about that now."

Quincy Rice, sitting cross-legged on the floor, puffed at his pipe. "How about me? I work in a primate lab, Ade. We experiment with chimpanzees when we can get them. Sometimes we test new medicines on them. Sometimes they die."

"Funny, isn't it," Ade asked, "when the shoe is on the other foot?"

"We don't *know* that."

"Don't we?"

"I read a piece in the *Times* this morning. Seems the alien life-forms just got indigestion from old Mother Earth. Statistics and everything. Very scientific."

"And the blue lights?"

"Atmospheric phenomena, my boy. Five leading astronomers have *proved* . . ."

Ade put down his empty glass, clasped his hands behind his head. "Quincy, I think we saved the world, or a good part of it."

"You'll never prove that."

"We may not have to."

Quincy stroked his beard. "Meaning?"

Ade uncoiled himself, sat forward. "What if we were right? What if that animal of ours really exists? What if we *did* make contact with it? Where does that leave us?"

Quincy grinned. "Behind the well-known eight ball."

"Exactly. Quincy, *we're* the dinosaurs now—or at least the apes. We don't know anything about those hypothetical animals of ours, but we know what they can *do.* They may not stay put on that island forever. I don't think they're hostile toward men, or we would have heard from them before. But they're just beginning. They may want some more room before long."

"And then?"

Ade shrugged. "Depends on what they think of us. Look, we don't hate apes, do we? Of course not. We like them. We think apes are pretty sharp. But the apes are headed for extinction, just the same."

"Be kind to your web-footed friends," Quincy said.

Ade laughed, reached for a cigarette'. "It's out of our hands, of course. And it won't happen in our time. It might even be that we could be useful to them, somehow. Just the same, Quincy, I kind of like men. I happen to be one. I don't think we're through yet."

Quincy killed the rest of his Scotch. "It did come at an interesting time, didn't it?"

Ade nodded. "Whenever man gets himself into a hole, his culture gives him something so he can dig himself out again. I've heard a lot of prayers lately, and maybe we ought to offer thanks for technology. We're on the verge of going out into space.

"We're going to need those spaceships, Quincy. Yes, those ships will give us time. We may lose the Earth, but the universe is a big place. I have a hunch that man hasn't reached the end of his road yet, not by a long shot. And next time we run into Them, we'll be ready."

"I hope you're right."

Ade got to his feet.

In his mind, he saw an animal. Furry, inconspicuous.

"I wonder what he thinks of us," he said quietly.

High in the jungle trees where the clean sunlight falls in mottled pools, an animal sits alone and not alone. It nibbles at a wild fruit with sharp white teeth.

It is a small animal, no larger than a rabbit. It has bright, alert eyes and its coat is soft and brown. It cocks its head as though listening.

A man, walking across the jungle floor far below.

Funny man!

The animal smiles, sharing a secret joke.

Men *are* comical!

Men are cute.

You have to give them that.

# THE LEECH

## by Robert Sheckley

*I don't thing I can do better than the original teaser blurb given this story when it appeared in* Galaxy: *"A visitor should be fed, but this one could eat you out of house and home . . . literally!"*

⁂

***Robert Sheckley*** *(1928-2005) seemed to explode into print in the early 1950s with stories in nearly every science fiction magazine on the newsstands. Actually, the explosion was bigger than most realized, since he was simultaneously writing even more stories under a number of pseudonyms. For example, "The Leech" was originally published as by "Phillip Barbee." His forte was humor, wild and unpredictable, often absurdist, much like the work of Douglas Adams three decades later. His work has been compared to the Marx Brothers by Harlan Ellison®, to Voltaire by both Brian W. Aldiss and J.G. Ballard, and Neil Gaiman has called Sheckley "Probably the best short-*

*story writer during the 1950s to the mid-1960s working in any field." "The Leech" is a suspenseful and scary yarn, and it's a pleasure to bring it back in book form.*

**THE LEECH** was waiting for food. For millennia it had been drifting across the vast emptiness of space. Without consciousness, it had spent the countless centuries in the void between the stars. It was unaware when it finally reached a sun. Life-giving radiation flared around the hard, dry spore. Gravitation tugged at it.

A planet claimed it, with other stellar debris, and the leech fell, still dead-seeming within its tough spore case.

One speck of dust among many, the winds blew it around the Earth, played with it, and let it fall.

On the ground, it began to stir. Nourishment soaked in, permeating the spore case. It grew—and fed.

Frank Conners came up on the porch and coughed twice. "Say, pardon me, Professor," he said.

The long, pale man didn't stir from the sagging couch. His horn-rimmed glasses were perched on his forehead, and he was snoring very gently.

"I'm awful sorry to disturb you," Conners said, pushing back his battered felt hat. "I know it's your restin' week and all, but there's something damned funny in the ditch."

The pale man's left eyebrow twitched, but he showed no other sign of having heard.

Frank Conners coughed again, holding his spade in one purple-veined hand. "Didja hear me, Professor?"

"Of course I heard you," Micheals said in a muffled voice, his eyes still closed. "You found a pixie."

"A what?" Conners asked, squinting at Micheals.

"A little man in a green suit. Feed him milk, Conners."

"No, sir. I think it's a rock."

Micheals opened one eye and focused it in Conners' general direction.

"I'm awfully sorry about it," Conners said. Professor Micheals' resting week was a ten-year-old custom, and his only eccentricity. All winter Micheals taught anthropology, worked on half a dozen committees, dabbled in physics and chemistry, and still found time to write a book a year. When summer came, he was tired.

Arriving at his worked-out New York State farm, it was his invariable rule to do absolutely nothing for a week. He hired Frank Conners to cook for that week and generally make himself useful, while Professor Micheals slept.

During the second week, Micheals would wander around, look at the trees and fish. By the third week he would be getting a tan, reading, repairing the sheds and climbing mountains. At the end of four weeks, he could hardly wait to get back to the city.

But the resting week was sacred.

"I really wouldn't bother you for anything small," Conners said apologetically. "But that damned rock melted two inches off my spade."

Micheals opened both eyes and sat up. Conners held out the spade. The rounded end was sheared cleanly off. Micheals swung himself off the couch and slipped his feet into battered moccasins.

"Let's see this wonder," he said.

* * *

The object was lying in the ditch at the end of the front lawn, three feet from the main road. It was round, about the size of a truck tire, and solid throughout. It was about an inch thick, as far as he could tell, grayish black and intricately veined.

"Don't touch it," Conners warned.

"I'm not going to. Let me have your spade." Micheals took the spade and prodded the object experimentally. It was completely unyielding. He held the spade to the surface for a moment, then withdrew it. Another inch was gone.

Micheals frowned, and pushed his glasses tighter against his nose. He held the spade against the rock with one hand, the other held close to the surface. More of the spade disappeared.

"Doesn't seem to be generating heat," he said to Conners. "Did you notice any the first time?"

Conners shook his head.

Micheals picked up a clod of dirt and tossed it on the object. The dirt dissolved quickly, leaving no trace on the gray-black surface. A large stone followed the dirt, and disappeared in the same way.

"Isn't that just about the damnedest thing you ever saw, Professor?" Conners asked.

"Yes," Micheals agreed, standing up again. "It just about is."

He hefted the spade and brought it down smartly on the object. When it hit, he almost dropped the spade. He had been gripping the handle rigidly, braced for a recoil. But the spade struck that unyielding surface and stayed. There was no perceptible give, but absolutely no recoil.

"Whatcha think it is?" Conners asked.

"It's no stone," Micheals said. He stepped back. "A leech drinks blood. This thing seems to be drinking dirt. And spades." He struck it a few more times, experimentally. The two men looked at each other. On the road, half a dozen Army trucks rolled past.

"I'm going to phone the college and ask a physics man about it," Micheals said. "Or a biologist. I'd like to get rid of that thing before it spoils my lawn."

They walked back to the house.

Everything fed the leech. The wind added its modicum of kinetic energy, ruffling across the gray-black surface. Rain fell, and the force of each individual drop added to its store. The water was sucked in by the all-absorbing surface.

The sunlight above it was absorbed, and converted into mass for its body. Beneath it, the soil was consumed, dirt, stones and branches broken down by the leech's complex cells and changed into energy. Energy was converted back into mass, and the leech grew.

Slowly, the first flickers of consciousness began to return. Its first realization was of the impossible smallness of its body.

It grew.

When Micheals looked the next day, the leech was eight feet across, sticking out into the road and up the side of the lawn. The following day it was almost eighteen feet in diameter, shaped to fit the contour of the ditch, and covering most of the road. That day the sheriff drove up in his model A, followed by half the town.

"Is that your leech thing, Professor Micheals?" Sheriff Flynn asked.

"That's it," Micheals said. He had spent the past days looking unsuccessfully for an acid that would dissolve the leech.

"We gotta get it out of the road," Flynn said, walking truculently up to the leech. "Something like this, you can't let it block the road, Professor. The Army's gotta use this road."

"I'm terribly sorry," Micheals said with a straight face. "Go right ahead, Sheriff. But be careful. It's hot." The leech wasn't hot, but it seemed the simplest explanation under the circumstances.

Micheals watched with interest as the sheriff tried to shove a crowbar under it. He smiled to himself when it was removed with half a foot of its length gone.

The sheriff wasn't so easily discouraged. He had come prepared for a stubborn piece of rock. He went to the rumble seat of his car and took out a blowtorch and a sledgehammer, ignited the torch and focused it on one edge of the leech.

After five minutes, there was no change. The gray didn't turn red or even seem to heat up. Sheriff Flynn continued to bake it for fifteen minutes, then called to one of the men.

"Hit that spot with the sledge, Jerry."

Jerry picked up the sledgehammer, motioned the sheriff back, and swung it over his head. He let out a howl as the hammer struck unyieldingly. There wasn't a fraction of recoil.

In the distance they heard the roar of an Army convoy.

"Now we'll get some action," Flynn said.

Micheals wasn't so sure. He walked around the periphery of the leech, asking himself what kind of substance would react that way. The answer was easy—no substance. No known substance.

The driver in the lead jeep held up his hand, and the long convoy ground to a halt. A hard, efficient-looking officer stepped out of the jeep. From the star on either shoulder, Micheals knew he was a brigadier general.

"You can't block this road," the general said. He was a tall, spare man in suntans, with a sunburned face and cold eyes. "Please clear that thing away."

"We can't move it," Micheals said. He told the general what had happened in the past few days.

"It must be moved," the general said. "This convoy must go through." He walked closer and looked at the leech. "You say it can't be jacked up by a crowbar? A torch won't burn it?"

"That's right," Micheals said, smiling faintly.

"Driver," the general said over his shoulder. "Ride over it."

Micheals started to protest, but stopped himself. The military mind would have to find out in its own way.

The driver put his jeep in gear and shot forward, jumping the leech's four-inch edge. The jeep got to the center of the leech and stopped.

"I didn't tell you to stop!" the general bellowed.

"I didn't, sir!" the driver protested.

The jeep had been yanked to a stop and had stalled. The driver started it again, shifted to four-wheel drive, and tried to ram forward. The jeep was fixed immovably, as though set in concrete.

"Pardon me," Micheals said. "If you look, you can see that the tires are melting down."

The general stared, his hand creeping automatically toward his pistol belt. Then he shouted, "Jump, driver! Don't touch that gray stuff."

White-faced, the driver climbed to the hood of his jeep, looked around him, and jumped clear.

There was complete silence as everyone watched the jeep. First its tires melted down, and then the rims. The body, resting on the gray surface, melted, too.

The aerial was the last to go.

The general began to swear softly under his breath. He turned to the driver. "Go back and have some men bring up hand grenades and dynamite."

The driver ran back to the convoy.

"I don't know what you've got here," the general said. "But it's not going to stop a U.S. Army convoy."

Micheals wasn't so sure.

The leech was nearly awake now, and its body was calling for more and more food. It dissolved the soil under it at a furious rate, filling it in with its own body, flowing outward.

A large object landed on it, and that became food also. Then suddenly—

A burst of energy against its surface, and then another, and another. It consumed them gratefully, converting them into mass. Little metal pellets struck it, and their kinetic energy was absorbed, their mass converted. More explosions took place, helping to fill the starving cells.

It began to sense things—controlled combustion around it, vibrations of wind, mass movements.

There was another, greater explosion, a taste of real food! Greedily it ate, growing faster. It waited anxiously for more explosions, while its cells screamed for food.

But no more came. It continued to feed on the soil and on the Sun's energy. Night came, noticeable for its lesser energy possibilities, and then more days and nights. Vibrating objects continued to move around it.

It ate and grew and flowed.

Micheals stood on a little hill, watching the dissolution of his house. The leech was several hundred yards across now, lapping at his front porch.

Good-by, home, Micheals thought, remembering the ten summers he had spent there.

The porch collapsed into the body of the leech. Bit by bit, the house crumpled.

The leech looked like a field of lava now, a blasted spot on the green Earth.

"Pardon me, sir," a soldier said, coming up behind him. "General O'Donnell would like to see you."

"Right," Micheals said, and took his last look at the house.

He followed the soldier through the barbed wire that had been set up in a half-mile circle around the leech. A company of soldiers was on guard around it, keeping back the reporters and the hundreds of curious people who had flocked to the scene. Micheals wondered why he was still allowed inside. Probably, he decided, because most of this was taking place on his land.

The soldier brought him to a tent. Micheals stooped and went in. General O'Donnell, still in suntans, was seated at a small desk. He motioned Micheals to a chair.

"I've been put in charge of getting rid of this leech," he said to Micheals.

Micheals nodded, not commenting on the advisability of giving a soldier a scientist's job.

"You're a professor, aren't you?"

"Yes. Anthropology."

"Good. Smoke?" The general lighted Micheals' cigarette. "I'd like you to stay around here in an advisory capacity. You were one of the first to see this leech. I'd appreciate your observations on—" he smiled—"the enemy."

"I'd be glad to," Micheals said. "However, I think this is more in the line of a physicist or a biochemist."

"I don't want this place cluttered with scientists," General O'Donnell said, frowning at the tip of his cigarette. "Don't get me wrong. I have the greatest appreciation for science. I am, if I do say so, a scientific soldier. I'm always interested in the latest weapons. You can't fight any kind of a war any more without science."

O'Donnell's sunburned face grew firm. "But I can't have a team of longhairs poking around this thing for the next month, holding me up. My job is to destroy it, by any means in my power, and at once. I am going to do just that."

"I don't think you'll find it that easy," Micheals said.

"That's what I want you for," O'Donnell said. "Tell me why and I'll figure out a way of doing it."

"Well, as far as I can figure out, the leech is an organic mass-energy converter, and a frighteningly efficient one. I would guess that it has a double cycle. First, it converts mass into energy, then back into mass for its body. Second, energy is converted directly into the body mass. How this takes place, I do not know. The leech is not protoplasmic. It may not even be cellular—"

"So we need something big against it," O'Donnell interrupted. "Well, that's all right. I've got some big stuff here."

"I don't think you understand me," Micheals said. "Perhaps I'm not phrasing this very well. The leech eats energy. It can consume the strength of any energy weapon you use against it."

"What happens," O'Donnell asked, "if it keeps on eating?"

"I have no idea what its growth-limits are," Micheals said. "Its growth may be limited only by its food source."

"You mean it could continue to grow probably forever?"

"It could possibly grow as long as it had something to feed on."

"This is really a challenge," O'Donnell said. "That leech can't be totally impervious to force."

"It seems to be. I suggest you get some physicists in here. Some biologists also. Have them figure out a way of nullifying it."

The general put out his cigarette. "Professor, I cannot wait while scientists wrangle. There is an axiom of mine which I am going to tell you." He paused impressively. "Nothing is impervious to force. Muster enough force and anything will give. Anything.

"Professor," the general continued, in a friendlier tone, "you shouldn't sell short the science you represent. We have, massed under North Hill, the greatest accumulation of energy and radioactive weapons ever assembled in one spot. Do you think your leech can stand the full force of them?"

"I suppose it's possible to overload the thing," Micheals said doubtfully. He realized now why the general wanted him around. He supplied the trappings of science, without the authority to override O'Donnell.

"Come with me," General O'Donnell said cheerfully, getting up and holding back a flap of the tent. "We're going to crack that leech in half."

After a long wait, rich food started to come again, piped into one side of it. First there was only a little, and then more and more. Radiations, vibrations, explosions, solids, liquids—an amazing variety of edibles. It accepted them all. But the food was coming too slowly for the starving cells, for new cells were constantly adding their demands to the rest.

The ever-hungry body screamed for more food, faster!

Now that it had reached a fairly efficient size, it was fully awake. It puzzled over the energy-impressions around it, locating the source of the new food massed in one spot.

Effortlessly it pushed itself into the air, flew a little way and dropped on the food. Its super-efficient cells eagerly gulped the rich radioactive substances. But it did not ignore the lesser potentials of metal and clumps of carbohydrates.

"The damned fools," General O'Donnell said. "Why did they have to panic? You'd think they'd never been trained." He paced the ground outside his tent, now in a new location three miles back.

The leech had grown to two miles in diameter. Three farming communities had been evacuated.

Micheals, standing beside the general, was still stupefied by the memory. The leech had accepted the massed power of the weapons for a while, and then its entire bulk had lifted in the air. The Sun had been blotted out as it flew leisurely over North Hill, and dropped. There should have been time for evacuation, but the frightened soldiers had been blind with fear.

Sixty-seven men were lost in Operation Leech, and General O'Donnell asked permission to use atomic bombs. Washington sent a group of scientists to investigate the situation.

"Haven't those experts decided yet?" O'Donnell asked, halting angrily in front of the tent. "They've been talking long enough."

"It's a hard decision," Micheals said. Since he wasn't an official member of the investigating team, he had given his information and left. "The physicists consider it a biological matter, and the biologists seem to think the chemists should have the answer. No one's an expert on this, because it's never happened before. We just don't have the data."

"It's a military problem," O'Donnell said harshly. "I'm not interested in what the thing is—I want to know what can destroy it. They'd better give me permission to use the bomb."

Micheals had made his own calculations on that. It was impossible to say for sure, but taking a flying guess at the leech's mass-energy absorption rate, figuring in its size and apparent capacity for growth, an atomic bomb might overload it—if used soon enough.

He estimated three days as the limit of usefulness. The leech was growing at a geometric rate. It could cover the United States in a few months.

"For a week I've been asking permission to use the bomb," O'Donnell grumbled. "And I'll get it, but not until after those jackasses end their damned talking." He stopped pacing and turned to Micheals. "I am going to destroy the leech. I am going to smash it, if that's the last thing I do. It's more than a matter of security now. It's personal pride."

That attitude might make great generals, Micheals thought, but it wasn't the way to consider this problem. It was anthropomorphic of O'Donnell to see the leech as an enemy. Even the identification, "leech," was a humanizing factor. O'Donnell was dealing with it as he would any physical obstacle, as though the leech were the simple equivalent of a large army.

But the leech was not human, not even of this planet, perhaps. It should be dealt with in its own terms.

"Here come the bright boys now," O'Donnell said.

From a nearby tent a group of weary men emerged, led by Allenson, a government biologist.

"Well," the general asked, "have you figured out what it is?"

"Just a minute, I'll hack off a sample," Allenson said, glaring through red-rimmed eyes.

"Have you figured out some scientific way of killing it?"

"Oh, that wasn't too difficult," Moriarty, an atomic physicist, said wryly. "Wrap it in a perfect vacuum. That'll do the trick. Or blow it off the Earth with anti-gravity."

"But failing that," Allenson said, "we suggest you use your atomic bombs, and use them fast."

"Is that the opinion of your entire group?" O'Donnell asked, his eyes glittering.

"Yes."

The general hurried away. Micheals joined the scientists.

"He should have called us in at the very first," Allenson complained. "There's no time to consider anything but force now."

"Have you come to any conclusions about the nature of the leech?" Micheals asked.

"Only general ones," Moriarty said, "and they're about the same as yours. The leech is probably extraterrestrial in origin. It seems to have been in a spore-stage until it landed on Earth." He paused to light a pipe. "Incidentally, we should be damned glad it didn't drop in an ocean. We'd have had the Earth eaten out from under us before we knew what we were looking for."

They walked in silence for a few minutes.

"As you mentioned, it's a perfect converter—it can

transform mass into energy, and any energy into mass." Moriarty grinned. "Naturally that's impossible and I have figures to prove it."

"I'm going to get a drink," Allenson said. "Anyone coming?"

"Best idea of the week," Micheals said. "I wonder how long it'll take O'Donnell to get permission to use the bomb."

"If I know politics," Moriarty said, "too long."

The findings of the government scientists were checked by other government scientists. That took a few days. Then Washington wanted to know if there wasn't some alternative to exploding an atomic bomb in the middle of New York State. It took a little time to convince them of the necessity. After that, people had to be evacuated, which took more time.

Then orders were made out, and five atomic bombs were checked out of a cache. A patrol rocket was assigned, given orders, and put under General O'Donnell's command. This took a day more.

Finally, the stubby scout rocket was winging its way over New York. From the air, the grayish-black spot was easy to find. Like a festered wound, it stretched between Lake Placid and Elizabethtown, covering Keene and Keene Valley, and lapping at the edges of Jay.

The first bomb was released.

It had been a long wait after the first rich food. The greater radiation of day was followed by the lesser energy of night many times, as the leech ate away the earth beneath it, absorbed the air around it, and grew. Then one day—

An amazing burst of energy!

Everything was food for the leech, but there was always the possibility of choking. The energy poured over it, drenched it, battered it, and the leech grew frantically, trying to contain the titanic dose. Still small, it quickly reached its overload limit. The strained cells, filled to satiation, were given more and more food. The strangling body built new cells at lightning speed. And—

It held. The energy was controlled, stimulating further growth. More cells took over the load, sucking in the food.

The next doses were wonderfully palatable, easily handled. The leech overflowed its bounds, growing, eating, and growing.

That was a taste of real food! The leech was as near ecstasy as it had ever been. It waited hopefully for more, but no more came.

It went back to feeding on the Earth. The energy, used to produce more cells, was soon dissipated. Soon it was hungry again.

It would always be hungry.

O'Donnell retreated with his demoralized men. They camped ten miles from the leech's southern edge, in the evacuated town of Schroon Lake. The leech was over sixty miles in diameter now and still growing fast. It lay sprawled over the Adirondack Mountains, completely blanketing everything from Saranac Lake to Port Henry, with one edge of it over Westport, in Lake Champlain.

Everyone within two hundred miles of the leech was evacuated.

General O'Donnell was given permission to use hydrogen bombs, contingent on the approval of his scientists.

"What have the bright boys decided?" O'Donnell wanted to know.

He and Micheals were in the living room of an evacuated Schroon Lake house. O'Donnell had made it his new command post.

"Why are they hedging?" O'Donnell demanded impatiently. "The leech has to be blown up quick. What are they fooling around for?"

"They're afraid of a chain reaction," Micheals told him. "A concentration of hydrogen bombs might set one up in the Earth's crust or in the atmosphere. It might do any of half a dozen things."

"Perhaps they'd like me to order a bayonet attack," O'Donnell said contemptuously.

Micheals sighed and sat down in an armchair. He was convinced that the whole method was wrong. The government scientists were being rushed into a single line of inquiry. The pressure on them was so great that they didn't have a chance to consider any other approach but force—and the leech thrived on that.

Micheals was certain that there were times when fighting fire with fire was not applicable.

Fire. Loki, god of fire. And of trickery. No, there was no answer there. But Micheals' mind was in mythology now, retreating from the unbearable present.

Allenson came in, followed by six other men.

"Well," Allenson said, "there's a damned good chance of splitting the Earth wide open if you use the number of bombs our figures show you need."

"You have to take chances in war," O'Donnell replied bluntly. "Shall I go ahead?"

Micheals saw, suddenly, that O'Donnell didn't care if he did crack the Earth. The red-faced general only knew that he was going to set off the greatest explosion ever produced by the hand of Man.

"Not so fast," Allenson said. "I'll let the others speak for themselves."

The general contained himself with difficulty. "Remember," he said, "according to your own figures, the leech is growing at the rate of twenty feet an hour."

"And speeding up," Allenson added. "But this isn't a decision to be made in haste."

Micheals found his mind wandering again, to the lightning bolts of Zeus. That was what they needed. Or the strength of Hercules.

Or—

He sat up suddenly. "Gentlemen, I believe I can offer you a possible alternative, although it's a very dim one."

They stared at him.

"Have you ever heard of Antaeus?" he asked.

The more the leech ate, the faster it grew and the hungrier it became. Although its birth was forgotten, it did remember a long way back. It had eaten a planet in that ancient past. Grown tremendous, ravenous, it had made the journey to a nearby star and eaten that, replenishing the cells converted into energy for the trip.

But then there was no more food, and the next star was an enormous distance away.

It set out on the journey, but long before it reached the food, its energy ran out. Mass, converted back to energy to make the trip, was used up. It shrank.

Finally, all the energy was gone. It was a spore, drifting aimlessly, lifelessly, in space.

That was the first time. Or was it? It thought it could remember back to a distant, misty time when the Universe was evenly covered with stars. It had eaten through them, cutting away whole sections, growing, swelling. And the stars had swung off in terror, forming galaxies and constellations.

Or was that a dream?

Methodically, it fed on the Earth, wondering where the rich food was. And then it was back again, but this time above the leech.

It waited, but the tantalizing food remained out of reach. It was able to sense how rich and pure the food was.

Why didn't it fall?

For a long time the leech waited, but the food stayed out of reach. At last, it lifted and followed.

The food retreated, up, up from the surface of the planet. The leech went after as quickly as its bulk would allow.

The rich food fled out, into space, and the leech followed. Beyond, it could sense an even richer source.

The hot, wonderful food of a sun!

O'Donnell served champagne for the scientists in the

control room. Official dinners would follow, but this was the victory celebration.

"A toast," the general said, standing. The men raised their glasses. The only man not drinking was a lieutenant, sitting in front of the control board that guided the drone spaceship.

"To Micheals, for thinking of—what was it again, Micheals?"

"Antaeus." Micheals had been drinking champagne steadily, but he didn't feel elated. Antaeus, born of Ge, the Earth, and Poseidon, the Sea. The invincible wrestler. Each time Hercules threw him to the ground, he arose refreshed.

Until Hercules held him in the air.

Moriarty was muttering to himself, figuring with slide rule, pencil and paper. Allenson was drinking, but he didn't look too happy about it.

"Come on, you birds of evil omen," O'Donnell said, pouring more champagne. "Figure it out later. Right now, drink." He turned to the operator. "How's it going?"

Micheals' analogy had been applied to a spaceship. The ship, operated by remote control, was filled with pure radioactives. It hovered over the leech until, rising to the bait, it had followed. Antaeus had left his mother, the Earth, and was losing his strength in the air. The operator was allowing the spaceship to run fast enough to keep out of the leech's grasp, but close enough to keep it coming.

The spaceship and the leech were on a collision course with the Sun.

"Fine, sir," the operator said. "It's inside the orbit of Mercury now."

"Men," the general said, "I swore to destroy that thing.

This isn't exactly the way I wanted to do it. I figured on a more personal way. But the important thing is the destruction. You will all witness it. Destruction is at times a sacred mission. This is such a time. Men, I feel wonderful."

"Turn the spaceship!" It was Moriarty who had spoken. His face was white. "Turn the damned thing!"

He shoved his figures at them.

They were easy to read. The growth-rate of the leech. The energy-consumption rate, estimated. Its speed in space, a constant. The energy it would receive from the Sun as it approached, an exponential curve. Its energy-absorption rate, figured in terms of growth, expressed as a hyped-up discontinuous progression.

The result—

"It'll consume the Sun," Moriarty said, very quietly.

The control room turned into a bedlam. Six of them tried to explain it to O'Donnell at the same time. Then Moriarty tried, and finally Allenson.

"Its rate of growth is so great and its speed so slow—and it will get so much energy—that the leech will be able to consume the Sun by the time it gets there. Or, at least, to live off it until it can consume it."

O'Donnell didn't bother to understand. He turned to the operator.

"Turn it," he said.

They all hovered over the radar screen, waiting.

The food turned out of the leech's path and streaked away. Ahead was a tremendous source, but still a long way off. The leech hesitated.

Its cells, recklessly expending energy, shouted for a decision. The food slowed, tantalizingly near.

The closer source or the greater?

The leech's body wanted food now.

It started after it, away from the Sun.

The Sun would come next.

"Pull it out at right angles to the plane of the Solar System," Allenson said.

The operator touched the controls. On the radar screen, they saw a blob pursuing a dot. It had turned.

Relief washed over them. It had been close!

"In what portion of the sky would the leech be?" O'Donnell asked, his face expressionless.

"Come outside; I believe I can show you," an astronomer said. They walked to the door. "Somewhere in that section," the astronomer said, pointing.

"Fine. All right, Soldier," O'Donnell told the operator. "Carry out your orders."

The scientists gasped in unison. The operator manipulated the controls and the blob began to overtake the dot. Micheals started across the room.

"Stop," the general said, and his strong, commanding voice stopped Micheals. "I know what I'm doing. I had that ship especially built."

The blob overtook the dot on the radar screen.

"I told you this was a personal matter," O'Donnell said. "I swore to destroy that leech. We can never have any security while it lives." He smiled. "Shall we look at the sky?"

The general strolled to the door, followed by the scientists.

"Push the button, Soldier!"

The operator did. For a moment, nothing happened. Then the sky lit up!

A bright star hung in space. Its brilliance filled the night, grew, and started to fade.

"What did you do?" Micheals gasped.

"That rocket was built around a hydrogen bomb," O'Donnell said, his strong face triumphant. "I set it off at the contact moment." He called to the operator again. "Is there anything showing on the radar?""Not a speck, sir."

"Men," the general said, "I have met the enemy and he is mine. Let's have some more champagne."

But Micheals found that he was suddenly ill.

It had been shrinking from the expenditure of energy, when the great explosion came. No thought of containing it. The leech's cells held for the barest fraction of a second, and then spontaneously overloaded.

The leech was smashed, broken up, destroyed. It was split into a thousand particles, and the particles were split a million times more.

The particles were thrown out on the wave front of the explosion, and they split further, spontaneously.

Into spores.

The spores closed into dry, hard, seemingly lifeless specks of dust, billions of them, scattered, drifting. Unconscious, they floated in the emptiness of space.

Billions of them, waiting to be fed.

# ROUGH BEAST

## by Roger Dee

*The escaped* Thing *was so dangerous that the aliens had revealed their secret existence to a horrified Earth. What could possibly stop the monster?*

❂ ❂ ❂

***Roger Dee Aycock*** *(1914-2004), who wrote SF under his first two names, began selling SF stories with "The Wheel is Death" in the Fall 1949* Planet Stories. *He was a prolific contributor to the SF magazines, particularly in the 1950s, until the 1970s, when his last story, "Perfect Match," appeared in the Spring 1971* Worlds of Tomorrow. *He sold one novel,* An Earth Gone Mad, *to Ace Books in 1954, an expansion of his novelet with the same title in the November 1952* Startling Stories. *According to the Internet Speculative Fiction Database, he published a total of 53 stories, and while no book collections of his stories have been published, a number of his stories are available online at Project Gutenberg. Biographical* *information about Mr. Avcock is scarce, and I'd like to know more about one of the many unsung, or not very sung authors of stories in the decades when SF paid little and was written by people just for fun.*

**THE FIELD** of the experimental Telethink station in the Florida Keys caught the fleeing Morid's attention just as its stolen Federation lifeboat plunged into the outer reaches of nightside atmosphere.

The Morid reacted with the instant decision of a harried wolf stumbling upon a dark cave that offers not only sanctuary but a lost lamb for supper as well. With the pursuing Federation ship hot on its taloned heels, the Morid zeroed on the Telethink signals—fuzzy and incomprehensibly alien to its viciously direct mentality, but indicating life and therefore food—and aimed straight for their source.

The lifeboat crashed headlong in the mangroves fringing Dutchman's Key, perhaps ten miles west of the Oversea Highway and less than two from the Telethink station. The Morid emerged in snarling haste, anticipating the powerplant's explosion by a matter of seconds, and vanished like a magenta-furred juggernaut into the moonlit riot of vegetation that crowded back from the mangroved strip of beach. The Morid considered it a success.

The lifeboat went up in a cataclysmic roar and flare of bluish light that brought Vann, the Telethink operator on duty, out of his goldberg helmet with a prickly conviction of runaway range missiles. It all but blinded and deafened

Ellis, his partner, who was cruising with a portable Telethink in the station launch through a low-lying maze of islands a quarter of a mile from Dutchman's Key.

Their joint consternation was lost on the Morid because both at the moment were outside its avid reach. The teeming welter of life on Dutchman's Key was not. The Morid headed inland, sensing abundant quarry to satisfy the ravening hunger that drove it and, that craving satisfied, to offer ample scope to its joy of killing.

The Morid's escape left Xaxtol, Federation ship's commander, in a dilemma bordering upon the insoluble.

It would have been bad enough to lose so rare a specimen even on a barren world, but to have one so voracious at large upon one so teeming—as the primitive Telethink signals demonstrated—with previously unsuspected intelligence was unthinkable.

This, at the outset, was Xaxtol's problem:

Forbidden by strictest Galactic injunction, he could not make planetfall and interfere with a previously unscouted primitive culture. Contrariwise, neither could civilized ethic condone his abandoning such an unsuspecting culture to the bloody mercies of a Morid without every effort to correct his blunder.

Hanging in stationary orbit in order to keep a fixed relation to the Morid's landing site, the Federation commander debated earnestly with his staff until a sudden quickening of the barbarous Telethink net made action imperative.

Two of the autochthons were isolated on a small island with the Morid. Unwarned, they were doomed.

So he grouped his staff about him—sitting, crouching, coiling or hovering, as individual necessity demanded—and as one entity put the whole into rapport with the all-but-meaningless signals that funneled up from the Telethink station in the Florida Keys.

And, in doing so, roused a consternation as great as his own and infinitely more immediate.

The flash brought Vann away from the Telethink console and out of the quonset station to stare shakenly across the tangle of mangroved islands to the west. Weyman came out a moment later, on the run, when the teeth-jarring blast of the explosion woke him. They stood together on the moon-bright sand and Vann relayed in four words the total of his information.

"It fell over there," Vann said.

A pale pinkish cloud of smoke and steam rose and drifted phosphorescently toward a noncommittal moon.

"Second key out," Weyman said. "That would be Dutchman's, where the hermit lives."

Vann nodded, drawing minimal reassurance from the fact that there had been no mushroom. "It shouldn't be atomic."

The Gulf breeze was steady out of the west, freighted with its perpetual salt-and-mangrove smell.

"The Geigers will tell us soon enough," Weyman said. "Not that it'll help us, with Ellis out in the launch."

They looked at each other in sudden shock of joint realization.

"The launch," Vann said. "Ellis is out there with the

portable Telethink rig. We were working out field-strength ratios for personal equipment—"

They dived for the quonset together. Vann, smaller and more agile than the deliberate Weyman, reached the Telethink first.

"Nothing but the regular standby carrier from Washington," Vann said. "Ellis may have been directly under the thing when it struck. He was working toward Dutchman's Key, hoping for a glimpse of the hermit."

"Maybe he wasn't wearing the Telethink when the blast came," Weyman said. Then, with characteristic practicality: "Better image Washington about this while we're waiting for Ellis to report in. Can't use the net radio—we'd start a panic."

Vann settled himself at the console.

"I'll try. That is, if I can get across anything beyond the sort of subliminal rot we've been trading lately."

He signaled for contact and felt the Washington operator's answering surge of subconscious resentment at being disturbed. With the closing of the net the now-familiar giddiness of partial rapport came on him, together with the oppressive sense of bodily sharing.

There was a sudden trickle of saliva in his mouth and he resisted the desire to spit.

"Washington is having a midnight snack," Vann said. "Rotted sardines and Limburger, I think."

He made correction when the Washington operator radiated indignation. "Goose liver and dill pickles, then, but you wouldn't guess it. Salt tastes like brass filings."

Weyman said shortly, "Get on with it. You can clown later."

Vann visualized the flare of explosion and winced at the panicky hammer-and-sickled surmise that came back to him.

"How would I know?" he said aloud. "We have a man out—"

He recalled the inherent limitation of phonetics then and fell back upon imagery, picturing Ellis' launch heading toward an island luridly lighted by the blast. For effect he added, on the key's minuscule beach, a totally imaginary shack of driftwood, complete with bearded hermit.

He knew immediately when authority arrived at the other end of the net. There was a mental backwash of conversation that told him his orders even before the Washington operator set himself for their relay.

"They want an eyewitness account from Ellis," he told Weyman. "As if—"

Ellis broke into the net at that moment, radiating a hazy image—he was still partially blinded from the glare of the blast—of a lowering key overhung by a dwindling pall of pinkish smoke. In the foreground of lagoon and mangroves stood a stilted shack not unlike the one Vann had pictured, but without the hermit.

Instead, the rickety elevation of thatched porch was a blot of sable darkness relieved only by a pair of slanted yellow eyes gleaming close to the floor.

Climactically, Xaxtol entered the net then with an impact of total information that was more than the human psyche, conditioned to serialized thinking by years of phonetic communication, could bear.

The Washington operator screamed and tore off his helmet, requiring restraint until he could compose himself enough to relay his message.

Ellis, in his launch, fainted dead away and ran the boat headlong aground on the beach of Dutchman's Key.

Vann reeled in his chair, teetering between shock and lunacy, until Weyman caught him and slid the Telethink from his head. It was minutes before Vann could speak; when he did, it was with a macabre flippancy that Weyman found more convincing than any dramatics.

"It's come," Vann said. "There's an interstellar ship out there with a thousand-odd crew that would give Dali himself nightmares."

Weyman had to shake him forcibly before he could continue.

"They're sorry they can't put down and help us," Vann said. "Galactic regulations, it seems. But they feel they should warn us that they've let some sort of bloodthirsty jungle monster—a specimen they were freighting to an interplanetary zoo—escape in a lifeboat. It's loose down here."

"Dutchman's Key," Weyman breathed. "What kind of brute could live through a blast like that?"

"It left the lifeboat before the power plant blew," Vann said. "They're tracking its aura now. It's intelligent to a degree—about on par with ourselves, I gather—and it's big. It's the largest and most vicious life form they've met in kilo-years of startrading."

He frowned over a concept unsuited to words. "Longer than thousands. Their culture goes back so far that the term doesn't register."

"Ellis," Weyman said. "Tell him to sheer off. Tell him to keep away from that island."

Vann clapped on the Telethink helmet and felt real panic when he found the net vacant except for a near-hysterical Washington operator.

"Aliens are off the air," he said. "But I can't feel Ellis."

"Maybe he isn't wearing his Telethink. I'll try his launch radio."

He had the microphone in his hand when Vann said, "They got the message in Washington, and they're petrified. I asked for a copter to pick up Ellis—and the hermit, if they can reach them before this thing does—but they're thinking along different lines. They're sending a squadron of jet bombers with nonatomic HE to make sure the beast doesn't escape to the mainland and devastate the countryside."

Weyman said incredulously, "They'll blow the key to bits. What about Ellis and the hermit?"

"Ellis is to evacuate him if possible. They're giving us twenty minutes before the jets come. After that—"

He didn't have to finish.

At midnight old Charlie Trask was wading knee-deep in the eastside grass flats of his private lagoon, methodically netting shrimp that darted to the ooze-clouded area stirred up by his ragged wading shoes. An empty gunny sack hung across one shoulder, ready for the coon oysters he would pick from mangrove roots on his way back to his shack.

In his dour and antisocial way, Charlie was content. He had nearly enough shrimp for boiling and for bait, with the prospect of coon oyster stew in the offing. He had tobacco for his pipe and cartridges for his single-shot .22 rifle and a batch of potent homebrew ready for the bottling.

What more could a man want?

The blast and glare of the Morid's landing on the western fringe of his key jarred Charlie from his mellow mood like a clear-sky thunderbolt. The concussion rattled what teeth remained to him and brought a distant squall from his cat, a scarred and cynical old tom named Max, at the shack.

Damn rockets, was Charlie's instant thought. Fool around till they blow us all to hell.

The rosy phosphorescence drifting up from the mangroves a quarter of a mile away colored his resentment with alarm. A blast like that could start a fire, burn across the key and gut his shack.

Grumbling at the interruption of his midnight foray, Charlie crimped the lid tight on his shrimp bucket and stalked back along the lagoon toward his shack. The coon oysters would have to wait.

Five minutes later he reached his personal castle, perched on precarious piling in a gap hewn from the mangroves. The moon made it, to Charlie, a thing of black-and-silver beauty, with Max's yellow eyes gleaming from the porch floor like wicked, welcoming beacons.

Still muttering, Charlie waded out of the shallow-water ooze and stumped in squishing shoes up the ladder to his shack. The shrimp bucket he hung on a wall peg out of Max's calculating reach. He found his pipe in the kitchen and loaded and lighted it, deliberately because the capacity for haste was not in him. His homebrew crock bubbled seductively and he took time out to raise the grimy toweling that covered it and sniff appreciatively.

"Ready to cap by the time I come back and get the shrimp graded," he told Max.

He changed his dripping brogans for a pair of snake-proof boots and took down his .22 rifle from its pegs, not because he really imagined that anyone might have lived through such a blast but because strangers—them radio fellows two keys east, for instance—might take it into their heads to come prying around.

He was halfway across the key when the drone of Ellis' launch entering his lagoon justified his suspicions.

Charlie's investigation was soon over.

A dying plume of steam rising from a circle of battered mangroves told him that no danger of fire impended, and he turned back in relief. It did not occur to him that the pilot of his hypothetical rocket might be lying desperately injured in the shallow water, at the mercy of sharks and crocodiles. If it had, he would not have moved to help. Any fool who got himself into such a spot, in Charlie's rude philosophy, could get himself out.

The drone of the launch's engine was loud when he reached his shack. The boat, handled by a pilot grotesque in what Charlie took at first for a diver's helmet, was heading directly for his landing at an unsafe speed.

"Serve him right if he shoals on a oyster bed and rips his bottom," Charlie said.

As if on cue, the boat swerved sharply. Its pilot came half erect, arms flung wide in a convulsive gesture. The engine roared wildly; the boat heeled, slamming its occupant against the right gunwale, and blasted straight for Charlie's shack.

Miraculously, it missed the shack's piling and lunged half its length upon the sand. The engine-roar died instantly. The pilot was thrown headlong overside, goldberg helmet flying off in mid-arc, to lie stunned at the foot of Charlie's ladder.

Callously, Charlie stepped over Ellis' twitching form and stumped up the ladder to his shack. Max, who had taken to the porch rafters at the crash of the launch, came meowing gingerly down to meet him.

"It's all right," Charlie told him. "Just some fool that don't know how to handle a boat."

He leaned his rifle against the wall and brought a split-bamboo chair from the kitchen. He was not too late; the bucket, when he took it from its peg, still slithered satisfactorily with live shrimp.

The squawking of the launch radio roused Ellis. He groaned and sat up, dazed and disoriented by the combined shock of Xaxtol's telepathic bombshell and his own rude landing, just as Weyman gave up his attempt at radio contact. In the silence that fell, Ellis would have fainted again except for the chilling knowledge that he was unarmed and afoot on the same key with a man-eating alien monster that might make its appearance at any moment.

He collected wits and breath to stave off the black pall of shock that still threatened.

"Come down from there and help me push the launch off," he called up to Charlie Trask. "We've got to get off this key. Fast!"

Charlie separated a menu-sized shrimp from his bucket.

"You grounded her," he said sourly. "Push her off yourself."

"Listen," Ellis said desperately. "That blast was a ship from space, from another star. A wild animal escaped from it, something worse than you ever dreamed of. We've got to get out of here before it finds us."

Charlie grunted and chose another shrimp.

The Morid, as Xaxtol had pictured it, rose vividly in Ellis' memory, fanged and shaggy and insatiably voracious, a magenta-furred ursine embodiment of blood-lust made the worst by its near-human intelligence.

He described it in dogged haste, his eyes frozen to the tangle of inland underbrush behind the shack.

"No such varmint in these kays," old Charlie said.

The launch radio blared again in Weyman's voice, speaking urgently of jet bombers and deadlines. A glance at his watch brought Ellis up from the sand in galvanic resolution.

"In twelve minutes," he said grimly, "a squadron of planes will pinpoint this key and blast it out of the water. I'm not going to be eaten alive or blown to bits arguing with you. If I can't push the launch off alone, I'll swim."

He scooped up his fallen Telethink helmet and ran for the launch. At the fourth step his foot caught in the iron-hard stump of a mangrove root that had been chopped off inches above the sand and he fell heavily. Pain blinded him; his right ankle lanced with fire and went numb.

He fought to rise and fell again when the ankle collapsed under him.

"Hell," he said, just before blackness claimed him for the second time. "I've broken my leg!"

His twelve minutes had dwindled to seven when Ellis roused. He tried to stand, his twisted ankle momentarily forgotten, and gave it up when the mangroves spun dizzily before his eyes. He couldn't afford to pass out again.

He made one last-ditch bid for help.

"My leg's broken," he yelled up at old Charlie Trask. "Get down here and lend a hand!"

Charlie glowered and said nothing.

Max bounded down the ladder, tail stiffly erect and scarred ears cocked at the underbrush in baleful curiosity.

"The thing is coming this way," Ellis called. "Your cat scents it. Will you let us all be killed?"

Charlie Trask graded another shrimp.

Swearing bitterly, Ellis caught up his Telethink helmet and slid it over his head. He found the net in a welter of confusion. Washington demanded further information; Vann, at the station, was calling him frantically. His own scramble for help-images only added to the mental babel.

On the Federation ship, confusion was nearly as rampant.

Xaxtol's dilemma still held: he could not make planetfall—time was too short for aid now, in any case—but neither could he, with clear Galactic conscience, desert the harried primitives below while hope remained.

Ellis' predicament forced Xaxtol to decision; he could only follow the Morid's aura and relay its progress.

It could not be helped that the relayed image was

blurred of definition and weirdly askew; the Morid's visual and auditory range differed so sharply from either human or Galactic that even over the ship's wonderfully selective telecommunicator little of the Morid's immediate surroundings came through clearly. Its aura arrived with a burning intensity that turned Xaxtol and his group faint with empathetic horror, but the fact that the Morid had just made its first kill obliterated all detail for the moment beyond a shocking welter of blood and torn flesh.

Ellis fared a little better under the second telepathic blast than under the first—he managed to snatch off his Telethink helmet just in time.

"The thing just killed something out there," he yelled at Charlie Trask. "It's coming this way. Are you going to sit there and—"

Charlie graded his last edible shrimp, took up his bucket and went inside. The leisurely clinking of homebrew bottles drifted after him, clear and musical on the still, hot air.

Ellis looked at his watch and considered prayer. He had three minutes left.

When the Morid came, Ellis was sitting dumbly on the sand, nursing his broken ankle and considering with a shock-detached part of his mind a fragmentary line of some long-forgotten schooldays poem.

What rough beast is this . . . the rest eluded him.

The underbrush beyond the shack rustled and the Morid's ravening image sprang to Ellis' mind with a clarity that shook his three net-participants to the core—one of them past endurance.

Vann, in the station, said "Dear God," and braced himself for the end. In Washington, the operator fainted and had to be dragged from his console.

Aboard the Federation ship, Xaxtol radiated a shaken "Enough!" and tentacled a stud that sent his craft flashing on its way through subspace.

At Charlie Trask's shack, Max bounded across the clearing and into the brush. There followed a riot of squalling and screaming that brought Charlie out of his shack on the run. Ellis sat numbly, beyond shock, waiting for the worst.

Unaccountably, the worst was delayed.

Charlie came back, clutching a protesting Max by the scruff of the neck, and threw down something at Ellis' feet. Something small and limp and magenta-furred, smeared with greenish blood and very, very dead.

"There's your varmint," said Charlie.

With one minute remaining before the promised bombers roared over, Ellis, with a frozen clarity he had not dreamed he possessed, radiated a final message before he fainted again.

"Call off the jets," he said, in effect. "It's over. The beast is dead. The hermit's cat killed it."

An hour later at the station, his ankle bandaged and his third cup of coffee in hand, Ellis could review it all with some coherence.

"We didn't consider the business of relative size," he said. "Neither did our Galactic friends. Apparently they're small, and so are all the species they've met with before. Maybe we're something unique in the universe, after all.

And maybe it's a good thing they didn't land and learn how unique."

"It figures," Weyman said. "Washington let it out on the air that DF stations made a fix on the spaceship before it jumped off. It measured only twenty-two feet."

Vann said wonderingly, "And there were hundreds of them aboard. Gentlemen, we are Brobdingnagians in a universe of Lilliputians."

"I've been trying," Ellis said irrelevantly, "to recall a poem I read once in school. I've forgotten the author and all the verse but one line. It goes—"

"What rough beast is this," Vann quoted. "You were thinking about it hard enough when the debacle in the brush took place. The image you radiated was rough enough—it shocked the pants off us."

"And off the Galactics," Weyman said. "The shoe is on the other foot now, I think."

He went to the quonset door and looked out and up, listening. "Jets. The Washington brass on its way to cross-examine us."

"The other foot?" Vann said. "Don't be cryptic, man. Whose foot?"

"Theirs," Ellis said. "Don't you see? One of these days we'll be going out there to make our own place in the galaxy. With our size and disposition, how do you think we'll seem to those gentle little people?"

Vann whistled in belated understanding.

"Rough," he said.

# LOVE ME TRUE

## by Gordon R. Dickson

*We've seen a number of hideous* Things *now, but there's no law that says a* Thing *from space has to be a Lovecreftian horror. And cuteness could disguise a more subtle menace.*

***Gordon R. Dickson*** *(1923-2001) was one of the leading writers of science fiction from the late 1940s until the late 1990s, by which time he had produced, with his friend Poul Anderson, a couple of book's worth of stories of those screwball Teddy-bear-like aliens, the Hokas, and several volumes of his celebrated Childe cycle, also known as the Dorsai series (though the Dorsai part of the saga, was originally only intended to be a third of the cycle) in novels, including* Dorsai!, Necromancer, The Tactics of Mistake, Soldier, Ask Not *among others, and several shorter pieces about those fascinating galactic mercenary* *soldiers, the Dorsai. His writing won him three Hugo Awards and a Nebula Award, and in 2000 he was inducted into the Science Fiction Hall of Fame. In 1976 he wrote the fantasy novel,* The Dragon and the George *(expanded and considerably altered from an earlier novelet, "St. Dragon and the George"). The popularity of that novel led to a string of "Dragon" sequels. They were enjoyable light-hearted fantasy adventure stories, but one might wish that he instead had written more of the Childe Cycle. Still, we should be grateful for the impressive number of novels and shorter works that Dickson left us; such as this one.*

**ON THE WAY** to the Colonel's office, Ted Holman asked the MP to take him around by the laboratories so he could get a look at Pogey.

"You think I'm nuts?" said the MP. "I can't do that. Anyway we haven't got time. And anyway, they wouldn't let you in there. All we could do is look in through the door."

"All right. I can see him through the door, anyway," said Ted. The MP hesitated. He was a lean, dark young kid from Colorado; and he looked older than Ted, who was a tow-headed, open-faced young soldier of the type who never looks quite grown up. But Ted had been to Arcturus IV and back; while the MP had never been farther than Washington, D.C.

So they went to the laboratories; and the MP stood to one side while Ted peered through the wire and glass of the small window set high in the door to the experimental section. Inside were cages with white rats, and rabbits, some rhesus monkeys and a small, white-haired, terrier-looking bitch. The speaker grill above the door brought to Ted's ears the rustling sound of the creatures in their cages.

"I can't see him," said Ted.

"In the corner," said the MP.

Ted pressed closer to the door and caught sight of a cage in the corner containing what looked like some woman's silver fox fur neckpiece, including the black button nose and the bead eyes. It was all curled up.

"Pogey!" said Ted. *"Pogey!"*

"He can't hear you," said the MP. "That speaker's one way, so the night guards can check, in the labs."

A white-coated man came into the room from a far door, carrying a white enamel tray with fluffy cotton and three hypodermic syringes lying in it. The little bitch and Pogey were instantly alert and pressing their nose to the bars of their cages. The bitch wagged her stub tail and whined.

"Love me?" said Pogey. "Love me?"

The white-coated man paid no attention. He left his tray and went out again. The bitch whined after him. Pogey drooped. Ted's hands curled into fists against the slick metal face of the door.

"He could've said something!" said Ted. "He could've spoke!"

"He was busy," said the MP nervously. "Come on—we got to get going."

They went on over to the Colonel's office. When they

came to the door of the outer office, the MP slid his gun around on his belt so it was out of sight under his jacket. Then they went in. A small girl with startlingly beautiful green eyes in a blue summer-weight suit, a civilian, was seated on one of the hard wooden benches outside the wooden railing, waiting. She looked closely at Ted as he and the MP came through the railing.

"He's waiting for you. Go on in," said the lieutenant behind the railing. They passed on, through a brown door and closed it behind them, into a rectangular office with a good-looking dark wood desk, a carpet, and a couple of leather chairs this side of the desk.

"You can wait outside, Corporal," said the Colonel, from behind the desk. The MP went out again, leaving Ted standing stiff and facing the desk. "You fool, Ted!" said the Colonel.

"He's mine," said Ted.

"You just get that notion out of your head," said the Colonel. "Get it out right now." He was a dark little man with a nervous mustache.

"I want him back."

"You're getting nothing back. It's tough enough as it is. All right, we all went to Arcturus together, and we're the first outfit to do something like that and so we're not going to let one of our own boys get slapped by regulations when we can handle it among ourselves. But you just get it straight you aren't getting that antipod back."

Ted said nothing.

"You listen to me good now," said the Colonel. "Do you know what they can do to you for striking a commissioned officer? Instead of getting out, today, you could be starting fifteen years hard labor. Plus what you'd get for smuggling the antipod back."

Ted still said nothing.

"Well, you're lucky," said the Colonel. "You're just plain lucky. The whole outfit went to bat for you. We got the necessary papers faked to make the antipod an experimental animal the outfit brought back—not you, the outfit. And Curry—*Lieutenant* Curwen, Ted, you might remember—is going to pretend you didn't try to half-kill him when he came to take the antipod away from you. *I* was going to make you go over and apologize to him; but he said no, he didn't blame you. You're just lucky."

He stopped and looked at Ted.

"Well?" he said.

"You don't understand," said Ted. "They die if they don't have somebody to love them. I was at that weather observation point all by myself for six months. I know. Pogey'll die."

"Look . . . oh, go out and get drunk, or something!" exploded the Colonel. "I tell you we've done the best we can. Everybody's done the best they can; and you're lucky to be walking out of here with a clean record." He picked up the phone on his desk and began punching out a number. "Get out."

Ted went out. Nobody stopped him. He went back to the temporary barracks the expedition had been assigned to, changed into civilian clothes and left the base. He was in about his fifth bar that evening when a woman sat down on the stool next to him.

"Hi there, Ted," she said.

He turned around and looked at her. Her eyes were as green as a well-watered lawn at sunset, her hair was somewhere between brunette and blond and she wore a tailored blue suit. Then he recognized her as the girl in the Colonel's outer office. With her face only a foot or so away she looked older than she had in the office; and she saw he saw this, for she leaned back a little from him.

"I'm June Malyneux," she said, "from *The Recorder*. I'm a newspaperwoman." Ted considered this, looking at her.

"You want a drink, or something?" he said.

"That'd be wonderful," she said. "I'd like a Tom Collins."

He bought her a Tom Collins and they sat there side by side in the dim bar looking at each other and drinking.

"Well," she said, "what did you miss most when you were twenty-three and a half quadrillion miles from home?"

"Grass," said Ted. "That is, at first. After a while I got used to the sand and the creepers. And I didn't miss it so much anymore."

"Did you miss getting drunk?"

"No," said Ted.

"Then why are you doing it?"

He stopped drinking to look at her.

"I just feel like it, that's all," he said. She reached out and laid a hand on his arm.

"Don't be mad," she said. "I know about it. It's pretty hard to keep secrets from newspaper people. What are you going to do about it?"

He pulled his arm out from under her hand and had another swallow from his glass.

"I don't know," he said. "I don't know what to do."

"How'd you happen to get the . . . the—"

"Antipod. When they hunch their back to walk it looks like the front pair of legs're working against the back pair."

"Antipod. How'd you make a pet of it in the first place?"

"I was alone at this weather observation point for a long time." Ted was turning his glass around and around, and watching the rim revolve like a hoop of light. "After a while, Pogey took to me."

"Did any of the other men make pets out of them?"

"Nobody I know of. They'll come up to you; but they're real shy. They scare off easy. Then after that they won't have anything to do with you."

"Did you scare any off?" June said.

"I must have," he shrugged, "—at first. I didn't pay any attention to them for a long time. Then I began to notice how they'd sit and watch me and my shack and the equipment. Finally Pogey got to know me."

"How did you do it?" she asked.

He shrugged again.

"Just patient, I guess," he said.

The bar was filling up around them. A band had started up in the supper club attached, and it was getting noisy.

"Come on," June said. "I know a quieter place where we can hear ourselves talk." She got up; and he got up and followed her out.

They took a taxi and went down to a place on the beach called Digger's Inn. It had a back porch overlooking the surf which was washing upon the sand, some fifteen feet below. The porch had a thatched roof, and the small round tables on it were lit by candles and the moonlight coming in across the waves. They had switched to rum drinks and Ted was getting quite drunk. It annoyed him; because he was trying to tell June what it had been like and his thickened tongue made talking clumsy.

". . . The farther away you get," he was saying. "I mean—the farther you go, the smaller you get. You understand?" She sat, waiting for him to tell her. "I mean . . . suppose you were born and grew up and never went more than a block from home. You'd be real big. You know what I mean? Put you and that block side by side, like on a table, and both of you'd show." He drew a circle and a dot with his forefinger on the dampness of the table between them to illustrate. "But suppose you traveled all over the city, then you'd look *this* big, side by side with it. Or the world, or the solar system—"

"Yes," she said.

". . . But you go someplace like Alpha Centauri, you go twenty-three quadrillion, four hundred trillion miles from home, and"—he held up thumb and forefinger nails pinched together—"you're all alone out there for months. What's left of you then?" He shook the thumb and forefinger before her eyes. "You're that small. You're nothing."

She glanced from his pinched fingers to his face without moving anything but her eyes. His elbow was on the table, his thumb and forefinger inches before her face. She reached up and put her own hand gently over his fingers.

"No, listen—" he insisted shaking his hand loose. "What's left when you're that small? What's left?"

"You are," she said.

He shook his head, hard.

"No!" he said. "I'm not. Only what I can do? But what can I do when I'm that high?" He closed his hand earnestly around her arm. "I'm little and I do little things. Everything I do is too little to count—"

"Please," she was softly prying at his fingers with her other hand, "you're hurting—"

". . . I can love," he said. "I can give my love."

Her fingers stilled. They stopped trying to loosen his. She looked up at him and he looked drunkenly down at her. Her eyes searched his face almost desperately.

"How old are you?" she whispered.

"Twenty-five," he said.

"You don't look that old. You look—younger than I am," she said.

"Doesn't matter how old I am," said Ted. "It just matters what I can do."

"Please," she said. "You're squeezing too hard. My arm—"

He let go of her.

"Sorry," he said. He went back to his drinking.

"No, tell me," she said. Her right hand massaged the arm he had squeezed. "How did you get him out?"

"Pogey?" he said. "We practiced. I wrapped him around my waist, under my shirt and jacket."

"And he didn't show? And you got him on the ship that way when you came back."

"They weighed us on," said Ted, dully. "But I'd thought of that. I'd taken off twelve pounds. And exercised so I wouldn't look gaunted down. Pogey weighs just about eleven."

"And they didn't know it until you got here?"

"Sneak inspection. To beat the government teams to it, so nobody'd be embarrassed. Colonel ordered it; but Curry pulled it—Lieutenant Curwen—and he found him, and—" Ted ran down staring at his glass.

"What would you have done?" June said. "With—Pogey, I mean?"

He looked over at her, surprised.

"I would have kept him. With me. I would have taken care of him." He looked at her. "Don't you understand? Pogey *needs* me."

"I understand," she said. "I do." She moved a little toward him, so that her shoulder rubbed against the sleeve of his arm. "I'll help you get him out."

"You?" He said.

"Oh, yes!" she said, quickly. "Yes, I can!"

"How?" he said. And then—"Why? We've been talking here all this time; and now all of a sudden you want to help Pogey and me. Why? It isn't that newspaper of yours—"

"No, *no!*" she said. "I didn't really care at first, that was it. I mean it was a good story, that was all. Just that. And then, something about the way you talk about him . . . I don't know. But I changed sides, all of a sudden. Ted, you believe me, don't you?"

"I don't know," he said thickly.

"Ted," she said. "Ted." She moved close to him, her head was tilted back, her eyes half-closed. He stared stupidly down at her for a moment; then, clumsily, he put his arms around her and bent his own head and kissed her. He felt her tremble in his arms.

He let her go at last. She drew back a little from him and wiped the corners of her eyes, with her forefinger.

"Now," she said shakily, "do you believe me?"

"Yes," he said. He watched her for a second as she got out handkerchief, lipstick and compact. "But how're we going to do it? They've got him."

"There're ways," she said, sliding the lipstick around her upper lip carefully. She rolled her upper lip against the lower, and blinked a little, examining the result in the mirror. "I'm quite good, you know," she said to the compact. "I can manage all sorts of things. And I . . . I want to manage this for you."

"How?" he said.

"You have to know what's going on." She folded the compact and put it away with a sharp snap. "That expedition of yours to Alpha Centauri cost forty billion dollars."

"I know," he said. "But what's that got to do—"

"The military's sold on the idea of further stellar exploration and expansion. They want a program of three more expeditions of increasing size, one that would cost a hundred-fifty billion during the next twenty years." She glanced at him the way a schoolteacher might. "That's a lot of money. But now's the ideal time to ask for it. All of you have just got back. Popular interest is high . . . so on."

"Sure." he said. "But what's that got to do with Pogey?"

"They don't want a fuss. No scandal. Nothing that'll start an argument at this stage in the game. Now tell me," she turned to face him, "you're released from service now, aren't you?"

"Yes," Ted nodded, frowning at her. "They signed me out today before they took me to see the colonel. I'm a civilian."

"All right. Fine," she said. "And you know where Pogey is. Can you go get him and get him outside the base?"

"Yeah," he said. "Yeah, I thought of that. But I was saving it for last—if I couldn't think of a better way where they couldn't come after us."

"They won't. You leave that part of it to me. Pogey was your pet; and his kind was listed harmless by the expedition when they were on Alpha Centauri. There's enough of a case there to make good weepy newspaper copy. I'll have a little talk with your colonel and some others."

"But what good'll that do if they just take him back anyway?"

"They won't. Legally, they've got you, Ted. But they'll let you get away with it rather than risk the publicity. Wait and see."

"You think so?" he said, his face lighting up. "You really think they will?"

"I promise," she answered, watching him. He surged to his feet. The little round table before them rocked. "I'll go get him right now."

"You better have some coffee first."

"No. No. I'm sober." He took a deep breath and straightened up; and the fuzziness from the liquor seemed to burn out of his head.

"You'll need some place to bring him," she said. "I've got an apartment—" He shook his head.

"I'll call you," he said. "We may just move around. I'll call you tomorrow. When'll you be seeing the colonel?" He was already backing away from her.

"First thing in the morning." She got up hurriedly and came after him. "But wait—I'm coming."

"No . . . no!" he said. "I don't want you mixed up in it. I'll call you. Where'll I call you?"

"Parketon 5-45-8321—the office," she called after him. And then he was gone, through the entrance to the interior bar of the Inn. She reached the entrance herself just in time to see his tow head and square shoulders moving beyond the drinkers at the bar and out the front door of the place.

Outside, Holman called a cab.

"Richardson Space Base," he told the driver. His permanent pass was good to the end of the week; and they passed through the gates of the Base, when they reached them, with only a nod and a yawn from the guard.

He left the cab outside the laboratories and stepped off into the shadows. He followed along paths of darkness until he came to the section where Pogey was being kept. A night guard came out of the door just before he reached it, swinging his arm with the machine pistol clipped to one wrist, and looking ahead down the corridor with the sleepy young face of a new recruit. Ted stood still in the shadows until the door of the next section had swung to behind the guard, then went inside.

He found the door he had looked through earlier. A light burned inside the room and most of the animals in the cages were curled up with their heads tucked away from the glare of it. The door was locked, but there was an emergency handle under glass above it. Ted broke the glass, turned the handle and went in; and the animals woke at the noise and looked at him wonderingly.

He opened the door to Pogey's cage.

"Pogey . . . Pogey . . . ." he said; and the antipod leaped up and came into his arms like a child and clung there. Together they went out into the night. When he got back into the cab, Ted bulged a little around the waist under his shirt; but that was all.

The sky was paling into dawn as they got back into the city. Ted paid off the cab and took the public tubes. Wedged into a corner seat, he drowsed against the soft cushions, feeling Pogey stir warmly now and again around his waist; until, waking with a start he looked at the watch on his wrist and saw that it was after eleven a.m. He had been shuttling back and forth beneath the city for seven hours.

He got stiffly off the tubes and phoned the number June had given him. She was not in, they told him at the other end, but she should be back shortly. He hung up and found a restaurant and had breakfast. When he called for the second time, he heard her voice answer him over the phone.

"It's all right," she said. "But you better stay out of sight for a while anyway. Where can I meet you?"

He thought.

"I'm going to get a hotel room," he said. "I'll register under the name of—William Wright. Where's a good hotel where they have individual entrances and lobbies for the room groups?"

"The Byngton," she said. "One hundred and eighty-seventh and Chire Street—fourth level. I'll meet you there in half an hour."

"All right," he said, and hung up.

He went to the Byngton and registered. He had just gone up to his room and let Pogey out on the bed, when the talker over the door to the room told him he had a visitor.

"There she is—" he said to Pogey, and went out alone, closing the door of the room carefully behind him. June was waiting for him in the bright sunlight of the little glassed-in lobby a dozen yards from his door; and she ran to him as he appeared. He found himself holding her.

"We did it! We did it!" She clung to him tightly. Awkwardly, but a little gently, he disengaged her arms so that he could see her face.

"What happened?" he said.

"I phoned ahead—before I went out at nine this morning," she said, laughing up at him. "When I got there, your colonel was there, and General Daton—and some other general from the United Services. I told them you'd taken Pogey—but they knew that; and I told them you were going to keep him. And I showed them some copy I'd written." She almost pirouetted with glee. "And oh, they were angry! I'd stay out of their way for a long time, Ted. But you can keep him. You can keep Pogey!"

She hugged him again. Once more he put her arms away.

"It sounds awful easy. You sure?" he said.

"You've got to keep him quiet. You've got to keep him out of sight," she said. "But if you don't bother them, they'll leave you alone. The power of the Fourth Estate—of course it helps if you're on the national board of the Guild."

"Guild?"

"Newspaperman's Guild," she said. "Didn't I tell you, darling? Of course, I didn't. But I've been northwestern sector representative to the Guild for fourteen"—she stumbled suddenly, caught herself on the word, and the animation of her face crumpled and fled—"years," she finished, barely above a whisper, her eyes wide and palely watching upon his face.

But he only frowned impatiently.

"Then it's set for sure," he said. "I mean—from now on they'll leave us alone?"

"Oh, yes!" she said. "Yes! You and Pogey are safe, from now on."

He sighed so deeply and heavily that his shoulders heaved.

"Pogey's safe then," he murmured. Then he looked back at her. He took her hand in his. "I . . . don't know how to thank you," he said.

She stared at him, pale-faced, wide-eyed.

"Thank me!" she said.

"You did an awful lot," he said. "If it hadn't been for you . . . but we had to have faith somebody'd come through." He shook her hand, which went lifelessly up and down in his. "I just can't thank you enough. If there's ever anything I can do to pay you back." He let go of her hand and stepped backward. "I'll write you," he said. "I'll let you know how we make out." He took another step backward and turned toward the door of his room. "Well, so long—and thanks again."

*"Ted!"* Her voice thrust at him like an icepick, sharply, bringing him back around to face her. "Aren't you," she moved her lips stiffly with the words, "going to invite me in?"

He rubbed the back of his neck with one hand, clumsily.

"Well," he said, "I was up all night and I had all those drinks and Pogey is pretty shy with strangers—" He turned a hand palm out toward her. "I mean, I know he'd like you, but some other time, huh?" He smiled at her wooden face. "Give me a call tomorrow, maybe? I tell you, I'm out on my feet right now. Thanks again."

He turned and opened the door to his room and went in, closing it behind him, leaving her there. Once on the inside he set the door on lock and punched the DO NOT DISTURB sign. Then he turned to the bed. Pogey was still curled up on it, and at the sight of the antipod Ted's face softened. He knelt down by the side of the bed and put his face down on a level with Pogey's. The antipod humped like an otter playing and shoved its own button nose and bead eyes close to his.

"Love me?" said Pogey.

"Love you," breathed Ted. "We're all right now, Pogey, just like we knew we'd be, aren't we?" He put his face down sideways on the coverlet of the bed and closed his eyes. "Love Pogey," he whispered. "Love Pogey."

Pogey put out a small pink tongue and stroked Ted's forehead with it.

"What now?" murmured Ted, sleepily.

Pogey's button-eyes glowed like two small flames of jet.

"Now," Pogey said, "we go to Washington—for more like you."

# DEVOLUTION

## by Edmond Hamilton

*These* Things *didn't bear humans any malice (let's not mention digust and contempt, though), but their arrival was still Very Bad News.*

***Edmond Hamilton** (1904-1977) was one of the most prolific contributors to* Weird Tales, *which published 79 of his stories between 1926 and 1948. Unusually for a* WT *mainstay, most of his work was science fiction (or, as the magazine tagged it initially, "weird-scientific") rather than fantasy. He was also prolific outside the pages of* WT, *with stories in many other pulps, sometimes under pseudonyms. In the late 1940s, as interest in adventure SF waned, Hamilton developed a more serious style, with deeper characterizations, notably in his 1952 short story, "What's It Like Out There?" and his 1960 novel,* The Haunted Stars. *During the 1950s, he was also a prolific writer for such D.C. comic books as* The Legion of Super-Heroes.

*He continued writing into the 1970s, with stories in the SF magazines and new novels in paperback. He was a writer's writer, with a gift for tales of adventure. Some critics may have felt that such tales were insignificant, but that is their loss. Readers should be grateful for such a good and prolific writer.*

**ROSS HAD ORDINARILY** the most even of tempers, but four days of canoe travel in the wilds of North Quebec had begun to rasp it. On this, their fourth stop on the bank of the river to camp for the night, he lost control and for a few moments stood and spoke to his two companions in blistering terms.

His black eyes snapped and his darkly unshaven handsome young face worked as he spoke. The biologists listened to him without reply at first. Gray's blond young countenance was indignant but Woodin, the older biologist, just listened impassively with his gray eyes level on Ross's angry face.

When Ross stopped for breath, Woodin's calm voice struck in. "Are you finished?"

Ross gulped as though about to resume his tirade, then abruptly got hold of himself. "Yes, I'm finished," he said sullenly.

"Then listen to me," said Woodin, like a middle-aged father admonishing a sulky child.

"You're working yourself up for nothing. Neither Gray nor I have made one complaint yet. Neither us has once said that we disbelieve what you told us."

"You haven't said you disbelieve, no!" Ross exclaimed with anger suddenly re-flaring. "But don't suppose I can tell what you're thinking?

"You think I told you a fairy story about the things I saw from my plane, don't you? You think I dragged you two up here on the wildest wild-goose chase, to look for incredible creatures that could never have existed. You believe that, don't you?"

"Oh, damn these mosquitoes!" said Gray, slapping viciously at his neck and staring with unfriendly eyes at the aviator.

Woodin took command. "We'll go over this after we've made camp. Jim, get out the dufflebags. Ross, will you rustle firewood?"

They both glared at him and at each other, but grudgingly they obeyed. The tension eased for the time.

By the time darkness fell on the little riverside clearing, the canoe was drawn up on the bank, their trim little balloon-silk tent had been erected, and a fire crackled in front of it. Gray fed the fire with fat knots of pine while Woodin cooked over it coffee, hot cakes, and the inevitable bacon.

The firelight wavered feebly up toward the tall trunks of giant hemlocks that walled the little clearing on three sides. It lit up their three khaki-clad, stained figures and the irregular white block of tent. It gleamed out there on the ripples of the McNorton, chuckling softly as it flowed on toward the Little Whale.

They ate silently, and as wordlessly cleaned the pans with bunches of grass. Woodin got his pipe going, the other two lit crumpled cigarettes, and then they sprawled for a time by the fire, listening to chuckling, whispering river-sounds, the sighing sough of the higher hemlock branches, the lonesome cheeping of insects.

Woodin finally knocked his pipe out on his boot-heel and sat up.

"All right," he said, "now we'll settle this argument we were having."

Ross looked a little shamefaced. "I guess I got too hot about it," he said subduedly. Then added, "But all the same, you fellows do more than half disbelieve me."

Woodin shook his head calmly. "No, we don't, Ross. When you told us that you'd seen creatures unlike anything ever heard of while flying over this wilderness, Gray and I both believed you.

"If we hadn't, do you think two busy biologists would have dropped their work to come up here with you into these unending woods and look for the things you saw?"

"I know, I know," said the aviator unsatisfiedly. "You think I saw something queer and you're taking a chance that it will be worth the trouble of coming up here after.

"But you don't believe what I've told you about the look of the things. You think that sounds too queer to be true, don't you?"

For the first time Woodin hesitated in answering. "After all, Ross," he said indirectly, "one's eyes play tricks when you're only glimpsing things for a moment from a plane a mile up."

"Glimpsing them?" echoed Ross. "I tell you, man, I saw them as clearly as I see you. A mile up, yes, but I had my big binoculars with me and was using them when I saw them.

"It was near here, too, just east of the fork of the McNorton and the Little Whale. I was streaking south in a hurry for I'd been three weeks up at that government mapping survey on Hudson's Bay. I wanted to place myself by the river fork, so I brought my plane down a little and used my binoculars.

"Then, down there in a clearing by the river, I saw something glisten and saw—the things. I tell you, they were incredible, but just the same I saw them clear! I forgot all about the river fork in the moment or two I stared down at them.

"They were big, glistening things like heaps of shining jelly, so translucent that I could see the ground through them. There were at least a dozen of them and when I saw them they were gliding across that little clearing, a floating, flowing movement.

"Then they disappeared under the trees. If there'd been a clearing big enough to land in within a hundred miles, I'd have landed and looked for them, but there wasn't and I had to go on. But I wanted like the devil to find out what they were, and when I took the story to you two, you agreed to come up here by canoe to search for them. But I don't think now you've ever fully believed me."

Woodin looked thoughtfully into the fire. "I think you saw something queer, all right, some queer form of life. That's why I was willing to come up on this search.

"But things such as you describe, jelly-like, translucent, gliding over the ground like that—there's nothing like that since the first protoplasmic creatures, the beginning of life on earth, glided over our young world ages ago."

"If there were such things then, why couldn't they have left descendants like them?" Ross argued.

Woodin shook his head. "Because they all vanished ages ago, changed into different and higher forms of life, starting the great upward climb of life that has reached its height in man.

"Those long-dead, single-celled protoplasmic creatures were the start, the crude, humble beginnings of our life. They passed away and their descendants were unlike them. We men are their descendants."

Ross looked at him, frowning. "But where did they come from in the first place, those first living things?"

Again Woodin shook his head. "That is one thing we biologists do not know and can hardly speculate upon, the origin of those first protoplasmic forms of life.

"It's been suggested that they rose spontaneously from the chemicals of earth, yet this is disproved by the fact that no such things rise spontaneously now from inert matter. Their origin is still a complete mystery. But, however they came into existence on earth, they were the first of life, our distant ancestors."

Woodin's eyes were dreaming, the other two forgotten, as he stared into the fire, seeing visions.

"What a glorious saga it is, that wonderful climb up from crude protoplasm creatures to a man! A marvelous series of changes that has brought us from that first low form to our present splendor.

"And it might not have occurred on any other world but earth! For science is now almost sure that the cause of evolutionary mutations is the radiations of the radioactive deposits inside the earth, acting upon the genes of all living matter."

He caught a glimpse of Ross's uncomprehending face, and despite his raptness smiled a little.

"I can see that means nothing to you. I'll try to explain. The germ-cell of every living thing on earth contains in it a certain number of small, rod-like things which are called chromosomes. These chromosomes are made up of strings of tiny particles which we call genes. And each of these genes have a potent and different controlling effect upon the development of the creature that grows from that germ-cell.

"Some of these genes control the creature's color, some control his size, some the shape of his limbs, and so on. Every characteristic of the creature is predetermined by the genes in its original germ-cell.

"But now and then the genes in a germ-cell will be greatly different from the genes normal to that species, and when that is so, the creature that grows from that germ-cell will be greatly different from the fellow-creatures of its species. He will be, in fact, of an entirely new species. That is the way in which new species come into existence on earth, the method of evolutionary change.

"Biologists have known this for some time and they have been searching for the cause of these sudden great changes, these mutations, as they are called. They have tried to find out what it is that affects the genes so radically. They have found experimentally that X-rays and chemical rays of various kinds, when turned upon the genes of a germ-cell, will change them greatly. And the creature that grows from that germ-cell will thus be a greatly changed creature, a mutant.

"Because of this, many biologists now believe that the radiation from the radioactive deposits inside earth, acting upon all the genes of every living thing on earth, is what causes the constant change of species, the procession of mutations, that has brought life up the evolutionary road to its present height.

"That is why I say that on any other world but earth, evolutionary progress might never have happened. For it may be that no other world has similar radioactive deposits within to cause by gene-effect the mutations. On any other world, the first protoplasmic things that began life might have remained forever the same, down through endless generations.

"How thankful we ought to be that it was not so on earth! That mutation after mutation has followed, life ever changing and progressing into new and higher species, until the first crude protoplasm things have advanced through countless changing forms into the supreme achievement of man!"

Woodin's enthusiasm had carried him away as he talked, but now he stopped, laughing a little as he relit his pipe.

"Sorry that I lectured you like a college freshman, Ross. But that's my chief subject of thought, my *idée fixe*, that wonderful upward climb of life through the ages."

Ross was staring thoughtfully into the fire. "It does seem wonderful the way you tell it. One species changing into another, going higher all the time—"

Gray stood up by the fire and stretched. "Well, you two can wonder over it, but this crass materialist is going to emulate his remote invertebrate ancestors and return to a prostrate position. In other words, I'm going to bed."

He looked at Ross, a doubtful grin on his young blond face, and said, "No hard feelings now, feller?"

"Forget it." The aviator grinned back. "The paddling was hard today and you fellows look mighty skeptical. But you'll see! Tomorrow we'll be at the fork of the Little Whale and then I'll bet we won't scout an hour before we run across those jelly-creatures."

"I hope so," said Woodin yawningly. "Then we'll see just how good your eyesight is from a mile up, and whether you've yanked two respectable scientists up here for nothing."

Later as he lay in his blankets in the little tent, listening to Gray and Ross snore and looking sleepily out at the glowing fire embers, Woodin wondered again about that. What had Ross actually seen in that fleeting glimpse from his speeding plane? Something queer, Woodin was sure of that, so sure that he'd come on this hard trip to find it. But what exactly?

Not protoplasmic things such as he described. That couldn't be, of course. Or could it? If things like that had existed once, why couldn't they—couldn't they—?

Woodin didn't know he'd been sleeping until he was awakened by Gray's cry. It wasn't a nice cry, was the hoarse yell of someone suddenly assaulted by bone-freezing terror.

He opened his eyes at that cry to see the Incredible looming against the stars in the open door of the tent. A dark, amorphous mass humped there in the opening, glistening all over in the starlight, and gliding into the tent. Behind it were others like it.

Things happened very quickly then. They seemed to Woodin to happen not consecutively but in a succession of swift, clicking scenes like the successive pictures of a motion picture film.

Gray's pistol roared red flame at the first viscous monster entering the tent, and the momentary flash showed the looming, glistening bulk of the thing, and Gray's panic-frozen face, and Ross clawing in his blankets for his pistol.

Then that scene was over and instantly there was another one, Gray and Ross both stiffening suddenly as though petrified, both falling heavily over. Woodin knew they were both dead now, but didn't know how he knew it The glistening monsters were coming on into the tent.

He ripped up the wall of the tent and plunged out into the cold starlight of the clearing. He ran three steps, he didn't know in what direction, and then he stopped. He didn't know why he stopped dead, but he did.

He stood there, his brain desperately urging his limbs to fly, but his limbs would not obey. He couldn't even turn, could not move a muscle of his body. He stood, his face toward the starlit gleam of the river, stricken by a strange and utter paralysis.

Woodin heard rustling, gliding movements in the tent behind him. Now from behind, there came into the line of his vision several of the glistening things. They were gathering around him, a dozen of them it seemed, and he now could see them quite clearly.

They weren't nightmares, no. They were real as real, poised here around him, humped, amorphous masses of viscous, translucent jelly. Each was about four feet tall and three in diameter, though their shapes kept constantly changing slightly, making dimensions hard to guess.

At the center of each translucent mass was a dark, disk-like blob or nucleus. There was nothing else to the creatures, no limbs or sense-organs. He saw that they could protrude pseudopods, though, for two who held the bodies of Gray and Ross in such tentacles, were now bringing them out and laying them down beside Woodin.

Woodin, still quite unable to move a muscle, could see the frozen, twisted faces of the two men, and could see the pistols still gripped in their dead hands. And then as he looked on Ross's face he remembered.

The things the aviator had seen from his plane, the jelly-creatures the three had come north to search for, they were the monsters around him! But how had they killed Ross and Gray, how were they holding him petrified like this, who were they?

"We will permit you to move, but you must not try to escape."

Woodin's dazed brain numbed further with wonder. Who had said those words to him?

He had heard nothing, yet he had thought he heard.

"We will let you move but you must not attempt to escape or harm us."

He did hear those words in his mind, even though his ears heard no sound. And now his brain heard more.

"We are speaking to you by transference of thought impulses. Have you sufficient mentality to understand us?"

Minds? Minds in these things? Woodin was shaken by the thought as he stared at the glistening monsters.

His thought apparently had reached them. "Of course we have minds," came the thought answer into his brain. "We are going to let you move now, but do not try to flee."

"I-I won't try," Woodin told himself mentally.

At once the paralysis that held him abruptly lifted. He stood there in the circle of the glistening monsters, his hands and body trembling violently.

There were ten of them, he saw now. Ten monstrous, humped masses of shining, translucent jelly, gathered around him like cowled and faceless genii come from some haunt of the unknown. One stood closer to him than the others, apparently spokesman and leader.

Woodin looked slowly around their circle, then down at his two dead companions. In the midst of the unfamiliar terrors that froze his soul, he felt a sudden aching pity as he looked down at them.

Came another strong thought into Woodin's mind from the creature closest to him. "We did not wish to kill them, we came here simply to capture and communicate with the three of you.

"But when we sensed that they were trying to kill us, we slew quickly. You, who did not try to kill us but fled, we harmed not."

"What-what do you want with us, with me?" Woodin asked. He whispered it through lips, as well as thinking it.

There was no mental answer this time. The things

stood unmoving, a silent ring of brooding, unearthly figures. Woodin felt his mind snapping under the strain of silence and he asked the question again, screamed it.

This time the mental answer came. "I did not answer, because I was probing your mentality to ascertain whether you are of sufficient intelligence to comprehend our ideas.

"While your mind seems of an exceptionally low order, it seems possible that it can appreciate enough of what we wish to convey to understand us.

"Before beginning, however, I warn you again that it is quite impossible for you to escape or to harm any of us and that attempts to do so will result disastrously for you. It is apparent you know nothing of mental energy, so I will inform you that your two fellow-creatures were killed by the sheer power of wills, and that your muscles were held unresponsive to your brain's commands by the same power. By our mental energy we could completely annihilate your body, if we chose."

There was a pause, and in that little space of silence, Woodin's dazed brain clutched desperately for sanity, for steadiness.

Then came again that mental voice that seemed so like a real voice speaking in his brain.

"We are children of a galaxy whose name, as nearly as it can be approximated in your tongue, is Arctar. The galaxy of Arctar lies so many million light-years from this galaxy that it is far around the curve of the sphere of the three-dimensional cosmos.

"We came to dominance in that galaxy long ages ago. For we were creatures who could utilize our mental energy for transport, for physical power, for producing almost any effect we required. Because of this we rapidly conquered and colonized that galaxy, traveling from sun to sun without need of any vehicle.

"Having brought all the matter of the galaxy Arctar under our control, we looked out upon the realms beyond. There are approximately a thousand million galaxies in the three-dimensional cosmos, and it seemed fitting to us that we should colonize them all so that all the matter in the cosmos should in time be brought under our control.

"Our first step was to proliferate our numbers so as to multiply our number to that required for the great task of colonization of the cosmos. This was not difficult since, of course, reproduction with us is a matter of mere fission. When the requisite number of us were ready, they were divided into four forces.

"Then the whole sphere of the three-dimensional cosmos was quartered out among those four forces. Each was to colonize its division of the cosmos and so in their tremendous hosts they set out from Arctar, in four different directions.

"A part of one of these forces came to this galaxy of yours eons ago and spread out deliberately to colonize all its habitable worlds. All this took great lengths of time, of course, but our lives are of length vastly exceeding yours, and we comprehend that racial achievement is everything and individual achievement is nothing. In the colonization of this galaxy, a force of several million Arctarians came to this particular sun and, finding but this one planet of its nine nearer worlds habitable, settled here.

"Now it has been the rule that the colonists of all these

worlds throughout the cosmos have kept communication with the original home of our race, the galaxy Arctar. In that way, our people, who now hold the whole cosmos, are able to concentrate at one point all their knowledge and power, and from that point go forth commands that shape great projects for the cosmos.

"But from this world no communications have ever been received since shortly after the force of colonizing Arctarians came here. When this was first noted the matter was deferred, it being thought within a few more million years reports would surely be made from this world, too. But still no word came, until after more than a thousand million years of this silence the directing council at Arctar ordered an expedition sent to this world to ascertain the reason for such silence on the part of its colonists.

"We ten form that expedition and we started from one of the worlds of the sun you call Sirius, a short distance from your own sun, where we too are colonists. We were ordered to come with full speed to this world and ascertain why its colonists had made no report. So, wafting ourselves by mental energy through the void, we crossed the span from sun to sun and a few days ago arrived on your world.

"Imagine our perplexity when we floated down here on your world! Instead of a world peopled every square mile by Arctarians like ourselves, descended from the original colonists, a world completely under their mental control, we find a planet that is largely a wilderness of weird forms of life.

"We remained at this spot where we had landed and for some time sent our vision forth and scanned this whole globe mentally. And our perplexity increased, for never had we seen such grotesque and degraded forms of life as presented themselves to us. And not one Arctarian was to be seen on this whole planet.

"This has sorely perplexed us, for what could have done away with the Arctarians who colonized this world? Our mighty colonists and their descendants surely could never have been overcome and destroyed by the pitifully weak mentalities that now inhabit this globe. Yet where, when, are they?

"That is why we sought to seize you and your companions. Low as we knew your mentalities must be, it seemed that surely even such as you would know what had become of our colonists who once inhabited this world."

The thought-stream paused a moment, then raced into Woodin's mind with a clear question.

"Have you not some knowledge of what became of our colonists? Some clue as to their strange disappearance?"

The numbed biologist found himself shaking his head slowly. "I never-I never heard before of such creatures as you, such minds. They never existed on earth that we know of, and we now know almost all of the history of earth."

"Impossible!" exclaimed the thought of the Arctarian leader. "Surely you must have some knowledge of our mighty people if you know all the history of this planet."

From another Arctarian's mind came a thought, directed at the leader but impinging indirectly on Woodin's brain.

"Why not examine the past of the planet through this creature's brain and see what we can see for ourselves!"

"An excellent idea!" exclaimed the leader. "His mentality will be easy enough to probe."

"What are you going to do?" cried Woodin shrilly, panic edging his voice.

The answering thoughts were calming, reassuring. "Nothing that will harm you in the least. We are simply going to probe your racial past by unlocking the inherited memories of your brain.

"In the unused cells of your brain lie impressed inherited racial memories that go back to your remotest ancestors. By our mental power of command we shall make those buried memories temporarily dominant and vivid in your mind.

"You will experience the same sensations, see the same scenes, that your remote ancestors of millions of years ago saw. And we, here around you, can read your mind as we now do, and so see what you seeing, looking into the past of this planet.

"There is no danger. Physically you will remain standing here, but mentally you will leap back across the ages. We shall first push your mind back to a time approximating that when our colonists came to this world, to see what happened to them."

No sooner had this thought impinged on Woodin's mind than the starlit scene around him, the humped masses of the Arctarians, suddenly vanished and his consciousness seemed whirling through gray mist.

He knew that physically he was not moving, yet mentally he had a sense of terrific velocity of motion. It was as though his mind was whirling across unthinkable gulfs, his brain expanding.

Then abruptly the gray mists cleared. A strange new

scene took hazy form inside Woodin's mind. It was a scene that he sensed, not saw. By other senses than sight did it present itself to his mind; it was nonetheless real and vivid.

He looked with those strange senses upon a strange earth, a world of gray seas and harsh continents of rock without any speck of life upon them. The skies were heavily clouded and rain fell continually.

Down upon that world Woodin felt himself dropping, with a host of weird companions.

They were each an amorphous, glistening, single-celled mass, with a dark nucleus at its center. They were Arctarians and Woodin knew that he was an Arctarian, and that he had come with the others a long way through space toward this world.

They landed in hosts upon the harsh and lifeless planet. They exerted their mentalities and by sheer telekinetic force of mental energy they altered the material world to suit them. They reared great structures and cities, cities that were not of matter but of *thought*. Weird cities built of crystalized mental energy.

Woodin could not comprehend a millionth of the activities he sensed going on in those alien Arctarian cities of thought. He realized a vast ordered mass of inquiry, investigation, experiment, and communication, but all beyond his present human mind in motives and achievement. Abruptly all dissolved in gray mists again.

The mists cleared almost at once and now Woodin looked on another scene. It was later in time, this one. And now Woodin saw that time had worked strange changes upon the hosts of Arctarians, of which he still was one.

They had changed from unicellular to multicellular beings. And they were no longer the same. Some were sessile, fixed in one spot, others mobile. Some betrayed a tendency toward the water, others toward the land. Something had changed the bodily form of the Arctarians as generations passed, branching them out in different lines.

This strange degeneration of their bodies had been accompanied by a kindred degeneration of their minds. Woodin sensed that. In the thought-cities the ordered process of search for knowledge and power had become confused, chaotic. And the thought-cities themselves were vanishing, the Arctarians having no longer sufficient mental energy to maintain them.

The Arctarians were trying to ascertain what was causing this strange bodily and mental degeneration in them. They thought it was something that was affecting the genes of their bodies, but what it was they could not guess. On no other world had they ever degenerated so!

That scene passed rapidly into another much later. Woodin now saw the scene, for by then the ancestor, whose mind he looked through, had developed eyes. And he saw that the degeneration had now gone far, the Arctarians' multicellular bodies more and more stricken by the diseases of complexity and diversification.

The last of the thought-cities now were gone. The once mighty Arctarians had become hideous, complex organisms degenerating ever further, some of them creeping and swimming in the waters, others fixed upon the land.

They still had left some of the great original mentality of their ancestors. These monstrously degenerated creatures of land and sea, living in what Woodin's mind recognized as the late Paleozoic age, still made frantic and futile attempts to halt the terrible progress of their degradation.

Woodin's mind flashed into a scene later still, in the Mesozoic. Now the spreading degeneration made of the descendants of the colonists a still more horrible group of races. Great webbed and scaled and taloned creatures they were now, reptiles living in land and water.

Even these incredibly changed creatures possessed a faint remnant of their ancestors' mental power.

They made vain attempts to communicate with Arctarians far on other worlds of distant suns, to apprise them of their plight. But their minds were now too weak.

There followed a scene in the Cenozoic. The reptiles had become mammals; the downward progress of the Arctarians had gone further. Now only the merest shreds of the original mentality remained in these degraded descendants. And now this pitiful posterity had produced a species even more foolish and lacking in mental power than any before, ground-apes that roamed the cold plain in chattering, quarreling packs. The last shreds of Arctarian inheritance, the ancient instincts toward dignity and cleanliness and forbearance, had faded out of these creatures.

And then a last picture filled Woodin's brain. It was the world of the present day, the world he had seen through his own eyes. But now he saw and understood it as he never had before, a world in which degeneration had gone to the utmost limit.

The apes had become even weaker bipedal creatures, who had lost almost every atom of inheritance of the old Arctarian mind. These creatures had lost, too, many of the senses which had been retained by the apes before them.

And these creatures, these humans, were now degenerating with increasing rapidity. Where at first they had killed like their animal forebears only for food, they had learned to kill wantonly. And had learned to kill each other in groups, in tribes, in nations and hemispheres. In the madness of their degeneracy they slaughtered each other until earth ran with their blood.

They were more cruel even than the apes who had preceded them, cruel with the utter cruelty of the mad. And in their progressive insanity they came to starve in the midst of plenty, to slay each other in their own cities, to cower beneath the lash of superstitious fears as no creatures had before them.

They were the last terrible descendants, the last degenerated product, of the ancient Arctarian colonists who once had been kings of intellect. Now the other animals were almost gone. These, the last hideous freaks, would soon wind up the terrible story entirely by annihilating each other in their madness.

Woodin came suddenly to consciousness. He was standing in the starlight in the center of the riverside clearing. And around him still were poised the ten amorphous Arctarians, a silent ring.

Dazed, reeling from that tremendous and awful vision that had passed through his mind with incredible vividness, he turned slowly from one to the other of the Arctarians. Their thoughts impinged on his brain, strong, somber, shaken by terrible horror and loathing.

The sick thought of the Arctarian leader beat into Woodin's mind.

"So that is what became of our Arctarian colonists who came to this world! They degenerated, changed into lower and lower forms of life, until these pitiful insane things, who now swarm on this world, are their last descendants.

"This world is a world of deadly horror! A world that somehow damages the genes of our race's bodies and changes them bodily and mentally, making them degenerate further each generation. Before us we see the awful result."

The shaken thought of another Arctarian asked, "But what can we do now?"

"There is nothing we can do," uttered their leader solemnly. "This degeneration, this awful change, has gone too far for us ever to reverse it now.

"Our intelligent brothers became on this poisoned world things of horror, and we cannot now turn back the clock and restore them from the degraded things their descendants are."

Woodin found his voice and cried out thinly, shrilly.

"It isn't true!" he cried. "It's all a lie, what I saw! We humans aren't the product of downward devolution, we're the product of ages of upward evolution! We must be, I tell you! Why, we wouldn't want to live, I wouldn't want to live, if that other tale was true. It can't be true!"

The thought of the Arctarian leader, directed at the other amorphous shapes, reached his raving mind. It was tinged with pity, yet strong with a superhuman loathing.

"Come, my brothers," the Arctarian was saying to his fellows. "There is nothing we can do here on this soul-sickening world.

"Let us go, before we too are poisoned and changed. And we will send warning to Arctar that this world is poisoned, a world of degeneration, so that never again may any of our race come here and go down the awful road that those others went down.

"Come! We return to our own sun."

The Arctarian leader's humped shape flattened, assumed a disk-like form, then rose smoothly upward into the air. The others too changed and followed, in a group, and a stupefied Woodin stared at them, glistening dots lifting rapidly into the starlight.

He staggered forward a few steps, shaking his fist insanely up at the shining, receding dots.

"Come back, damn you!" he screamed. "Come back and tell me it's a lie!

"It must be a lie—it must—"

There was no sign of the vanished Arctarians now in the starlit sky. The darkness was brooding and intense around Woodin.

He screamed up again into the night, but only a whispering echo answered. Wild-eyed, staggering, soul-smitten, his gaze fell on the pistol in Ross's hand. He seized it with a hoarse cry.

The stillness of the forest was broken suddenly by a

sharp crack that reverberated a moment and died rapidly away. Then all was silent again save for the chuckling whisper of the river hurrying on.

# OPERATION STINKY

## by Clifford D. Simak

*And here's another* cute Thing, *which even purrs. Of course, it had a hidden agenda.*

***Clifford D. Simak*** *(1904-1988) published his first SF story, "The World of the Red Sun" in 1931, and went on to become one of the star writers during John W. Campbell's Golden Age of Science Fiction in the 1940s, notably in the series of stories which he eventually combined into his classic novel* City. *Other standout novels include* Time and Again, Ring Around the Sun, Time is the Simplest Thing, *and the Hugo-winning* Way Station. *Altogether, Simak won three Hugo Awards, a Nebula Award, and was the third recipient of the Grand Master Award of the Science Fiction Writers of America for lifetime achievement. He also received the Bram Stoker Award for lifetime achievement from the Horror Writers Association. He was noted for stories written with a warm* *pastoral feeling, though he could also turn out a chilling horror story, such as "Good Night, Mr. James," which was made into an episode of the original* Outer Limits. *His day job was newspaperman, joining the staff of the* Minneapolis Star and Tribune *in 1939, becoming its news editor in 1949, and retiring in 1976. He once wrote that "My favorite recreation is fishing (the lazy way, lying in a boat and letting them come to me)."*

**I WAS SITTING** on the back stoop of my shack, waiting for the jet with the shotgun at my right hand and a bottle at my left, when the dogs began the ruckus.

I took a quick swig from the bottle and lumbered to my feet. I grabbed a broom and went around the house.

From the way that they were yapping, I knew the dogs had cornered one of the skunks again and those skunks were jittery enough from the jets without being pestered further.

I walked through the place where the picket fence had fallen down and peered around the corner of the shack. It was getting dusk, but I could see three dogs circling the lilac thicket and from the sound of it, another had burrowed half-way into it. I knew that if I didn't put an end to it, all hell was bound to pop.

I tried to sneak up on them, but I kept stumbling over old tin cans and empty bottles and I decided then and there, come morning, I'd get that yard cleaned up. I had studied on doing it before, but it seemed there always was some other thing to do.

* * *

With all the racket I was making, the three dogs outside the thicket scooted off, but the one that had pushed into the lilacs was having trouble backing out. I zeroed in on him and smacked him dead center with the broom. The way he got out of there – well, he was one of those loose-skinned dogs and for a second, I swear, it looked like he was going to leave without his hide.

He was yelping and howling and he came popping out like a cork out of a bottle and he ran straight between my legs. I tried to keep my balance, but I stepped on an empty can and sat down undignified. The fall knocked the breath out of me and I seemed to have some trouble getting squared around so I could get on my feet again.

While I was getting squared around, a skunk walked out of the lilac bush and came straight toward me. I tried to shoo him off, but he wouldn't shoo. He was waving his tail and he seemed happy to find me there and he walked right up and rubbed against me, purring very loudly.

I didn't move a muscle. I didn't even bat my eyes. I figured if I didn't move, he might go away. The skunks had been living under the shack for the last three years or so and we got along fine, but we had never been what you'd call real close. I'd left them alone and they'd left me alone and we both were satisfied.

But this happy little critter apparently had made up his mind that I was a friend. Maybe he was just plumb grateful to me for running off the dogs.

He walked around me, rubbing against me, and then he climbed up in my lap and put his feet against my chest and looked me in the face. I could feel his body vibrating with the purring noise that he was making.

He kept standing there, with his feet against my chest, looking in my face, and his purring kept getting soft and loud, fast and slow. His ears stood straight up, like he expected me to purr back at him, and all the time his tail kept up its friendly waving.

Finally I reached up a hand, very gingerly, and patted him on the head and he didn't seem to mind. I sat there quite a while, patting him and him purring at me, and he still was friendly.

So I took a chance and pushed him off my lap.

After a couple of tries, I made it to my feet and walked around the shack, with the skunk following at my heels.

I sat down on the stoop again and reached for the bottle and took a healthy swig, which I really needed after all I had been through, and while I had the bottle tilted, the jet shot across the treeline to the east and zoomed above my clearing and the whole place jumped a foot or two.

I dropped the bottle and grabbed the gun, but the jet was gone before I got the barrel up.

I put down the gun and did some steady cussing.

I had told the colonel only the day before that if that jet ever flew that close above my shack again, I'd take a shot at it and I meant every word of it.

"It don't seem right," I told him. "A man settles down and builds himself a shack and is living peaceable and contented and ain't bothering no one. Then the government comes in and builds an air base just a couple miles away and there ain't no peace no more, with them jets flying no more than stove-pipe high. Sometimes at night they bring a man plumb out of bed, standing at attention in the middle of the room, with his bare feet on the cold floor."

The colonel had been real nice about it. He had pointed out how we had to have air bases, how our lives depended on the planes that operated out of them and how hard he was trying to arrange the flight patterns so they wouldn't upset folks who lived around the base.

I had told him how the jets were stirring up the skunks and he hadn't laughed, but had been sympathetic, and he told me how, when he was a boy in Texas, he had trapped a lot of skunks. I explained that I wasn't trapping these skunks, but that they were, you might say, sort of living with me, and how I had become attached to them, how I'd lay awake at night and listen to them moving around underneath the shack and when I heard them, I knew I wasn't alone, but was sharing my home with others of God's creatures.

But even so, he wouldn't promise that the jets would stop flying over my place and that was when I told him I'd take a shot at the next one that did.

So he pulled a book out of his desk and read me a law that said it was illegal to shoot at any aircraft, but he didn't scare me none.

So what happens when I lay for a jet? It passes over while I'm taking me a drink.

I quit my cussing when I remembered the bottle, and when I thought of it, I could hear it gurgling. It had rolled underneath the steps and I couldn't get at it right away and I almost went mad listening to it gurgle.

Finally I laid down on my belly and reached underneath the steps and got it, but it had gurgled dry. I tossed it out into the yard and sat down on the steps, glum.

The skunk came out of the darkness and climbed the stairs and sat down beside me. I reached out and patted him kind of absent-minded and he purred back at me. I stopped fretting about the bottle.

"You sure are a funny skunk," I said. "I never knew skunks purred."

We sat there for a while and I told him all about my trouble with the jets, the way a man will when there's nobody better around than an animal to do the listening, and sometimes even when there is.

I wasn't afraid of him no more and I thought how fine it was that one of them had finally gotten friendly. I wondered if maybe, now that the ice was broken, some of them might not come in and live with me instead of living under the shack.

Then I got to thinking what a story I'd have to tell the boys down at the tavern. Then I realized that no matter how much I swore to it, they wouldn't believe a word of what I said. So I decided to take the proof along.

I picked up the friendly skunk and I said to it: "Come along. I want to show you to the boys."

I bumped against a tree and got tangled up in an old piece of chicken wire out in the yard, but finally made it out front where I had Old Betsy parked.

Betsy wasn't the newest or the best car ever made, but she was the most faithful that any man could want. Me and her had been through a lot together and we understood each other. We had a sort of bargain—I polished and fed her and she took me where I wanted to go and always brought me back. No reasonable man can ask more of a car than that.

I patted her on the fender and said good evening to her, put the skunk in the front seat and climbed in myself.

Betsy didn't want to start. She'd rather just stayed home. But I talked to her and babied her and she finally started, shaking and shivering and flapping her fenders.

I eased her into gear and headed her out into the road.

"Now take it easy," I told her. "The state coppers have got themselves a speed trap set up somewhere along this stretch and we don't want to take no chances."

Betsy took it slow and gentle down to the tavern and I parked her there and tucked the skunk under my arm and went into the place.

Charley was behind the bar and there were quite a lot of customers – Johnny Ashland and Skinny Patterson and Jack O'Neill and half a dozen others.

I put the skunk on the bar and it started walking toward them, just like it was eager to make friends with them.

They took one look and they made foxholes under chairs and tables. Charley grabbed a bottle by the neck and backed into a corner.

"Asa," he yelled, "you take that thing out of here!"

"It's all right," I told him. "It's a friendly cuss."

"Friendly or not, get the hell out with it!"

"Get it out!" yelled all the customers.

I was plenty sore at them. Imagine being upset at a friendly skunk!

But I could see I was getting nowhere, so I picked it up and took it out to Betsy. I found a gunny sack and made a nest and told it to stay right there, that I'd be right back.

It took me longer than I had intended, for I had to tell my story and they asked a lot of questions and made a lot of jokes and they wouldn't let me buy, but kept them set up for me.

When I went out, I had some trouble spotting Betsy and then I had to set a course to reach her. It took a little time, but after tacking back and forth before the wind, I finally got close enough in passing to reach out and grab her.

I had trouble getting in because the door didn't work the way it should, and when I got in, I couldn't find the key. When I found it, I dropped it on the floor, and when I reached down to get it, I fell flat upon the seat. It was so comfortable there that I decided it was foolish to get up. I'd just spend the night there.

While I was lying there, Betsy's engine started and I chuckled. Betsy was disgusted and was going home without me. That's the kind of car she was. Just like a wife'd act.

She backed out and made a turn and headed for the road. At the road, she stopped and looked for other cars, then went out on the highway, heading straight for home.

I wasn't worried any. I knew I could trust Betsy. We'd been through a lot together and she was intelligent, although I couldn't remember she'd ever gone home all by herself before.

I lay there and thought about it and the wonder of it was, I told myself, that it hadn't happened long before.

A man is as close to no machine as he is to his car. A man gets to understand his car and his car gets to understand him and after a time a real affection must grow up between them. So it seemed absolutely natural to me that the day had to come when a car could be trusted just the way a horse or dog is, and that a good car should be as loyal and faithful as any dog or horse.

I lay there feeling happy and Betsy went head high down the road and turned in at the driveway.

But we had no more than stopped when there was a squeal of brakes and I heard a car door open and someone jump out on the gravel.

I tried to get up, but I was a bit slow about it and someone jerked the door open and reached in and grabbed me by the collar and hauled me out.

The man wore the uniform of a state trooper and there was another trooper just a little ways away and the police car stood there with its red light flashing. I wondered why I hadn't noticed it had been following us and then remembered I'd been lying down.

"Who was driving that car?" barked the cop who was holding me.

Before I could answer, the other cop looked inside Betsy and jumped back about a dozen feet.

"Slade!" he yelled. "There's a skunk in there!"

"Don't tell me", said Slade, "that the skunk was drivin'."

And the other one said, "At least the skunk is sober."

"You leave that skunk alone!" I told them. "He's a friend of mine. He isn't bothering no one."

I gave a jerk and Slade's hand slipped from my collar and I lunged for Betsy. My chest hit the seat and I grabbed the steering post and tried to pull myself inside.

Betsy started up with a sudden roar and her wheels spun gravel that hit the police car like machine-gun fire. She lurched forward and crashed through the picket fence, curving for the road. She smashed into the lilac thicket and went through it and I was brushed off.

I lay there, all tangled up with the smashed-down lilac bushes and watched Betsy hit the road and keep on going. She done the best she could, I consoled myself. She had tried to rescue me and it wasn't her fault that I had failed to hang onto her. Now she had to make a run for it herself. And she seemed to be doing pretty well. She sounded and went like she had an engine of a battleship inside her.

The two state troopers jumped into their car and took off in pursuit and I settled down to figure out how to untangle myself from the lilac thicket.

I finally managed it and went over to the front steps of the shack and sat down. I got to thinking about the fence, and decided it wasn't worth repairing. I might just as well uproot it and use what was left of it for kindling.

And I wondered about Betsy and what might be happening to her, but I wasn't really worried. I was pretty sure she could take care of herself.

I was right about that, for in a little while the state troopers came back again and parked in the driveway. They saw me sitting on the steps and came over to me.

"Where's Betsy?" I asked them.

"Betsy who?" Slade asked.

"Betsy is the car," I said.

Slade swore. "Got away. Travelling without lights at a hundred miles an hour. It'll smash into something, sure as hell."

I shook my head at that. "Not Betsy. She knows all the roads for fifty miles around."

Slade thought I was being smart. He grabbed me and jerked me to my feet. "You got a lot to explain." He shoved me at the other trooper and the other trooper caught me. "Toss him in the back seat, Ernie, and let's get going."

Ernie didn't seem to be as sore as Slade. He said: "This way, Pop."

Once they got me in the car, they didn't want to talk with me. Ernie rode in back with me and Slade drove. We hadn't gone a mile when I dozed off.

When I woke up, we were just pulling into the parking area in front of the state police barracks. I got out and tried to walk, but one of them got on each side of me and practically dragged me along.

We went into a sort of office with a desk, some chairs and a bench. A man sat behind the desk.

"What you got there?" he asked.

"Damned if I know," said Slade, all burned up. "You won't believe it, Captain."

Ernie took me over to a chair and sat me down. "I'll get you some coffee, Pop. We want to talk with you. We have to get you sober."

I thought that was nice of him.

I drank a lot of coffee and I began to see a little better and things were in straight lines instead of going round in circles—things I could see, that is. It was different when

I tried to think. Things that had seemed okay before now seemed mighty queer, like Betsy going home all by herself, for instance.

Finally they took me over to the desk and the captain asked me a lot of questions about who I was and how old I was and where I lived, until eventually we got around to what was on their minds.

I didn't hold back anything. I told them about the jets and the skunks and the talk I had with the colonel. I told them about the dogs and the friendly skunk and how Betsy had got disgusted with me and gone home by herself.

"Tell me, Mr. Bayles," said the captain, "are you a mechanic? I know you told me you are a day laborer and work at anything that you can get. But I wonder if you might not tinker around in your spare time, working on your car."

"Captain," I told him truthfully, "I wouldn't know which end of a wrench to grab hold of."

"You never worked on Betsy, then?"

"Just took good care of her."

"Has anyone else ever worked on her?"

"I wouldn't let no one lay a hand on her."

"Then you can't explain how that car could possibly operate by itself?"

"No, sir. Betsy is a smart car, Captain—"

"You're sure you weren't driving?"

"I wasn't driving. I was just taking it easy while Betsy took me home."

The captain threw down his pencil in disgust. "I give up!"

He got up from the desk. "I'm going out and make some more coffee," he said to Slade. "You see what you can do."

"There's one thing," Ernie said to Slade as the captain left. "The skunk--"

"What about the skunk?"

"Skunks don't wave their tails," said Ernie. "Skunks don't purr."

"This skunk did," Slade said sarcastically. "This was a special skunk. This was a ring-tailed wonder of a skunk. Besides, the skunk hasn't got a thing to do with it. He was just out for a ride."

"You boys haven't got a little nip?" I asked. I was feeling mighty low.

"Sure," said Ernie. He went to a locker in one corner of the room and took out a bottle.

Through the windows, I could see that the east was beginning to brighten. Dawn wasn't far away.

The telephone rang. Slade picked it up.

Ernie motioned to me and I walked across to where he stood by the locker. He handed me the bottle.

"Take it easy, Pop," he advised me. "You don't want to hang one on again."

I took it easy. About a tumbler and a half, I'd reckon.

Slade hollered, "Hey!" at us.

"What's going on?" asked Ernie.

He took the bottle from me, not by force exactly, but almost.

"A farmer found the car," said Slade. "It took a shot at his dog."

"It took a what—a shot at his dog?" Ernie stuttered.

"That's what the fellow says. Went out to get in the cows. Early. Going fishing and was anxious to get the morning chores done. Found what he thought was an abandoned car at the end of a lane."

"And the shot?"

"I'm coming to that. Dog ran up barking. The car shot out a spark—a big spark. It knocked the dog over. He got up and ran. Car shot out another spark. Caught him in the rump. Fellow says the pooch is blistered."

Slade headed for the door. "Come on, the both of you."

"We may need you, Pop," said Ernie.

We ran and piled into the car.

"Where is this farm?" asked Ernie.

"Out west of the air base," said Slade.

The farmer was waiting for us at the barnyard gate. He jumped in when Slade stopped.

"The car's still there," he said. "I been watching. It hasn't come out."

"Any other way it could get out?"

"Nope. Woods and fields is all. That lane is dead end."

Slade grunted in satisfaction. He drove down the road and ran the police car across the mouth of the lane, blocking it entirely.

"We walk from here," he said.

"Right around that bend," the farmer told us.

We walked around the bend and saw it was Betsy, all right.

"That's my car," I said.

"Let's scatter out a bit," said Slade. "It might start shooting at us."

He loosened the gun in his holster.

"Don't you go shooting up my car," I warned him, but he paid me no mind.

Like he said, we scattered out a bit, the four of us, and went toward the car. It seemed funny that we should be acting that way, as if Betsy was an enemy and we were stalking her.

She looked the same as ever, just an old beat-up jalopy that had a lot of sense and a lot of loyalty. And I kept thinking about how she always got me places and always got me back.

Then all at once she charged us. She was headed in the wrong direction and she was backing up, but she charged us just the same.

She gave a little leap and was running at full speed and going faster every second and I saw Slade pull his gun.

I jumped out in the middle of the lane and waved my arms. I didn't trust that Slade. I was afraid that if I couldn't get Betsy stopped, he'd shoot her full of holes.

But Betsy didn't stop. She kept right on charging us and she was going faster than an old wreck like her had any right to go.

"Jump, you fool!" shouted Ernie. "She'll run over you!"

I jumped, but my heart wasn't in the jump. I thought that if things had come to the pass where Betsy'd run me down there wasn't too much left for me to go on living for.

I stubbed my toe and fell flat on my face, but even while I was falling, I saw Betsy leave the ground as if she was going to leap over me. I knew right away that I'd never been in any danger, that Betsy never had any intention of hitting me at all.

She sailed right up into the sky, with her wheels still spinning, as if she was backing up a long, steep hill that was invisible.

I twisted around and sat up and stared at her and she sure was a pretty sight. She was flying just like an airplane. I was downright proud of her.

Slade stood with his mouth open and his gun hanging at his side. He never even tried to fire it. He probably forgot that he even had a gun in his hand.

Betsy went up above the treeline and the Sun made her sparkle and gleam—I'd polished her only the week before last—and I thought how swell it was she had learned to fly.

It was then I saw the jet and I tried to yell a warning for Betsy, but my mouth dried up like there was alum in it and the yell wouldn't come out.

It didn't take more than a second, probably, although it seemed to me that days passed while Betsy hung there and the jet hung there and I knew they would crash.

Then there were pieces flying all over the sky and the jet was smoking and heading for a cornfield off to the left of us.

I sat there limp in the middle of the lane and watched the pieces that had been Betsy falling back to Earth and I felt sick. It was an awful thing to see.

The pieces came down and you could hear them falling, thudding on the ground, but there was one piece that didn't fall as fast as the others. It just seemed to glide.

I watched, wondering why it glided while all the other pieces fell and I saw it was a fender and that it seemed to be rocking back and forth, as if it wanted to fall, too, only something held it back.

It glided down to the ground near the edge of the woods. It landed easy and rocked a little, then tipped over. And when it tipped over, it spilled something out of it. The thing got up and shook itself and trotted straight into the woods. It was the friendly skunk!

By this time, everyone was running. Ernie was running for the farmhouse to phone the base about the jet and Slade and the farmer were running toward the cornfield, where the jet had plowed a path in the corn wide enough to haul a barn through.

I got up and walked off the lane to where I had seen some pieces falling. I found a few of them – a headlight, the lens not even broken, and a wheel, all caved in and twisted, and the radiator ornament. I knew it was no use. No one could ever get Betsy back together.

I stood there with the radiator ornament in my hand and thought of all the good times Betsy and I had had together – how she'd take me to the tavern and wait until I was ready to go home, and how we'd go fishing and eat a picnic lunch together, and how we'd go up north deer hunting in the fall.

While I was standing there, Slade and the farmer came down from the cornfield with the pilot walking between them. He was sort of rubber-legged and they were holding him up. He had a glassy look in his eyes and he was babbling a bit.

When they reached the lane, they let loose of him and he sat down heavily.

"When the hell," he asked them, "did they start making flying cars?"

They didn't answer him. Instead, Slade yelled at me, "Hey, Pop! You leave that wreckage alone. Don't touch none of it."

"I got a right to touch it," I told him. "It's my car."

"You leave it alone! There's something funny going on here. That junk might tell us what it is if no one monkeys with it."

So I dropped the radiator ornament and went back to the lane.

The four of us sat down and waited. The pilot seemed to be all right. He had a cut above one eye and some blood had run down across his face, but that was all that was the matter with him. He asked for a cigarette and Slade gave him one and lit it.

Down at the end of the lane, we heard Ernie backing the police car out of the way. Pretty soon he came walking up to us.

"They'll be here right away."

He sat down with us. We didn't say anything about what had happened. I guess we were all afraid to talk.

In less than fifteen minutes, the air base descended on us. First there was an ambulance and they loaded the pilot aboard and left in a lot of dust.

Behind the ambulance was a fire rig and behind the fire rig was a jeep with the colonel in it. Behind the colonel's jeep were other jeeps and three or four trucks, all loaded with men, and in less time than it takes to tell it, the place was swarming.

The colonel was red in the face and you could see he was upset. After all, why wouldn't he be? This was the first time a plane had ever collided in mid-air with a car.

The colonel came tramping up to Slade and he started hollering at Slade and Slade hollered right back at him and I wondered why they were sore at one another, but that wasn't it at all. That was just the way they talked when they got excited.

All around, there was a lot of running here and there and a lot more hollering, but it didn't last too long. Before the colonel got through yelling back and forth with Slade, the entire area was ringed in with men and the situation was in Air Force hands.

When the colonel finished talking with Slade, he walked over to me.

"So it was your car," he said. The way he said it, you'd thought it was my fault.

"Yes, it was," I told him, "and I'm going to sue you. That was a darn good car."

The colonel went on looking at me as if I had no right to live, then suddenly seemed to recognize me.

"Say, wait a minute," he said. "Weren't you in to see me the other day?"

"I sure was. I told you about my skunks. It was one of them that was in Old Betsy."

"Hold up there, old-timer," said the colonel. "You lost me. Let's hear that again."

"Old Betsy was the car," I explained, "and the skunk

was in her. When your jet crashed into it, he rode a fender down."

"You mean the skunk—the fender—the—"

"It just sort of floated down," I finished telling him.

"Corporal," the colonel said to Slade, "have you further use for this man?"

"Just drunkenness," said Slade. "Not worth mentioning."

"I'd like to take him back to the base with me."

"I'd appreciate it," Slade said in a quivery kind of voice.

"Come on, then," said the colonel and I followed him to the jeep.

We sat in the back seat and a soldier drove and he didn't waste no time. The colonel and I didn't talk much. We just hung on and hoped that we'd live through it. At least, that's the way I felt.

Back at the base, the colonel sat down at his desk and pointed at a chair for me to sit in. Then he leaned back and studied me. I was sure glad I had done nothing wrong, for the way he looked at me, I'd just have had to up and confess it if I had.

"You said some queer things back there," the colonel started. "Now suppose you just rear back comfortable in that chair and tell me all about it, not leaving out a thing."

So I told him all about it and I went into a lot of detail to explain my viewpoint and he didn't interrupt, but just kept listening. He was the best listener I ever ran across.

When I was all finished, he reached for a pad and pencil.

"Let's get a few points down," he said. "You say the car had never operated by itself before?"

"Not that I know of," I answered honestly. "It might have practiced while I wasn't looking, of course."

"And it never flew before?"

I shook my head.

"And when it did both of these things, there was this skunk of yours aboard?"

"That's right."

"And you say this skunk glided down in a fender after the crash?"

"The fender tipped over and the critter ran into the woods."

"Don't you think it's a little strange that the fender should glide down when all the other wreckage fell ker-plunk?"

I admitted that it did seem slightly strange.

"Now about this skunk. You say it purred?"

"It purred real pretty."

"And waved its tail?"

"Just like a dog," I said.

The colonel pushed the pad away and leaned back in his chair. He crossed his arms and sort of hugged himself.

"As a matter of personal knowledge," he told me, "gained from years of boyhood trapping, I can tell you that no skunk purrs or ever wags its tail."

"I know what you're thinking," I said, indignant, "but I wasn't that drunk. I'd had a drink or two to while away the time I was waiting for the jet. But I saw the skunk real plain and I knew he was a skunk and I can remember that he purred. He was a friendly cuss. He acted as if he liked me and he—"

"Okay," the colonel said. "Okay."

We sat there looking at one another. All at once, he grinned.

"You know," he said, "I find quite suddenly that I need an aide."

"I ain't joining up," I replied stubbornly. "You couldn't get me within a quarter mile of one of them jets. Not if you roped and tied me."

"A civilian aide. Three hundred a month and keep."

"Colonel, I don't hanker none for the military life."

"And all the liquor you can drink."

"Where do I sign?" I asked.

And that is how I got to be the colonel's aide.

I thought he was crazy and I still think so. He'd been a whole lot better off if he'd quit right there. But he had an idea by the tail and he was the kind of gambling fool who'd ride a hunch to death.

We got along just fine, although at times we had our differences. The first one was over that foolish business about confining me to base. I raised quite a ruckus, but he made it stick.

"You'd go out and get slobbered up and gab your head off," he told me. "I want you to button up your lip and keep it buttoned up. Why else do you think I hired you?"

It wasn't so bad. There wasn't a blessed thing to do. I never had to lift my hand to do a lick of work. The chow was fit to eat and I had a place to sleep and the colonel kept his word about all the liquor I could drink.

For several days, I saw nothing of him. Then one afternoon, I dropped around to pass the time of day. I hadn't more than got there when a sergeant came in with a bunch of papers in his hand. He seemed to be upset.

"Here's the report on that car, sir," he said.

The colonel took the papers and leafed through a few of them. "Sergeant, I can't make head nor tail of this."

"Some of it I can't, either, sir."

"Now this?" said the colonel, pointing.

"That's a computer, sir."

"Cars don't have computers."

"Well, sir, that's what I said, too. But we found the place where it was attached to the engine block."

"Attached? Welded?"

"Well, not exactly welded. Like it was a part of the block. Like it had been cast as a part of it. There was no sign of welding."

"You're sure it's a computer?"

"Connally said it was, sir. He knows about computers. But it's not like any he's ever seen before. It works on a different principle than any he has seen, he says. But he says it makes a lot of sense, sir. The principle, that is. He says—"

"Well, go on!" the colonel yelled.

"He says its capacity is at least a thousand times that of the best computer that we have. He says it might not be stretching your imagination too far to say that it's intelligent."

"How do you mean—intelligent?"

"Well, Connally says a rig like that might be capable of thinking for itself, sir."

"My God!" the colonel said.

He sat there for a minute, as if he might be thinking. Then he turned a page and pointed at something else.

"That's another part, sir," the sergeant said. "A drawing of the part. We don't know what it is."

"Don't know!"

"We never saw anything like it, sir. We don't have any idea what it might be for. It was attached to the transmission, sir."

"And this?"

"That's an analysis of the gasoline. Funny thing about that, sir. We found the tank, all twisted out of shape, but there was some gas still left in it. It hadn't –"

"But why an analysis?"

"Because it's not gasoline, sir. It is something else. It was gasoline, but it's been changed, sir."

"Is that all, Sergeant?"

The sergeant, I could see, was beginning to sweat a little. "No, sir, there's more to it. It's all in that report. We got most all the wreckage, sir. Just bits here and there are missing. We are working now on reassembling it."

"Reassembling –"

"Maybe, sir, pasting it back together is a better way to put it."

"It will never run again?"

"I don't think so, sir. It's pretty well smashed up. But if it could be put back together whole, it would be the best car that was ever made. The speedometer says 80,000 miles, but it's in new-car condition. And there are alloys in it that we can't even guess at."

The sergeant paused. "If you'll permit me, sir, it's a very funny business."

"Yes, indeed," the colonel said. "Thank you, Sergeant. A very funny business."

The sergeant turned to leave.

"Just a minute," said the colonel.

"Yes, sir."

"I'm sorry about this, Sergeant, but you and the entire detail that was assigned to the car are restricted to the base. I don't want this leaking out. Tell your men, will you? I'll make it tough on anyone who talks."

"Yes, sir," the sergeant said, saluting very polite, but looking like he could have slit the colonel's throat.

When the sergeant was gone, the colonel said to me: "Asa, if there's something that you should say now and you fail to say it and it comes out later and makes a fool of me, I'll wring your scrawny little neck."

"Cross my heart," I said.

He looked at me funny. "Do you know what that skunk was?"

I shook my head.

"It wasn't any skunk," he said. "I guess it's up to us to find out what it is."

"But it isn't here. It ran into the woods."

"It could be hunted down."

"Just you and me?"

"Why just you and me when there are two thousand men right on this base?"

"But—"

"You mean they wouldn't take too kindly to hunting down a skunk?"

"Something like that, Colonel. They might go out, but they wouldn't hunt. They'd try not to find it."

"They'd hunt if there was five thousand dollars waiting for the man who brought the right one in."

I looked at him as if he'd gone off his rocker.

"Believe me," said the colonel, "it would be worth it. Every penny of it."

I told you he was crazy.

I didn't go out with the skunk hunters. I knew just how little chance there was of ever finding it. It could have gotten clear out of the county by that time or found a place to hole up where one would never find it.

And, anyhow, I didn't need five thousand. I was drawing down good pay and drinking regular.

The next day, I dropped in to see the colonel. The medical officer was having words with him.

"You got to call it off!" the sawbones shouted.

"I can't call it off," the colonel yelled. "I have to have that animal."

"You ever see a man who tried to catch a skunk barehanded?"

"No, I never have."

"I got eleven of them now," the sawbones said. "I won't have any more of it."

"Captain," said the colonel, "you may have a lot more than eleven before this is all over."

"You mean you won't call it off, sir?"

"No, I won't."

"Then I'll have it stopped."

"Captain!" said the colonel and his voice was deadly.

"You're insane," the sawbones said. "No court martial in the land—"

"Captain."

But the captain did not answer. He turned straight around and left.

The colonel looked at me. "It's sometimes tough," he said.

I knew that someone better find that skunk or the colonel's name was mud.

"What I don't understand," I said, "is why you want that skunk. He's just a skunk that purrs."

The colonel sat down at his desk and put his head between his hands.

"My God," he moaned, "how stupid can men get?"

"Pretty stupid," I told him, "but I still don't understand—"

"Look," the colonel said, "someone jiggered up that car of yours. You say you didn't do it. You say no one else could have done it. The boys who are working on it say there's stuff in it that's not been even thought of."

"If you think that skunk—"

The colonel raised his fist and smacked it on the desk.

"Not a skunk! Something that *looks* like a skunk! Something that knows more about machines than you or I or any human being will ever get to know!"

"But it hasn't got no hands. How could it do what you think?"

He never got to answer. The door burst in and two of the saddest sacks outside the guardhouse stumbled in. They didn't bother to salute.

"Colonel, sir," one of them said, heaving hard "Colonel, sir, we got one. We didn't even have to catch it We whistled at it and it followed us."

The skunk walked in behind them, waving its tail and purring. It walked right over to me and rubbed against my legs. When I reached down and picked it up, it purred so loud I was afraid it would go ahead and explode.

"That the one?" the colonel asked me.

"He's the one," I said.

The colonel grabbed the phone. "Get me Washington. General Sanders. At the Pentagon."

He waved his hand at us. "Get out of here!"

"But, Colonel, sir, the money –"

"You'll get it. Now get out of here."

He looked exactly like you might imagine a man might look right after he's been told he's not going to be shot at dawn.

We turned around and got out of there.

At the door, four of the toughest-looking hombres this side of Texas were waiting, with rifles in their hands.

"Don't pay no attention to us, Mac," one of them said to me. "We're just your bodyguards."

They were my bodyguards, all right. They went every place I went. And the skunk went with me, too. That, of course, was why they stuck around. They didn't care a rap about me. It was the skunk that was getting the bodyguarding.

And that skunk stuck closer to me than paper to the wall. He followed at my heels and walked between my feet, but mostly he wanted me to carry him or to let him perch on my shoulder. And he purred all the blessed time. Either he figured I was the only true friend he had or he thought I was a soft touch.

Life got a little complicated. The skunk slept with me and the four guards stayed in the room. The skunk and one of the guards went to the latrine with me while the others kept close. I had no privacy at all. I said it wasn't decent. I said it was unconstitutional. It didn't make no difference. There was nothing I could do. There were, it turned out, twelve of them guards and they worked in eight-hour shifts.

For a couple of days, I didn't see the colonel and I thought it was funny how he couldn't rest until he'd found the skunk and then paid no attention to it.

I did a lot of thinking about what the colonel had said about the skunk not being a skunk at all, but something that only looked like a skunk and how it might know more, some ways, than we did. And the more I lived with it, the more I began to believe that he might be right. Although it still seemed impossible that any critter without hands could know much about machinery in the first place, let alone do anything about it.

Then I got to remembering how me and Betsy had understood each other and I carried that a little further, imagining how a man and machine might get to know one another so well, they could even talk together and how the man, even if he didn't have hands, might help the machine to improve itself. And while it sounds somewhat far-fetched just telling it, thinking of it in the secrecy of one's mind made it sound all right and it gave a sort of warm feeling to imagine that one could get to be downright personal friendly with machines.

When you come to think of it, it's not so far-fetched, either.

Perhaps, I told myself, when I had gone into the tavern and had left the skunk bedded down in Betsy, the skunk might have looked her over and felt sorry for such a heap of junk, like you or I would feel sorry for a homeless cat or an injured dog. And maybe the skunk had set out, right then and there, to fix her up as best he could, probably cannibalizing some metal here and there, from places where it would not be missed, to grow the computer and the other extra pieces on her.

Probably he couldn't understand, for the life of him, why they'd been left off to start with. Maybe, to him, a machine was no machine at all without those pieces on it. More than likely, he thought Betsy was just a botched-up job.

The guards began calling the skunk Stinky and that was a libel because he never stunk a bit, but was one of the best-mannered, even-tempered animals that I have ever been acquainted with. I told them it wasn't right, but they just laughed at me, and before long the whole base knew about the name and everywhere we went they'd yell "Hi, Stinky" at us. He didn't seem to mind, so I began to think of him as Stinky, too.

I got it figured out to my own satisfaction that maybe Stinky could have fixed up Betsy and even why he fixed up Betsy. But the one thing I couldn't figure out was where he'd come from to start with. I thought on it a lot and came up with no answers except some foolish ones that were too much for even me to swallow.

I went over to see the colonel a couple of times, but the sergeants and the lieutenants threw me out before I could get to see him. So I got sore about it and decided not to go there any more until he sent for me.

One day, he did send for me and when I got there, the place was crowded with a lot of brass. The colonel was talking to an old gray-haired, eagle-beaked gent who had a fierce look about him and a rat-trap jaw and was wearing stars.

"General," said the colonel, "may I introduce Stinky's special friend?"

The general shook hands with me. Stinky, who was riding on my shoulder, purred at him.

The general took a good look at Stinky.

"Colonel," he said, "I hope to God you're right. Because if you aren't and this business ever leaks, the Air Force goose is cooked. The Army and the Navy would never let us live it down and what Congress would do to us would be a crimson shame."

The colonel gulped a little. "Sir, I'm sure I'm right."

"I don't know why I let myself get talked into this," the general said. "It's the most hare-brained scheme I have ever heard of."

He had another squint at Stinky.

"He looks like a common skunk to me," the general said.

The colonel introduced me to a bunch of other colonels and a batch of majors, but he didn't bother with the captains if there were any there and I shook hands with them and Stinky purred at them and everything was cozy.

One of the colonels picked up Stinky, but he kicked up quite a fuss trying to get back to me.

The general said to me, "You seem to be the one he wants to be with."

"He's a friend of mine," I explained.

"I be damned," the general said.

After lunch, the colonel and the general came for me and Stinky and we went over to a hangar. The place had been cleared out and there was only one plane in it, one of the newer jets. There was a mob of people waiting for us, some of them military, but a lot of them were technicians in ordinary clothes or in dungarees. Some of them had clipboards tucked under their arms and some were carrying tools or what I imagined must be tools, although never before have I ever seen contraptions such as those. And there were different pieces of equipment scattered here and there.

"Now, Asa," the colonel said to me, "I want you to get into that jet with Stinky."

"And do what?" I asked.

"Just get in and sit. But don't touch anything. You might get the detail all fouled up."

It seemed a funny business and I hesitated.

"Don't be afraid," the general assured me. "There won't nothing happen. You just get in and sit."

So I did and it was a foolish business. I climbed up where the pilots sit and sat down in his seat and it was a crazy-looking place. There were instruments and gadgets and doodads all over. I was almost afraid to move for fear of touching one of them because God knows what might have happened if I had.

❖ ❖ ❖

I got in and sat and I kept myself interested for a time by just looking at all the stuff and trying to figure out what it was for, but I never rightly got much of it figured out.

But finally I had looked at everything a hundred times and puzzled over it and there wasn't anything more to do and I was awful bored. But I remembered all the money I was pulling down and the free drinking I was getting and I thought if a man just had to sit in a certain place to earn it, why, it was all right.

Stinky didn't pay any attention to any of the stuff. He settled down in my lap and went to sleep, or at least he seemed to go to sleep. He took it easy, for a fact. Once in a while, he opened an eye or twitched an ear, but that was all he did.

I hadn't thought much about it at first, but after I'd sat there for an hour or so, I began to get an idea of why they wanted me and Stinky in the plane. They figured, I told myself, that if they put Stinky in the ship, he might feel sorry for it, too, and do the same kind of job on it as he had done on Betsy. But if that was what they thought, they sure were getting fooled, for Stinky didn't do a thing except curl up and go to sleep.

We sat there for several hours and finally they told us that we could get out.

And that is how Operation Stinky got off to a start. That is what they called all that foolishness. It does beat hell, the kind of names the Air Force can think up.

It went on like that for several days. Me and Stinky would go out in the morning and sit in a plane for several hours, then take a break for noon, then go back for a few hours more. Stinky didn't seem to mind. He'd just as soon be there as anywhere. All he'd do would be curl up in my lap and in five minutes he'd be dozing.

As the days went on, the general and the colonel and all the technicians who cluttered up the hangar got more and more excited. They didn't say a word, but you could see they were aching to bust out, only they held it back. And I couldn't understand that, for as far as I could see, there was nothing whatsoever happening.

Apparently their work didn't end when Stinky and I left. Evening after evening, lights burned in the hangar and a gang was working there and they had guards around three deep.

One day they pulled out the jet we had been sitting in and hauled in another and we sat in that and it was just the same as it had been before. Nothing really happened. And yet the air inside that hangar was so filled with tension and excitement, you could fairly light a fire with it.

It sure beat me what was going on.

Gradually the same sort of tension spread throughout the entire base and there were some funny goings-on. You never saw an outfit that was faster on its toes. A construction gang moved in and started to put up buildings and as soon as one of them was completed, machinery was installed. More and more people kept arriving until the base began to look like an anthill with a hotfoot.

On one of the walks I took, with the guards trailing along beside me, I found out something else that made my eyes bug. They were installing a twelve-foot woven fence, topped with barbed wire, all around the area.

And inside the fence, there were so many guards, they almost walked on one another.

I was a little scared when I got back from the walk, because from what I saw, this thing I'd been pitchforked into was bigger and more important than I had ever dreamed. Up until then, I'd figured it was just a matter of the colonel having his neck stuck out so far, he could never pull it back. All along, I had been feeling sorry for him because that general looked like the kind of gent who would stand for just so much tomfoolery before he lowered the boom.

It was about this time that they began to dig a big pit out in the center of one of the runways. I went over one day to watch it and it didn't make no sense at all. Here they had a nice, smooth runway they'd spent a lot of money to construct and now they were digging it up to make what looked like a swimming pool. I asked around about it, but the people that I talked to either didn't know or they weren't talking.

Me and Stinky kept on sitting in the planes. We were on our sixth one now. And there wasn't any change. I sat, bored stiff, while Stinky took it easy.

One evening the colonel sent a sergeant over to say he'd like to see me.

I went in and sat down and put Stinky on the desk. He lay down on top of it and looked from one to the other of us.

"Asa," said the colonel, "I think we got it made."

"You mean you been getting stuff?"

"We've got enough we actually understand to give us unquestioned air superiority. We're a good ten years, if not a hundred, depending on how much we can use, ahead of the rest of them. They'll never catch us now."

"But all Stinky did was sleep!"

"All he did," the colonel said, "was to redesign each ship. In some instances, there were principles involved that don't make a bit of sense, but I'll bet they will later. And in other cases, what he did was so simple and so basic that we're wondering why we never thought of it ourselves."

"Colonel, what is Stinky?"

"I don't know," he said.

"You got an idea, though."

"Sure, an idea. But that's all it is. It embarrasses me even to think of it."

"I don't embarrass easy."

"Okay, then—Stinky is like nothing on Earth. My guess is that he's from some other planet, maybe even some other solar system. I think he crossed space to us. How or why, I have no notion. His ship might have been wrecked and he got into a lifeboat and made it here."

"But if there was a lifeboat—"

"We've combed every foot of ground for miles around."

"And no lifeboat?"

"No lifeboat," said the colonel.

Getting that idea down took a little doing, but I did it. Then I got to wondering about something else.

"Colonel," I said, "you claim Stinky fixed up the ships, made them even better. Now how could he have done that with no hands and just sleeping and never touching a thing?"

"You tell me," said the colonel. "I've heard a bunch of guesses. The only one that makes any kind of sense—and cockeyed sense at that—is telekinesis."

I sat there and admired that word. "What's it mean, Colonel?" I wanted to use it on the boys at the tavern, if I ever got back there, and I wanted to get it right.

"Moving things by the power of thought," he said.

"But there wasn't nothing moved," I objected. "All the improvements in Betsy and the planes came from right inside them, not stuff moved in."

"That could be done by telekinesis, too."

I shook my head, thoughtful-like. "Ain't the way I see it."

"Go ahead," he sighed. "Let's hear your theory. No reason you should be an exception."

"I think Stinky's got a kind of mental green thumb for machines," I said. "Like some people got green thumbs for plants, only he's got—"

The colonel took a long, hard frown at me. Then he nodded very slowly. "I see what you mean. Those new parts weren't moved in or around. They were *grown*."

"Something like that. Maybe he can make a machine come kind of alive and improve itself, grow parts that'll make it a better and happier and more efficient machine."

"Sounds silly when you say it," the colonel said, "but it makes a lot more sense than any of the other ideas. Man's been working with machines—real machines, that is—

only a century or two. Make that ten thousand or a million years and it might not seem so silly."

We sat in silence while the twilight crept into the room and I think the both of us must have been thinking the same thing. Thinking of the black night that lay out beyond Earth and of how Stinky must have crossed it. And wondering, too, about what kind of world he came from and why he might have left it and what happened to him out in the long dark that forced him to look for asylum on Earth.

Thinking, too, I guess, about the ironic circumstance that had cast him on a planet where his nearest counterpart was a little animal that no one cared to have much to do with.

"What I can't understand," the colonel said, "is why he does it. Why does he do it for us?"

"He doesn't do it for us," I answered. "He does it for the planes. He feels sorry for them."

The door burst open and the general came tramping in. He was triumphant. Dusk had crept into the room and I don't think he saw me.

"We got an okay!" he gloated. "The ship will be in tomorrow. The Pentagon agrees!"

"General," said the colonel, "we're pushing this too hard. It's time for us to begin to lay some sort of grounds for basic understanding. We've grabbed what we can grab the quickest. We've exploited this little cuss right up to the hilt. We have a lot of data—"

"Not all we need!" the general bellowed. "What we have been doing has been just sort of practice. We have no data on the A-ship. That is where we need it."

"What we need as well is an understanding of this creature. An understanding of how he does it. If we could talk to him—"

"Talk!" the general shouted.

"Yes, talk!" the colonel shouted back. "He keeps purring all the time. That may be his means of communication. The men who found him simply whistled and he came. That was communication. If we had a little patience—"

"We have no time for patience, Colonel."

"General, we can't simply wring him dry. He's done a lot for us. Let's give the little guy a break. He's the one who has had the patience—waiting for us to communicate with him, hoping that someday we'll recognize him for what he is!"

They were yelling at one another and the colonel must have forgotten I was there. It was embarrassing. I held out my arms to Stinky and he jumped into them. I tiptoed across the room and went out as quietly as I could.

That night, I lay in bed with Stinky curled up on the covers at my feet. The four guards sat in the room, quiet as watchful mice.

I thought about what the colonel had said to the general and my heart went out to Stinky. I thought how awful it would be if a man suddenly was dumped into a world of skunks who didn't care a rap about him except that he could dig the deepest and slickest burrows that skunks had ever seen and that he could dig them quick. And there were so many burrows to be dug that not one of the skunks would take the time to understand this man, to try to talk with him or to help him out.

I lay there feeling sorry and wishing there was something I could do. Then Stinky came walking up the covers and crawled in under them with me and I put out my hand and held him tight against me while he purred softly at me. And that is how we went to sleep.

The next afternoon, the A-ship arrived. The last of three that had been built, it was still experimental. It was a monster and we stood far back behind a line of guards and watched it come mushing down, settling base-first into the water-filled rocket pit they'd dug out on the runway. Finally it was down and it stood there, a bleak, squat thing that somehow touched one with awe just to look at it.

The crew came down the ladder and the launch went out to get them. They were a bunch of cocky youngsters and you could sense the pride in them.

Next morning, we went out to the ship. I rode in the launch with the general and the colonel, and while the boat bobbed against the ladder, they had another difference of opinion.

"I still think it's too risky, General," said the colonel. "It's all right to fool around with jets, but an atomic ship is a different matter. If Stinky goes fooling with that pile—"

The general said, tight-lipped: "We have to take the chance."

The colonel shrugged and went up the ladder. The general motioned to me and I went up with Stinky perched on my shoulder. The general followed.

Whereas Stinky and I before this had been in a ship

alone, this time a picked crew of technicians came aboard as well. There was plenty of room and it was the only way they could study what Stinky might be doing. And I imagined that, with an A-ship, they'd want to keep close check.

I sat down in the pilot's chair and Stinky settled himself in my lap. The colonel stayed with us for a while, but after a time he left and we were alone.

I was nervous. What the colonel had said made good sense to me. But the day wore on and nothing happened and I began to feel that perhaps the colonel had been wrong.

It went on for four days like that and I settled into routine. I wasn't nervous any longer. We could depend on Stinky, I told myself. He wouldn't do anything to harm us.

By the way the technicians were behaving and the grin the general wore, I knew that Stinky must be performing up to expectations.

On the fifth day, as we were going out, the colonel said: "This should wind it up."

I was glad to hear it.

We were almost ready to knock off for noon when it happened. I can't tell you exactly how it was, for it was a bit confusing. It was almost as if someone had shouted, although no one had. I half rose out of the chair, then sat back again. And someone shouted once more.

I knew that something was about to happen. I could feel it in my bones. I knew I had to get out of the A-ship and get out fast. It was fear—unreasoning fear. And over and above the fear, I knew I could not leave. It was my job to stay. I had to stick it out. I grabbed the chair arms and hung on and tried my best to stay.

Then the panic hit me and there was nothing I could do. There was no way to fight it. I leaped out of the chair, dumping Stinky from my lap. I reached the door and fought it open, then turned back.

"Stinky!" I shouted.

I started across the room to reach him, but halfway across the panic hit me again and I turned and bolted in blind flight.

I went clattering down the catwalk and from below me came the sound of running and the yells of frightened men. I knew then that I had been right, that I had not been cowardly altogether—there was something wrong.

Men were pouring out of the port of the big A-ship when I got there and scrambling down the ladder. The launch was coming out to pick them up. One man fell off the ladder into the water and began to swim.

Out on the field, ambulances and fire rigs were racing toward the water pit and the siren atop the operations building was wailing like a stepped-on tomcat.

I looked at the faces around me. They were set and white and I knew that all the men were just as scared as I was and somehow, instead of getting scareder, I got a lot of comfort from it.

They went on tumbling down the ladder and more men fell in the drink, and I have no doubt at all that if someone had held a stopwatch on them, there'd have been swimming records falling.

I got in line to wait my turn and I thought again of Stinky and stepped out of line and started back to save him. But halfway up the catwalk, my courage ran plumb out and I was too scared to go on. The funny thing about it was that I didn't have the least idea what there was to scare me.

I went down the ladder among the last of them and piled into the launch, which was loaded so heavily that it barely crept back to solid ground.

The medical officer was running around and shouting to get the swimmers into decontamination and men were running everywhere and shouting and the fire rigs stood there racing their motors while the siren went on shrieking.

"Get back!" someone was shouting. "Run! Everybody back!"

So, of course, we ran like a flock of spooked sheep.

Then a wordless yell went up and we turned around.

The atomic ship was rising slowly from the pit. Beneath it, the water seethed and boiled. The ship rose steadily, gracefully, without a single shudder or shake. It went straight up into the sky, up and out of sight.

Suddenly I realized that I was standing in dead silence. No one was stirring. No one was making any noise. Everybody just stood and stared into the sky. The siren had shut off.

I felt someone tap me on the shoulder. It was the general.

"Stinky?" he asked.

"He wouldn't come," I answered, feeling low. "I was too scared to go and get him."

The general wheeled and headed off across the field.

For no reason I can think of, I turned and followed him. He broke into a run and I loped along beside him.

We stormed into operations and went piling up the stairs to the tracking room.

The general bellowed: "You got a fix on it?"

"Yes, sir, we're tracking it right now."

"Good," the general said, breathing heavily. "Fine. We'll have to run it down. Tell me where it's headed."

"Straight out, sir. It still is heading out."

"How far?"

"About five thousand miles, sir."

"But it can't do that!" the general roared. "It can't navigate in space!"

He turned around and bumped into me.

"Get out of my way!" He went thumping down the stairs.

I followed him down, but outside the building I went another way. I passed administration and there was the colonel standing outside. I wasn't going to stop, but he called to me. I went over.

"He made it," said the colonel.

"I tried to take him off," I said, "but he wouldn't come."

"Of course not. What do you think it was that drove us from the ship?"

I thought back and there was only one answer. "Stinky?"

"Sure. It wasn't only machines, Asa, though he did wait till he got hold of something like the A-ship that he could make go out into space. But he had to get us off it first, so he threw us off."

I did some thinking about that, too. "Then he *was* kind of like a skunk."

"How do you mean?" asked the colonel, squinting at me.

"I never did get used to calling him Stinky. Never seemed right somehow, him not having a smell and still having that name. But he did have a smell—a mental one, I guess you'd say—enough to drive us right out of the ship."

The colonel nodded. "All the same, I'm glad he made it." He stared up at the sky.

"So am I," I said.

Although I was a little sore at Stinky as well. He could have said good-bye at least to me. I was the best friend he had on Earth and driving me out along with the other men seemed plain rude.

But now I'm not so sure.

I still don't know which end of a wrench to take hold of, but I have a new car now—bought it with the money I earned at the air base—and it can run all by itself. On quiet country roads, that is. It gets jittery in traffic. It's not half as good as Betsy.

I could fix that, all right. I found out when the car rose right over a fallen tree in the road. With what rubbed off on me from being with Stinky all the time, I could make it fly. But I won't. I ain't aiming to get treated the way Stinky was.

# THE HUNTING GROUND

## by David Drake

*Time to close out the book with a no-holds-barred malevolent* Thing from Outer Space. *Accept no substitutes.*

***David Drake,*** *author of the best-selling Hammer's Slammers future mercenary series, is often referred to as the Dean of military science fiction, but is much more versatile than that label might suggest, as shown by his epic fantasy series that began with Lord of the Isles (Tor), and his equally popular Republic of Cinnabar Navy series (Baen) starring the indefatigable team of Leary and Mundy. His recent collection of horror and fantasy stories,* Night & Demons *(Baen), has a generous helping of monsters, all* Things *in good standing, though I don't advise your standing too close to them. He lives near Chapel Hill, NC, with his family.*

**THE PATROL CAR'S TIRES** hissed on the warm

asphalt as it pulled to the curb beside Lorne. "What you up to, snake?" asked the square-bodied policeman. The car's rumbling idle and the whirr of its air conditioner through the open window filled the evening.

Lorne smiled and nodded the lighted tip of his cigarette. "Sitting on a stump in my yard, watching cops park on the wrong side of the street. What're you up to, Ben?"

Instead of answering, the policeman looked hard at his friend. They were both in their late twenties; the man in the car stocky and dark with a close-cropped mustache; Lorne slender, his hair sand-colored and falling across his neck brace. "Hurting, snake?" Ben asked softly.

"Shit, four years is enough to get used to anything," the thinner man said. Though Lorne's eyes were on the chime tower of the abandoned Baptist church a block down Rankin Street, his mind was lost in the far past. "You know, some nights I sit out here for a while instead of going to bed."

Three cars in quick succession threw waves of light and sound against the rows of aging houses. One blinked its high beams at the patrol car briefly, blindingly. "Bastard," Ben grumbled without real anger. "Well, back to the war against crime." His smile quirked. "Better than the last war they had us fighting, hey?"

Lorne finished his cigarette with a long drag. "Hell, I don't know, sarge. How many jobs give you a full pension after two years?"

"See you, snake."

"See you, sarge."

The big cruiser snarled as Ben pulled back into the

traffic lane and turned at the first corner. The city was on a system of neighborhood police patrols, an attempt to avoid the anonymous patrolling that turned each car into a miniature search and destroy mission. The first night he sat on the stump beside his apartment, Lorne had sworn in surprise to see that the face peering from the curious patrol car was that of Ben Gresham, his squad leader during the ten months and nineteen days he had carried an M60 in War Zone C.

And that was the only past remaining to Lorne.

The back door of Jenkins's house banged shut on its spring. A few moments later heavy boots began scratching up the gravel of the common drive. Lorne's seat was an oak stump, three feet in diameter. Instead of trying to turn his head, he shifted his whole body around on the wood. Jenkins, a plumpish, half-bald man in his late sixties, lifted a pair of canned Budweisers. "Must get thirsty out here, warm as it is."

"It's always thirsty enough to drink good beer," Lorne smiled. "I'll share my stump with you."

They sipped for a time without speaking. Mrs. Purefoy, Jenkins's widowed sister and a matronly Baptist, kept house for him. Lorne gathered that while she did not forbid her brother to drink an occasional beer, neither did she provide an encouragingly social atmosphere.

"I've seen you out here at 3 a.m.," the older man said. "What'll you do when the weather turns cold?"

"Freeze my butt for a while," Lorne answered. He gestured his beer toward his dark apartment on the second floor of a house much like Jenkins's. "Sit up there with the light on. Hell, there's lots of VA hospitals, I've *been* in lots of them. If North Carolina isn't warm enough, maybe they'd find me one in Florida." He took another swallow and said, "I just sleep better in the daytime, is all. Too many ghosts around at night."

Jenkins turned quickly to make sure of the smile on the younger man's face. It flashed at his motion. "Not quite that sort of ghost," Lorne explained. "The ones I bring with me . . . ." And he kept his smile despite the sizzle of faces in the white fire sudden in his mind. The noise of popping, boiling flesh faded and he went on, "There was something weird going on last night, though—" he glanced at his big Japanese wristwatch—"well, damn early this morning."

"A Halloween ghost with a white sheet?" Jenkins suggested.

"Umm, no, down at the church," said Lorne, fumbling his cigarettes out. Jenkins shrugged refusal and the dart of butane flame ignited only one. "The tower there was—I don't know, I looked at it and it seemed to be vibrating. No sound, though, and then a big red flash without any sound either. I thought sure it'd caught fire, but it was just a flash and everything was back to normal. Funny. You know how you hold your fingers over a flashlight and it comes through, kind of? Well, the flash was like that, only through a stone wall."

"I never saw anything like that," Jenkins agreed. "Old church doesn't seem the worse for it, though. It'll be ready to fall down itself before the courts get all settled about who owns it, you know."

"Umm?"

"Fellowship Baptist built a new church half a mile

north of here, more parking, and anyhow, it was going to cost more to repair that old firetrap than it would to build a new one." Jenkins grinned. "Mable hasn't missed a Sunday in forty years, so I heard all about it.

"The city bought the old lot for a boys' club or some such fool thing—I want to spit every time I think of my property taxes, I do—but it turns out the Rankins, that's who the street's named after, too, they'd given the land way back before the Kaiser's War. Damn if some of them weren't still around to sue to get the lot back if it wasn't going to be a church anymore. So that was last year, and it's like to be a few more before anybody puts money into tearing the old place down."

"From the way it's boarded up and padlocked, I figured it must have been a reflection I saw," Lorne admitted. "But it looked funny enough," he added sheepishly, "that I took a walk down there last night."

Jenkins shrugged and stood up. He had the fisherman's trick of dropping the pull tab into his beer before drinking any. Now it rattled in the bottom. "Well," he said, picking up Lorne's can as well, "it's bed time for me, I suppose. You better get yourself off soon or the bugs'll carry you away."

"Thanks for the beer and the company," Lorne said. "One of these nights I'll bring down an ice chest and we'll really tie one on."

Lorne's ears followed the old man back, his boots a friendly, even sound in the warm April darkness. A touch of breeze caught the wisteria hedge across the street and spread its sweetness, diluted, over Lorne. He ground out his cigarette and sat quietly, letting the vines breathe on him.

Jenkins's garbage can scrunched open and one of the empties echoed into it. The other did not fall. "What the hell?" Lorne wondered aloud. But there was something about the night, despite its urban innocence, that brought up memories from past years more strongly than ever before.

In a little while Lorne began walking. He was still walking when dawn washed the fiery pictures from his mind and he returned to his apartment to find three police cars parked in the street.

The two other tenants stored their cars in the side yard of the apartment house. Lorne had stepped between them when he heard a woman scream, "That's him! Don't let him get away!"

Lorne turned. White-haired Mrs. Purefoy and a pair of uniformed policemen faced him from the porch of Jenkins's house. The younger man had his revolver half-drawn. A third uniformed man, Ben, stepped quickly around from the back of the house. "I'm not going anywhere but to bed," Lorne said, spreading his empty hands. He began walking toward the others. "Look, what's the matter?"

The oldest, heaviest of the policemen took the porch steps in a leap and approached Lorne at a barely restrained trot. He had major's pips on his shoulder straps. "Where have you been, snake?" Ben asked, but the major was between them instantly, growling, "I'll handle this, Gresham. Mr. Charles Lorne?"

"Yes," Lorne whispered. His body flashed hot, as though the fat policeman were a fire, a towering sheet of orange rippling with the speckles of tracers cooking off . . . .

". . . and at any time during the questioning you may withdraw your consent and thereafter remain silent. Do you understand, Mr. Lorne?"

"Yes."

"Did you see Mr. Jenkins tonight?"

"Uh-huh. He came out—when did you leave me, Ben? 10:30?" Lorne paused to light another cigarette. His flame wavered like the blade of a kris. "We each drank a beer, shot the bull. That's all. What happened?"

"Where did you last see Mr. Jenkins?"

Lorne gestured. "I was on the stump. He walked around the back of the house—his house. I guess I could see him. Anyway, I heard him throw the cans in the trash and . . . that's all."

"Both cans?" Ben broke in despite his commander's scowl.

"No, you're right—just one. And I didn't hear the door close. It's got a spring that slams it like a one-oh-five going off, usually. Look, what happened?"

There was a pause. Ben tugged at a corner of his mustache. Low sunlight sprayed Lorne through the trees. Standing, he looked taller than his six feet, a knobbly staff of a man in wheat jeans and a green-dyed T-shirt. The shirt had begun to disintegrate in the years since it was issued to him on the way to the war zone. The brace was baby-flesh pink. It made him look incongruously bullnecked, alien.

"He could have changed clothes," suggested the young patrolman. He had holstered his weapon but continued to toy with the butt.

"He didn't," Ben snapped, the signs of his temper

obvious to Lorne if not to the other policemen. "He's wearing now what he had on when I left him."

"We'll take him around back," the major suddenly decided. In convoy, Ben and the other, nervous, patrolman to either side of Lorne, and the major bringing up the rear, they crossed into Jenkins's yard following the steep downslope. Mrs. Purefoy stared from the porch. Beneath her a hydrangea bush graded its blooms red on the left, blue on the right, with the carefully tended acidity of the soil. It was a mirror for her face, ruddy toward the sun and gray with fear in shadow.

"What's the problem?" Lorne wondered aloud as he viewed the back of the house. The trash can was open but upright, its lid lying on the smooth lawn beside it. Nearby was one of the Budweiser empties. The other lay alone on the bottom of the trash can. There was no sign of Jenkins himself.

Ben's square hand indicated an arc of spatters six to eight feet high, black against the white siding. "They promised us a lab team but hell, it's blood, snake. You and me've seen enough to recognize it. Mrs. Purefoy got up at four, didn't find her brother. I saw this when I checked and . . . ." He let his voice trail off.

"No body?" Lorne asked. He had lighted a fresh cigarette. The gushing flames surrounded him.

"No."

"And Jenkins weighs what? 220?" He laughed, a sound as thin as his wrists. "You'd play hell proving a man with a broken neck ran off with him, wouldn't you?"

"Broke? Sure, we'll believe that!" gibed the nervous patrolman.

"You'll believe *me,* meatball!" Ben snarled. "He broke it and he carried me out of a fucking burning Shithook while our ammo cooked off. And by God—"

"Easy, sarge," Lorne said quietly. "If anybody needs shooting, I'll borrow a gun and do it myself."

The major flashed his scowl from one man to the other. His sudden uncertainty was as obvious as the flag pin in his lapel: Lorne was now a veteran, not an aging hippy.

"I'm an outpatient at the VA hospital," Lorne said, seeing his chance to damp the fire. "Something's fucking up some nerves and they're trying to do something about it there. Wish to hell they'd do it soon."

"Gresham," the major said, motioning Ben aside for a low-voiced exchange. The third policeman had gone red when Ben snapped at him. Now he was white, realizing his mortality for the first time in his twenty-two years.

Lorne grinned at him. "Hang loose, turtle. Neither Ben or me ever killed anybody who didn't need it worse than you do."

The boy began to tremble.

"Mr. Lorne," the major said, his tone judicious but not hostile, "we'll be getting in touch with you later. And if you recall anything, anything at all that may have bearing on Mr. Jenkins's disappearance, call us at once."

Lorne's hands nodded agreement. Ben winked as the lab van arrived, then turned away with the others.

Lorne's pain was less than usual, but his dreams awakened him in a sweat each time he dropped off to sleep. When at last he switched on the radio, the headline news was that three people besides Jenkins had disappeared during the night, all of them within five blocks of Lorne's apartment.

The air was very close, muffling the brilliance of the stars. It was Friday night and the roar of southbound traffic sounded from Donovan Avenue a block to the east. The three northbound lanes of Jones Street, the next one west of Rankin, were not yet as clotted with cars as they would be later at night, but headlights there were a nervous darting through the houses and trees whenever Lorne turned on his stump to look. Rankin Street lay quietly between, lighted at alternate blocks by blue globes of mercury vapor. It was narrow, so that cars could not pass those parked along the curb without slowing, easing; a placid island surrounded by modern pressures.

But no one had disappeared to the east of Donovan or the west of Jones.

Lorne stubbed out his cigarette in the punky wood of the stump. It was riddled with termites and sometimes he pictured them, scrabbling through the darkness. He hated insects, hated especially the grubs and hidden things, the corpse-white termites . . . but he sat on the stump above them. A perversely objective part of Lorne's mind knew that if he could have sat in the heart of a furnace like the companions of Daniel, he would have done so.

From the blocky shade of the porch next door came the creak of springs: Mrs. Purefoy, shifting her weight on the cushions of the old wing-back chair. In the early evening Lorne had caught her face staring at a parlor window, her muscles flat as wax. As the deeper darkness blurred and pooled, she had slipped out into its cover. Lorne felt her burning eyes, knowing that she would never forgive him for her brother's disappearance, not if it were proven that Jenkins had left by his own decision. Lorne had always been a sinner to her; innocence would not change that.

Another cigarette. Someone else was watching. A passing car threw Lorne's angled shadow forward and across Jenkins's house. Lorne's guts clenched and his fingers crushed the unlit cigarette. *Light. Twelve men in a rice paddy when the captured flare bursts above them. The pop-pop-pop of a gun far off, and the splashes columning around Lt. Burnes—*

"Christ!" Lorne shouted, standing with an immediacy that laced pain through his body. Something was terribly wrong in the night. The lights brought back memories, but they quenched the real threat that hid in the darkness. Lorne knew what he was feeling, *knew* that any instant a brown face would peer out of a spider hole behind an AK-47 or a mine would rip steel pellets down the trail . . .

He stopped, forcing himself to sit down again. If it was his time, there was nothing he could do for it. A fresh cigarette fitted between his lips automatically and the needle-bright lighter focused his eyes.

And the watcher was gone.

Something had poised to kill Lorne, and had then passed on without striking. It was as unnatural as if a wall collapsing on him had separated in midair to leave him unharmed. Lorne's arms were trembling, his cigarette tip an orange blur. When Ben's cruiser pulled in beside him,

Lorne was at first unable to answer the other man's, "Hey, snake."

"Jesus, sarge," Lorne whispered, smoke spurting from his mouth and nostrils. "There's somebody out here and he's a *bad* fucker."

Carrier noise blatted before the car radio rapped a series of numbers and street names. Ben knuckled his mustache until he was sure his own cruiser was not mentioned. "Yeah, he's a bad one. Another one gone tonight, a little girl from three blocks down. Went to the store to trade six empties and a dime on a coke. Christ, I saw her two hours ago, snake. The bottles we found, the kid we didn't . . . . Seen any little girls?"

There was an upright shadow in front of Ben's radio: a riot gun, clipped to the dashboard. "Haven't seen anything but cars, sarge. Lots of police cars."

"They've got an extra ten men on," Ben agreed with a nod. "We went over the old Baptist church a few minutes ago. Great TAC Squad work. Nothing. Damn locks were rusted shut."

"Think the Baptists've taken up with baby sacrifice?" Lorne chuckled.

"Shit, there's five bodies somewhere. If the bastard's loading them in the back of a truck, you'd think he'd spread his pickups over a bit more of an area, wouldn't you?"

"Look, baby, anybody who packed Jenkins around on his back—I sure don't want to meet him."

"Don't guess Jenkins did either," Ben grunted. "Or the others."

"PD to D-5," the radio interrupted.

Ben keyed his microphone. "Go ahead."

"10-25 Lt. Cooper at Rankin and Duke."

"10-4, 10-76," Ben replied, starting to return the mike to its holder.

"D-5, acknowledge," the receiver ordered testily.

"Goddamn fucker!" Ben snarled, banging the instrument down. "Sends just about half the fucking time!"

"Keep a low profile, sarge," Lorne murmured, but even had he screamed, his words would have been lost in the boom of exhaust as Ben cramped the car around in the street, the left wheels bumping over the far curb. Then the accelerator flattened and the big car shot toward the rendezvous.

In Viet Nam, Lorne had kept his death wish under control during shelling by digging in and keeping his head down. Now he stood and went inside to his room. After a time, he slept. If his dreams were bright and tortured, then they always were. . . .

"Sure, you knew Jackson," Ben explained, the *poom-poom-poom* of his engine a live thing in the night. "He's the blond shit who . . . didn't believe you'd broken your neck. Yesterday morning."

"Small loss, then," Lorne grinned. "But you watch your own ass, hear? If there's nobody out but cops, there's going to be more cops than just Jackson disappearing."

"Cops and damned fools," Ben grumbled. "When I didn't see you out here on my first pass, I thought maybe you'd gotten sense enough to stay inside."

"I was going to. Decided . . . oh, hell. What's the box score now?"

"Seven gone. Seven for sure," the patrolman corrected himself. "One got grabbed in the time he took to walk from his girl's front porch back to his car. That bastard's lucky, but he's crazy as hell if he thinks he'll stay that lucky."

"He's crazy as hell," Lorne agreed. A spring whispered from Jenkins's porch and Lorne bobbed the tip of his cigarette at the noise. "She's not doing so good either. All last night she was staring at me, and now she's at it again."

"Christ," Ben muttered. "Yeah, Major Hooseman talked to her this morning. You're about the baddest man ever, leading po' George into smoking and drinking and late hours before you killed him."

"Never did get him to smoke," Lorne said, lighting Ben's cigarette and another for himself. "Say, did Jackson smoke?"

"Huh? No." Ben frowned, staring at the closed passenger-side windows and their reflections of his instruments. "Yeah, come to think, he did. But never in uniform, he had some sort of thing about that."

"He sheered off last night when I lit a cigarette," Lorne said. "No, not Jackson—the other one. I just wondered . . . ."

"You saw him?" Ben's voice was suddenly sharp, the hunter scenting prey.

Lorne shook his head. "I just felt him. But he was there, baby."

"Just like before they shot us down," the policeman said quietly. "You squeezing my arm and shouting over the damn engines 'They're waiting for us, they're waiting for us!' And not a fucking thing I could do—I didn't order the assault and the captain sure wasn't going to call it off because my machine gunner said to. But you were right, snake."

"The flames . . ." Lorne whispered, his eyes unfocused.

"And you're a dumb bastard to have done it, but you carried me out of them. It never helped us a bit that you knew when the shit was about to hit the fan. But you're a damn good man to have along when it does."

Lorne's muscles trembled with memory. Then he stood and laughed into the night. "You know, sarge, in twenty-seven years I've only found one job I was any good at. I didn't much like that one, and anyhow—the world doesn't seem to need killers."

"They'll always need us, snake," Ben said quietly. "Some times they won't admit it." Then; "Well, I think I'll waste some more gas."

"Sarge—" The word hung in the empty darkness. There was engine noise and the tires hissing in the near distance and—nothing else. "Sarge, Mrs. Purefoy was on her porch a minute ago and she didn't go inside. But she's not there now."

Ben's five-cell flashlight slid its narrow beam across the porch: the glider, the wing-back chair. On the far railing, a row of potted violets with a gap for the one now spilled on the boards as if by someone vaulting the rail but dragging one heel . . . .

"Didn't hear it fall," the policeman muttered, clacking open the car door. The dome light spilled a startling yellow pool across the two men. As it did so, white motion trembled half a block down Rankin Street.

"Fucker!" Ben said. "He couldn't jump across the

street, he threw something so it flashed." Ben was back in the car.

Lorne squinted, furious at being blinded at the critical instant. "Sarge, I'll swear to God he headed for the church." Lorne strode stiffly around the front of the vehicle and got in on the passenger side.

"Mother *fuck!*" the stocky policeman snarled, dropping the microphone that had three times failed to get him a response. He reached for the shift lever, looked suddenly at Lorne as the slender man unclipped the shotgun. "Where d'ye think *you're* going?"

"With you."

Ben slipped the transmission into Drive and hung a shrieking U-turn in the empty street. "The first one's birdshot, the next four are double-ought buck," he said flatly.

Lorne jacked the slide twice, chambering the first round and then shucking it out the ejector. It gleamed palely in the instrument light. "Don't think we're going after birds," he explained.

Ben twisted across the street and bounced over the driveway cut. The car slammed to a halt in the small lot behind and shielded by the bulk of the old church. It was a high, narrow building with two levels of boarded windows the length of the east and west sides; the square tower stood at the south end. At some time after its construction, the church had been faced with artificial stone. It was dingy, a gray mass in the night with a darkness about it that the night alone did not explain.

Ben slid out of the car. His flash touched the small door to the right of the tower. "Nothing wrong with the padlock," Lorne said. It was a formidable one, set in a patinaed hasp to close the church against vandals and derelicts.

"They were all locked tight yesterday, too," the patrolman said. "He could still be getting in one of those windows. We'll see." He turned to the trunk of the car and opened it, holding his flashlight in the crook of his arm so his right hand could be free for his drawn revolver.

Lorne's quick eyes scanned the wall above them. He bent back at the waist instead of tilting his head alone. "Got the key?" he asked.

The stocky man chuckled, raising a pair of folding shovels, army surplus entrenching tools. "Keep that cornsheller ready," he directed, holstering his own weapon. He locked the blade of one shovel at 90° to the shaft and set it on top of the padlock. The other, still folded, cracked loudly against the head of the first and popped the lock open neatly. "Field expedients, snake," Ben laughed. "If we don't find anything, we can just shut the place up again and nobody'll know the difference."

He tossed the shovels aside and swung open the door. The air that puffed out had the expected mustiness of a long-closed structure with a sweetish overtone that neither man could have identified. Lorne glanced around the outside once more, then followed the patrolman within. The flames in his mind were very close.

"Looks about like it did last night," Ben said.

"And last year, I'd guess." The wavering oval of the flashlight picked over the floor. The hardwood was warping, pocked at frequent intervals by holes.

"They unbolted the old pews when they moved," Ben

explained. "Took the stained glass, too, since the place was going to be torn down."

The nave was a single narrow room running from the chancel in the north to the tower which had held the organ pipes and, above, the chimes. The main entrance was by a side aisle, through double doors in the middle of the west wall. The interior looked a gutted ruin.

"You checked the whole building?" Lorne asked. The pulpit had been ripped away. The chancel rail remained though half-splintered, apparently to pass the organ and altar. Fragments of wood, crumpled boxes, and glass littered the big room.

"The main part. We didn't have the key to the tower and the major didn't want to bust in." Ben took another step into the nave and kicked at a stack of old bulletins.

*White heat, white fire*—"Ben, did you check the ceiling when you were here last night?"

"Huh?" The narrow Gothic vault was blackness forty feet above the ground. Ben's flashlight knifed upward across painted plaster to the ribbed and paneled ceiling that sloped to the main beam. And—"Jesus!"

A large cocoon was tight against the roof peak. It shimmered palely azure, but the powerful light thrust through to the human outline within. Long shadows quivered on the wood, magnifying the trembling of the policeman's wrist as the beam moved from the cocoon to another beside it, to the third—

"Seven of the fuckers!" Ben cried, taking another step and slashing the light to the near end of the room where the south wall closed the inverted V of the ceiling. Above the door to the tower was the baize screen of the pipe loft.

The cloth fluttered behind Mrs. Purefoy, who stood stiffly upright twenty feet in the air. Her face was locked in horror, framed by her tousled white hair. Both arms were slightly extended but were stone-rigid within the lace-fringed sleeves of her dress.

"She—" Lorne began, but as he spoke and Ben's hand fell to the butt of his revolver, Mrs. Purefoy began to fall, tilting a little in a rustle of skirts. Beneath the crumpled edge of the baize curtain, spiked on the beam of Ben's flashlight, gleamed the head and foreclaws of what had been clutching the woman.

The eyes glared like six-inch opals, fierce and hot in a dead-white exoskeleton.

The foreclaws clicked sideways. As though they had cocked a spring, the whole flat torso shot down at Ben.

An inch long and scuttling under a rock, it might have passed for a scorpion, but this lunging monster was six feet long without counting the length of the tail arced back across its body. Flashing legs, flashing body armor, and the fluid-jeweled sting that winked as Lorne's finger twitched in its killer's reflex—

Lorne's body screamed at the recoil of the heavy charge. The creature spun as if kicked in midair, smashing into the floor a yard from Ben instead of on top of the policeman. The revolver blasted, a huge yellow bottle-shape flaring from the muzzle. The bullet ripped away a window shutter because a six-inch pincer had locked Ben's wrist. The creature reared onto the back two pairs of its eight jointed legs. Lorne stepped sideways for a clear shot, the slide of his weapon slick-snacking another round into the chamber. On the creature's white belly was a smeared asterisk—the load of buckshot had ricocheted off, leaving a trail like wax on glass.

Ben clubbed his flashlight. It cracked harmlessly between the glowing eyes and sprang from his hand. The other claw flashed to Ben's face and trapped it, not crushingly but hard enough to immobilize and start blood-trails down both cheeks. The blades of the pincer ran from nose to hairline on each side.

Lorne thrust his shotgun over Ben's right shoulder and fired point-blank. The creature rocked back, jerking a scream from the policeman as the claws tightened. The lead struck the huge left eye and splashed away, dulling the opal shine. The flashlight still glaring from the floor behind the creature silhouetted its sectioned tail as it arched above the policeman's head. The armed tip plunged into the base of his neck. Ben stiffened.

Lorne shouted and emptied his shotgun. The second dense red bloom caught like a strobe light the dotted line of blood droplets joining Ben's neck to the withdrawn injector. A claw seized Lorne's waist in the rolling echo of the shotgun blasts. His gunbutt cracked on the creature's armor, steel sparking as it slid off. The extending pincer brushed the shotgun aside and clamped over Lorne's face, half-shielding from him the sight of the rising sting.

Then it smashed on Lorne's neck brace, and darkness exploded over him in a flare of coruscant pain.

The oozing ruin of Mrs. Purefoy's face stared at Lorne through its remaining eye when he awoke. Everything swam in blue darkness except for one bright blur. He blinked and the blur suddenly resolved into a streetlight glaring up through a shattered board. Lorne's lungs burned and his stiffness seemed more than even unconsciousness and the pain skidding through his nerve paths could explain. He moved his arm and something clung to its surface; the world quivered.

Lorne was hanging from the roof of the church in a thin, transparent sheath. Mrs. Purefoy was a yard away, multiple wrappings shrouding her corpse more completely. With a strength not far from panic, Lorne forced his right fist into the bubble around him. The material, extruded in broad swathes by the creature rather than as a loom of threads, sagged but did not tear. The clear azure turned milky under stress and sucked in around Lorne's wrist.

He withdrew his hand. The membrane passed some oxygen but not enough for an active man. Lorne's hands patted the outside of his pockets finding, as he had expected, nothing with a sharp edge. He had not recently bitten off his thumbnails. Thrusting against the fire in his chest, he brought his left hand in front of his body. With a fold of the cocoon between each thumb and index finger, he thrust his hands apart. A rip started in the white opacity beneath his right thumb. Air, clean and cool, jetted in.

"Oh, Jesus," Lorne muttered, even the pain in his body forgotten as he widened the tear upwards to his face. The cocoon was bobbing on a short lead, rotating as the rip changed its balance. Lorne could see that he had become ninth in the line of hanging bodies, saved from their paralysis by the chance of his neck brace. Ben, his face blurred by the membrane holding him next to Lorne, had been less fortunate.

Ten yards from where Lorne hung and twenty feet below the roof beam, the baize curtain of the pipe loft twitched. Lorne froze in fearful immobility.

The creature had been able to leap the width of a street carrying the weight of an adult; its strength must be as awesome as was the rigidity of its armor. Whether or not it could drive its sting through Lorne's brace, it could assuredly rip him to collops if it realized he was awake.

The curtain moved again, the narrow ivory tip of a pincer lifting it slightly. The creature was watching Lorne.

Ben carried three armor-piercing rounds in his .357 Magnum for punching through car doors. Lorne tried to remember whether the revolver had remained in Ben's hand as he fell. There was no image of that in Lorne's mind, only the torchlike muzzle blasts of his own shotgun. Slim as it was, his only hope was that the jacketed bullets would penetrate the creature's exoskeleton though the soft buckshot had not.

Lorne twisted his upper torso out of the hole for a closer look at Ben, making his own cocoon rock angrily. The baize lifted further. The streetlight lay across it in a pale band. Why didn't the creature scuttle out to finish the business?

Brief motion waked a flash of scintillant color from the pipe loft. The curtain flapped closed as if a volley of shots had ripped through it. Lorne recognized the reflex: the panic of a spider when a stick thrusts through its web. Not an object, though; the light itself, weak as it was, had slapped the creature back.

Ben's bright flashlight had not stopped it when necessity drove, but the monster must have felt pain at human levels of illumination. Its eyes were adapted to starlight or the glow of a sun immeasurably fainter than that of Earth. "Where did you come from, you bastard?" Lorne whispered.

Light. It gave him an idea and he fumbled out his butane lighter, adjusting it to a maximum flame. The sheathes were relatively thin over the victims' faces to aid transpiration. At the waist, though, where a bulge showed Ben's arm locked to his torso, the membrane was thick enough to be opaque in the dim light. Lorne bent dangerously over, cursing the stiffness of his neck brace. Holding the inch-high jet close, he tried to peer through Ben's cocoon. Unexpectedly the fabric gave a little and Lorne bobbed forward, bringing the flame in contact with the material sheathing Ben.

The membrane sputtered, kissing Lorne's hand painfully. He jerked back and the lighter flicked away. It dropped, cold and silent until it cracked on the floor forty feet below. Despite the pattern of light over it, the curtain to the loft was shifting again. Lorne cursed in terror.

A line of green fire sizzled up the side of Ben's cocoon from the point at which the flame had touched it. The material across his face flared. The policeman gave no sign of feeling his skin curl away. The revolver in his hand winked green.

Lorne screamed. His own flexible prison lurched and sagged like heated polyethylene. Ben was wrapped in a cancerous hell that roared and heaved against the roofbeams as a live thing. Green tongues licked yellow-orange flames from the dry wood as well. Lorne's cocoon and that to the other side of Ben were deforming in the furnace heat. Another lurch and Lorne had slipped twenty feet, still gripped around the waist in a sack of blue membrane. He was gyrating like a top.

The loft curtain had twitched higher each time it spun past his vision.

The bottom of Ben's cocoon burned away and he plunged past Lorne, face upward and still afire. Bone crunched as he hit. The body rebounded a few inches to fall again on its face. The roar of the flames muffled Lorne's wail of rage. His own elongated capsule began to flow. Flames grasped at Lorne's support. Before they could touch the sheathing, the membrane pulled a last few inches and snapped like an overstretched rubber band. The impact of the floor smashed Lorne's jaw against his neck brace, grinding each tortured vertebra against the next. He did not lose consciousness, but the shock paralyzed him momentarily as thoroughly as the creature's sting could have done.

Bathed in green light and the orange of the blazing roof panels, the scorpion-thing thrust its thorax into the nave. Its walking legs gripped the flat surface, dimpling the plaster. The creature turned upward toward the fire, three more cocoons alight and their hungry flames lapping across the beams. Then, partly colored by the illumination, its legs shifted and the opal eyes trained on Lorne. The light must be torture to it; muffling in indecision its responses, but it was about to act.

A small form wrapped in a flaming shroud dropped to thump the floor beside Lorne. His arms would move again. He used them to strip the remaining sheathing from his legs. It clung as the heat of the burning corpse began to melt the material. Something writhed from a crackling tumor on the child's neck. The thing was finger-long and seemed to paw the air with a score of tiny legs; its opalescent eyes proved its parentage. The creature brought more than paralysis to its victims: it was a gravid female.

Green flame touched the larva. It burst in a pustulant smear.

The adult went mad. Its legs shot it almost the length of the nave to rebound from a sidewall in a cloud of plaster. The creature's horizontally flattened tail ruddered it instinctively short of the fire as it leapt upward to the roof peak. It clung there in pale horror against the wood, eyes on the advancing flames. Three more bodies fell, splashing like ginkgo fruits.

Lorne staggered upright. The fire hammered down at him without bringing pain. His body had no feeling whatever. Ben's hair had burned. His neck and scalp were black where skin remained, red where it had cracked open to the muscle beneath. The marbled background showed clearly the tiny, pallid hatchling trying to twist across it.

Lorne's toe brushed the larva onto the floor. His boot heel struck it, struck again and twisted. Purulent ichor spurted between the leather and the boards. Lorne knelt. In one motion he swung Ben across his shoulders and stood, just as he had after their helicopter had nosed into the trees and exploded. Logic had been burned out of Lorne's mind, leaving only a memory of friendship. He did not look up. As his mechanical steps took him and his burden through the door they had entered, a shadow wavered across them. The creature had sprung back into the loft.

Lorne stumbled to his knees in the parking lot. The church had been rotten and dry. Orange flames fluffed through the roof in several places, thrusting corkscrews of sparks into the night sky. Twelve feet of roof slates thundered into the nave. Flame spewed up like a secondary explosion. There were sirens in the night.

Without warning, the east facade of the tower collapsed into the parking lot. Head-sized chunks of Tennessee-stone smashed at the patrol car, one of them missing Lorne by inches. He looked up, blank-eyed, his hands lightly touching the corpse of his friend. Of its own volition, the right hand traced down Ben's shoulder to the raw flesh of his elbow. The tower stairs spiraled out of the dust and rubble, laid bare to the steel framework when the wall fell. On the sagging floor of the pipe loft rested a machine like no other thing on Earth, and the creature was inside it. Tubes of silvery metal rose cradle-form from a base of similar metal. The interstices were not filled with anything material, but the atmosphere seemed to shiver, blurring the creature's outline.

And Lorne's hand was unwrapping Ben's stiff fingers from the grips of his revolver.

Lorne stood again, his left hand locking his right on the butt of the big magnum. He was familiar with the weapon: it was the one Ben had carried in Nam, the same tool he had used for five of his thirteen kills. It would kill again tonight.

Even in the soaring holocaust the sharp crack of Lorne's shot was audible. Lorne's forearms rocked up as a unit with the recoiling handgun. The creature lurched sideways to touch the shimmering construct around it. A red surface discharge rippled across the exoskeleton from the point of contact. Lorne fired again. He could see the armor dull at his point of aim in the center of the thorax.

Again the creature jumped. Neither bullet had penetrated, but the splashing lead of the second cut an upright from the machine. The creature spun, extending previously unglimpsed tendrils from the region of its mouth parts. They flickered over a control plate in the base. Machinery chimed in response.

The shivering quickened. The machine itself and the thing it enclosed seemed to fade. Lorne thumb-cocked the magnum, lowered the red vertical of the front sight until it was even with the rear notch; the creature was a white blur beyond them. The gun bucked back hard when he squeezed; the muzzle blast was sharper, flatter, than before. The first of the armor-piercing bullets hit the creature between the paired tendrils. The exoskeleton surrounding them shattered like safety glass struck by a brick.

The creature straightened in silent agony, rising onto its hind legs with its tail lying rigidly against its back. Its ovipositor was fully extended, thumb-thick and six inches long.

"Was it fun to kill them, bug?" Lorne screamed. "Was it as much fun as this is?" His fourth shot slammed, dimpling a belly plate which then burst outward in an ugly gush of fluids. The creature's members clamped tightly about its spasming thorax. The tail lashed the uprights in red spurts. The machine was fading and the torn paneling of the loft was beginning to show through the dying creature's body.

There was one shot left in the cylinder and Lorne steadied his sights on the control plate. He had already begun taking up the last pressure when he stopped and lowered the muzzle. No, let it go home, whatever place or time that might be. Let its fellows see that Earth was not their hunting ground alone. And if they came back anyway—*if they only would!*

There was a flash as penetrating as the first microsecond of a nuclear blast. The implosion dragged Lorne off his feet and sucked in the flames so suddenly that all sound seemed frozen. Then both sidewalls collapsed into the nave and the ruins of the tower twisted down on top of them. In the last instant, the pipe loft was empty of all but memory.

A fire truck picked its way through the rubble in the parking lot. Its headlights flooded across the figure of a sandy-haired man wearing scorched clothing and a neck brace. He was kneeling beside a body, and the tears were bright on his face.

# If You Like... You Should Try...

DAVID DRAKE
David Weber

DAVID WEBER
John Ringo

JOHN RINGO
Michael Z. Williamson
Tom Kratman

ANNE MCCAFFREY
Mercedes Lackey
Liaden Universe® by Sharon Lee & Steve Miller

MERCEDES LACKEY
Wen Spencer, Andre Norton
Andre Norton
James H. Schmitz

LARRY NIVEN
Tony Daniel
James P. Hogan
Travis S. Taylor

ROBERT A. HEINLEIN
Jerry Pournelle
Lois McMaster Bujold
Michael Z. Williamson

HEINLEIN'S "JUVENILES"

Rats, Bats & Vats series by Eric Flint & Dave Freer

HORATIO HORNBLOWER OR PATRICK O'BRIAN

David Weber's Honor Harrington series

David Drake's RCN series

HARRY POTTER

Mercedes Lackey's Urban Fantasy series

THE LORD OF THE RINGS

Elizabeth Moon's *The Deed of Paksenarrion*

H.P. LOVECRAFT

Larry Correia's Monster Hunter series

P.C. Hodgell's Kencyrath series

*Princess of Wands* by John Ringo

GEORGETTE HEYER

Lois McMaster Bujold

Catherine Asaro

Liaden Universe® by Sharon Lee & Steve Miller

GREEK MYTHOLOGY

*Pyramid Scheme* by Eric Flint & Dave Freer

*Forge of the Titans* by Steve White

*Blood of the Heroes* by Steve White

NORSE MYTHOLOGY

*Northworld Trilogy* by David Drake

# If You Like... You Should Try...

DAVID DRAKE
David Weber
Tony Daniel
John Lambshead

DAVID WEBER
John Ringo
Timothy Zahn
Linda Evans
Jane Lindskold
Sarah A. Hoyt

JOHN RINGO
Michael Z. Williamson
Tom Kratman
Larry Correia
Mike Kupari

ANNE MCCAFFREY
Mercedes Lackey
Lois McMaster Bujold
Liaden Universe® by Sharon Lee & Steve Miller
Sarah A. Hoyt
Mike Kupari

MERCEDES LACKEY
Wen Spencer
Andre Norton
James H. Schmitz

LARRY NIVEN
Tony Daniel
James P. Hogan
Travis S. Taylor
Brad Torgersen

ROBERT A. HEINLEIN
Jerry Pournelle
Lois McMaster Bujold
Michael Z. Williamson

HEINLEIN'S "JUVENILES"
Rats, Bats & Vats series by Eric Flint & Dave Freer
Brendan DuBois' *Dark Victory*
David Weber & Jane Lindskold's Star Kingdom Series
Dean Ing's *It's Up to Charlie Hardin*
David Drake & Jim Kjelgaard's *The Hunter Returns*

HORATIO HORNBLOWER OR PATRICK O'BRIAN
David Weber's Honor Harrington series
David Drake's RCN series
Alex Stewart's *Shooting the Rift*

HARRY POTTER
Mercedes Lackey's Urban Fantasy series

JIM BUTCHER
Larry Correia's The Grimnoir Chronicles
John Lambshead's *Wolf in Shadow*

## TECHNOTHRILLERS
Larry Correia & Mike Kupari's Dead Six Series
Robert Conroy's *Stormfront*
Eric Stone's *Unforgettable*
Tom Kratman's Countdown Series

## THE LORD OF THE RINGS
Elizabeth Moon's *The Deed of Paksenarrion*
*Shattered Shields* ed. by Schmidt and Brozek
P.C. Hodgell
Ryk E. Spoor's Phoenix Rising series

## A GAME OF THRONES
Larry Correia's *Son of the Black Sword*
David Weber's fantasy novels
Sonia Orin Lyris' *The Seer*

## H.P. LOVECRAFT
Larry Correia's Monster Hunter series
P.C. Hodgell's Kencyrath series
John Ringo's Special Circumstances Series

## ZOMBIES
John Ringo's Black Tide Rising Series
Wm. Mark Simmons

## GEORGETTE HEYER
Lois McMaster Bujold
Catherine Asaro
Liaden Universe® by Sharon Lee & Steve Miller
Dave Freer